LINE OF
DEMARCATION

ALSO BY TOM CLANCY

The Hunt for Red October
Red Storm Rising
Patriot Games
The Cardinal of the Kremlin
Clear and Present Danger
The Sum of All Fears
Without Remorse
Debt of Honor
Executive Orders
Rainbow Six
The Bear and the Dragon
Red Rabbit
The Teeth of the Tiger
Dead or Alive (with Grant Blackwood)
Against All Enemies (with Peter Telep)
Locked On (with Mark Greaney)
Threat Vector (with Mark Greaney)
Command Authority (with Mark Greaney)
Tom Clancy Support and Defend (by Mark Greaney)
Tom Clancy Full Force and Effect (by Mark Greaney)
Tom Clancy Under Fire (by Grant Blackwood)
Tom Clancy Commander in Chief (by Mark Greaney)
Tom Clancy Duty and Honor (by Grant Blackwood)
Tom Clancy True Faith and Allegiance (by Mark Greaney)
Tom Clancy Point of Contact (by Mike Maden)
Tom Clancy Power and Empire (by Marc Cameron)
Tom Clancy Line of Sight (by Mike Maden)
Tom Clancy Oath of Office (by Marc Cameron)
Tom Clancy Enemy Contact (by Mike Maden)
Tom Clancy Code of Honor (by Marc Cameron)
Tom Clancy Firing Point (by Mike Maden)
Tom Clancy Shadow of the Dragon (by Marc Cameron)
Tom Clancy Target Acquired (by Don Bentley)
Tom Clancy Chain of Command (by Marc Cameron)
Tom Clancy Zero Hour (by Don Bentley)
Tom Clancy Red Winter (by Marc Cameron)
Tom Clancy Weapons Grade (by Don Bentley)
Tom Clancy Command and Control (by Marc Cameron)
Tom Clancy Act of Defiance (by Andrews & Wilson)
Tom Clancy Shadow State (by M. P. Woodward)
Tom Clancy Defense Protocol (by Andrews & Wilson)

TOM CLANCY
LINE OF DEMARCATION

M. P. WOODWARD

SPHERE

SPHERE

First published in the United States in 2025 by G. P. Putnam's Sons
(an imprint of Penguin Random House LLC)
First published in Great Britain in 2025 by Sphere

5 7 9 10 8 6 4

Copyright © The Estate of Thomas L. Clancy, Jr.; Rubicon, Inc.;
Jack Ryan Enterprises, Ltd.; and Jack Ryan Limited Partnership 2025

The moral right of the author has been asserted.

*All characters and events in this publication, other than those
clearly in the public domain, are fictitious and any resemblance
to real persons, living or dead, is purely coincidental.*

All rights reserved.
No part of this publication may be reproduced, stored in a
retrieval system, or transmitted, in any form or by any means, without
the prior permission in writing of the publisher, nor be otherwise circulated
in any form of binding or cover other than that in which it is published
and without a similar condition including this condition being
imposed on the subsequent purchaser.

A CIP catalogue record for this book
is available from the British Library.

Hardback ISBN 978-1-4087-3274-8
Trade Paperback ISBN 978-1-4087-3275-5

Printed and bound in Great Britain by
Clays Ltd, Elcograf S.p.A.

Papers used by Sphere are from well-managed forests
and other responsible sources.

Sphere	The authorised representative
An imprint of	in the EEA is
Little, Brown Book Group	Hachette Ireland
Carmelite House	8 Castlecourt Centre
50 Victoria Embankment	Dublin 15, D15 XTP3, Ireland
London EC4Y 0DZ	(email: info@hbgi.ie)

An Hachette UK Company
www.hachette.co.uk

www.littlebrown.co.uk

PRINCIPAL CHARACTERS

UNITED STATES GOVERNMENT
MARY PAT FOLEY: Director of National Intelligence
SYDNEY O'KEEFE: Ambassador to Guyana

THE CAMPUS ("BLACK SIDE") AND HENDLEY ASSOCIATES ("WHITE SIDE")
JOHN CLARK: Director of Operations; Hendley Chief Security Officer
DOMINGO "DING" CHAVEZ: former CIA officer, operator
JACK RYAN, JR.: lead Campus operator; Hendley venture capitalist
KENDRICK MOORE: former SEAL, operator
AMANDA "MANDY" COBB: former FBI, operator
LISANNE ROBERTSON: former Marine, operator; Hendley Logistics Director
GAVIN BIERY: information technology specialist; Hendley Cybersecurity Director
STEVEN "CHILLY" EDWARDS: former SWAT officer, operator
CARY MARKS: active duty Green Beret, operator
JAD MUSTAFA: active duty Green Beret, operator
HOWARD BRENNAN: Hendley Chief Investment Officer

THE GUYANESE

ALI KHASIF: President
AUGUSTUS "GUTO" CASTILLO: Prime Minister
DR. ALBERTO QUINTERO, AKA "THE PROFESSOR": Minister of the Interior
AMANCIA QUINTERO: Alberto Quintero's wife
TALLULAH QUINTERO: Alberto Quintero's daughter
GUSTAVO QUINTERO: Alberto Quintero's nephew
ALEJANDRO ROMERO: Head of the National Intelligence and Security Agency (NISA)
HUGO SUÁREZ: Acting Attorney General and lead prosecutor

VENEZUELANS AND RUSSIANS

JUAN MACHADO AKA "TIBURÓN": Colombian drug lord operating in Venezuela
IGOR MOROZOV: Major in Russia's foreign intelligence service, the SVR
YEVGENY ZUKA: Russian Wagner Group combat leader
CARLOS CARAZA: combat leader of the Tiburónistas, Tiburón's mercenary group
VIKTOR ZHDANOV: CEO of the Russian oil company giant, Gazneft
MIKHAIL KROKHMAL: Captain First Rank of the Russian frigate *Admiral Gorshkov*

The day may dawn when fair play, love for one's fellow men, and respect for justice and freedom will enable tormented generations to march forth serene and triumphant from the hideous epoch in which we have to dwell.

Meanwhile, never flinch, never weary, never despair.

—Winston Churchill

PROLOGUE

ORINOCO BASIN, CARIBBEAN SEA
MARCH 1
0325

THE UNITED STATES COAST GUARD CUTTER *HARRY CLAIBORNE* WAS NOT A PRETTY ship. With her black hull, gawky foredeck crane, and overhanging pilothouse, it was plain to see that in the old naval architectural battle of form versus function, the latter had won.

As a Keeper-class buoy tender, the *Claiborne*—*Dirty Harry* to her crew—was slow, unarmed, and ungainly. Now a quarter-century old, she represented the unglamorous half of the U.S. Coast Guard that services thousands of buoys and navigation aids to make the nation's waterways safe. A vital mission to be sure—if not a pretty one.

In fairness, she'd had her glory moments. Once, *Dirty Harry* had ferried a First Lady at a New Orleans Fourth of July event. A few years later, she hauled up a previously missing World War II Navy PBY off the Atlantic floor, earning her way into the papers by dispelling a Bermuda Triangle myth. Plaques and news cutouts were framed in the passageways to mark these august occasions for the crew.

Such adornments were nice—but also telling. For the buoy tender would always be a far cry from the sleek, celebrated cutters that civilians normally envision when they think of the Coast Guard.

This was a source of regular embarrassment for Petty Officer Second Class Billy Gesparek of Spokane, Washington, the man at her helm on this clear South American night. Whenever Billy was back in Spokane on leave, some old-timer or former high school classmate would ask him how many rescues he'd performed. "None," he'd inevitably answer, followed by something defensive like "We do a lot more than that."

From a watch position at the far right of *Dirty Harry*'s bridge, Chief Bart Novak shot an irritated glance toward his helmsman. "Hey. Wake up, Gesparek. You're drifting." The chief then went back to sipping coffee from his enormous trucker-style travel mug.

Billy squeezed the wheel and tried to follow the little markers on the digital chart plotter to stay on course, while avoiding an urge to cuss. The rebuke seemed a little unfair to him.

As he saw it, it was damn near impossible to keep *Dirty Harry* moving in a straight line, especially in the waters of Guyana, a tiny sliver of a country on South America's northeastern shoulder. For starters, there were the strong Caribbean tides that came streaming into this muddy little bay. Then there were the coral reefs, submerged wrecks, and half-finished oil pipelines they were constantly steering to avoid. As if those hazards weren't enough, on nights like this one, when the sky was so clear that the Milky Way glowed like a cloud, the warm winds rolled in off the cooling sugarcane fields with such force that Billy could still smell the stalks.

Whenever that happened, the land breeze pushed *Dirty Harry*'s ugly crane and bulbous bow around like a bathtub toy. Even the autopilot couldn't keep up.

Billy, however, was a prime helmsman, requested by most watch officers for his skills. On this night, he soon had *Harry* back on course—a feat he would have accomplished with or without the chief's squawking. Before long, the watch officer had little to do other than sip his coffee, peer through his binoculars, and mumble an occasional complaint about the shallow seas.

After a while, the winds eased in the lee of a headland, and the bow behaved such that Billy could activate the autopilot again. That gave him the rare freedom to look out the bridge windows. He saw that the moon was getting low in the west and stared at the silvery waves until his eyes glazed over, dreaming of his next duty station.

When *Dirty Harry* eventually squeezed into her home berth in Mobile, Alabama, Billy would pack his two-room apartment and drive his Toyota pickup across the country in a northwest diagonal line that wouldn't end until he hit the Pacific. He had orders to Surfman—a dream he'd so coveted that he always kept the official dispatch from the communications shack in his breast pocket. Tonight, whenever the chief wasn't looking, he raised a hand from the wheel to touch the pocket with two fingers.

Officially called the National Motor Lifeboat School, Surfman was a training academy at the far west end of his home state of Washington, just off the deadly Columbia River Bar, otherwise known as "the graveyard of ships." Once he got up there, Billy hoped to become a coxswain on one of the fast forty-seven-foot motor lifeboats that charged into waves like a torpedo and, if toppled, could roll upright again with the ease of a river kayak. As a Surfman graduate, by God, he'd have a thing or two to tell the folks back home.

For now, though, he rechecked the course in the digital compass and watched the thin needles on the engine gauges. It irked him a little that the inrushing flood tide was slowing them down. To counter it, he goosed the throttles to get to nine knots, just three short of *Dirty Harry*'s pathetic top speed. As he saw it, the two thousand miles to Mobile couldn't tick down fast enough.

When Billy had first heard that *Dirty Harry* was deploying to the Caribbean, he'd envisaged gin-clear waters, sugar-white beaches, and sunbaked beauties. The reality had been depressingly different.

He'd spent his entire six-week assignment in a muddy river estuary outside the Guyanese capital of Georgetown, a city whose population was about the same as Spokane, equally as industrial, and a hell of a lot hotter. Throughout the deployment, Billy had found scant relief from Guyana's lashing sun. If there was even a sandy swimming beach, he'd never found it—let alone any sunbaked beauties.

Georgetown's only redeeming quality, it seemed to him, was that the world's largest natural gas reservoir had been discovered beneath its bay, as evidenced by the three towering drilling platforms—GOPLATs, as the Coast Guard called them—in and around which *Dirty Harry* had floated for the last month and a half.

Those GOPLATs had been the whole point of the mission. In their looming shadows, *Harry*'s crew had spent most days churning the dirty waters to auger buoy cables into the muck between the reefs. They'd marked dangerous shoals with posts and performed geological surveys for the chart makers at the National Oceanic and Atmospheric Administration. Having endured the racing tides, jagged rocks, and reeking mud for forty days and forty nights, Billy had decided NOAA and the oil companies could have this hellhole.

With the winds abating, he considered increasing the throttles again to get her to ten knots. He stopped himself for fear the chief would notice and settled on the notion that his only option was patience—a virtue which, like most men of twenty-five, he sorely lacked.

On the far side of the headland, a sudden gust knocked *Harry*'s bow to port. Billy switched off the autopilot and went back to his battle with the helm, mulling over the interminability of the voyage ahead of them.

He was comforted by the notion that the skipper planned a refueling stop in San Juan, Puerto Rico. Scuttlebutt held that the island had become the new spring break it-destination for Florida State coeds. While steering skillfully, Billy's mind blossomed with the same set of pleasant Caribbean images it had concocted six weeks earlier.

"Billy, steady up on three-zero-five. Let's get over this damn shoal."

"Aye, Chief. Steadying up on three-zero-five."

The helmsman swept his eyes over the instrument panel. It seemed to him that the trouble with night watches wasn't so much the lack of sleep as the utter boredom. It was easy for a man to fall into a mental distraction. That wasn't the case during the day. Then, he was usually too busy repairing slimy buoy cables, lifting rusted junk out of the water, hosing down the fouled deck, or chipping rust to think of anything except the mess in his hands. But standing the midnight to 0400 fired his imagination like a psychedelic drug.

With the bow under control again, he went back to looking at the water. A distant yellow light blinked on the formless horizon. The light could be mistaken for a flickering star, since there was no visual separation between sea and sky. But Billy knew what it was.

"Chief, I have a light on GOPLAT Marlin bearing zero-two-two, one mile," he announced. "At your two o'clock."

Bart Novak, ten years older than Billy and sporting an unfortunate deployment mustache, put down his big mug and swiveled his binoculars to the east. "Those guys are up early. I see welders' torches. My brother's a welder."

Billy waited a few seconds before responding. "He like it?"

Novak lowered the binoculars and scratched at his mustache, though he didn't answer the question. "Probably the last time we'll lay eyes on Marlin. You going to miss all this, Gesparek?"

"Miss Georgetown? Are you kidding me?"

"The work, I meant. You're not going to do any navaid stuff up there in Oregon. Until you flunk out of Surfman."

"Not flunking out of Surfman," Billy muttered.

"You better not. The pride of *Dirty Harry* is going there with you."

Billy swallowed, anxious to change the subject. "Chief, Marlin now bears zero-three-five. We're passing over one of her pipelines, depth forty-four feet."

Novak watched the faint flicker of the distant welders. The GOPLAT's builders called it Marlin. Two other GOPLATs, Mako and Mackerel, were just beyond it and still under construction.

All three were the product of a joint venture between the Guyanese government and a consortium of American oil giants. *Dirty Harry*'s mission had been to mark safe passage for the mammoth American tankers and processing ships that would arrive in these shallow, shoal-strewn waters in the next year or two.

The currents kept Billy busy at the wheel until he found a relative heading that kept her crabbing forward on a true course. His mind soon drifted, imagining himself out there in the Pacific surf, sweeping in on his motor lifeboat to rescue a handful of college girls from a sailboat caught in a riptide. Then the current beneath *Dirty Harry*'s keel shifted with the uneven seafloor.

"Gesparek, current's picking up again."

"I got it, Chief."

"Say position."

"Approaching the edge of the Orinoco Shelf." Billy glanced at the chart plotter to be precise. "Two hundred yards to King's Reef. Coming up on the Chute."

LINE OF DEMARCATION

Novak leaned closer to a display that showed him a sonar echo of the seafloor. It was a jagged line, interrupted by massive coral buildups. There was only one way through it—the so-called Chute. "Roger. Call out your depth at intervals. Steer to avoid hazards."

"Steer to avoid, aye, Chief." Gesparek repeated the numbers on the depth sounder as the water got shallower. "We're at forty. Thirty. Now twenty feet, Chief Novak."

"Twenty?"

"Yes, Chief. We're right over King's Reef."

"Right. All stop. Zero drift."

Gesparek snapped the throttles back to reverse, then idle. The massive twin diesels in the ship's bowels slowed to a steady hum. The chief walked behind the console and parked himself next to Billy. He stroked the wisps of his mustache and surveyed the chart plotter, mumbling to himself.

"Get to a more detailed view," he ordered.

Billy zoomed in tightly on their position. Together, they studied the squiggly brown lines that marked treacherous shoals.

"Goddamned maze," breathed the chief. "Set EOT for three knots."

"EOT for three knots, aye." Billy notched the throttles forward, barely.

In the old days, when bridge controls relayed commands to the engine room for workers to adjust the machinery, the throttle was appropriately called the engine order telegraph, EOT. *Dirty Harry*'s throttles were connected directly to the diesel engines, like any other modern boat. But in the hidebound maritime service, the old EOT name had stuck.

Billy was particularly good with the EOT and bow thruster controls. He'd navigated this maze twenty-five times when placing buoys between Marlin and Mako. He twirled the wheel and adjusted his throttles with the deftness of an airline pilot on approach. A few times he nosed *Harry* sideways with the bow thruster, then let her drift, before bringing her back on course.

"Sharp work," acknowledged Novak.

"Thanks, Chief."

Ignoring the seas outside, Billy kept his eyes on the chart plotter, scanning every sensor. Still, a single thought that distracted him for a few seconds managed to creep in. It was that maybe the chief had been right—maybe he would miss this after all. *Dirty Harry* was a uniquely maneuverable vessel.

While tubby above the waves, she was unexpectedly graceful below. Unlike the propeller and rudder that guided most ships, *Harry* moved with Z-drives—self-contained propulsion pods that could swivel beneath the hull in a full three-sixty. The result was incomparable maneuverability.

"Steady," warned Novak, pointing at the sonar display. A jagged hill loomed ahead on the sea surface. They would have marked it during their deployment, but the submerged peak was far enough away from the GOPLATs that it was outside their area of responsibility. Billy moved the ship swiftly around it.

"Morning, gents," said Hannah Mackenzie at the pilothouse door. "Sounds like you've got some real ship-driving going on up here."

"Morning, Skipper," Novak answered. With mock formality, he followed with "Captain on the bridge!"

She half smiled and looped her orange, rubberized binoculars around her neck. Billy had never seen his captain without them; he considered them an appendage.

The chief stroked his wispy mustache again. "You can catch up on your sleep, ma'am. We got this."

"Nah. Can't shake the adrenaline of the midnight departure. Where are we, anyway?"

"South edge of the Orinoco Shelf," answered the chief. "In the Chute."

She rubbed her eyes and adjusted her USCGC *Harry Claiborne* ball cap over her braided hair. Twenty-nine years old, she wore the double silver bars of a lieutenant on her dark blue fatigues.

She glanced at the helmsman. "How's she feel, Billy? Z-drives performing well?"

He dared not raise his eyes from the chart plotter as he maneuvered. "Yes, ma'am. Z-drives are four-oh."

"How much longer?"

"Six hundred yards left in the Chute. I should get us through it in about fifteen minutes."

Her face dimmed by the spare red light, the skipper nodded, then climbed into her elevated captain's chair near the windows. Billy had spent many a wistful hour looking at that chair—but only the captain was ever allowed to use it.

"Looks like they're already at work over on Marlin," she said, staring through her binoculars at the distant, flickering light.

"Yes, ma'am," the chief said.

"I'm surprised the gas and oil drilling unions allow it."

"My brother's a welder."

"You should tell him to work down here. These guys make a ton."

"Yeah. But he says there's a special certification for oil work. Can't afford the school. Catch-22."

The skipper kept the binoculars to her face and looked at the rest of the horizon.

Billy saw a black symbol blink on the chart plotter, which was unexpected. To keep the ship safe from the coral, he pulled the EOTs back to idle.

"Officer of the deck," he said. "Possible contact bearing two-six-three, five miles."

"Is it broadcasting?" asked the chief. Most maritime contacts sent out a signal to show the name and type of vessel.

"Negative, Chief. It's pure radar. Not broadcasting."

Chief Novak came to Billy's side for a look. The chart plotter was synced to the surface search radar on *Dirty Harry*'s mast. It was also possible to check the raw feed on the radarscope, though rarely required. Novak sidestepped to study it carefully. He then went back to the chart plotter.

"Captain," he announced. "We've got an unknown radar contact bearing two-six-three, five miles."

She looked west, though five miles was a long way for a visual, even at the elevated height of *Dirty Harry*'s bridge. "Surface contact? Boat?"

"Not sure. More like an object. From the nature of the radar return, looks to be a mast just coming up over the horizon. But if it's a boat, it ain't moving."

"Five miles to the west . . . Isn't that the edge of Orinoco Reef?" She hopped down from her chair and approached them. "Show me."

"Here, ma'am." Billy tapped the chart plotter. "It's right there, on the eastern edge of Orinoco Reef."

"Watch the coral," admonished Novak. "We don't want to drift onto it."

Billy worked on the engines while the chief directed the captain to the radarscope. "There, ma'am. See what I mean about a mast?" The dot, a representation of the energy from a reflected radio wave, was threaded by a jagged green line.

"Huh." She crossed her arms. "Put us in a hover, Gesparek."

Billy slipped the throttles to neutral and toggled the autopilot's hover setting. Using pinpoint GPS, *Dirty Harry*'s navigation computers would swivel the Z-drives to keep the cutter in the exact same spot in the ocean.

The silence grew long. "Orders, ma'am?" asked the chief.

Hannah Mackenzie was all of five and a half feet tall with ginger hair and freckles. Her thick-soled boots and ball cap provided another few inches. She cupped her chin with her hand. "Bart, I'm thinking that might be a stranded shrimp fisher."

"That far west? That shallow?"

"Could have run aground in transit," she said. "Anything on the guard freqs before this? Any radio traffic at all?"

"Negative, ma'am," said Novak and Gesparek in unison.

The captain uncrossed her arms and leaned on the console. "'Kay. Let's try a guard hail."

Billy unclipped the UHF radio mic and held it close to his lips, making sure he was broadcasting on the "guard" frequency that all marine traffic in the area was supposed to monitor. "Unknown vessel in the vicinity of Orinoco Reef. This is United States Coast Guard cutter *Harry Claiborne*, over."

In a stationary hover, the *Claiborne* rose and fell quietly on the dark coastal swell. Billy repeated the call three times, but there was no response.

Lieutenant Mackenzie was a graduate of the United States Coast Guard Academy in New London, Connecticut. Not counting her summer sea excursions as a cadet, she had six full years at sea under her belt. Abetting that, she'd been raised in Juneau, Alaska, the daughter of a king crab fisherman. She'd sooner die than ignore a stranded mariner.

"Someone's stuck out there," she decreed, fists balled at her sides. "How close can we get?"

"Let me figure it," the chief said.

He adjusted the chart plotter, zooming in and out of the area near the radar return. "We'd need to thread through these coral patches, here. It gets down to two feet in some spots. We might have five feet at this tide level—close enough to launch the motor whaleboat. We could drop the hook over here in the trough."

The motor whaleboat was a rubber Zodiac with an outboard—another outdated equipment name.

Mackenzie cast an impish grin, magnified by the red light of the bridge. "Billy, are you ready to try your first surf rescue?"

Gesparek's head snapped up. "Absolutely, ma'am!"

She chuckled. "Let's get him, boys. Chief, back up Gesparek on the controls. It's gonna get ugly in there among the reef breakers."

"Aye, aye, ma'am," the chief responded.

For the next twenty minutes, Gesparek worked the nimble *Claiborne* through the shallow seas with the chief at his side. He announced their position to Lieutenant Mackenzie when they were in a relatively deep trough with enough room to drop the anchor and swing safely.

"Okay," she replied from behind her binoculars. "Let's make sure before we get the sea-and-anchor detail out of the rack. Try 'em again, Billy."

Billy repeated the call on the guard frequency. Still no reply.

"Hit the lights," she ordered.

Billy cranked the knob for the powerful spotlights on *Dirty Harry*'s mast, directing them with a joystick to the thick of the reef, three hundred yards off their port bow. He saw the slosh of white water creaming over partially submerged rocks.

The captain swept her binoculars back and forth. "No navigation lights," she reported. "I got nothing but dark. Maybe we—"

She was cut off by a staticky screech from the radio speaker. The chief immediately cranked it down. "Damn. That was weird," he said.

"We've lost radar," Gesparek announced. "Screen's blanked."

"What do you mean blanked?" asked the captain, leaning back to see for herself.

"Screen's whited out, ma'am." Billy pointed to the glass scope. It was glowing brightly, like an old TV tube, ruining their night vision.

She dropped the binoculars to her chest and hurried to his side. "Chart plotter still functioning?"

"Yes, ma'am. I'm going to have to go hard to starboard to stay in this trough."

"Do it."

Beside her, the chief rotated through the radio channels and played with the squelches. Then he tried the long-range HF high-frequency band and the international maritime satellite phone called Inmarsat. "All comms down, ma'am. Nothing but static."

"What the hell?" she asked, running her fingers over the radio controls and getting the same result.

Gesparek had completed a turn to the east to stay in the trough. The foundering vessel they'd spotted on radar—if that's what it was—lay somewhere behind them now.

"This isn't right," the captain declared, one hand on her hip, orange binoculars hanging from her neck. She backed to the comms console and snagged the HF mic to broadcast in the blind. "This is United States Coast Guard cutter *Harry Claiborne*. We are at—"

A loud thud boomed behind them.

Simultaneously, the ship tilted suddenly forward as its stern bucked out of the water.

Thrown from the comms console, the skipper slammed into Gesparek. An instant later, like the whiplash from a car collision, they flew back as the stern splashed down. Warning lights all over the control panel blinked. A deafening fire alarm howled in a low wail that rose to a repeating high pitch.

The chief ran to the aft-facing starboard bridge wing. The captain shot a dismayed glance at Billy, while his hands flew over the ship's controls. "Steerage?" she yelled over the fire alarm.

"Negative, ma'am!"

"Power?"

"Unresponsive!"

Bracing herself against a sickening port list, Mackenzie grasped the microphone for the ship's intercom system, known as the 1MC. "This is the captain. All hands set condition Zebra throughout the ship. Damage control party alpha report ASAP. This is not a drill. Repeat, not a drill." She lowered the mic when the chief ran back inside from the bridge wing.

"Fire amidships!" he cried as he burst through the hatch. "Second deck! Starboard waist to stern!"

"What kind of fire?" she hollered back.

The chief convulsed with a wretch before answering. "Fuel oil!"

The captain put the 1MC mic close to her mouth. The list had kicked to the left another few degrees. "Fire teams one through four. Class B fire reported at stanchion twenty-six-tack-eight-tack-five. Set protective barrier around fuel bladders." Gesparek could hear her voice echoing behind him.

She put the mic back in its holder and cranked the volume on the walkie-talkies in the cradle below it. Static screeched at them.

Dirty Harry's port list had increased to ten degrees. The captain clutched a handhold on the comms panel to keep her balance. "Chief! Get back there. I need to know what's happening. Go! Now!"

The chief rushed out the hatch while the list ticked a few more alarming degrees to port. Billy clung to his station at the steering console. The captain tried to get back to the walkie-talkies.

She was nearly there when an air concussion blew her from her feet, bouncing her off the port bulkhead in a flash of blinding light.

Billy was blasted away from the wheel right along with her. Staggering to her knees, the captain crawled to the port bridge wing hatch, undogged it, and stumbled outside. She clutched the rail to get upright and looked back at the rest of her ship. She immediately coughed from the thick black smoke blowing into her.

"Ma'am!" Billy shouted next to her, his face bleeding, his head throbbing. He'd toppled into the emergency locker before following her. He shoved a bulky Day-Glo-orange life vest to his captain.

Shrugging into it, she stared down at black water reflecting yellow firelight. A sudden hot gust made her cough uncontrollably and turn away. Billy pulled his T-shirt over his nose and hacked furiously.

The captain turned and grappled over equipment in the uphill climb back onto the bridge. Billy pushed her from behind while she used her arms for leverage. Racked by coughs, they both made it inside. They could scarcely breathe.

"What's the depth here?" she sputtered.

"Forty feet, ma'am," Billy wheezed. "We're still in the trough—"

His face smeared with soot, Chief Novak nearly fell through the starboard hatch, coughing furiously and sliding into the steering console. The ball cap he'd been wearing was gone, but he'd found a life jacket. His wispy mustache had curled and blackened.

"Couldn't . . . make it very far back," he rasped, close to them. "Fire . . . coming up from the second deck. Fully evolved. Red-hot."

Straining to be heard over the fire alarm, the captain shouted through cupped hands. "Damage control report?"

"Couldn't see a goddamned thing, ma'am," the chief managed. "Smoke's too thick."

"Hull damage?"

Doubled over in a wretch, Novak nodded. When he straightened, his eyes looked like pools of blood. Billy saw smoke rising from his shoulders. "I . . . tried to make it to the crew mess and engine room. No go. We're taking on water."

Hannah Mackenzie's mouth parted in disbelief. She turned to Gesparek. "Could we have hit a reef?"

He shook his head forcefully. "Negative. No way, ma'am."

The chief had gained some control over his coughing fit. "That couldn't cause this, Captain. Something blew up." He rubbed his eyes and blew his nose into his shirttail.

"What then? A fuel line?"

Just as the chief was trying to answer, the bridge went completely dark.

A second later, yellow battle lanterns bolted to the ceiling girders clicked on. Billy could see blue smoke hovering before his eyes in the harsh white light. He touched the throttles and turned the wheel. He felt no resistance. The engine needles were dead.

"Maybe a power surge building in the engine room took the radios and radars offline," the chief hollered. "We're on backup DC power. Radios work yet?"

Hanging on to a stanchion, the captain grabbed the UHF radio microphone and dialed the frequency for the tiny Guyanese navy. They'd had several liaisons with their three American-made patrol boats over the prior six weeks.

"Mayday, Mayday, Mayday, this is U.S. Coast Guard cutter *Harry Claiborne*. We are in distress, listing, on fire . . ." She continued to describe their condition and rattled off their coordinates. She paused to listen for a response.

Nothing.

She dropped the mic. It swung at a slant.

"We're top-heavy," the chief warned, gripping a ceiling girder. "Might capsize."

As if to prove his point, the big crane on the foredeck broke loose from its tether lines. With a stomach-churning groan, it swung to port. Under the glare of the mast's bright lights, they could see its big heavy hook splash into the water. The port list notched a few degrees farther with the crane's weight.

Lieutenant Hannah Mackenzie, captain of the *Claiborne*, put the 1MC microphone close to her lips.

LINE OF DEMARCATION

Before she spoke, Billy watched her close her reddened eyes and swallow hard.

Finally, she thumbed the 1MC's microphone button. "This is the captain. Abandon ship. I say again, all hands abandon ship."

THOUGH THE SUN HADN'T YET RISEN, THE WATER WAS STILL WARM.

Just before *Dirty Harry* had rolled over, three crew members floated up, alive and unharmed. The three junior enlisted sailors had been on the starboard side, trying to free the motor whaleboat—until the fire had melted its rubber sponsons and tossed the boat on them like a burning tree.

Billy, the captain, the chief, and the three from the whaleboat crew bobbed silently on the sea. Billy could barely fathom the depths of strain on the captain. As though respecting her privacy, he kept his eyes on *Dirty Harry*'s slimy black hull, some thirty yards away. Flames from the floating fuel fire lit the four Z-drive pods. The propellers swiveled aimlessly, like windmills in a ghost town.

The young coastguardsman did the grim math. With six survivors, it meant twelve of his shipmates were trapped inside the overturned buoy tender. He'd heard the report from one of the survivors from the whaleboat. Flames had roared through the crew mess. Water had risen from the deck plates and into the crew quarters. They'd been drowned in their beds.

"Nearest land is the reef, a thousand yards west," the captain said, snugging a lifeline to string them together. "Form a line abreast."

For the next few minutes, they kicked and paddled in a single line, floating on their backs. Before long, they were quiet again, looking back at their ruined ship. The keel was at a thirty-degree angle to the waterline, and the bow had disappeared.

"She's going down," the captain decreed. "We need to get away from the suction. Keep an eye out for survivors. On your backs. Kick!"

While they churned the water, they stared through the floating flames at the overturned wreck. When they'd made it about fifty yards, they heard several loud pops. The captain quit kicking, and the rest followed her lead.

In the glow of the oil fire, they watched the United States Coast Guard cutter *Harry Claiborne* tilt vertically. Her stern hung suspended for a moment while air popped and gurgled at her waist. Then, as though entering a hot bath, *Dirty Harry* eased slowly beneath the waves.

She left nothing but boiling seafoam and flaming oil swirling behind her.

"Kick," the captain ordered.

For five full minutes, they kicked in silence. Billy passed the time by tilting his head back and studying the sky. He saw that the approaching dawn had blotted out the stars. It would be a clear day, he could see, yet another hot one. His mind drifted back to the explosion that had broken *Dirty Harry*'s back. As if speaking ill of the dead, none of them had said much about it.

"Keep kicking. We'll get picked up by sunrise," the captain exhorted.

She reminded them of her repeated Mayday calls and the usual daytime sea traffic in these waters. While they were out of sight of Marlin, she added, they would swim to the shrimp-fishing waters. Their life vests were equipped with whistles and shiny plastic signaling mirrors. As soon as the sun came up, they'd get rescued, she insisted.

A few minutes later, Billy Gesparek realized they wouldn't have to wait that long. Having grown up with boats on summer vacations to Priest Lake, Idaho, he thought he heard a familiar sound in the water—an outboard boat engine ticking along.

LINE OF DEMARCATION

To ensure it wasn't wishful thinking, he stopped kicking, held his breath, and tilted his head back to fully submerge his ears. The peculiar property of sound traveling through the water confirmed his suspicion. An engine was buzzing away in the distance.

"Stop kicking!" he shouted. "*Quiet!*" Once they were all floating and still, Billy dipped his head for more than ten seconds. He raised it excitedly and spit the salt water out of his mouth. "I hear a boat! It's coming this way!"

"Where?" asked the captain.

"Behind us." He watched the captain dip her head. "Hear it?" he asked when she came back up, spitting.

"Whistles, people!" she commanded as soon as she could, nodding. "Hard as you can blow!"

Their whistles screeched over the surf. It wasn't long before they could hear the outboard motor without dipping their heads. Moments later, a small searchlight blinked and scanned the swells near them, just a few hundred yards away.

"Splash!" the captain yelled.

As they'd been trained, the survivors flopped their arms to send water into the air. "Here!" they called and thrashed. "Over here! Over here!"

The searchlight stopped moving. It settled on them. The engine got louder as the boat came closer.

When it was just twenty yards away, Gesparek, squinting against the bright light, could discern the outlines of two men standing on the bow of the big metal boat. Without even realizing it, he briefly touched the Surfman orders that were still in his breast pocket. Deliverance was at hand. He whooped and waved his arms—partially to direct them in, but also because he was relieved, and it felt good to move.

But then he froze. Ecstasy was replaced by a cold stab of fear.

He saw that the men on the bow were holding objects up to

their faces. They were aiming assault rifles at them. They wore masks; only their eyes were visible.

"*Down!*" screamed Gesparek.

"Submerge and scatter!" roared the captain, suddenly seeing it, too.

The crew rolled awkwardly to remove the bulky life vests pinning them to the surface. Those who'd gotten loose swam crazily, roiling the water.

But it was all too late. The gunmen on the bow opened fire, rattling away on full automatic. *Dirty Harry*'s crew were sitting ducks. When their bodies stopped moving, the gunmen quit firing. The boat drove forward, pushing the floating Coast Guardsmen sideways in the bow wave.

Billy Gesparek had been hit in the shoulder. Knowing that his shipmates were all probably dead, he lay back on the waves and played possum, waiting for the boat to leave. He grit his teeth against the searing pain and breathed slightly through his nose, trying to keep his chest still.

He heard water swishing against the boat's hull. The wake covered his face, but he didn't open his eyes. The insides of his eyelids glowed red when the light settled on them.

He never felt the headshot that ended his young life.

At last, of the lost United States Coast Guard cutter *Harry Claiborne*, it could finally be said that she'd make her mark on history.

She'd just become the first Coast Guard cutter ever lost with all hands.

1

GEORGETOWN, GUYANA
MARCH 1, 0930

THE CHILL OF THE AIR-CONDITIONING AT GEORGETOWN'S MARRIOTT HOTEL WAS LONG forgotten by the time Jack Ryan, Jr., finished walking his first block. He had five more to go before he made it to his destination, the Guyanese Parliament building, and already he could feel sweat sliding down his armpits, back, and knees. He did his best to ignore it, for he had other things on his mind.

With a suit jacket slung over one shoulder and a messenger bag on the other, Jack strode down Water Street along the banks of the muddy, fast-flowing Demerara River. The mocha-colored water was narrow and deep, carrying so much silt from the inland jungles that it colored Georgetown's entire bay.

Below Jack, on the contrastingly green banks, he watched men cast lines, hoping to hook a peacock bass. Out in the river's center, where the current was strong, the occasional broken tree swirled by in a gurgle of tan bubbles. Often the logs were huge and sturdy, broken hulks from the thick rainforests upriver, caught in the slipstream, where they'd finish their fates as Atlantic driftwood. Each time one went by, Jack was amazed at how fast they traveled.

After a quarter mile, Water Street turned inland, pointing Jack to Georgetown's interior. He joined a family of pedestrians at a stoplight, waiting to cross the road. Here, farther from the river, the scant breeze had stopped. Jack flicked his thumb across his forehead, sluicing sweat away like a windshield wiper.

A woman smiled at him, her big teeth glowing white against her dark face. She had a light bonnet wrapped over her head to guard against the sun. Beside her, three young boys in school uniforms—white shirts over blue shorts—clung to her print dress.

"You need a hat," the largest of the boys said to Jack, peering up at him. Though only about ten, Jack noticed the boy already spoke with the faintly Caribbean-British accent he'd come to enjoy in Georgetown.

"You're probably right," Jack replied, shading his eyes.

The woman glanced at him. "You really should wear one. Your neck is already pink." She rested her hand on her youngest boy's shoulder. "We always keep an eye out for visitors here, don't we, boys?" Each nodded solemnly at her.

"I'm leaving today," Jack declared. "But thank you." He went back to watching the long line of traffic, still waiting for the light to change.

The woman regarded Jack curiously. "Where are you leaving for?"

"Washington, D.C."

"So you're going to the government buildings, then. Is that right?"

"Yes. That's right."

"And you walked all the way from the big American hotel?"

Jack could feel the boys' blinking eyes on him as they waited for him to answer. "Yes, I did. I happen to think it's good to get out and see a place," he said. "And I like Georgetown."

"May I ask what you like about it?"

LINE OF DEMARCATION

The mother's eyes lingered on Jack as he stared straight ahead, groping for an answer. In the few seconds of this chance encounter at an intersection, it seemed to him there was precious little time to express the thoughts running through his mind.

When he said he liked Georgetown, he didn't mean the weather, muddy river, or lashing rains that came over the sugarcane fields. Rather, he liked the people, the plucky attitude, the outright promise of the place unfolding before his eyes.

During a ten-day business trip, Jack had formed the view that Georgetown was that rare frontier settlement where something amazing was about to happen, where the rest of the world was about to come rushing in, like San Francisco before the gold rush. The charm lay in its innocence, the way its citizens didn't realize their coming significance, like a beautiful adolescent girl who had no time for mirrors. But he couldn't figure out how to say all of that to this young mother and her three boys.

The light turned green. One of the boys rummaged through his knapsack and produced a small white handkerchief. He held it out to Jack as he was about to cross the street. "For your head, sir," he said earnestly.

Jack knelt. Accepting it with dignity, he thanked the boy with a clap on the shoulder.

Before long, Jack found himself walking in a tightly packed grid of colonial buildings. Ahead of schedule, he slowed to watch a cricket match with players in their teens. The nearby school had mowed an oval in a vacant lot dotted with bowing palm trees.

Jack found a patch of shade with a mild Atlantic breeze and tried to make sense of the game, until he heard the church bells clanging from the belfry atop the whitewashed, Victorian St. George's Cathedral. That made it ten o'clock, time for his meeting.

He stood alone on the boulevard between the church and the

parliament building, again waiting for the traffic to clear. Then, stepping onto the pavement, he nearly got himself killed. As in all former British colonies, the Guyanese drove on the left side of the road. Distracted by the cricket match, Jack had looked the wrong way.

None the worse for wear, a minute later he stood before an impressive wrought-iron fence, wiping his forehead with the handkerchief the boy had given him.

The Guyanese parliament building before him was yet another reminder of the country's colonial roots and hidden charm. Though hardly the Palace of Westminster, Jack found its double rows of arches and soaring dome a reasonable representation of Victorian grandeur.

While approaching the heavy gates, he tightened his tie, shrugged into his jacket, and folded the boy's handkerchief into a neat, breast pocket square. Conscious of the two government guards who watched him, he smoothed his hair and buttoned his jacket. He then retrieved his passport from his trouser pocket and held it as he approached, making sure they knew he wasn't a threat.

The guards, two parade-ready officers of the Guyanese National Police Force, eyed him carefully. They wore spit-shined boots, jaunty black berets, and stubby MP5 machine guns slung over their shoulders.

"Good morning," Jack began, offering the passport. "I have an appointment with Dr. Quintero, the minister of the interior. We're supposed to meet here at ten o'clock."

The two guards twitched their eyes over Jack like a pair of Dobermans. One of them took the passport and stuck it to a clipboard, while the other ran a handheld metal detector over Jack's body.

"What is the name of your company?" Clipboard asked, while the other guard searched Jack's bag.

LINE OF DEMARCATION

Jack tugged one of the freshly printed business cards from his wallet. "I'm the chief executive officer of Athena Global Shipping Lines," he declared. "I've been here a time or two before." Though he didn't want to insult the guard, he'd been here four times in the prior ten days. Each time they went through the same rigmarole.

Clipboard studied the card carefully, just as he had during the previous instances. "It's an oil shipping company," the guard said.

Since Jack and the guard had graduated to a conversational level, he ventured a little more detail. "Ships for liquified natural gas, technically. Shallow draft bulk carriers designed for the Orinoco Basin. Three of them, to be exact."

Just as he had on Jack's previous visits, the guard made a note on the clipboard with a stubby golf pencil. His eyes lingered a little longer on the business card. "It says here your company is in San Juan, Puerto Rico."

"That's correct."

He handed Jack's passport back and lowered the clipboard to the table. "But you're an American."

"So are the Puerto Ricans. Feel free to keep the card."

Without another word, the guard pressed a buzzer and the heavy iron gate swung open. Jack stepped through it and strode the length of the curved driveway to the front door.

"Jack boy!" boomed the deep baritone of the Guyanese minister of the interior, Dr. Alberto Quintero.

"Good morning, Professor. Nice to see you again." Jack offered his hand.

Quintero, a big man of African Caribbean descent, shook it with an iron grip. At fifty-eight his tightly curled hair had gone gray. His advanced chemical engineering degree from the University of Chicago and subsequent tenure at a Guyanese university earned him the nickname Professor. "Where are your bags?" he asked, noting Jack's absence of luggage.

"With the bellhop at the hotel."

"You look hot. You didn't walk all the way here, did you?"

"I did."

The minister laughed. "Always with the walking." He then shook his gray head while his tone turned serious. "I'm sorry for getting you back so late last night. You probably didn't get much sleep."

"Oh, sure I did. I slept fine."

"You weren't . . . hungry?"

"No. I went to the lobby bar and got a burger. Please don't tell Amancia."

A grin creased Quintero's ebony face.

The previous evening, the Guyanese interior minister had hosted Jack at his country home, an organic farm twenty miles into the rainforest, where his wife hosted ecotours and expounded on the wonders of naturally grown foods. Quintero had explained on the long drive out there that the core complaint of every guest was that the raw foods were more akin to basic jungle survival than a hotel meal.

"What about you, Professor?" Jack asked, unable to keep a straight face. "Did you go to bed hungry?"

Partial to untucked, military-style khaki shirts, Quintero seized his belly with both hands. "Do I look like I only eat her cooking? I have a whole cupboard in the barn out by the llama pasture. Don't tell anyone."

"I won't," Jack agreed with a full-fledged grin. "Promise."

The minister led him to a staircase with a polished mahogany railing, speaking over his shoulder. "I won't keep you long. Your export license should be ready. Come on. Let's get to my office."

The floor was white marble bordered by black. It was an airy place, filled with the echoes of clicking feet and distant voices common to government halls the world over. Jack walked quickly, an eagerness in his step. As much as he liked the people of Guyana, he missed his fiancée, Lisanne, and looked forward to his business-class flight home that afternoon—so long as he had that export license in his bag.

"Are you still expecting your first ship to show up tomorrow?" Quintero asked after settling behind his capacious desk.

"I am," Jack answered with pride. "I checked in with San Juan this morning. The *Helena* is halfway here."

The *Helena* was Athena's best-maintained liquified natural gas transport ship. Jack had acquired the shipping company ninety days earlier as a new venture for Hendley Associates, the private equity firm for which he worked as an investment manager.

Athena's small fleet happened to be the only one in the world that could make it to the gas and oil platforms off the coast of Georgetown without dredging up the sensitive coral reefs—a firm requirement of the interior minister.

Jack's company, Hendley Associates, was not a typical private equity firm motivated purely by profit. While its capitalist "white-side" business was wholly legitimate, it served a dual purpose as a funding source and cover for a "black-side" covert organization: The Campus.

Similar to its like-minded brothers in the CIA's Special Activities Division, The Campus took direction from the President in national security direct-action missions that prized speed, discretion, and deniability above all else. But unlike the CIA, only the President, the director of national intelligence, and a handful of operators on Hendley's black side knew The Campus existed.

Jack was in Guyana on a profit-seeking business trip. His white-side boss, Howard Brennan, the firm's chief investment officer, didn't know of Jack's occasional black-side missions. And for Jack's dealings with Athena, Guyana, and Interior Minister Quintero, that was just fine.

"And what's the plan to mate it up to Marlin?" Quintero asked.

Marlin, the offshore drilling platform, had been built with public money from the Guyanese Treasury and private funds from American energy companies. Jack had spotted the opportunity to off-load to score the first export license when he heard that those American energy companies were dependent on pipelines to get the product into major oil ports—since the waters around the platforms were otherwise too shallow for tankers.

"It will just be a test," Jack explained. "The *Helena* will pull up alongside Marlin with empty LNG tanks, fill them up about halfway, and off-load them up in Houston at an Optimum facility." Optimum was the joint Guyanese-American consortium that had built the three offshore platforms Marlin, Mako, and Mackerel.

"Then I'd better get you that license," the minister said, swiveling to thumb the pages of a notebook.

While Quintero hunched over his credenza, Jack took note of the various pictures and memorabilia arranged to either side of him. There were the pictures of his wife, Amancia, and his daughter, Tallulah. Amancia was an American whom the professor had met in the circles of academia. Tallulah, Jack recalled, was a student at UC Berkeley, back home in Guyana for a final research project.

Beyond the family photos, Quintero's office wall was decked out with various awards and citations. One was a replica hard hat from ExxonMobil mounted to a plaque declaring Quintero an honorary roughneck. Another was a miniature golden pickax from British Petroleum naming him the world's foremost geologist. On the top right, Jack saw the large EIIR crest on an award from Queen Elizabeth, given before she passed. It recognized Quintero's natural conservation initiatives for the British Commonwealth.

The interior minister shifted from his notebook and studied his computer screen. "That license should be along any minute now," he extolled. He looked over his reading glasses at Jack and raised a graying eyebrow. "While we wait . . . I must say, Amancia was most impressed with your speech about preserving the coral reefs, Mr. Ryan."

Jack cocked his head. "Well, I wouldn't call it a speech. But—was she? Really?"

"Oh yes. She thinks you're the only man in this industry willing to respect our ecology and undersea diversity."

"Maybe not the only one," Jack said pridefully. "But there sure aren't many of us."

While he planned to exit the business in the next few months when he sold Athena Global Shipping Lines along with its newly acquired export license, Jack's lasting contribution to the enterprise would always be that he'd found a way for LNG carriers to get to the GOPLATs without touching the seafloor, respecting the interior minister's requirements. The big oil companies certainly had the wherewithal to do that, too, but they would rather use the scale of the large tankers they already had rather than invest in a niche business like shallow-water shipping. With the work Jack had done, he had made sure Guyana preserved its natural environment while allowing it to grow its wealth.

"The major energy companies are going to wait for those pipelines to get built," Jack added. "Or at least for the channels to get marked by the Coast Guard so some processing barges can come in."

"Or that I'll fold on my requirements first," the minister slyly remarked.

"You think so?"

"Oh, yes. The big energy firms know damn well I'm in the political hot seat. They've got armies of lobbyists swinging through those doors out there, trying to persuade me to back off."

The sixty-mile expanse of Orinoco Basin, a sandstone hydrocarbon field beneath the shallow waters of the Guyanese coastline, was presently considered the planet's largest untapped fossil fuel reserve. On a per capita basis, it would soon make the eight hundred thousand citizens of Guyana the world's richest people, which had led to heated political arguments about how the wealth should be managed.

"They don't realize you can take the heat," Jack declared, meaning it. He knew personally how committed Quintero was to preserving the local ecology.

Quintero harrumphed. "You got that right. I've got every major global oil company in the world vying for this first license, coming in with all kinds of proposals, money, investments in the local economy . . . Even a few outright bribes, I'm sorry to say."

Jack winced. "You turn any of them over to the national police force?"

The professor laughed. "Where do you think the businessmen got the idea that bribes work around here?"

Like many developing countries, Guyana battled corruption. The incoming wealth would only make it worse. Jack nodded in sad agreement.

"But," continued Quintero, "I tell all of them the same thing I told you when we first met—build a ship that doesn't require dredging to get to the platforms, and I'll consider an export license. *No dredging.*"

Jack glanced at the family pictures behind Quintero. "If they don't think you mean it, you should introduce them to your wife."

The minister rapped his desk twice and then pointed at Jack. "Exactly right. Now. My secretary should be bringing that license in a few minutes. You want a Cuban?" He pushed a dark humidor to the edge of his desk. Jack demurred. Quintero lit up with a brass Zippo and puffed.

While they discussed Jack's air-travel plans back to the States and the details of the *Helena*'s expected arrival in Georgetown Bay, Quintero's computer chirped. He studied the monitor. "Oh damn," he muttered, frowning after a lengthy read. "I'm sorry."

"Problem with the export license?"

"Yeah."

Jack pulled his sleeve up to glance at his well-worn Rolex Submariner. It was twenty past ten. He had an early afternoon flight back to D.C., connecting through Miami, and was anxious to be on it—with that export license.

"I'm sorry, Professor, what's the problem?"

Quintero sighed huskily through the smoke. "Well, you know President Khasif, my boss, is out of the country."

"Yes," said Jack. "You mentioned that he's in the Middle East, exploring OPEC membership or something like that."

"Correct. Which means the prime minister, Guto Castillo, is our acting chief executive. He's from the opposition party."

Jack inhaled shakily. "And . . . how does that affect granting the license?"

The interior minister stubbed out the cigar and placed it on the edge of his ashtray, apparently saving it for later. "It affects it because . . . Castillo is refusing to sign off on it."

Jack tried to play it cool.

Right at that moment, the *Helena* was churning across the Caribbean, burning through cash. If he couldn't secure this Guyanese government export license, he would have to hurriedly liquidate the otherwise unemployed shipping company, losing about thirty million dollars for Hendley Associates. The carefully calculated gamble he'd proposed to his boss, Howard Brennan, would go bust. It wouldn't be a big enough loss to seriously hurt Hendley Associates in the long run; but, as Jack saw it, the hit to his credibility as a new venture investor was inestimable.

"I don't understand," Jack said. "I've presented all the due diligence. This has been in the works for a month. You approved it yourself yesterday as interior minister. We toasted it last night—that homemade prickly-pear wine Amancia brought back from Chilé."

"Of course."

"In all that celebration, I didn't realize there was another hoop to jump through."

"There shouldn't be. Getting the executive leadership to sign it should be a formality, a rubber stamp."

"But . . . then why won't Prime Minister Castillo sign it?"

The minister raised his eyes to the slowly churning ceiling fan as though in prayer. "I'm not sure Job would have the patience for Guyanese government processes. I believe you know something of the fractured politics around here."

"I guess."

"Then you know Castillo is a socialist. He led the opposition to the privatization plan."

"Yes. I also know that the socialists lost the vote in parliament to nationalize the hydrocarbon field. I know that your party, along with your president's, won the right to develop the Orinoco Basin commercially."

"Exactly right."

"So what should we do to get Castillo to sign it?"

Quintero pushed himself up out of his chair with a grunt. "Why don't we go up and ask him? He's not all bad."

2

PARLIAMENT BUILDING, GEORGETOWN, GUYANA
1030

THE PRIME MINISTER'S OFFICE WAS ON THE LEFT WING OF THE BUILDING, UP THREE flights and down a long hallway.

"An honor to meet you, Mr. Ryan," Guto Castillo said, coming out from behind his desk with his hand extended. His office was large and plush, sporting royal-blue carpet, gold drapery, oil paintings, and a phalanx of Guyanese flags. It struck Jack that had the walls been curved, it would have looked a bit like the Oval Office.

Jack shook his hand. "Mr. Prime Minister. The pleasure is all mine." He guessed that Augustus "Guto" Castillo was in his early forties. The leader of the Guyanese Socialist Party looked the part of a South American politician right out of central casting. His bearing was patrician, his hair thick, his suit perfectly cut.

"Mr. Ryan, I have been impressed by your company's commitment to our coral reefs and our ecological environment in general," he said. "Very few of your peer companies operate with such . . . respect for the planet."

"Thank you, sir," Jack replied. Gesturing to Quintero, he added, "It is as important to me as it is to your interior minister."

Castillo acknowledged the comment and waved them to a sofa. The prime minister took a padded chair and crossed his legs.

"Now," he began. "What seems to be the issue, gentlemen? What can I do for you, Mr. Ryan?"

"Mr. Prime Minister," Quintero began. "I have awarded our first export license for the Orinoco Basin hydrocarbon field to Mr. Ryan's company—Athena Global Shipping Lines. Athena has ships with a shallow-enough draft to dock at the first completed offshore platform, Marlin, without dredging. After thorough due diligence by my staff, I am comfortable with the award."

"I see."

"Yes. And, Mr. Prime Minister, with President Khasif off in the Middle East—"

"The United Arab Emirates. Abu Dhabi, specifically," interrupted Castillo.

"Yes. Be that as it may, I need your signature on the license before Mr. Ryan can begin his first test shipment. He has a vessel approaching Guyana that embarked from, from . . ."

"San Juan," interjected Jack. "Puerto Rico. She'll be here in Georgetown Bay tomorrow. We're going to do the first natural gas off-load test on Marlin and then sell the LNG in Houston. The Guyanese Treasury will get its fair share of the revenue."

Castillo smoothed the fabric on his crossed thigh with his hand, looking down. "Yes. I saw the request for the license signature. I did not realize there was such a rush."

"That is why we're here," Quintero explained. "I told Jack I would deliver his license today. I cannot allow him to off-load the LNG without the export license."

The prime minister tented his fingers and held them before his nose. "I see. But I'm afraid I can't do that. There have been a few developments."

"What developments?" Quintero inquired. "This should be a formality."

Castillo took a deep breath before answering. "I have seen some recent legal arguments that would suggest otherwise."

Jack's heart pounded. As in all foreign ventures, he had expected political risks. But when it came to Guyana, he judged them as manageable.

The Guyanese government had passed a law allowing for the privatization of the hydrocarbon field. Moreover, Jack knew Guyana was strengthening its alliance with the United States. The State Department believed it was an important relationship because Guyana acted as a bulwark against the Russian-leaning Venezuelans.

To shore up the alliance, the Pentagon sold the Guyanese patrol boats, conducted joint military maneuvers, and visited naval ports. Two days ago, Jack saw a U.S. Coast Guard vessel in Georgetown Bay planting buoys for safe navigation.

For all these reasons, he didn't think the political risk of investing in Guyanese infrastructure was significant. Nor was he alone in that assessment—every energy giant from Houston to Riyadh was lining up to invest in Guyanese oil and gas.

With these thoughts flooding his head, the Hendley investor couldn't keep from speaking up. "But, Mr. Prime Minister, that's not right. You've passed a law. Many companies, including mine, have already—"

Quintero held up a thick hand, cutting Jack off. "Prime Minister Castillo. As a member of the executive branch, the president and I have the authority to grant the export licenses and contribute the fees to the Treasury. You suddenly doubt this?"

"As a matter of fact, Minister Quintero, yes, I do have my doubts."

"Why?"

"Last night, I read a new analysis from the judiciary. It seems there are . . . differing opinions on the law as currently passed. I can hardly act on it in good conscience. Certainly not without a much more thorough review."

Quintero's eyes flashed. "Oh? And where is the ambiguity, sir? We voted for the privatization of the Orinoco Basin. We backed it up with a referendum of the people. We all agreed we would set up a sovereign wealth fund to administer it. The law states that the minister of the interior—that would be me—has the jurisdiction, nay, the duty to execute private partnerships that maximize the value of the fund."

"Yes, Minister. I agree with all that," Castillo parried. "But the law on which we voted also says that such partnerships are, and I quote, 'subject to the national government's approval.'"

A veteran of many an academic debate, Quintero allowed an appreciative grin. "But in this case, that would mean the executive branch. For it is the president who *forms* said national government. You, yourself, sir, as the leader of the socialists, agreed to the coalition government."

"Or," countered Castillo, "the law might be interpreted to mean the approval of *the entire* national government. And if that is the case, then it would mean a national assembly vote."

Quintero's lips puckered in fresh appraisal of his political opponent.

The phone on the prime minister's desk trilled insistently.

Castillo ignored it. "Minister Quintero, I assume you've read the latest reports from the National Intelligence and Security Agency?"

"Yes," Quintero answered. "I read the NISA digest every morning."

"Then you have seen, sir, the diplomatic concerns of Guyanese oil and gas development harbored by the Bolivarian Republic of Venezuela."

Quintero crossed his legs and leaned back. "If you mean the Venezuelan dictatorship, then yes, I certainly have heard of those objections. But what you call 'diplomatic concerns' I call the posturing of a threatened regime. They're worried we'll bring down the price of oil and break their economy. Such are the risks, Prime Minister, of what economists call the 'Dutch disease,' or overreliance on a single commodity."

Castillo briskly shook his head. "Oh, that the verities of foreign relations were so simple as those taught in the classroom, Professor," he said wistfully. "The Bolivarian Republic of Venezuela is concerned with far more than crude oil prices. They've revived their territorial ambitions again. That means the Orinoco Basin has become, I regret, a matter of national security."

Observing the volley, Jack mentally revived his political risk calculations. He'd been reading about Venezuela's posturing for months. While the rhetoric was often heated, Jack considered it so much hot air. Given the growing U.S. presence in the country, the State Department's professional opinion was that it was unlikely the Venezuelans would ever act on their unsubstantiated territorial claims.

As if reading Jack's mind, Quintero made the same point. "The Venezuelans have been crying about Essequibo since Guyana got independence in 1966, for heaven's sake. This is nothing new. It's bluster."

"The discovery of the world's largest hydrocarbon reserve in the Orinoco Basin is new. The Venezuelans consider that part of the Essequibo region, what they call their 'lost province.'"

"You are making my point about the Dutch disease. The dictator can do nothing else. He is desperate. We must not suffer his same fate—precisely why we passed the privatization plan."

Comfortable with the ebb and flow of diplomacy, Castillo waited a polite moment before responding. "Nevertheless, Minister, I can tell you that the Socialist Party will formally object to the grant of a Guyanese export license without a vote of the legislature."

"I see," Quintero said, recognizing the tone. "And your position is solid, then."

"It is."

Quintero abruptly stood, nodded, and turned to exit. Jack and Castillo followed.

Having won the argument for the day, the prime minister warmed the atmosphere. "So . . . Mr. Ryan. Have you enjoyed your stay in Guyana?"

Jack knew enough about politics to treat Castillo with respect. He answered lightly, struggling to make his voice pleasant. "Very much, Prime Minister, thank you. I have found the people warm and inviting."

"Wonderful people, aren't they? Did you get to see some of the rainforest?"

"Yes, sir. I had the pleasure of dining with Minister Quintero's family at his ranch in the hills."

"Ah, yes. Mrs. Quintero prepared beetroot, butter squash, and tree bark or the like?" The prime minister grinned. "And you will be leaving today, as I understand it?"

The comment struck Jack. He'd been through Guyana's immigration queues like any other visitor. But it made little sense to him that Castillo should know Jack's travel plans off the top of his head.

He let it go. "Yes, Mr. Prime Minister. I have a flight at two o'clock."

"I assume you need to get back to your hotel to get your bags and so forth?"

"Yes, I need to pick up my bags from the front desk."

"Then, please. The least I can do is grant you the use of my car and driver. They'll get you back to the Marriott and over to the airport quickly. My chief of staff, Sheila, will handle it for you."

Before he knew it, the door was closed behind him, Quintero was hustling down the steps, and Sheila was bundling Jack into the back seat of a black SUV.

3

PARLIAMENT BUILDING, GEORGETOWN, GUYANA
1100

"THAT WAS THE AMERICAN AMBASSADOR ON THE PHONE EARLIER," SHEILA SAID after seeing Jack off and returning to Castillo's office.

"What?" he gasped, paling. "*That's* who was calling earlier? Are you serious?"

"Yes, she phoned twice while you were in the meeting."

"I told you always to put her through when the ambassador calls, Sheila."

"I did. That's why the phone was ringing."

The prime minister marched briskly to his desk. He parted the curtains so he could see the government Range Rover leave the gate with Jack Ryan aboard. Sheila waited at the threshold.

Her continued presence suddenly irritated Castillo. "Well, put her through, for God's sake," he barked.

"Madame Ambassador," the prime minister said into the phone handset a moment later, still standing at the window. "My deepest apologies for missing your calls earlier. I understand you're on your way to Suriname?"

"Yes," replied Sydney O'Keefe, a no-nonsense, career State Department foreign service officer who'd been elevated to the post of U.S. ambassador to Guyana by President Jack Ryan, Sr. "This isn't the best connection, I'm afraid. I hope you can hear me all right, Mr. Prime Minister?"

"I can tell you're on a cell phone, but you sound fine. My assistant said you have a matter of some urgency. What can I do for you?"

By now Castillo could see that the Range Rover had disappeared around the bright white angles of St. George's Cathedral. With the phone still cupped to his ear, he eased into his leather chair and swiveled behind his desk, basking in the satisfaction of having defeated Dr. Alberto Quintero in a legal debate. He also quite admired Sydney O'Keefe's long legs and hoped to deepen their relationship beyond the professional realm.

"Yes, that's right," continued the ambassador. "Listen, Mr. Prime Minister—"

"You have earned the right to address me as Guto when we are alone, Madame Ambassador."

In addition to Sydney's athletic legs, taut stomach, and ginger hair, Castillo found her position as the highest-ranking American in the country irresistibly attractive. And useful.

"Thank you, Mr. Prime Minister."

Disappointed that she hadn't used his first name, Castillo swiveled restlessly.

"Sir," she went on. "Our naval attaché has some concerns about a missing U.S. Coast Guard vessel that left the port of Georgetown at two o'clock this morning. Are you aware of the issue?"

Castillo stopped swiveling. "I'm sorry, Madame Ambassador. You're hitting me cold with this one. Have you any further details?"

"As you'll recall, sir, we had a cutter in Georgetown. The crew was installing navigation buoys to help ships approach the new oil platforms you're building. We ordered the cutter to Guyana at the request of President Khasif and Minister Quintero."

Remembering that Khasif had allowed the American Coast Guard to come to Guyana, Castillo twisted the phone cord tightly around his finger. It wasn't enough that men like Khasif and Quintero had sold them out with this privatization plan for the American oil companies. The U.S. was even leaning in with its own Coast Guard to establish the basics of maritime infrastructure—as if Guyana couldn't manage its own waters.

"I do recall," he replied smoothly, "that we approved buoy installations over the sensitive coral reef areas and that an American team would do the work. But forgive me, Madame Ambassador; I have hardly been close to the project."

"Of course, sir. I was simply reminding you that we had a cutter in Georgetown. And now, regrettably, I must also ask for your help. Our naval attaché tells me that some local fishermen reported an oil slick and wreckage debris in the area northwest of the offshore platforms. Given that the cutter isn't responding to radio calls, we've concluded that it may have been lost, perhaps wrecked on Orinoco Reef."

The mention of Orinoco Reef made Castillo sit up straight. He leaned forward on his elbows and sifted through a dozen responses. When he found the words he wanted, his mouth felt dry. "The waters around Orinoco Reef are famously dangerous, barely navigable, I'm told. Even for an American Coast Guard vessel."

"Yes," she said. "Our attaché agrees. But I have reason to believe there has been an incident at sea involving other mariners or, perhaps, some foul play."

An incident at sea . . . foul play . . . on Orinoco Reef. Castillo cleared his throat, faked a cough, and tried to sound calm. "What reasons?"

"The workers on the oil platform called Marlin heard the vessel radioing a distressed vessel, coming to its aid around three this morning. Then the oilmen said they heard an explosion."

The prime minister clamped a hand over his forehead in disbelief. "An explosion, you say?"

"Yes. Their words, not mine. And now the cutter—she's called the *Harry Claiborne*—is completely off the radio grid. I'm calling to see if you can mount a search and rescue operation. Immediately."

His hand still on his forehead, he answered, "Of course, Madame Ambassador. And on a personal level, may I extend my wishes to you that your crew is safe?"

"Thank you, Mr. Prime Minister. I am grateful for your concern."

"I will initiate a search immediately. You have my word on that."

After she hung up, he returned the phone to its cradle. He leaned back, tilted his face toward the ceiling, and closed his eyes.

The idiot, he seethed inwardly. *The goddamned, hotheaded idiot.*

His eyes sprang open. "Sheila!" he bellowed.

His chief of staff was at the door two seconds later. "Sir?"

"Get Alejandro Romero for me. Now."

Alejandro Romero was the director of the recently established Guyanese National Intelligence and Security Agency.

"Director Romero is in Costa Rica, sir. At that conference. You approved his trip."

Irritated that she should add the modifier that he approved Romero's travel himself, Castillo shot out of his chair and breezed past her, heading for the hallway. "Right. I'm going to get some air. I expect you to have Romero on the line before I get back."

He turned left past her desk and walked to the end of the hall, where he climbed two flights of fire stairs, heading for the roof. When he gained it, he paced on the gravel and cast his eyes toward the brown ribbon of the Demerara River, glinting in the late-morning sun under a cloudless sky. He dug through his trouser pocket and found the small burner flip phone buried there.

He lifted its lid and turned it on, expecting to find a message—especially after hearing what the American ambassador had to say. But seeing none, he stood motionless for a moment, wondering what to do. He grew peevish at his own indecision and the uncomfortable lack of shade. His thumb finally fell on the button that would dial the preprogrammed number.

Juan Machado, the drug lord better known as Tiburón, was the scariest person Castillo had ever met. To the prime minister, the drug lord was a hotheaded idiot. But a useful hotheaded idiot.

Castillo listened to the clicks of the mobile network that would connect him to the psychopath's Venezuelan refuge.

"Guto, my boy," Tiburón boomed on the third ring. "What can I get you? Are you already out of coke again?"

"Tiburón, I—"

"Not coke? Must be a woman, then. You like them, what, skinny, right? I know your pretty little wife has closed her legs to you."

Castillo shuddered. Only a month prior, his wife—a Spanish beauty he'd met on holiday in Ibiza—had indeed closed her legs to him. Isabela had also taken herself and their two boys to her native Spain when she'd caught Castillo in flagrante delicto with two naked Colombian ladies and an eight ball of cocaine in his supposedly secret hotel on Water Street.

"No, it's not about that," Castillo cut in while the sun warmed his head. He paced until he found a sliver of protection under a slanted air-conditioning duct. "I heard from—"

"Oh, I know what you want," Tiburón blustered from a hundred miles north of Georgetown. "You're worried about your daughters. Trust me, Senor Castillo, they are fine. Isabela found a nice place in Madrid, not far from that big square they have there, living well. Now, Isabela, I think she spends all her time shopping, they tell me, and lately, visiting some of those young *caballeros*, giving those boys anything they want. They come around for your daughters, but they like Isabela. She spends. Have you checked your accounts? Not the one you get from me. I mean the one with your pathetic government pay."

Castillo waited a few seconds before replying, reminding himself that many a great man had walked through sludge to attain the top seat in government. He wasn't so much concerned about losing Isabela. Their relationship had been going south for years, and he doubted it would recover since she'd caught him red-handed with Tiburón's prostitutes. For all his faults, Castillo loved his daughters. The thought that Tiburón even knew who they were scared him to death.

"Tiburón, listen to me," he said as firmly as he dared. "The U.S. ambassador called me this morning. She said an American ship, a Coast Guard cutter, has gone missing near Orinoco Reef. She said there was an explosion. They suspect foul play. Orinoco Reef, Tiburón."

"Aha. And what of it?"

"What of it?"

"Yes. There is no more ship at Orinoco Reef. It blew up. There is no more crew, either. My men took care of it."

Castillo inhaled sharply. Hazy in the distance on the tan bay, he could make out the three oil platforms built by Optimum, the joint venture between the Guyanese sovereign wealth fund and a bevy of American oil companies.

"What do you mean when you say you took care of it?"

"I mean that ship got too close to our people. They were busy unloading the weapons. The Coast Guard ship was coming to look at them. An *American* Coast Guard ship, *gilipollas*, you see?

You have nothing to worry about. I took care of it. I saved your ass, in fact."

Castillo couldn't believe his ears. "What did you do?" he asked weakly.

"My men struck. The Russian missiles. Think of it as an exercise, target practice. Think of it as protecting our interests. That's how a government man like you would put it, I think."

The prime minister used his free hand to pinch the bridge of his nose. With his eyes clenched shut, he chanced what he considered a reasonable question to the drug lord. "Tiburón, do you really think there will be no repercussions from sinking an American military vessel?"

Before Tiburón could answer, Castillo heard a clattering buzz over the phone. It was noisy enough that the drug lord had to raise his voice. "Listen, Guto. Our mutual friend Morozov is coming onto the *Gran Blanco* now. I'll discuss it with him."

"How does Morozov even know about this?" Castillo stammered, realizing it was a helicopter settling onto the bow of Tiburón's yacht, the *Gran Blanco*. "This needs to be kept quiet. We need a plan . . . a cover story . . . something. Fast."

"Don't worry," Tiburón shouted over the rising din.

The line went dead. Castillo stared at the phone in his hand for a few seconds. Thinking of Ambassador Sydney O'Keefe, he removed the phone's battery and SIM card. On the way back downstairs, he dumped the entire handful into a trash can.

"I have Director Romero on the line," Sheila said as he crossed by her desk in the anteroom, chuffing from the rush down the steps.

Gripped with worry, Castillo nodded brusquely as he passed.

But then he slowed in the few steps before his desk. There were two useful idiots in his orbit, he reminded himself.

Time to put the other one to use.

4

RITZ-CARLTON HOTEL, GUANACASTE, COSTA RICA
1015

ALEJANDRO LUIS ROMERO LAY SUPINE IN THE CHAISE BESIDE THE PRIVATE POOL OF his cliffside villa.

His shirtless torso was greased to the point that the sun broiled his naturally mocha-colored shoulders two shades darker. He tilted his head just far enough above the rolled towel to take a sip of his morning cocktail, a hair of the dog that was helping ease his nagging headache.

The phone on the table buzzed—again. He ignored it for the third time in an hour and let his free hand slide over the backside of the sleeping woman next to him. He cupped one of her butt cheeks in a lazy grope, moving aside a narrow stripe of spandex that under the strictest sense of the word might be called a bikini bottom.

Romero let his eyes drift from the glittering blue Pacific to the backs of her dark thighs, recalling the late night they'd spent together. Her name was Gabriela, a special gift sent down from Tiburón. She was part of the drug lord's Colombian harem, a group of about twenty women Tiburón shuttled between his yacht on the

Orinoco River and his mountain home in the foothills of Bogotá's Monserrate. Tiburón kept the women on a short leash in the usual way, stringing them out on drugs and threatening to murder their families.

Romero had a special appreciation for Gabriela, however, seeing her as different from the rest. She was in her mid-thirties, fifteen years younger than him, but old enough to know what was going on. There was something about the look in her eye whenever he took her to bed, as if complicit. Rumor held that her son had been fathered by Tiburón before she'd gotten too old for him. For reasons Romero didn't fully understand, he found that a major turn-on.

His hand slid up and down her sun-warmed back. He heard her groan softly.

She was still high, he guessed, but not so drugged that she didn't notice his hand. With the sun two hours from its zenith, Romero thought he might have a minute to lay her on the cool sheets inside.

The prospect aroused him, distracting him from the headache. He shifted his swimsuit to make himself more comfortable. He rose to an elbow and raised his arm, about to snap his fingers so the security man who stood at the pool gate could help carry Gabriela inside. A little cocaine was all it would take to revive her.

But just as forefinger met thumb, the phone on the table next to him buzzed for the fourth time. Romero raised his sunglasses and looked at the number, something he hadn't bothered to do until then. He grew instantly annoyed when he saw it was Castillo calling. He answered.

"Where the hell are you?" Prime Minister Guto Castillo shot.

Romero took another sip of his screwdriver. Castillo, with all his high-minded condescension, was a necessary evil—but one Romero wouldn't have to endure much longer if all went according to the plan they'd concocted with Tiburón.

"I am in Guanacaste, Costa Rica. The Intelligence Conference of the Americas. Don't you remember? You told me you wanted me to go."

Romero felt the answering silence as a modest victory. He loved subtly calling out Castillo whenever the supercilious prick slipped up.

"When are you getting back?"

Romero scratched his crotch. "Not sure yet. The ICA always has many meetings, most of them worthless."

Considering Gabriela, the villa, the view, and the unending flow of screwdrivers, the head of the Guyanese National Intelligence and Security Agency was in no particular hurry to fly back to Georgetown. And when it came to his boss, Castillo, he subscribed to a policy of vagueness when sharing his schedule.

"Are the Americans there at the conference?"

"Yes. They're here. That's why you wanted me to come in the first place, to stay close to them."

"Don't tell me why I wanted you to go. Who's there? Who exactly is representing them?"

Gabriela shifted positions, giving Romero a nice view of her tanned bosom while she drank from a water bottle. Romero watched her so intently that he forgot to answer his boss's question.

"Alejandro!"

"What?"

"What American official is there representing them?"

Gabriela got up and walked into the pool with swaying hips. Waist-deep, the Colombian beauty leaned over and splashed a little water on her leopard-print bikini top. Romero's eyes tracked her like a predator. "The American director of national intelligence herself, Mary Pat Foley, is here at the conference today. She's meeting with all of us, one-on-one, then speaking at the dinner tonight."

"So you have a meeting with Director Foley?"

"Yes."

"When?"

"Not until this evening. But I'm sure she'll be late in some kind of power play. So it could be late. I don't know."

"But you've seen the American delegation?"

Now Romero was genuinely annoyed. Here was Gabriela, virtually begging him to come and pull her legs around him in the pool. But instead of doing that, he had to sit here in the chaise and assuage his uptight boss.

"Everyone has seen them, Guto. Of course. The ICA is an American show. I think they organize it just to show how much they control us."

"I mean this morning," Castillo spat. "You've seen some of them this morning? Were they acting normal?"

Romero had been lazing in bed with Gabriela before going poolside. But there was no need for Castillo to know that. "I saw a few of them at the breakfast buffet," he lied. "It was some deputy CIA man and a couple of lackeys. They were normal. What the hell is the matter with you, Guto? Why the third degree? Why did you call on the encrypted line?"

He could hear Castillo sighing. "I just spoke to Tiburón. Something is happening. It could affect our operation."

"Hang on." Romero tore his eyes away from Gabriela and slid upright. "Let me get somewhere with a little more privacy."

He slipped into his sandals and went into the villa, shutting the glass door behind him. He plopped down on the couch so he could still see Gabriela, then, with reluctance, thought better of it.

As he'd just told his boss, the Intelligence Conference of the Americas was an American show. He wouldn't put it past the Yankees to have bugged each of the villas here at the Ritz-Carlton.

Romero went to the palatial bathroom, put the shower on full blast, and sat on the high toilet seat. When all that was done, he whispered into the phone. "Okay. I'm alone. Why are you talking directly to Tiburón? What's the matter with the operation?"

"We have a serious problem. The Tiburónistas were unloading weapons on Orinoco Reef with some of the Russians. The goddamned fools sunk a U.S. Coast Guard cutter that had been working here in Georgetown Bay."

The Guyanese intel chief snagged a towel to wipe the warm oil from his face. "Coast Guard? You mean that little ship that was installing the buoys out near the oil platforms?"

"Yes. That one."

"But it wasn't much more than a tugboat. Are there survivors? Do we have a hostage problem now?"

"Not as far I know."

"What does that mean?"

"It means Tiburón said he, quote, 'took care of it.' He wasn't more specific than that. But Sydney O'Keefe, the American ambassador, called me a half hour ago. She asked us to mount a rescue operation. I need you to get on it right now."

So much for spending another few hours with Gabriela. "As you wish," Romero said regretfully. "I'll take care of it. Do you want it to be like a real operation or . . . ?"

"Yes!" Castillo shot back with exasperation. "It has to be a real operation. But at the same time, you can't find anything."

"No problem," Romero said.

In the murky spaces between his official duties and the various conspiracies he'd orchestrated over the years, the veteran police officer had learned how to execute seemingly contradictory orders. He didn't find it all that difficult. Of the men who worked for and with him, he knew which ones to trust, bribe, or avoid.

Having climbed the ranks of the Guyanese National Police Force—a paramilitary group with sweeping powers—his network extended into all branches of government, including the army. If the prime minister wanted a high-profile search that produced absolutely nothing, then so be it. Romero had built a brilliant career doing things like that.

In his view, the problem was always Tiburón, whose rot extended into the same branches of the Guyanese services. The drug lord might or might not be on the same page.

Romero kept his voice even. "Guto, what did Tiburón mean when he said he took care of it? Does that mean he got rid of all the evidence? No dead Americans washing up on the beaches?"

"I can only assume," answered Castillo, "that the Tiburónistas and Russians did something with the bodies. I will leave it for you to follow up with them."

Of course you will, thought Romero in his cloud of steam.

As he saw it, Prime Minister Castillo wanted squeaky-clean hands with which to seize the reins of power in Guyana after their planned subterfuge with the Russians and Tiburónistas. Though just as guilty as the rest of them, Romero suspected the Cambridge-educated snob elevated himself far above the dirty work of killing people. Part of him wanted to force Castillo into admitting it.

"So, Prime Minister, what are your orders if there are American survivors?"

"I don't know," Castillo snapped at him. "This is all your business. I'm just telling you that all this needs to disappear. If you have to discuss a play-by-play, then call Tiburón yourself."

"But you said you spoke to him already. Why not call him back and ask him if he killed those sailors? Shouldn't you know for sure?"

Back in Georgetown on the rooftop of the colonial parliament building, Guto Castillo squeezed his fresh burner phone so hard that he nearly broke it. The sun was high and hot. A few tropical rain clouds had mushroomed over the distant sugarcane fields. He knew damned well that Romero was toying with him.

"Listen to me," Castillo grumbled, staring at the clouds. "You know I have to be kept arm's length from this thing. The investigation has started again."

"What investigation? You mean Hugo Suárez?"

"Of course I mean Suárez! It's not enough that you and Tiburón dispatched Martin Croom. Now Croom's replacement has restarted the investigation. I'll remind you that if he finds me, he'll find you. I can't protect you if I get implicated."

When Romero didn't agree immediately, Castillo kicked at the roof gravel, worrying that his argument had fallen flat. "Look, Alejandro," he continued. "When all is said and done, there will need to be some legitimacy left in this government. Because of Suárez's ongoing investigation, I shouldn't be speaking directly with Tiburón, especially not now. That will be important in the future to both of us. Am I being clear?"

Romero was still quiet, irritating Castillo. The prime minister's mood darkened.

Castillo had been the one to elevate Romero to the top job over President Khasif's objections. He'd done it because he knew the sleazy career policeman was bent as a crowbar, close to Tiburón yet subject to manipulation for all his past crimes. But now he, August Bolivar Castillo IV, had crossed the line himself. Here he was on a burner phone, in a quest for honor among thieves.

"Okay, Guto," Romero replied after a few seconds. "I will call Tiburón and ask him exactly what happened."

"And be sure he knows the Americans are a threat. Make sure Morozov knows, too."

"You want me to contact the Russians?"

Castillo put his palm over his face, speaking between his fingers. "Didn't you tell me that Morozov is a Russian intelligence officer?"

"Yes. He's a major in the SVR, their foreign spy service. Why?"

"Because Morozov is there with Tiburón. His helicopter flew onto the yacht this morning. He needs to know that the Americans are going to investigate this. I'm sure he can contact Moscow for extra resources if necessary."

"Did the ambassador say the Americans were going to investigate?"

"No. But Sydney O'Keefe isn't just going to lie down. She's going to ask for search elements from the American military to come in. Damn it, Alejandro, by the time Ali Khasif gets back from Abu Dhabi, he'll have U.S. Marines on our shores. Then we'll have the Yankees in our ports *and* Hugo Suárez breathing down our necks. You need to keep the Yankees from coming, beat O'Keefe at her own game."

"I can do the search you ask for. But I can't keep the Yankees from coming. They always do what they want."

"That's why we need to stay ahead of this. You said you're meeting with Director Foley tonight. You're our head of intelligence. Tell her that the Coast Guard sinking was a tragic matter of drug violence perpetrated by Tiburón. Tell her you're all over it, that you have an operation mounted. We only need to keep them at bay for another month or so."

"You want me to throw Tiburón under the bus? I'd rather not, thank you."

"For God's sake, Alejandro. The Americans have been going after Tiburón for twenty years. They know he's sitting there in Venezuela on the Orinoco River, propping up a dictator. So what if he lashed out at a Coast Guard cutter? It's the perfect cover. A tragedy. Let the Americans send Special Forces into Colombia and Venezuela to hunt him down. That will keep them out of our ports."

While the line stayed quiet, Castillo hoped Romero's vodka-addled brain would recognize the point. The planned meeting with Mary Pat Foley at the intelligence conference that night was a golden, fortuitous opportunity to make lemonade from the lemons of Tiburón's sour judgment.

"All right, Guto," Romero replied after a few seconds. "I will talk to Tiburón."

"And Morozov," Castillo prompted. "The SVR major."

"Yes. And the SVR major. I understand the strategy."

"It starts with you convincing Director Foley today that this was a matter of tragic Tiburónista drug violence. You have a good way with women. You can do that. And you aren't throwing Tiburón under the bus. Tell him you're enhancing his reputation with the Yankees. He'll like that."

"I understand, Guto. You don't have to tell me again. I get it."

"Good. And one more thing."

"What is that, Prime Minister?"

"Tell Tiburón about the Suárez problem. Remind him that Suárez's investigation could threaten our entire plan. See if he can make it go away."

"Make it go away?" Romero repeated with a mild grin, goading his boss once more. "You mean you want us to do to Suárez the same thing we did to Martin Croom?"

"You know exactly what I mean. Or should. Remember, if they find something on me, I can't protect you. The investigation has to go away. Suárez is a problem."

"I see," Romero chuckled. "I will address it with Tiburón. We'll figure something out."

"The sooner the better."

"Consider it done, Prime Minister."

5

GEORGETOWN AIRPORT, GUYANA
1310

JACK STOOD IN THE IMMIGRATION LINE WITH HIS WHEELED CARRY-ON BEHIND HIM, frustrated with the glacial pace.

As in similar lines worldwide, the uniformed officers behind the glass went about their work capriciously. Sometimes, they reached for the passport stamp before the traveler even crossed the red tape on the floor. More often, they looked endlessly into their computer screens with an abstruse scowl. Either way, they were moving one passenger through every two minutes, sometimes three.

Jack held his phone in his hand, debating whether to tell his shipping manager in San Juan to have the *Helena* turn around. While he mentally debated the merits of reversing course, his eyes drifted to the clock over the glass booths of the immigration officers. It was a little past one. His flight would leave in less than an hour, and three people were still in front of him.

His mind returned to the disastrous meeting with Castillo and his failure to obtain the export license that morning. There were several ramifications to game out.

For one, if he asked the *Helena* to return to San Juan and then managed to unstick the export license, Jack would simply be doubling the sea voyage, burning cash and killing his margins. Even more troubling, if he never got the export license, he would need to hurry up and find a buyer for the shipping company, losing a bundle.

Every day, Hendley Associates was paying Athena's employees, rent for the shipyards, and hefty ongoing maintenance fees. Jack had assured Howard Brennan, his "white-side" boss, that they would only have to operate the shipping business long enough to flip it to one of the big oil companies for a nice return. But without an export license, any buyer would pay the same Jack had paid for the shipping concern—maybe even less, given the looming maintenance headaches he'd heard from the foremen. In the event he broke even on a sale, he would still have burned through millions just operating the company over the prior three months.

And for what?

The line advanced to where he stood right in front of the immigration officer. "Passport and ticket," the officer demanded from behind the window.

Jack's brain flickered through the morning's events. A new idea flared.

The customs officer was scowling, clearly impatient. "Passport and ticket," he repeated with an edge.

Jack dropped his passport back into his suit pocket. "No thanks," he said. "I've decided to stay a little longer."

THE AIRPORT TAXI DEPOSITED HIM AT THE U.S. EMBASSY.

After getting through a security checkpoint run by two marine sergeants, Jack learned that the ambassador, Sydney O'Keefe, was out for the day. The front desk worker told him he could speak to the foreign service officer in charge of the Guyanese commercial interests section.

That FSO, though well-meaning, was of little help. But he showed Jack into the records room, where Jack buried himself in seventies-era microfiche machines.

By three o'clock, the Hendley investor thought he'd found the evidence he needed to support his latest idea. He walked the five blocks back to the Marriott under building storm clouds, ditched his bag with the bellman, and left a phone message with the interior minister's office. An hour later, he was standing on the pool deck, looking over a bay blotted with cloud shadows. Though he saw no lightning, he heard the rumble of thunder from somewhere up in the rainforest hills.

He paced the deck, waiting for Quintero's return call. Closer to the hotel, a brunette woman with a floppy sun hat and overlarge sunglasses took a table and buried her nose in a book. Jack went to the other side of the pool to stay out of earshot.

"I think I have a legal way for you to issue me a license," he told Quintero, when his phone finally rang.

"Where are you?" the minister asked.

"At the Marriott."

"What happened to your flight?"

"I skipped it, made a reservation for a later one."

"I don't understand. Why?"

"Like I said, Professor, I think I've figured out a way to make this export-licensing thing work where you won't need Castillo's approval."

Quintero replied with avuncular grace. "Jack, I love your persistence—but I'm afraid there's nothing more I can do for you. Castillo is digging in. When President Khasif gets back, he and I will take the matter to the judiciary for litigation. Come back then. We'll get a better meal next time."

"It will take months for litigation, won't it?"

"Yes, probably."

"And Khasif's not even back for another two weeks. Isn't that what you said?"

"Yes."

"Professor, when I show you what I have, I think you'll see it differently. I've been to the embassy and discovered a reason Castillo's argument won't hold water. You could call Khasif yourself for his signature, do it digitally."

"Calling Khasif's not an option, at least for now. He and his staff aren't in touch."

"Not in touch? How is that possible?"

"The Abu Dhabi people are taking the staff on some kind of road rally over the dunes. They're staying in luxurious Bedouin tents in the middle of nowhere, no phones allowed. It's all part of their effort to get us to join OPEC."

Jack fully understood the press from the OPEC members. If Guyana were to stay independent, it would break OPEC's price controls, something the mostly Arab members could ill afford, given Guyana's short transit routes to Europe and the U.S.

"Okay," Jack conceded. "So President Khasif's not in touch for a few days. But you're here. Maybe you could get the paperwork moving again—once you see what I'm talking about."

"I don't understand. What do you think you have?"

Jack moved closer to the seawall to stay out of earshot of the woman in the floppy hat. She wasn't dressed like a competitive oil executive, but one never knew. "It's a little complex to review on the phone," he said softly. "Could we meet in person?" He held his breath while waiting for the minister to answer.

"Well . . . I suppose . . . I'm at the fisheries building on the docks. I'll be wrapping up here in fifteen minutes."

"All right!" Jack exhorted with a fist pump. "That's close. I'll walk over to see you."

Just before Jack hung up, he added, "Oh, and one more thing,

Professor. Please don't tell Prime Minister Castillo that I'm still in town. I didn't quite like the way he shuffled me off this morning. If it's all the same to you, I'd prefer he not know I stayed."

"Jack, there are many things I choose not to share with Prime Minister Castillo. I'll see you when you get here."

THE CLANG OF HAMMERS AND THE BRIGHT GLOW OF TORCHES WERE THE BACKDROP for Jack's late-afternoon walk along the dock. The influx of oil money had already created a steady stream of work for the shipyards. Men and machines crammed the docks, crawling over all manner of hulks shouting, banging, and soldering. He found Quintero outside a corrugated-tin workshop the size of an airplane hangar, smoking a cigar. He invited Jack to walk along a vacant stretch of seawall. Distant workers were pouring concrete and erecting a flagpole. A banner with photos of happy strolling Guyanese citizens declared it would soon become a waterfront park.

The tide was out, exposing a hundred acres of brown, silty mud. As soon as it was quiet enough to hear each other, Jack launched into his explanation. "Minister, I believe I've found a loophole."

"I've been waiting with bated breath, Mr. Ryan."

"Let me explain. See, Optimum, the builder of those three platforms, is a joint venture with several American companies. The most prominent is Texron out of Houston. But none of those oil companies can approach the platforms without dredging."

"Yes. That's correct. What of it?"

"Well, Texron already *has* an old export license for Guyana from a spent well to the east near Suriname. I went to the embassy and dug it up. Here it is. See?"

Jack handed Quintero a flimsy computer printout from the microfiche. The minister squinted behind his large rectangular glasses and read while puffing on his cigar. Thunder boomed off in the hills, though no rain fell.

"I don't know why you are so excited," Quintero declared, handing the paper back. "You are not Texron. You are Athena Global, a small shipping concern out of San Juan."

Rather than accept the paper, Jack nudged it back. "No, Professor. Keep reading all the way down." Disliking the way that sounded, Jack politely gestured at the paragraph in question.

"The fine print of the export license the Guyanese government granted back then is still in effect," Jack explained. "And it says very clearly that the Guyanese government reserves the right to *transfer* its permission to any other oil company—should Texron fail to comply with Guyanese law."

Quintero removed the cigar from his mouth and studied the paragraph, blinking behind his glasses. Very slowly, his head rose and fell. He looked at Jack with a raised eyebrow.

Jack pressed his case. "Professor, here's the thing. Texron doesn't have the shallow-draft LNG ships that I do. Not yet, anyway. They require dredging, which, thanks to you, violates the Guyanese Marine Sanctuary Protection Act. *You*, Mr. Minister, therefore have the right to *transfer* this export license to another company—one like Athena that *does* meet your requirements. My ship, the *Helena*, can still pull into port tomorrow for that first test load to prove the case, just as we'd originally planned."

Quintero pressed his lips together, stroked his chin, and raised the paper before him. "May I keep this?"

"Yes, of course."

The interior minister crammed the paper in his pocket. "Good. Let me think about it."

Though he hadn't yet agreed with Jack's argument, he hadn't dismissed it, either. He kept walking along the partially constructed seawall, smoking his cigar and looking down at the muddy beach. Jack walked with him.

"I agree with the legal argument," Quintero announced after twenty yards. "I think the attorney general probably will, too. Castillo could sue on behalf of the socialists, I suppose, but I think the attorney general could give me the air cover to get this moving."

"Thank you," said Jack. "I'm happy to hear you say that."

"Well, you won't like this next part."

"Why?"

"Because I'm afraid that won't be the end of the matter. Not when it comes to Castillo. In Guyana, sadly, things aren't always as they seem."

The minister dropped the glowing stub of his cigar to the top of the masonry wall, stood on it, and looked around to ensure they were alone. Several cars were parked on the port's rim road across the vacant weedy lot.

A gray Kia sedan was squeezed between several beat-up vans, pickups, and derelict boat trailers at the edge of a workshop. It hadn't been there a minute ago, Jack noticed. Out of habits born from his black-side training, he narrowed his eyes and filed the sighting away for future consideration.

The interior minister turned his back to the street, facing the chocolate-colored mud. Jack rotated with him.

"Put simply," Quintero said into the humid sea breeze, "there are elements within this government that are under the influence of powerful people. They don't always operate with the best intentions for Guyana—only the best intentions for themselves. For all his fine talk, Castillo is one of them."

Now that the cigar smoke was gone, Jack missed it. He preferred it to the sulfury stench of the harbor. "You mean because he's a socialist?"

"No. I wish it were that simple. This isn't a matter of political philosophy or alignment. With the Orinoco Basin discovery, much money is at stake. The corrupt ones don't like the idea of a public trust fund. It means they'll miss their piece of the action."

"You're saying Castillo's corrupt?"

"We'll see," the minister mumbled obtusely.

"But you have the law on your side. You trust your president. Why not root out the corruption?"

"We've tried. It's why we lost our attorney general, Martin Croom, some months ago. He'd been closing in on a major corruption case. Then, suddenly, *poof.*"

"*Poof?*"

Quintero looked beyond the mud to the lapping water. "Poof. He disappeared from his Viking sport fishing boat off Trinidad. The body was never found. Quite a coincidence that he'd been closing in on his corruption investigation."

"And the case he'd been working on . . . it went away, too?"

The minister ruefully chuckled. "That depends on who you ask. And you'd better be careful about that."

"What if I asked you?"

"Then I'd say that some of us in this government—myself and President Khasif, certainly—want to make this oil discovery something beyond reproach. We want to create a new model, to raise our people out of . . ." He waved a tired arm at the crowded shanties on the hillside, where most of Georgetown's citizens lived, far from the charming colonial buildings.

"Others oppose your vision?" Jack asked. "Is that about money or power?"

Quintero offered a sad grin. "I find it charming that you think there's a difference."

"Okay. So you think that granting me the license might deprive Castillo of some sort of payoff, which is why he's dragging his feet?"

The minister leaned in; his voice lowered to a gravelly rumble. "I would be careful about saying that out loud."

Quintero straightened and raised his voice. "Look, Jack. I really do appreciate that you're the only company out there willing to respect my environmental requirements. With your approach, you're showing the major energy companies that it can be done. That's a great help to me. I thank you for it."

"You're welcome," Jack returned. "That was the idea behind my investment. To reap the rewards of a first mover."

The older man shoved his hands in his trouser pockets. "Precisely. I need creative guys like you in the game here. You're the type that gets the other ones to move."

"Thank you," Jack repeated.

The minister watched the distant brown water for a while, then shifted on his feet, pulled his hands from his pockets, and gestured with them. "Hey. How about this—I'll give you a memorandum of understanding on official letterhead. I can classify your incoming ship as a . . . 'proof of concept' test for LNG off-load. I don't think anyone in the government will mind. You think your ship *Helena* can really pull it off?"

"Yes," Jack replied hopefully. "My commitment to you, Minister, is that I'll prove it can be done without dredging."

Quintero's big teeth glowed when he smiled. "All right. Then an MOU it is. You'll eventually get your real license, and, in the meantime, I'll still get to show the big oil companies that it can be done. Do we have a deal?"

Jack seized the minister's hand, shaking it forcefully. "Deal, Professor. I won't let you down."

The minister laughed. "All right, all right, boy. Now don't tear my arm off." He removed a fresh cigar from his shirt pocket and clamped it between his teeth. But he didn't light it. "I'll need to give you that memo tonight so the working foremen out on the rigs have it. Are you going to be around? I know you were anxious to get back home."

"I've got a reservation for a flight out tonight. Connects through Panama. I'd like to be in the Hendley office in the morning to help coordinate everything. It would be good if I could leave here with that memorandum of understanding."

"I tell you what, then," Quintero said. "Let's meet in a few hours for dinner. I'll bring the MOU with me. That way we can both avoid my wife's cooking."

6

**MARRIOTT HOTEL, GEORGETOWN, GUYANA
1720**

"AH, MR. RYAN," SAID THE MAN BEHIND THE DESK AT THE MARRIOTT. "GOOD NEWS—your room is ready."

The clerk went about checking Jack in, which required him to hand over his passport and fill out a form. Jack found it a tiresome process, since he only intended to use the room for a few hours before catching a late flight out of the country. But a room was a room.

As he rolled his bag to the elevator, he passed by the lobby bar, which was filling up with groups of American businesspeople. Based on their Texas drawls, Jack knew one of the major oil companies was in town. He suspected they'd be off to see Minister Quintero tomorrow, trying to convince him that he was all wrong about the requirement for shallow-draft ships.

Finally in his room, Jack unzipped his bag and turned the air-conditioning down as far as it would go. He closed the curtains to blot out the dusky sun streaking below the clouds and took a seat at the desk with his legal pad and xeroxed microfiche. Arlington was an hour behind Guyana, so Howard Brennan, Jack's whiteside boss, would still be in the office.

LINE OF DEMARCATION

Jack soon learned that Howard thought an MOU was nice, but far short of the exclusive export license Jack had been seeking from the Guyanese government. The senior banker asked Jack to explore potentially selling the company early to limit the mounting expenses.

For that, Jack would need Gavin Biery, Hendley's top infotech specialist.

"So I hear you have a company to sell," Gavin said when Jack tracked him down a few minutes later.

Though Gavin also worked with Jack on black-side Campus operations, the infotech specialist's day job was to support the digital needs of the private equity business. After the strong effort he'd put into the last Hendley white-side deal in Vietnam, he was promoted. Gavin chose his new title as director of cyber operations, which he believed worked for both the black and the white side.

"Yes, that's right," Jack answered.

"Howard said you don't have the export license—and that we're burning through cash waiting for it."

Jack bristled at that. "I'm getting an MOU, Gav. Tonight. We should be able to sell the company at a profit if we choose to."

"I see. An MOU's not quite the same thing as an actual export license, though, is it?"

Jack rushed a sigh. "We're just exploring options. I need your help to look for potential buyers for Athena that could move quickly—just in case." He went through the parameters of a likely buyer of three shallow-draft ships and associated equipment. Jack explained that they should target midsize shipping companies with healthy balance sheets that were looking to broaden their portfolios. Gavin typed furiously, taking notes.

"I got it," the infotech specialist announced after a few questions. "So you want a company that will recognize the opportunity immediately and close a fast deal. They'll probably need to pay cash. Not a lot of midsize companies are going to be that liquid."

"Or they'd go to an underwriting bank, like we did in Vietnam."

"True. But banks are ballbusters when it comes to due diligence. They might not necessarily approve of a speculative buy for a risky opportunity in Guyana. Have you considered that?"

Jack bridled slightly at the notion that it was a risky opportunity. "Gav, one thing we know for sure is that Guyana is standing firm on its requirement for shallow-draft ships. We also know they're sitting on the world's largest hydrocarbon reserve. That part of the pricing analysis shouldn't be in doubt."

He could hear Gavin sucking on a straw, vacuuming up the remnants of one of the big iced soda drinks that seemed genetically attached to his hand. Jack remembered the four-hour time difference between Georgetown and Arlington. Gavin was just finishing his lunch.

"But the geopolitical risk seems a little fluid to me," Gavin countered. "Any investment bank is going to sniff that out."

"Geopol problems are already priced into the model I created when I valued Athena for Hendley."

"Yeah, Jack, but your numbers are three months old. I saw in the papers that Venezuela is making noise over Guyana. I would think the risk coefficient has gone up, lowering the overall selling price for Athena."

Unlike in his conversations with Howard, Jack could slip into his black-side role with Gavin. He lowered his voice. "Hey, going black-side for a second here, I checked on the Venezuelan order of battle before I flew down by looking at imagery from NGA."

NGA was the National Geospatial-Intelligence Agency, the DoD's top reconnaissance satellite organization. The Campus maintained a feed into American intelligence resources, as enabled by the director of national intelligence, Mary Pat Foley. By "going black-side," Jack was putting Gavin on notice that they were discussing the classified half of the Hendley enterprise, something they typically avoided unless preparing for an op.

"Okay," Gavin replied. "We're black." Jack went on. "You're correct, Gav. It's true that the Venezuelan army has moved a handful of tanks down to Anacoco Island on the Essequibo River, close to Guyana. But they're just four old Russian T-72s that'll get bogged down in the river marshes as soon as they try to do anything. It's not a serious invasion force. It's performative. Bluster. Keep that between you and me—obviously, Howard can't know about it. The State Department came to the same conclusion in an unclassified report. You can reference that with him."

Since Gavin Biery spent his days manipulating machines that tended to be more reliably intelligent than humans, he was difficult to impress. "Maybe the Venezuelan army action's not down there on the river."

"What do you mean?"

"Maybe the Venezuelans aim to seize the oil fields at sea. That Orinoco Basin backs right up to their maritime border. If they did that, then your export license won't be worth the paper it's written on. I would think any buyer of the company is going to put a hefty risk multiple on that."

"You're right, Gav. I priced that risk in, too. But it's a matter of probabilities. Don't you think the odds of Venezuela seizing oil wells that are half-owned by the United States would be pretty low?"

"Okay, okay," Gavin relented. "I see your point."

"I see yours, too," said Jack. "Perception is reality. If moving Venezuelan tanks are in the papers, then the banks are going to raise the risk price. We may as well reflect it, too. So go ahead and raise the risk coefficient a few basis points. I'm just looking for some companies to call to get the conversations started. And, of course, they're not going to have the intelligence resources of The Campus informing their decisions."

The phone in Jack's hand buzzed. When he glanced at the display, he saw that it was Quintero calling. "Hey, Gav, I have to go. Important call coming in. Thanks for your help. Email whatever prospects you come up with. And remember: keep it white-side."

Jack pressed the button to switch calls. "Hi, Professor. We still on for dinner I hope?"

The interior minister answered in a surprisingly hushed tone.

"Jack," he whispered hoarsely. "Something has come up. We're switching restaurants. I know a place with an outside patio where the tourists go. We'll meet later, after sundown."

"Why? What's wrong?"

"Let's not talk on the phone. I'll text you the restaurant and time. And make sure no one follows you. Take one of those walks you're so fond of—maybe in a roundabout manner this time."

Jack's Campus experience kicked in by reflex. "Don't say another word, Professor. Let me check something." He went to the window overlooking the hotel's parking lot and looked down at the twenty or thirty cars there.

Along the back row, he saw a gray Kia sedan, just as he'd seen when they were talking on the docks.

7

**ABOARD THE *ADMIRAL GORSHKOV*, SOUTH ATLANTIC OCEAN
1830**

CAPTAIN FIRST RANK MIKHAIL KROKHMAL WALKED STEADILY ALONG THE EDGE OF the flight deck. Here and there, he had to raise his foot to step over one of the chains that tethered the hulking Mi-8 army helicopter, bristling with missiles, to the deck. Occasionally, he had to raise his hand to steady himself against the ship's roll. But never once did he have to get out of someone's way.

Though the sun lay on the horizon, the wind in this southern, central part of the Atlantic Ocean was warm and hot, churning a dark green sea with whitecaps. The northeasterly trade winds that came roaring out of the Sahara raked the waves. There were times when Krokhmal thought he could smell the dust and camel shit in the air.

The frigate *Admiral Gorshkov* was the initial combatant of her class, a thoroughly modern vessel with the first keel laid since the fall of the Soviet Union. Taking design cues from the West, she was narrow and sleek, five-hundred-fifty feet long.

Her hull angled back from the water as though forged of a single piece of steel, seemingly stretching to the superstructure, leaving none of her weapons systems exposed. Her thirty-two antiair and sixteen cruise missile tubes were flush with the foredeck, visible only from above like so many manhole covers.

The naval designers had buried the weapons and shaped the hull in continuous angles to lessen radar reflectivity and improve stealth. As Krokhmal saw it, a second, unheralded advantage of the hull design was that on blustery Atlantic crossings like this one, he could walk from the flight deck to the forward missile tubes in complete shelter.

"*Dvigat'sya!*" shouted a sailor as he hefted the lever of a watertight hatch and stepped into the passage. The cry was the Russian equivalent of the American Navy's "gangway," the warning to press your butt cheeks to the bulkhead at the captain's approach, lest the great man should have to alter his course.

Krokhmal barged through. Shielded from the wind in the metal cave of the weather deck, the fifty-eight-year-old marched against the pitching ship. He felt the frigate roll a few degrees to the right and hoped the sailors who chained the visiting army helicopter had done it right. An army helicopter had never flown out to them from Africa before. Krokhmal still didn't know why the fleet admiral had sent it to him. He grabbed a cable to steady himself.

A young sailor grinned at him as though finding it funny that his salty old captain might not have his sea legs. Krokhmal scowled at the seaman, noted the name on his jersey to give to the boatswain, and kept trudging up the deck.

He dogged the exit hatch at the foredeck and stood in the swirling wind. The Atlantic spray stung his forehead. Dusk had thickened to slate gray. He interrupted a working party in blue coveralls who were welding a bent cleat. They scattered when they saw him like gazelles before a lion.

The captain looked down at the missile tube covers as the wind made his pant legs snap like flags. The deck was still black and sooty from the blast a few hours earlier.

He knelt and touched the black streaks, nodding slowly with satisfaction. The hatches were scorched and burned. The paint at the heavy metal hinges had melted away. Even the nonskid surface of the foredeck was streaked a darker shade of black.

These were the small details Krokhmal had come forward to see with his own eyes. Yes, he'd watched the Zircon hypersonic missile launch earlier that day from the bridge—but there was something special about feeling the remnants of the missile exhaust on the scorched tubes.

Krokhmal had never been a man to trust abstractions. To him, the tactile world mattered. As he'd come to believe, one should not mistake seeing for believing. There were too many ways to manipulate video. To truly accept a given instance in the modern world, the captain believed that one must touch it, smell it, hear it, dirty one's hands with it.

Clinging to that belief like a religious tenet, he widened his knees to brace against another ship's roll and shoved his finger around the sooty streaks. He held them close to his nose and sniffed them, recognizing the odor of spent rocket fuel.

That scent told him that the Zircon missile was no longer some abstract system on an engineer's drawing board or a bureaucrat's wish list. The missile he launched that afternoon was as real as the whitecaps whipping past the hull. He could finally believe that he was in command of an arsenal of genuine, over-the-horizon ship killers, better than anything the American Navy had—indeed, the best in the world.

He recounted the launch he'd witnessed when standing on the bridge. The missile had roared out of the belowdecks magazines in a blaze of fire, then disappeared as fast as a lightning strike.

According to the telemetry data, the Zircon had achieved a speed of Mach 8, nearly six thousand miles per hour, one-point-seven miles per second, twice as fast as a rifle bullet.

In just five minutes, the Zircon had flown four hundred ninety miles and drilled into its target, an old Russian trawler towed into the center of the South Atlantic. Its speed had been so intense that the *Gorshkov*'s own phased array radar had lost track of it seconds after it launched, disappearing over the horizon like a comet.

Captain Mikhail Krokhmal had seen many things in his long life at sea, but he'd never seen anything like that. It had been so shocking that only the soot on his finger made it real. And on top of that, the fleet admiral had ordered an army helicopter over from Africa for an as-yet-undisclosed operation. In all his years at sea, he'd never seen that, either.

"We are back," he said to himself, knowing no one could hear him over the wind. He kept his face pointed at the deck so the men couldn't see his mouth moving—or the light in his eyes.

He got up from the deck and kept walking forward, passing the bow-mounted gun—just a thing for show, really, considering the rest of his arsenal. He made it to the narrowest point of the bow and grasped a lifeline in each hand, staring westward. He saw that the sun was squatting low on the horizon, glowing in the haze like a hot coal. Thinking of the army helicopter and the lethal Zircon, he wanted nothing more than to stand by himself and enjoy the moment.

But solitude on a cramped warship was scarce, even for a captain. After a few minutes, his executive officer approached with a clipboard and handed him paper dispatches from the radio room. He dismissed his XO and stood there in the wind, reading them in the thin gray light of the fading dusk.

The first was from his admiral, the head of the Northern Fleet in freezing Severomorsk, thousands of miles to the north. It was a rare congratulations on a job well done in testing the Zircon. As a reward, it said, Krokhmal was to proceed west to Havana Harbor, where he would show the Russian flag among his ideological brothers, his *compañeros*, and let his men enjoy a few days in port.

The second dispatch, which the XO had sealed in an envelope, had been issued a few minutes later. It was marked SROCHNY, urgent, superseding all prior orders, an eyes-only message for the captain. That surprised him.

The SROCHNY told the *Gorshkov* to proceed directly to the western Caribbean, then on to the South Atlantic, where he was to assume a patrol position in a battle box precisely defined by four coordinates. He was to prepare for flight operations for the army helicopter. The message noted that the ship's patrol area should remain outside the twelve-nautical-mile territorial waters abutting Aruba, Grenada, Trinidad, and Venezuela.

The *Gorshkov*'s narrow bow dipped into a trough, sending a salty spray into Krokhmal's eyes. The water was warm here—a far cry from the ice bath he was accustomed to off the freezing Kola Peninsula.

Without wiping the drops from his face, he balled the Havana order in his fist and tossed it over the side. He folded the sacred SROCHNY dispatch and tucked it away in the left breast pocket of his black and khaki uniform shirt, right over his heart.

He kept facing forward, enjoying the dip and rise of the bow as it plundered the waves. He knew the officers up on the bridge were watching his back, wondering why their captain stood at the ship's prow, staring forward into the setting sun. He also knew they couldn't see his face.

That reminded him of a dictum an old warhorse mentor had given him during the Cold War: *Never let them see you smile.*

8

**KING GEORGE CAFÉ, GEORGETOWN, GUYANA
1930**

JACK FOUND MINISTER QUINTERO SITTING AT A CANDLELIT TABLE AT THE EDGE OF THE restaurant's open-air courtyard. The night sky was pricked with stars, but the city's baked pavement and cloying humidity kept things warm. Across from the minister sat a bearded man in a khaki suit with an open-necked white shirt.

The King George Café was along the Demerara River road bordering the city's west side. To get there, Jack walked a jagged surveillance detection route, weaving through the seedier parts of town with narrow alleys and little vehicle traffic. To counter the night heat, he opted for a short-sleeved linen shirt, jeans, and white-soled brown leather casual sneakers. His messenger bag was hanging from his shoulder.

Though on a white-side mission with a legitimate business purpose, Jack still traveled with a few tools of his black-side trade to avoid surveillance. One of them was a Sony digital recording device not much larger than a deck of cards. Though it functioned as it should—letting him record voice memos to himself for business purposes—it had been further modified by the CIA's personal technology group as a specialized electromagnetic (EM) frequency receiver and transmitter. As soon as he'd hung up with Quintero at the Marriott and seen the Kia in the parking lot, Jack had flipped it on and passed it around his room. He'd found no surveillance bugs and tossed it into his bag.

When Jack approached, both men stood up at the small iron table. Over their heads dangled crossing strings of Edison bulbs that cast a warm orange glow. The courtyard floor was made of rough brick pavers. Jack set his messenger bag on the bricks and sat in a metal chair.

Out of habit, he threw a darting glance at the rest of the diners—twelve tables, half occupied, all couples. More customers were dining within the single-story building—a former house from the looks of it—with beige stucco walls and turquoise wooden shutters.

"You came on foot? You weren't followed?" Quintero asked quietly.

Preferring to stay quiet, Jack nodded.

Quintero gestured to his table companion. "Jack Ryan, this is the colleague I told you about on our walk earlier—Deputy Attorney General Hugo Suárez."

Suárez extended his hand across the table. He was a compact man, well put-together. Between the Edison lights above and the candles below, his bearded face was cast in shadows.

"An honor to meet you, Mr. Ryan," he said with a faintly Spanish accent that wasn't unusual in Georgetown. "I want to—"

A middle-aged but trim waiter in black pants and a white shirt arrived at the table, interrupting him.

They endured his presentation of the specials and wine pairings. Afterward, the minister leaned over the table, speaking softly.

"As I mentioned earlier, Jack, Hugo took over Martin Croom's investigation. He's our acting attorney general now."

Jack and Suárez exchanged nods.

"And there's something new?" Jack asked.

Suárez smoothed his napkin over his lap. They were at the last outdoor table, closest to Water Street. The traffic noise was good cover. Jack leaned forward to hear the attorney general.

"For the last year, Mr. Ryan, I've worked with your Drug Enforcement Administration," he began.

"Okay."

"Your government believes the drug lord Tiburón manufactures cocaine—and now fentanyl—in the ungoverned rainforests, maybe forty miles up that river. My people have provided reports to the DEA man at your embassy."

"I understand."

Before his visit to Guyana, Jack had read one of those DEA reports. The U.S. government had a standing arrest warrant for Tiburón and had worked closely with the Colombian army to track him. But Tiburón and much of his operation had sheltered under the protection of the hostile Venezuelan dictatorship.

Suárez went on. "I'm sure you know that your government has been chasing Tiburón for years. His Tiburónista gang came out of the Bogotá area. Now they're spread across Venezuela and Guyana, though Tiburón himself never sets foot in our country."

A noisy set of motorcycles roared down Water Street. Jack sipped his water, waiting for the din to subside. "I'm only in Georgetown for an export license," he said warily.

Suárez gave him a hard look.

Jack continued in a hushed voice. "Hey—I realize Tiburón is a problem. But I'm a private equity investor here for business. What does it have to do with me?"

The waiter was back. He took their orders, writing carefully on a pad. Jack noticed that the waiter had a strange habit of letting his eyes wander over the table while he wrote. When Jack ordered his grilled sea bass, the waiter glanced briefly at his face, then resumed his ocular sweep of the table.

"There are opposing forces at play here in Guyana, Mr. Ryan," Suárez said when they were alone again. "Those of us in the legitimate government see a powerful, just future. The oil riches we've uncovered will propel us into it. Others, we know, are in Tiburón's grip. Call it the invisible hand."

"I still don't see—"

The waiter was back. He deposited an ice bucket on the table, uncorked a Chilean sauvignon blanc, and offered Quintero a taste. The waiter poured three glasses, then shoved the bottle into the ice bucket, swaddled in cloth.

Afterward, Suárez said, "You must understand. I have been conducting a wide-ranging operation to expose Tiburón's reach into our government." He stopped to look left and right, ensuring they were well out of earshot. "A surveillance operation."

Suárez tilted his body with his arm below the table. He pushed a soft canvas bag toward Jack.

"In that bag," he added, "is the result."

Jack looked first at Suárez, then at Quintero.

"I don't understand why you're giving this to me," he said.

Quintero cleared his throat. "That's on me. I told Hugo you were flying to the U.S. tonight."

"Why does that matter?" asked Jack.

"Because," Quintero said, "we both think that the output of Hugo's surveillance is of a nature that should get to the top of the American government immediately."

Jack didn't move. "I'm not a government official. You should take this to our embassy."

"That would take too long to get it to the right people in your government," countered Suárez.

"Whatever you have at my foot, Mr. Suárez, could go in the diplomatic courier pouch. It could be on the next flight to the U.S."

"Which would be tomorrow," rebutted Suárez. "There is only one direct U.S. carrier flight to the U.S. every day. That's what your embassy uses. This evidence is more urgent than that. Trust me."

Jack felt the hairs on the back of his neck stand up. "Evidence that can't wait until tomorrow? Why?"

"The Tiburónistas attacked one of your Coast Guard vessels at sea this morning. They murdered the entire crew. When you review the evidence, you'll see that senior elements in our government were part of it. And that they're planning a wider operation."

"What wider operation?"

Suárez and Quintero exchanged a look. Quintero answered. "We don't know exactly. Not yet. But we fear it will be very soon. It is much more urgent than we realized."

Jack crossed his arms. "Gentlemen, this is clearly a matter for the ambassador."

"No," said Suárez, his eyes steady.

"No?"

"Mr. Ryan. You are, of course, highly connected to senior elements of your government. If . . . not in an official capacity, then in a personal one."

Jack stared back at Suárez, saying nothing. Out of a personal honor code, he refused to let his family, even his famous father, influence his business. To Jack, that was true on both the white and black side of his dealings. Still, he couldn't just tell Suárez to go away. "So these are digital recordings," he said. "Surveillance evidence."

Holding Jack's gaze, Suárez's nod was almost imperceptible.

"Then it was dangerous to bring it here," Jack said.

A fifty-something couple came through the Water Street gate, breezing past them.

Suárez leaned back in his chair. Quintero pulled his cigar tin from his breast pocket, withdrew a long Cuban, and picked up the candle to light it. "We've taken additional precautions," he said after the couple passed.

Jack thought through what he'd seen at the small embassy building that afternoon. Though he'd only touched base with a low-level FSO, he suspected that at least a few people from the CIA were on official diplomatic cover in the annex building off the back side. Guyana wasn't large enough to have an agency chief of station, but it should at least have a chief of base, he thought.

"Look," he began. "I'm not equipped for this—not right now. There are people at the embassy who . . ." He shut his mouth. Looking into the dim dining room, he saw their waiter leaning against a wall, looking straight out at the street. It seemed an odd posture to Jack. The waiter raised his hand near his ear, as though scratching it.

Jack held two fingers to his lips, gesturing to Suárez and Quintero to keep quiet. From his shirt pocket, he removed his pen and scrawled on a cocktail napkin:

SAY NOTHING ELSE

He passed the napkin between them, then reached into his messenger bag. He retrieved his digital voice recorder and toggled the hidden switch that converted it into a passive EM detection device. He put it on the table and saw the single red LED light blinking slowly.

"The wine's really good," he said in a conversational tone.

The LED light blinked faster. To Jack, that meant a bug somewhere near them had picked up his voice and transmitted it.

He pushed the device toward the wine bucket. Again he raised his voice and said, "Should we get a second bottle, gentlemen?" This time the LED went from blinking to a steady state.

The bug was in the cloth around the ice bucket.

Jack grabbed his pen and was about to add a line to the napkin, telling them they should proceed immediately to the U.S. embassy with the evidence. But by the time he'd written the first few letters, a movement caught his eye.

The waiter was coming toward him—with a machine pistol in his hand.

9

ARLINGTON, VIRGINIA
1530

AS SOON AS JACK HAD ENDED HIS PHONE CALL WITH GAVIN BIERY, THE INFOTECH specialist got busy trying to devise a competitive sale price for Athena Global Shipping Lines.

He started by noting the market capitalization of the public oil and LNG shipping companies he could find—but they were all far too large to invite comparison. Then he looked at the registry of ships within Lloyd's of London, Athena's insurance company. But when he tried to see how much insurance peer companies carried—which he considered a fair way to value Athena's assets—he was stopped by a Lloyd's firewall.

Not that that was a problem for a hacker like Gavin.

Without delay, he launched an internet protocol tool to see that he was dealing with a packet-filtering firewall. Understanding the nature of the blockage, he redirected his queries through a UK proxy server and played around with various router ports. After some trial and error, he saw a stream of packets with a Canadian IP address that the firewall accepted. Gavin mimicked the four sets of numbers on the Canadian IP address as though they were his own.

He was behind the Lloyd's firewall in a matter of minutes.

Once in the database, he found six companies that met Jack's parameters and built a table for insurance comparisons. As it turned out, Jack's own analysis of the value of Athena's assets was fairly close to similar companies in the Lloyd's database.

But Gavin couldn't see how Lloyd's had evaluated geopolitical risk, the wild card in the whole thing. For that, he hopped through another firewall to get to a secondary, internal Lloyd's application server that housed their live risk model. He saw that Lloyd's used a breakdown by country. The coefficient for Guyana was higher than the median, but not off the charts—again, not dissimilar from Jack's thinking.

But Gavin, naturally possessive of a skepticism rooted in the ultrarational world of computer science, wasn't willing to take Lloyd's subjective coefficient as a final answer. He went to the Campus national intelligence feed for the latest reports on Guyana. Jack had done the same thing, but intelligence was ever-changing so it made sense to Gavin to check the feed again.

He quickly grew impatient. In his view, reading the dense prose of intelligence in the normal, human way was highly inefficient. As he saw it, it was a problem of computational processing speed. The average human could read at an intake rate of about forty bits per second—a pathetically slow data rate. A machine learning algorithm could do the relevant reporting much faster.

For that, he fired up an AI bot he'd been toying with for the last few months. He developed it from open-source code freely available to anyone on the internet. He had already trained its language capabilities by feeding it thousands of old intelligence reports from the various agencies. It still wasn't perfect, he knew, but it was getting better all the time. He named the bot Princess, after his cat.

LINE OF DEMARCATION

He asked it to comb the national intelligence feeds by using a plain language query: *Princess, tell me about geopolitical threats to Guyana within the past twenty days.*

Princess came back with forty data hits from the DEA, the Office of Naval Intelligence, the DIA, the CIA, and the NSA. But the one from the DIA's naval attaché in Guyana shocked him, especially when mated with a second report from the CIA's Russia desk.

He called Jack, but got no answer.

Gavin stood up and headed to the door.

It was time to bring the head of The Campus into this.

"I THINK THE VENEZUELANS SUNK A COAST GUARD CUTTER THIS MORNING," GAVIN declared in John Clark's office. "And I think the Russians are in on it."

Clark was behind his desk, reading glasses low on his nose. He, too, had been thinking a lot about Venezuela—but for a different reason.

"Don't you know to knock?"

Gavin plopped his substantial bulk into the only other chair in Clark's office, facing the storied SEAL from across his desk. "Sorry. I don't knock when an American ship has been sunk."

"Gav, what are you talking about?"

The infotech specialist threw his laptop on the end of Clark's desk and tilted it. "I was researching potential valuations for Jack's company, Athena, the shipping firm Hendley bought with the hope of flipping it for a big return."

"Yeah, I'm aware of the deal."

"Okay, so, in doing that for Jack, I wanted to update the geopolitical risk coefficient for pricing purposes . . ." He went on to explain his process.

"So," he said when finished, "I used my bot, Princess—"

"Your what?"

"I made an AI bot to pick through all the gobbledygook of the intelligence databases," he explained. "It's just easier. I named it Princess."

"Okay. Go on."

"Well, Princess picked up this reporting from the Guyanese naval attaché that says a Coast Guard cutter bound from Georgetown to its home port in Mobile, Alabama, may have been lost. Its last position was estimated in the waters of the Orinoco Basin. I think you know, Mr. C., that Venezuela claims that area. They've even been moving troops to an island in the Essequibo River called Ankoko. There's also this other report from the DIA that . . ."

By now, Clark had removed his glasses. As Gavin went through his litany of findings, he leaned back in his chair, polishing them, trying to look unconcerned. The posture belied what he really thought.

"Wait," Clark interrupted. "Go back to that last thing you said—about the Wagner Group and all that stuff about the Russians."

Gavin paged up through his Princess findings.

"Here. See this? There's a CIA report from a base they have in Colombia called Windward Station. It says that suspected, quote, 'former Wagner commanders' have been coming and going to a base in the Orinoco river delta, sixty nautical miles west of the Guyanese border. Princess mated that up to a generic Air Force intelligence report that tracked a Russian An-124 cargo flight between the Central African Republic and Havana. Then there's this other NSA intercept that shows a Russian frigate, the *Gorshkov*, just got a high-priority flash order to head to the same area."

"Hold on. One thing at a time," Clark said. "Does Princess list the names of the suspected Wagner people in that report?"

"Not yet. But she will. Give me a second."

Gavin's estimated second turned into two minutes of intense typing.

"Here," the infotech specialist announced. "Princess came back with a deeper CIA dive. There's a Russian SVR major, Igor Morozov. It says he did a stint with the Wagner Group, working in the Central African Republic."

"Right. And do we know what Morozov is doing in Venezuela?"

"That's back in the other report from Windward. Let me ask Princess." He typed again. "There is an unnamed clandestine asset from the Office of the Director of National Intelligence who says Morozov has been meeting with the drug lord Tiburón at the Orinoco delta base. Another report from the DEA says Tiburón is making fentanyl and smuggling it to the U.S. to—"

Clark held up his palm. "I got it." He swiveled away from Gavin, put his reading glasses on his nose, and went back to work at his keyboard.

"Wait—Mr. C., that's it?"

"Yeah. Thanks for the report, Gav. I don't know how, exactly, you put all that into a valuation for Jack's company, but it's very thorough work. Just make sure the valuation doesn't include any of the classified stuff."

Gavin's lips parted. "You're not worried about the sunken Coast Guard cutter? Or the Russians?"

Clark remained still. "As I understand it, that cutter was a noncombatant, a buoy tender. You said it was a Keeper class, right?"

"Right."

"They're small ships. They operate in shallow, hazardous waters. It may have had a legitimate incident, like running into a reef. Tragic, but highly probable."

"And the Russian cargo plane?"

"You said it's in Havana. That's not Caracas."

"What about this Morozov guy? And the Russian frigate?"

"Sounds to me like the CIA has a handle on the situation. If they weren't reporting it, you wouldn't be reading it now, would you? Don't get me wrong. I think your analysis is interesting—but hardly unique. Let the pros handle it."

Gavin's mouth had yet to close. Clark realized the infotech specialist wasn't going to be mollified so easily. "Look, Gav. Jack's been in Guyana for almost two weeks. Lisanne said he'll be in the office in the morning. Let's debrief him when he lands and get his thoughts on your Princess readout. Some genuine on-the-ground HUMINT might give it all a different flavor."

Gavin still hadn't left his chair. "Why wait for human intelligence? A satellite report showed that a Russian frigate, the *Gorshkov*, fired a Zircon earlier today. You're not worried that it has a flash order to sail to Venezuela?"

Clark stared impassively at Gavin.

Though a peaceful gesture, the hard look in the old SEAL's eyes was enough to make the infotech specialist close his laptop and leave the room without another word.

10

RITZ-CARLTON HOTEL, GUANACASTE, COSTA RICA
1745

MARY PAT FOLEY CARRIED THREE PHONES, EACH ENCRYPTED VIA A HARDWIRED microprocessor designed by the NSA.

The first was her private phone, dedicated to her family—two adult sons and a retired husband. The second was her duty phone, connected to the watch officer at her Liberty Crossing operations center. The watch officer triaged all incoming calls from the seventeen U.S. government intelligence agencies under her purview as the director of national intelligence.

The third—the bat phone, as she called it—was for the exclusive use of the White House. Only four people had its number: President Jack Ryan, Sr.; his private secretary, Alma Winters; his chief of staff, Arnie Van Damm; and John Clark, operations director of The Campus.

The rhythm of the buzz in her handbag told her it was John Clark calling on the bat phone.

She immediately excused herself from a hushed conversation with the Panamanian director of intelligence. She retrieved the phone on an empty veranda with a view of distant shipping lights on the fading reflected light of the Pacific.

"We have a serious problem," Clark said gruffly.

"Where?" she asked without preamble.

"Not far from your current position. Venezuela. Are you free to talk?"

She looked back through the glass doors at the assembled members of the Intelligence Conference of the Americas, all portly Latin men. The purpose of the conference was to shore up cooperative ties with the various intelligence agencies from the friendly countries of North, Central, and South America. Few civilians realized just how important those ties were in creating a net of surveillance to prevent bad actors from running amok in the Western Hemisphere. Her bodyguard, a Secret Service agent named Brett Johnson, stood with his back to the door. He had cleared the veranda so she'd have a private place to take calls.

"I can talk," she said. "What's up?"

"Gavin Biery was in here a few minutes ago. He put together an analysis that has me a little worried."

"Why are you worried?"

"It's about Ding."

She replied in a whisper. "TALON?"

"Yes."

Months ago, she and Clark had created a cover for Ding Chavez to get into the Colombian-Venezuelan drug network, specifically targeting Tiburón, a violent psychopath who'd been developing ties with the Venezuelan dictator. The CIA's so-called Legend Factory built years of records that painted Ding as a crooked Colombian army Special Forces colonel. He'd since defected to the Tiburónistas and earned his way into Tiburón's primary tier of advisors.

Blessed by Mary Pat, Ding's mission was to root out a link between the drug lord and the Russians. Based on peripheral intelligence, she suspected the Russians were using the Tiburónistas as a proxy, building them up as a Latin version of the Wagner Group. The new axis of Russia, China, and Iran had been employing such tactics to develop shadow forces all over the world to the point that she'd given the effort a code name: TALON. Her tool to expose it without escalation through direct American forces was to use The Campus wherever possible.

"Do we have a problem?"

"Maybe. Ding's last report syncs with the spot analysis Gavin just gave me."

Far below her, Mary Pat heard the screech of a tropical bird. She leaned on the brick railing, looking down on jungle treetops. "What's your analysis?"

"The Russian TALON initiative in Venezuela might be further along than we thought."

"Damn. Brief me."

"Sure," Clark agreed. "Ding's last coded message to me said the Tiburónistas were unloading crates from a Wagner front company, distributing them on boats. He said they were all gathering down at a makeshift base around Tiburón's yacht on the Orinoco River, apparently preparing for some operation."

"What's the operation?"

"He doesn't know yet. They keep him in the dark. His only job is to give Tiburón information on the Colombian army when asked."

"Can he confirm that Wagner is involved?"

"Yes. He sees trucks coming and going with the logos associated with Playa Del Sol, a known Wagner front company. He also reported that ex-Spetsnaz advisors are conducting some training."

"Should we pull Ding out?"

"His cover's solid and he knows how to take care of himself.

He's got a good solo exfil plan if things get hot. What worries me is that Gavin may have connected a few dots, including the reporting coming in from Ding. Things might be about to go kinetic a lot faster than we realized."

Mary Pat groaned. "How the hell could Gavin Biery, your infotech specialist, see something that the thousands of people I have working for me in the professional intelligence field missed?"

"He built some AI bot to crawl through all your databases. That's how. He named it Princess, after his cat."

"Oh, for Christ's sake."

"I know. But listen. The analysis is credible. Ding told us about that Russian SVR major with Wagner connections, Morozov, flying in to meet with Tiburón via helo. Gavin's bot saw a link between Morozov and some Russian heavy-lift flights between the Central African Republic and Havana. The bot also connected those activities to a Russian frigate, the *Admiral Gorshkov*, which just got orders to steam into the western Atlantic. I checked on the raw CIA and NSA reporting. He's right."

Mary Pat remained silent, listening to the bird. Through the glass door, she could see Brett's eyes sweeping the room. She noticed that he checked his watch twice and realized she was falling behind her schedule. She still had some one-on-one meetings to get through with her Central American counterparts. The next morning, she was to deliver a breakfast address on narco-trafficking.

"*Gorshkov*," she repeated in a whisper. "I got an update from my watch officer on that one. We're putting it in tomorrow's presidential daily brief. That's the ship that test-fired a Zircon hypersonic off Angola this morning. Scary stuff."

"Right. Gavin's bot caught an NSA intercept depicting two sets of orders coming out of the Russian Northern Fleet headquarters for *Gorshkov*. The first ordered her to Havana as a port visit. The second was a high-priority eyes-only message for the captain, ordering him to proceed immediately to a patrol area near Venezuela. It mentioned something about air operations with an army helicopter."

"Got it. I'll have my people dig into NSA to see if there's anything else."

"Good."

"So tell me what you think all this means, John. Why do you think this is about to go kinetic?"

"I haven't told you the kicker," Clark replied.

"Shit."

"Yeah. Get this, a Coast Guard cutter called the *Harry Claiborne* went missing off Guyana this morning. She's a buoy tender that was down there installing navaids around those oil platforms. I just spoke with the local naval attaché down there. Witnesses on those platforms said they heard an explosion. The *Claiborne* hasn't been heard from since. There have been reports of wreckage—but no survivors."

"Could be an accident. If the *Claiborne* was installing buoys, then she was in hazardous waters."

"I doubt it. We've never lost a Coast Guard vessel with all hands. Doesn't feel right."

"Is anyone looking for survivors?"

"Our ambassador in Guyana, Sydney O'Keefe, has asked the Guyanese to mount a search."

"I know Sydney. Career FSO, not a political appointee. She's good."

"What about the Guyanese? You know any of them? Can they do a competent search?"

"As a matter of fact, I'm scheduled to meet with the head of the new Guyanese intelligence agency, NISA, tonight. I'm running behind schedule, so he'll probably be pissed at me when I finally meet with him. He'll think it's a power play when, in fact, it's just my terrible schedule management."

"Okay. Well, maybe talk to him about this."

"Not yet. He's new to the NISA job. Let's see what he says to me first."

"Roger that, M.P. You know best how to manage the foreign spooks. I'll let you go."

"John, wait. We need some actual *human* intelligence reporting on this thing—not some AI bot named after Gavin Biery's cat."

"I know. As it turns out, Jack Junior has been down in Georgetown for the last week and a half working a white-side deal. He's on a red-eye home tonight, so we'll get a real-time picture of Georgetown."

"Good. What about Ding?"

"I'll send a message to Ding to get an update."

"Get him out. We need the briefing now and things could get a lot hotter for him. The Legend Factory built him a good cover, but nothing's bulletproof."

"On it. I'll shoot him the code as soon as we're done."

Mary Pat exhaled slowly. "John, why do I get the feeling that *artificial* intelligence is suddenly smarter than *real* intelligence people?"

"Because it probably is," Clark said before hanging up.

11

ORINOCO RIVER DELTA, VENEZUELA
1950

DOMINGO "DING" CHAVEZ FELT THREE SUBTLE THUMPS ON HIS WRIST WHILE WALKING along the splintered, floating dock in the thickening dusk.

The watch, a Garmin Tactix Pro Ballistics edition, was a whiz of technology. Among the usual smartwatch features—already impressive—it used pressure, temperature, humidity, and windage sensors to calculate a perfect minute of angle for a given caliber and rifle. It also had the processing horsepower to act as a satellite transceiver, connected to the orbiting military communications bird from which John Clark's coded message had just bounced.

Ding shoved his hand in his pocket to ensure that Carlos Caraza, the Tiburónista henchman carrying the AK-12 assault rifle behind him, didn't notice the buzz. Feeling it thump three more times in his pocket, Ding's memory flashed back to the debate over the sophisticated gear on his wrist when he had assumed the nonofficial cover of a Colombian army colonel named Luis Diaz.

That debate had arisen when Langley's Legend Wizards—who never left a detail to chance—objected to the Garmin as part of

Luis Diaz's persona. As far as they could tell, the real Diaz had worn a Seiko.

The Seiko in question was presently buried in an unmarked grave east of Bogotá along with Diaz himself. The colonel's throat had been slit by a Colombian counterintelligence officer who'd discovered the outlaw's drug consulting business, where he took in substantial fees in exchange for the detailed movements of the Colombian counter-narc forces.

Like a zombie, however, Diaz lived on, thanks to the counterintelligence officer who'd killed him. Since there were no witnesses to his execution and since he had no wife, Bogotá's counterintelligence group kept the colonel's career alive with paperwork that said he was deep undercover and had disappeared—which, given his burial, held a grain of truth. They weren't sure they would ever use Diaz's vacated identity, but it was always good to have a few lying around just in case.

Consequently, when the Legend Wizards called the Colombian Dirección Nacional de Inteligencia to find a cover for Domingo Chavez, the Colombian intelligence people offered army colonel Luis Diaz.

To bring him back to life, Ding had to learn the colonel's habits and memorize a roster of consorts from the deceased's career in the Lanceros, the equivalent of the U.S. Army Rangers. Already fluent in Spanish, Ding learned a Bogotá accent at Monterey's Defense Language Institute, picked up the special lingo of the Lanceros, and familiarized himself with the puts and takes of the Colombian drug trade.

When he went for his final exam, Ding had the Garmin strapped to his wrist. The Legend Wizards told him it was a mistake to go into cover with it; Ding didn't care. It was his ass on the line out there and he needed a remote satellite transceiver, since he didn't know where, exactly, he would end up.

LINE OF DEMARCATION

By the time he crossed the Venezuelan border in January and sought out a Tiburónista kingpin, he had spent so much time getting into character that he had forgotten all about the watch controversy.

It all came flooding back, though, on the floating dock that led to Tiburón's long white yacht. He hoped the three thumps on his wrist had been subtle enough that Caraza didn't notice.

"Wait here," Caraza said as he walked around Ding, tilting the floating dock. Ding stood before a sentry while Caraza hustled up the slanted gangplank and went aboard the yacht. The sentry, also armed with an AK-12, glanced at Ding and then listlessly watched the dark river flowing by. Ding waited a half minute to make sure Caraza was out of sight before he snatched a glimpse at his watch, pressing two buttons simultaneously to open the secure queue.

Clark's message read: 5 6 1 2.

"Diaz," called Caraza from the yacht's aft deck. "He's waiting. Let's go."

Ding dropped his arm to his side, thinking about the numbers. He walked up the steep metal ramp and stepped onto the *Gran Blanco*'s main deck.

Waiting for him, Caraza scowled at Ding. "*Zapatos.*"

Ding sat on the bench and removed his green nylon boots, one of Tiburón's rules for guests boarding the yacht. Over these, he wore cheap denim jeans and a floppy, short-sleeved plaid shirt—standard Tiburónista garb. He took his time untying, stealing glances at the boat. Caraza watched him with slitted eyes.

Once down to his socks, Ding endured a frisk from one of Tiburón's closest security guards while Caraza waited. With the security guard leading and Caraza following, they led him through the sliding glass door of the main salon, then up two flights of cherrywood steps to the glass-enclosed sky bridge, where Tiburón liked to conduct his business. The entire time, Ding was thinking of the message—*5 6 1 2*.

The 5 meant it was directly from Clark. The 6-1 told Ding that he was to report in with fresh intelligence. Neither of those was surprising. It was the last digit that worried him—because the 2 was an order to exfil as soon as possible. That was bad.

"Diaz," Tiburón growled from his slouch in the corner of the bridge's sofa. The drug lord had both tattooed arms spread out along the tops of the settee.

"*Jefe*," Ding replied. "What can I do for you?" he asked in Spanish.

Tiburón didn't answer. Rather, he rolled his head to his left and spoke to the man next to him.

"This is the one I was telling you about," Tiburón said with a lazy hand gesture toward Ding. "Ask him anything. He knows exactly what the *yanquis* will do."

Ding, as the traitorous Colonel Luis Diaz, had proven once or twice during his nine-week embed with the Tiburónistas that he knew the detailed behavior of American and Colombian counternarc forces. He'd done so with accurate yet harmless intelligence fed to him by Clark for exactly that purpose.

Ding made a quick assessment of the man next to Tiburón. He'd seen a few Russian Wagner thugs around the river base, always keeping to themselves. It seemed to Ding that he was probably looking at Igor Morozov, the SVR commander in charge of them. His skin was pale, his hair nearly black. He was younger than Ding thought he would be, mid-thirties.

"*Qué quieres saber?*" asked Ding. What do you want to know?

"In English," Tiburón said. "My friend's Spanish is only so-so."

For all of his coaching in Monterey to affect a Colombian accent, Ding had to wing it when it came to simulating a non-native

LINE OF DEMARCATION

English speaker. He addressed the Russian haltingly. "What . . . would you like to know, *patron*?"

Igor Morozov, a Russian SVR major who'd begun his career as a business protégé of the late Yevgeny Prigozhin, eyed Ding suspiciously. In Morozov's opinion, Tiburón was a mediocre judge of character. The drug lord's practice was to hire indiscriminately and kill anyone who didn't give him the results he was looking for.

Morozov, by contrast, was a careful man. He'd run his checks through SVR back channels and seen that Luis Diaz was a crooked colonel who'd climbed the ranks of the Lanceros. The colonel had so far provided a few useful—and accurate—bits of intelligence on American military movements in South America. But Morozov didn't rise from his junior position at Wagner to the head of SVR's Latin America desk by missing details.

Tiburón became annoyed at the Russian's contemplative silence. "Ask him, Igor. Go ahead. He's a whiz."

Morozov decided to start with the basics. Over the years, he'd learned that an unexpectedly simple question could sometimes throw a spy off track.

"Who are you?" he began, pegging his gray eyes on Ding.

Ding looked back at the Russian, taking him in. His previous sightings had been from the aft deck of the floating barge the Tiburónistas were using as a temporary barracks. To Ding, Morozov looked like a banker. He wore a dark suit and a Hermès tie. He supposed that was because the SVR man had to keep his legitimate beverage business in Venezuela operating and needed to look the part.

"I'm Colonel Luis Diaz," Ding replied.

"How did you come to be here?"

"I was recruited."

Tiburón's stark laugh nearly made Ding flinch. "Recruited! Ha!

He wanted the good life—the whores and coke like the rest of them."

Both Morozov and Ding ignored the interruption. When it was quiet again, Morozov asked Ding what infantry unit he was with as a Colombian army regular.

Ding cast his eyes down to play the part of a guilty man. "I was . . . working in CCOPE. I decided to stop and work for Tiburón."

Pronounced see-ko-pay, the Spanish acronym CCOPE stood for Commando Conjunto de Operaciónes Especiales, the Colombian Special Forces command organization. Based in Bogotá, CCOPE regularly worked with American special ops teams.

"What did you do there?" asked Morozov.

"I ran joint American-Colombian counter-narcotics airborne operations."

By now, Ding understood what this was. Internally, he was on high alert. Fooling Tiburón was one thing; fooling an SVR major was quite another.

"And before that?" asked Morozov.

"Lanceros."

"Who was your commanding officer in the Lanceros?"

Ding looked into the Russian's placid gray eyes. "What year?"

"Twenty-eighteen."

"That was Colonel Miguel Garza."

"And five years before that?"

"I was a captain then. Andres Cholla was my commanding officer."

Igor Morozov kept staring at Ding, looking for the tiny twitch of his pupils that would indicate a lie. He was leaning toward acceptance.

The Wagner men circulating among the Tiburónistas on the base ashore had told Morozov that Diaz knifed a Tib for trying to steal some of his food while still carrying himself apart—as would be expected of a Colombian officer. Morozov doubted a foreign spy could carry off a cover so coolly among the violent Tiburónistas.

"And how did you get here?" Morozov persisted.

For his part, Ding had decided it was time to feign outrage. He shot an angry glance at Tiburón. Though he was playing a crooked Colombian army colonel, he still needed to portray a proud Latin man with a brass set of *cojones*. "I'm not going to be subject to this," he snapped to Tiburón in rapid Spanish. "Either you want my expertise, or you don't. I have better things to do than to talk to this *hijo de puta*."

Tiburón's eyes flashed. Few people talked back to him.

Ding caught the angered response and built on it. The more he could sell his cover, the safer he would be. He addressed Morozov. "You address me as Colonel Diaz. We both know you're the spy here, not me." Then he turned to Tiburón and swore at him.

Tiburón nodded at Caraza, who reared and punched Ding in the jaw. Ding was thrown back against the flybridge's engine controls. He sprung back up with a sidekick that nailed Caraza in the chest, ramming the man's AK-12 painfully against his trachea.

Two bodyguards jumped into the breach and seized Ding's arms.

"What's his problem?" the Russian asked Tiburón as Ding grunted against them.

"He thought he'd be in a Caracas penthouse by now, snorting coke out of whores' navels. Instead, I've stuck him on that shit-pot of a barge. He's not getting paid or laid until we're done with the operation. If he lives that long."

Still held by the bodyguards, Ding glared at Tiburón. "What do you want to know? Ask me or get me out of here. I'm sick of living in this prison."

Tiburón raised an eyebrow at the Russian.

Morozov was nearly satisfied. Taking a shot at Tiburón was the kind of insane thing a defecting colonel would do. In the interlude, however, he had received another factoid from Luis Diaz's personnel file. He said to Ding, "One more question. What was your grandmother's maiden name on your mother's side?"

The question caught Ding cold. Four months ago, he'd learned it once during the quiz sections from the woman who'd come out to Monterey from the Legend Factory. His mind tumbled over the complicated family tree of the late Luis Diaz. It was either Salazar or Gonzalez.

Here goes nothing.

"Salazar," he seethed angrily. "She was from Quito, in case you were going to ask that next."

He swallowed a wad of bloody spit and waited. The Russian checked his phone with the nonchalance of a man waiting on an Uber. Morozov looked at Tiburón. "You didn't clear this man with me for the operation."

"He's not in the operation. We keep him like a pet in a cage, eh, Diazito?" Tiburón, who was always the first to laugh at his own jokes, shook jovially. The bodyguards and even Caraza chuckled in imitation. Tiburón turned to examine Ding, speaking to him as a hunter might speak to a promising bird dog. "You like the dinero, don't you Diazito?" He loved to add the diminutive modifier "*ito*" to Ding's cover name as a way to belittle him.

Ding cursed and asked again what they wanted from him.

Morozov nodded once at Tiburón, who asked, "We want to know what the *yanquis* would do if we were to sink one of their Coast Guard boats. You worked with the Coast Guard, *sí* or *no*?"

"*Sí*," Ding answered. "There was a Coast Guard officer in see-ko-pay. They run law enforcement operations off Mexico and in the Gulf Coast, the Caribbean. They've established a communications protocol with the Colombian navy."

The drug lord grinned and leaned back. He wore a blue silk

shirt, two buttons open to reveal the thick gold chain on his hairy chest. He'd cut his black hair short and grown an impressive, gray-streaked goatee. With all the time he'd spent cruising in the Caribbean on the *Gran Blanco*, the fifty-four-year-old's skin had grown lined and dark, nearly maroon.

"And," Tiburón continued with his question to Ding, "if I had a cargo boat headed north and a single Coast Guard ship challenged it . . . and let's just say that the Tiburónistas held their own . . . that they fought back and sunk it. What would the *yanquis* do?"

Thinking like Diaz, but also trying to tease out the origin of the question, Ding answered, "It depends on how it went down. If it was a small rubber boat, then it might simply be considered a casualty of war, like a cop killed in the line of duty. But the Coast Guard has very large cutters, too, almost like a destroyer. The bigger the boat, the bigger the *yanqui* response."

Tiburón dropped his mock cheerfulness, revealing, for a moment, the cold eyes of a killer. Once, decades ago, an American F-18 on a covert solo mission had dropped a laser-guided two-thousand-pound cellulose-encased bomb, targeting Ernesto Escobedo. It missed Escobedo. But it murdered ten families gathered for a birthday celebration—among them, Tiburón's parents.

"What if," the Russian asked Ding, "the American Coast Guard vessel had strayed into foreign waters. Perhaps by mistake. And the foreign navy sunk the boat."

"I doubt that would happen, *patron*."

"Just suppose it did."

"Then," replied Ding, "I believe it would be like other incidents. A few years ago the yanquis let a big expensive drone the size of a jetliner stray into Iranian airspace. The Iranians shot it down and the yanquis did nothing in response."

"What was the American protocol for flying Air Force reconnaissance routes in Colombia?" asked Morozov. "Suppose one of the U.S. eavesdropping planes had gone down? Would they put forces on the ground to protect the aircrew?"

"They would not, *patron*. They would ask the Lanceros to rescue the crew. The yanquis are very sensitive about a direct response in Colombia."

"You see?" Tiburón extolled with an amused glance at Morozov. "They won't do anything."

Morozov continued studying Ding. Something felt a little off, and he wasn't sure what it was.

Ding crossed his arms as he met the Russian's eyes, attempting a pose to show his impatience at being summoned to a meeting where he knew next to nothing. It also happened to be the correct posture to expose the one-millimeter digital camera lens at the top of the Garmin's watch face. If Ding's job had been to establish a TALON link between the Russian SVR and the Tiburónistas, then a picture of Major Igor Morozov on Tiburón's yacht was going to be worth far more than a thousand words.

The Campus operative furtively pressed the watchband near the buckle to trigger the exposure. *Say cheese, asshole.*

A second later Morozov nodded to Tiburón.

"Raz, take him back to his room," Tiburón said to Caraza, who remained standing near the door, massaging his bruised throat.

Ding dropped his arms and pivoted on his socks to follow Caraza through the door. On his way, he heard Tiburón say in English to Morozov, "I told you. It was a tiny Coast Guard boat in Venezuelan waters and there are no survivors. Anyone who suspects anything will be taken care of. Romero is already seeing to it. There is no more Suárez problem in Guyana."

Ding didn't know who Romero or Suárez were, but he memorized the names as he was led away.

Whatever the Russian's response, he was too far down the *Gran Blanco*'s staircase to hear it.

12

**KING GEORGE CAFÉ, GEORGETOWN, GUYANA
1955**

THE FIRST FEW SHOTS FROM THE MACHINE PISTOL CUT THE AIR LIKE A CHAIN SAW.

Jack threw the iron table over by reflex, forming a shield. He heard several automatic rounds plink off the thick metal. He yanked Quintero by the forearm and pulled him to the bricks.

"*Stay down!*" he roared at the minister. Beside them lay the bloodied corpse of Hugo Suárez, who'd taken a half dozen 9-millimeter rounds in a diagonal line that ran from his neck to his hip. The blood puddle under him was three feet wide and spreading.

Jack took quick stock of his options. The waiter with the machine pistol was sure to vault over the table and spray a deadly fusillade down on them. At best, Jack had the scattered cutlery on the brick pavers to use for defense—but he couldn't spot a decent knife. Running out of the courtyard to Water Street didn't seem like an option, either. While he might have the speed, Quintero didn't.

Jack checked the tables to either side, trying to find anything else he could use. The civilian diners were cowering behind scattered metal chairs. A few sets of wide eyes met his. He ignored them.

"Who sent them?" he barked at Quintero.

"Tiburón," the minister rasped, his chest heaving as he scrunched into a fetal position to stay behind the tabletop. "They all work for Tiburón."

Jack heard a woman scream. Staying low, he stole a glance around the table. He saw two feet pounding forward, coming for him. Jack rolled to a crouch, seized a toppled chair, and swung it at the attacker, knocking him sideways. The gunman went down four feet from the table, landing on his hip.

Jack was about to lunge for him to wrestle the machine pistol free of his hand when he saw the attacker aiming. He instantly dropped to the bricks and ducked behind a set of overturned chairs. The gun burped, sparking five rapid rounds off the metal. It fell silent.

Jack recognized the Glock 18 automatic. As far as he'd seen, the clip looked normal, factory-issue, ten-round capacity. The pause meant the killer was changing mags.

Now.

Jack sprang to his feet and attacked. As expected, the man was slamming a fresh clip home. He was lying on his side, two feet from another diner's table, swinging his reloaded gun toward Jack.

Jack seized the table edge and whipped it over. He could hear bullets clanging. Sparks danced in front of him as he smashed the heavy tabletop directly onto the gunman. Jack dove on it, driving it down like a hammer, squashing the assaulter.

Bones crunched. The gunman screamed.

Speed was everything now. The assailant was crawling away on his stomach with the machine pistol still in his right hand. Jack pounced on the assassin, landing on his back. He slammed the killer's face into the bricks with his palm spread over the back of his head. The assassin rolled just far enough to tilt the weapon at Jack. Jack went for the gun as it fired.

LINE OF DEMARCATION

Two short bursts cooked off next to his head, disorienting him. The cordite burned his nose. His ears rang. Jack slammed the man's arm to the bricks and pried the gun loose from his hand. Shaking with adrenaline, he aimed and pulled the trigger.

The burst nearly cut the man's head in half. The waiter's bloody jaw dangled from the rest of his face by a goopy string of red tendons. The gun's empty breach remained open and smoking.

Jack heard screams around him. Horrified, the other diners had found their chance to run for it. He ignored them and went back to Quintero, tossing the spent machine pistol aside and crawling on hands and knees. Quintero lay prostrate, right where Jack had left him, next to Hugo Suárez's body. Blood surrounded him, drenching the edge of his khaki shirt—whether it was from Suárez or Quintero, Jack couldn't tell.

Jack turned him over and did a blood sweep with his hands. He found a wet depression high on the minister's chest. Quintero's head lolled, turning sideways. Jack held his face up. Red bubbles inflated and popped on Quintero's pale lips as he tried to breathe.

"I'm getting you out of here," Jack said, using his fingers to clear the airway. Jack surmised that the round had entered Quintero's back, torn through a lung, and exited his chest. There was still a chance to save him with only one lung damaged.

Quintero's eyes followed Jack. He tried to say something and coughed, spewing blood.

"Don't," Jack urged. "I'm getting you to the closest hospital." He picked up the pen he'd used to write the note to them earlier. He unscrewed the cap, thinking it might have to do as an emergency tracheotomy tube. "Conserve your energy." He slid his arm under Quintero's back, intent on lifting him and getting him out to the street.

Quintero raised his forearm. Jack heard something metal fall on the bricks next to him. It was a cigar tin. "Take it," wheezed the professor, angling his eyes toward the case. "It's important. Go to my family. Amancia will need it. Please. Take it . . ." He stopped speaking when blood filled his mouth. Jack tilted the professor's head to empty it.

"I don't think she smokes," Jack replied, shoving the tin in his breast pocket. He raised a knee to brace himself, preparing to lift Quintero. "Now let's go. As soon as I get you to safety, I'll go to Amancia. First, we're going to—"

"No . . ." he gurgled. "They'll—"

The crack of two rapid gunshots made Quintero's body leap in Jack's arms. Jack's head snapped up.

Beneath the Edison lights, he saw a second man dashing for cover at the edge of the building with a pistol. The gunman was holding it with both hands, barrel down, taking cover behind a porch pillar.

Jack lowered Quintero to the brick pavers, taking cover behind the table. He checked the minister's face. The eyes were lifeless. He was gone.

At a loss, Jack flinched when he heard a tearing sound behind him, thinking it was another machine pistol. A second later, he realized it was a noisy two-stroke engine, the type used on old motorcycles. It was getting louder, closer, headed down Water Street.

He risked a glance at the assaulter near the building. Except for three dead men and Jack, the patio had cleared out. The killer was short with a dark complexion and closely shorn hair. He wore a black shirt and blue jeans. He moved to a corner column to get a better shooting angle.

The rasp of the two-stroke engine was just outside. In another few seconds, it would be gone. Unarmed, with scant cover and an assaulter nearby, it might be his last chance.

Keeping his shoulders hunched, Jack leaped to his feet and darted for Water Street. A chip of masonry stung his cheek on his way through the courtyard gate. The killer on the porch had barely missed.

The street was dim except for a single headlight. The motorcycle was nearly abeam Jack's position, sputtering along at about twenty miles per hour. Without breaking stride, Jack lowered his shoulder and slammed into the rider. The shocked man flew off the bike, landing on the curb with a yelp. The front wheel turned sideways, making the motorcycle fall awkwardly about twenty feet farther down the street. It petered out in a stall.

Jack ran for the bike. He heaved it upright and swung his leg over it. On the handlebar, he saw an ignition key, a green light, and a red button. He squeezed the clutch with his left hand and pushed the ignition button with his right. The engine came to life. With his left toe, he shoved the gear lever down.

He heard another gunshot over his shoulder and felt a bullet thud into the seat two inches behind him. Without another thought, Jack twisted the throttle all the way back. The engine screamed. He let the clutch out too fast.

Like a viciously spurred horse, the bike reared and jerked. It moved with such force that Jack was nearly flung off. He hung on to the handlebars as the machine heaved forward in an accidental wheelie, trying to keep it from falling on him. He got a foot to the street and managed to get the front wheel down with a bounce.

A 9-millimeter round whizzed past his ear. Jack leaned as far over the handlebars as he could and raced away, killing the lights.

13

RITZ-CARLTON HOTEL, GUANACASTE, COSTA RICA
1815

MARY PAT FOLEY GULPED WATER FROM THE PLASTIC BOTTLE BRETT JOHNSON HAD handed her.

"Thanks, Brett," she said, passing it back empty.

"You've been on your feet, talking all day," he said. "Good to stay hydrated."

Johnson was an athletic six-three thirty-five-year-old. The last time he and the woman in his charge had been in Central America, they'd been dodging a murderous gang in a Panamanian jungle. Surviving that had earned him a permanent billet at the DNI's side.

"I'm coming up on my last meeting," she said. "Thank God."

"I'll have Mike Hopkins sweep your villa now so we can get some rest as soon as your speech is done. Are we still wheels up tomorrow morning? Ten-hundred?"

"Yup. Breakfast address to the plenary session," she said. "And then we're outta here. Here comes my guy—Alejandro Romero, head of Guyanese intelligence."

"Roger that, ma'am."

LINE OF DEMARCATION

Johnson checked out the man walking toward them. He wore a light gray suit with a black tie, loose at the neck. He had the dark complexion of a native South American, though his eyes were blue. "I'll be in position," said the agent. "If you need me to fake an evacuation, tug your ear." He receded to a corner.

"Madame Director," said Romero, introducing himself as the head of NISA, the recently created Guyanese intelligence service.

Mary Pat performed her habitual physical assessment. Romero was about her height, a little paunchy. She thought he smelled faintly of coconut oil, like he'd lounged by the pool all day.

She recalled the dossier her team had prepared. Romero had worked his way up through the Guyanese National Police Force. A few months ago, he'd been promoted to control both the police and NISA. According to Ambassador Sydney O'Keefe, he was said to be politically connected and close to the prime minister, Castillo.

His handshake was firm, which she appreciated. She hated few things more than a condescending squish handshake just because of her sex.

"Shall we sit down?" he asked. "I believe we have a few urgent matters to discuss." He gestured toward one of the empty tables in the main ballroom, where the plenary sessions had concluded for the day.

Too exhausted for small talk, she crossed her legs. "Where would you like to start?"

"With a drink, perhaps?" Without waiting for her reply, he turned his head, spotted his security man, and snapped his fingers.

"Not on duty, thank you," she replied. "And as you mentioned, we have some urgent matters to review."

"Tonic water only. I promise. I brought you some." The guard set down two icy glasses. Romero poured from a can. He spoke with a curious accent, half-British, half-Latin, like his country.

"The Coast Guard cutter *Harry Claiborne*," he began after a sip. "Your ambassador informed the prime minister that it went missing early this morning. Per her request, I have since had people out scouring the waters."

"And?"

"I am afraid, Madame Director, that the news is not good. I've come prepared to share everything I know."

Mary Pat quietly appreciated three things about Romero so far: he hadn't patronized her with a weak handshake, had planned the drinks correctly, and had volunteered to begin with the facts.

"Thank you, Director Romero," she said. "Whenever you're ready."

"Very well. First, let me apologize for not relaying this a few hours ago when I got the initial report. I wanted to confirm everything."

"Understandable."

He unleashed a long, rueful sigh. "I wish I had more precise information. But here I will give it to you unvarnished. At three thirty this morning, a shrimp fisherman heard a UHF radio call from the cutter *Harry Claiborne*. It was to an unknown vessel attempting to render aid. After that, the radio went quiet."

"The radio call wasn't answered?"

"We don't know. All we know is that the fisherman didn't hear a reply."

"Where was the fisherman?"

"About twenty clicks to the east of the oil platforms. Guyanese waters."

"So it's possible the hail was to a vessel farther to the west, putting the fisherman out of range."

"Yes."

"What else?" she asked.

"My team interviewed workers on the oil platform called Marlin. They heard a distant explosion at about zero-three-thirty. They weren't sure what it was."

"They didn't call it in?"

"No. This time of year, we get frequent storms near the coast. They thought it was thunder."

Mary Pat nodded slowly. "But you have other boats out there looking?"

Romero went on. "Yes. Unfortunately, this afternoon, one of them reported a major oil slick. It was in an area called the Graveyard, strewn with rocks and a strong seaward current from the Essequibo River delta. Technically, the area of the slick is in the waters claimed by Venezuela."

He stopped speaking and settled his blue eyes on her.

"Those are all your facts?" she asked. "Everything?"

"Yes. But you and I are in the intelligence business. Facts are only half the story."

"Correct."

"So let me tell you what I think, as an intelligence officer."

After a few gulps of the soda, he cleared his throat and tugged on the end of his tie. "My professional intuition tells me that this was likely the work of Tiburón. I suspect that his Tiburónistas were running a big shipment of drugs through the area, coming out of one of their protected ports in Venezuela. My guess is that your Coast Guard vessel came within range of them and . . . Well, I think you can imagine. Your Coast Guard has quite a reputation with the Tiburónistas. Tiburón himself, of course, despises all things American."

"The *Claiborne* was a buoy tender," she replied. "She wouldn't have been chasing down a gang of smuggling Tiburónistas."

"Regardless . . . I believe their paths intersected. And the smugglers probably wouldn't care. They hate the Coast Guard. The explosion, the rapid radio silence, and the disappearance of survivors can only mean to me that it was a case of mistaken identity."

Mary Pat held his gaze, saying nothing.

So far, she had no reason to believe he was holding anything back—other than her long experience as a spy. She assumed every foreign official lied out of well-worn habit, especially to her. She made a mental note to to check with the NSA on intercepted radio transmissions in the area.

"And the crew?" she returned. "No bodies have been found?"

"Regrettably . . . no. Our search grid has expanded to the limits of our territorial waters. We will keep looking, of course, but . . . I am not hopeful." He briefly touched her elbow with his index finger. "I'm terribly sorry for this tragedy and for the families of these sailors. Given the work they were doing for Guyana, our government will make reasonable amends if we can."

"Thank you," she replied. Then, after a beat, "I would ask that you turn all available evidence over to the United States. Whatever you have. If it was Tiburón, I'd like inviolate proof."

"Of course, Madame Director." He drummed his fingers on the table linen next to his drink as though dissatisfied with the facts.

"You know," he resumed, "I have spent nearly my entire career trying to break the backs of the Tiburónistas operating their drug labs in Guyana. I believe you're aware that Tiburón assassinated our attorney general, Martin Croom, a few months ago?"

"Yes. I've been briefed on that."

"The good news is that his replacement, Hugo Suárez, is closing in on links to Tiburón. I'll give you whatever he finds, especially if we can prove Tiburón was involved in this sinking."

She nodded. "Thank you for that. But I'd also add that we're going to mount our own search of those waters, of course," she said, bluffing.

LINE OF DEMARCATION

It was likely that President Jack Ryan would order the Coast Guard to dispatch a C-130 long-range search aircraft from the air station in Puerto Rico. But she'd only said it to gauge Romero's reaction.

"That will require my president's permission, Madame Director. I will seek it immediately."

"Given the cooperation between our governments," she persisted, "why wait? Where is President Khasif?" After a message exchange with Sydney O'Keefe, Mary Pat knew exactly where President Khasif was—on a dune buggy ride across the Abu Dhabi desert—but she considered it rude to say as much.

"He's in the Middle East," answered Romero. "The prime minister and I will brief him as soon as we can. I would ask that you formalize a request for the movement of forces through Ambassador O'Keefe. In the meantime, we will keep up the search. You have my word on that."

"Thank you, Director Romero."

Unbidden, he continued. "As you know, Madame Director, we are very appreciative of the work your Coast Guard was doing for us, paving the way for the successful export of gas and oil from the Orinoco Basin field. I will not let the Tiburónistas interfere with our alliance. Attorney General Suárez will root out any corruption."

"I appreciate that, Director."

"Yes. And may I also say . . . Oh, pardon me, Madame Director." The phone in the breast pocket of his jacket trilled insistently. He reached for it and glanced at the phone's face.

Out of the corner of her eye, Mary Pat saw Brett Johnson snap his head toward them, triggered by the sudden shift of Romero's hand. She gave him a reassuring wave.

"One moment," said Romero. "I must take this." The head of NISA stood and walked a few paces away for privacy.

Watching Romero with the phone to his ear, Mary Pat recalled her earlier conversation with Clark. Ding Chavez had reported a TALON link between the Russians and Tiburón. The Russian frigate *Admiral Gorshkov* was steaming toward Venezuela. Russian cargo planes chartered to a Wagner front company had crossed the Atlantic from Africa to land in Havana.

And her new Guyanese colleague, Alejandro Romero, head of the National Intelligence and Security Agency, hadn't mentioned any of that.

Of course, she considered further, the NISA was a brand-new organization with weak capabilities. If anything, she should be alerting Romero to these happenings, not the other way around.

Then what was it? she asked herself. Why did she feel uncomfortable bringing up any of those intelligence findings?

The answer occurred to her with a jolt. It was because he paused when she suggested they would do their own search. He seemed so eager for her to accept his explanation: Tiburón, open and shut, evidence forthcoming.

That was it, she thought, sipping some of the tonic water. Romero had been selling her.

"Madame Director," he said when he returned. "I'm afraid I have more bad news." He shook his head bitterly. "The scourge of the Tiburónistas continues on what has become a very dark day for Guyana."

"Oh?"

"Yes, Madame Director. It appears that Tiburón has struck again."

She frowned. "How?"

"The Tiburónistas have assassinated Attorney General Suárez in a Georgetown restaurant." Romero rapped his fist on the table. "They shot him in cold blood." He clenched his jaw before adding,

"I'm doubly sad to tell you that they also killed the minister of the interior, Alberto Quintero."

After an appropriate expression of sorrow, Mary Pat saw him off. Romero left muttering pledges about justice in Guyana.

As he passed over the wide ballroom carpet, it struck her as odd that he wasn't hurrying or picking up a phone to give instructions to some lieutenant. He seemed to be strolling at an easy pace to the lobby with an occasional nod to a Latin peer.

Pondering that, she went outside to the veranda and stood at its outer wall. Below it, there was a lit path crowded by lush jungle landscaping. She could see Romero walking along it, heading toward his villa, talking to his security man.

Though too far away to make out a word, Mary Pat could tell that the conversation was rapid and light. Then she heard something that chilled her.

Laughter.

"To the villa, ma'am?" Brett asked. He'd slipped out the glass doors to check on her.

"No," she responded, turning. "Bring my car around instead. We're going to the airport. Deputy Director Pratt can do my speech in the morning. I want to get back to Liberty Crossing."

"What? We're leaving? Now?"

"Yes. Now."

"Something changed, ma'am?"

"Yes, Brett, it has. I do believe I've just been played."

14

ORINOCO RIVER DELTA, VENEZUELA
2030

THE FLOATING BARRACKS WHERE THE TIBURÓNISTAS KEPT A SHARP EYE ON DING were two stories of cheap plywood rooms stacked on an old barge.

Ten days earlier, Tiburón had ordered the men to this riparian base, an outpost on the Orinoco's northern shore. The compound had once been owned by a company that exported soybeans to Europe—but like most Venezuelan firms that weren't in the oil business, it had gone bust when the dictators seized power. A few miles downriver, the muddy waters flowed into the Atlantic, which served it well for exports.

Before his arrival at the Orinoco camp, Ding was living in an apartment in San Felipe, a town on the Colombia-Venezuela border, where he sold information on the Colombian military for money, continuing the business of his dead predecessor.

Ding knew he was trading with Tiburónistas, but it wasn't until he was thrown into a truck, blindfolded, and subjected to a full day's drive to the Orinoco that he met Tiburón face-to-face. Tiburón, it seemed, liked Ding's intelligence and wanted him as a personal advisor for a special operation.

LINE OF DEMARCATION

Over the ten days since Ding's arrival, the facilities had steadily adopted a military look. Old warehouses got bunks and porta-potties. A shower facility was set up in the former crop-processing center. Meals were served in a run-down house by a staff of old women trucked in daily. The compound's perimeter fence was topped with razor wire, as much to keep curious villagers out as to keep the Tiburónistas in.

The *Gran Blanco* was moored just upriver of the barge. From it, Tiburón ordered his men to prepare for, as he put it, "a major shipment to the yanquis." Under the guidance of the Russians, his faithful henchmen collected cell phones and weapons as a security precaution. The Wagner mercenaries and a few veteran Tiburónistas moved cargo from trucks to docks to boats.

Ding noticed that the boats left with crates and returned empty. The estuary was too broken up with tidal islands and sandbars to tell exactly where they were going. He assumed they were meeting an offshore freighter.

Along with most of the men on the barge, Ding wasn't privy to the contents of the unmarked crates. The presence of the Russians had made him suspect they were more than just drugs. Though he'd seen Clark's message to exfil, he was determined to figure it out.

There weren't many Wagner men. He thought there were about ten, but could never be sure. They berthed ashore in a derelict bean storage building, staying separated from the Tiburónistas and leaving on the boats for long periods. On the three occasions when Morozov's helicopter landed on the *Gran Blanco*, Ding noted that two Russians went up the gangplank to meet him.

Ding also saw that the Tiburónistas living ashore differed from the young men from the jungle processing plants. Whereas those men were of average to poor physical builds, the workers who lived ashore were hard and lean. In Ding's view, an informal caste system had begun to develop with the Russians at the top, trusted Tiburónistas like Caraza in the middle, and lowly jungle drug factory workers at the bottom. Ding was in a category all his own—a turncoat Colombian army officer whom no one trusted.

Still, he was allowed to walk the pier, hit the latrines or showers, and eat with the rest of the men. Through his various interactions, he had come to learn that many of the shore-berthed Tiburónistas had done jail time in Colombia. Some, he learned, came straight from the notorious Venezuelan Tocoron prison, which operated more like an outlaw city than a jail.

Here on the river, for the most part, Ding saw the various sects behaving under the strict camp rules. The prisoners considered Tiburón worthy of loyalty, since he'd given them each varying degrees of freedom and money.

But devoted or not, the toxic brew of confined quarters, alcohol, and idiocy made conflict inevitable. Three nights after Ding arrived from his shanty apartment in San Felipe, a druggie scumbag had gotten sideways with him due to Ding's legend as a defected Colombian counter-narc officer.

After a very public fight that ended with the point of Ding's switchblade against the Venezuelan's jugular, they'd since left him alone. Ding spoke only when spoken to and portrayed himself as an important source for Tiburón.

Ding went down the ladderway to get out to the barge's fantail. His reason for doing so was to send in a new report to Clark to let him know he'd received the 5-61-2 message and would comply when able. He also wanted to get the picture with Morozov back to The Campus to confirm the link between the Russians and the Tiburónistas.

When he got to the bottom of the ladder, Caraza saw him from his usual spot on his bunk.

"What are you doing?"

"*Baño*," Ding said without slowing down. He headed to the back of the barge. A sentry sat at its edge with an AK-12 across his knees. "*Baño*," Ding repeated to the sentry.

When he went to the porta-potty door, he saw that it was locked. That was okay with Ding, since he needed a clear line of sight to the starry sky over his head for the Garmin's transmitter to work. He stood near the sentry and fiddled with his watch, getting the image queued up.

"Where you from?" he asked the sentry, raising his hands over his head and clasping them in a relaxed, shooting-the-breeze posture so the watch would transmit freely.

"Bogotá," came the reply.

"How long you work for Tiburón?"

"*Toda mi vida*," came the answer. My whole life.

Ding waited for the Garmin to finish transmitting. "This guy's taking forever," he said to the guard with a nod to the porta-potty. He checked his watch and then put his hands over his head again. The narrow data channel was irritatingly slow. It had uploaded about twenty percent of the file. He put his hands back on his head.

"Hey, Diaz. I like your watch."

Shit, thought Ding, recognizing the voice. It was Caraza.

Ignoring the remark, Ding leaned back, looking up at the stars. "You hear me, Diaz?" asked Caraza. "I said I like your watch."

"*Gracias*," muttered Ding, still looking up at the stars.

"*Dámelo*." Give it to me.

Ding breathed deeply. With Tiburón's obvious trust, Carlos Caraza was high up in the Tiburónista caste system. During the lockdown, he'd acted as a combination enforcer, den mother, and landlord on the barge.

The young sentry was only a few feet away. He'd heard the whole exchange, the AK-12 still across his knees.

"No," Ding answered bluntly. "This watch was a gift from my unit. Not giving it up."

Caraza approached and squeezed Ding's elbow. "*Dámelo.*"

With his arms already over his head, Ding's next action was quick. He brought his right hand down in a lightning chop to Caraza's Adam's apple while his left fist hammered the Tiburónista's balls.

Caraza gasped and doubled over. Ding was about to kick him over the edge of the barge when he heard the sentry's AK click with a freshly chambered round.

"*Congela!*" shouted the sentry, aiming the rifle at Ding's chest.

The Campus operative froze.

Caraza recovered, his hands on his knees at first, then standing upright. His chest heaved as he spoke to the sentry. "Ayee, Pedro. *Buen hombre.* If this *hijo de puta* does anything else, blow his head off." Then he turned to Ding and spat on the ground. "Diaz, give me the watch."

Ding unstrapped the Garmin from his left wrist and held it out. When Caraza came forward to grab it, Ding threw it far into the brown river current.

"Guess you had something you didn't want me to see," Caraza seethed, spitting. He then turned to the sentry. "If he comes out of his room, shoot him."

The sentry nodded.

Back on his thin mattress on the barge's second floor, Ding lay still, hoping the photo had made it up to the satellite. If nothing else, he'd managed to long-press his emergency egress button before his only link to The Campus had disappeared into the river.

So much for delaying the exfil, he thought.

15

ARLINGTON, VIRGINIA
1815

CLARK COULD HEAR THE GROWL OF AN ENGINE OVER THE LINE AS SOON AS MARY PAT Foley picked up her secure phone.

"You going somewhere?" he asked her.

"Yeah. I met with Romero, the new head of the Guyanese intelligence service."

"And?"

"He volunteered information about the lost Coast Guard cutter. He's pinning it all on Tiburón. Says it was a smuggling run-in that went bad. But he doesn't have any solid evidence."

"Did he mention any concerns about the Russian frigate? Or the suspected Russian TALON link to Tiburón?"

"No. Not a word about that."

"Huh. Where are you going now?" asked Clark. Of the twenty or so investment bankers who worked on Hendley's white side, he could see through his interior office window that only a few were left at their desks. The rest of the floor was empty.

"I'm headed home," Mary Pat said. "I left behind a deputy to cover the rest of the conference."

"Why?"

Clark could hear her vehicle accelerating in the background as she answered. "As I was meeting with Romero, he informed me that the Guyanese attorney general and minister of the interior were both assassinated tonight."

Clark winced. "What was his reaction to that?"

"Not what you would expect. He didn't seem to be in a hurry. That's why I'm headed back to the ranch."

"You think he knew?"

"Not sure. Have you spoken with Jack Junior yet?"

"Negative. His phone went to voicemail. I'm told he's on a long, complicated series of flights to get back in CONUS. Did Romero finger anyone for the hit?"

"Tiburón, of course."

"You don't believe him?"

"John, I just think there's something off. There are too many coincidences between the Russian movements and the assassinations. Have you got Ding out of the country yet?"

"That's actually why I called," said Clark, who'd picked up Ding's emergency beacon. "He—"

"Wait, hold on," she interrupted. "I have a call coming in. Be right back."

Clark studied the image on his computer while he waited. It was a satellite image of Tiburón's camp on the Orinoco River. He could see Tiburón's yacht tied to the main pier with the Russian's helicopter on the bow-mounted helipad. Clark could also see the long river barge where Ding had been sequestered—and the spot behind the barge where the distress beacon had originated.

"Hey, John," said Mary Pat after another fifteen seconds. "I've got Sydney O'Keefe on the line. It would be good for the three of us to discuss this." She introduced Clark to Ambassador O'Keefe, calling Clark the president's special security advisor.

Once the niceties were out of the way, Mary Pat got down to business. "Sydney, Mr. Clark and I have a few concerns about the situation in Guyana. You already know about the *Harry Claiborne* disappearing off the coast with reports of an explosion. Add to that some potential Russian Wagner Group movements in Venezuela and a Russian frigate that's on a course to the western Caribbean. Now we have the murder of a couple of pro-American government people. Your thoughts on the situation there?"

As a professional diplomat, Ambassador O'Keefe took a few moments to compose her answer. "Director Foley, here's what I can tell you. I've been in touch with the prime minister since the *Claiborne* went missing this morning. The Guyanese initiated a search. An hour ago, Prime Minister Castillo told me they believe the boat was hit by—"

"Tiburón," Mary Pat said, cutting her off. "Romero, their head of NISA said the same thing to me in the last hour."

"As expected," confirmed O'Keefe. "Prime Minister Castillo said Romero was meeting with you."

"But what about this assassination? What's Castillo got to say about that?"

"Castillo said Romero's team is investigating. They suspect it was Tiburón, since Hugo Suárez, the new attorney general, had been closing in on Tiburón's network in Guyana."

"Ambassador," Clark interrupted, "how well do you know this prime minister . . . Castillo is it?"

"Yes, Augustus Castillo. Goes by Guto. I know him fairly well."

"Why are we dealing with him instead of the Guyanese president?"

"Because," answered O'Keefe, "President Khasif is in Abu Dhabi right now."

"Yes—but can't you get to him?" Mary Pat asked.

"I've got an official request to speak to him as soon as he's available. We have a strong relationship with Khasif. He supported the privatization of the Orinoco Basin and cleared the Coast Guard to come in and set up the work required to off-load gas from the offshore platforms."

"Was Castillo a supporter of that?" asked Clark.

"No. Castillo is head of the opposition party, the socialists. They were vehemently opposed to privatization. Which is why I'd much rather be dealing with President Khasif."

"And what about this interior minister, Quintero? Why was he killed?"

"Mr. Clark, according to Prime Minister Castillo, Quintero was just in the wrong place at the wrong time. They believe Suárez was the target."

"What do we know about Quintero?" Mary Pat asked.

"Before his death, Quintero was a vocal opponent of the socialists."

The line hissed while Mary Pat and Clark digested the ambassador's update. The DNI asked, "So what would happen if POTUS ordered a couple of C-117s stuffed with Marines to the Guyana airport to help protect our assets down there? We could say they're assisting in the search for the cutter."

Again Sydney O'Keefe took a few moments to respond. "Madame Director, legally, Guyanese law would require President Khasif to approve that."

"What if we did it anyway? President Ryan could order it as Commander in Chief, declaring the developing turmoil in Guyana a clear and present danger to American citizens in the region."

"He could, certainly. But I must tell you, it would feed the narrative the socialists here are always pushing—that America is the big bully, that we do nothing but rape and pillage. I can say that Marines patrolling in plain sight would be an ugly image. It might even push the socialists into power. If that happens, we could lose Guyana to the Russians and Venezuelans. If POTUS were to ask Secretary of State Adler, I believe he would agree with me."

LINE OF DEMARCATION

"I appreciate your perspective," Mary Pat said, finishing up. "Please keep trying to get through to President Khasif."

"Yes, Madame Director."

"Well, there you have it," Mary Pat concluded when it was just herself and Clark left on the line. "Mighty coincidental timing. Russian arms shipments, Wagner Group staging, Venezuelan troop movements. But I'm still uncomfortable going to POTUS with this without any decent human intelligence. I really need some ground truth coming in from Ding. What's the latest from him?"

"Exactly why I called you. I sent Ding the coded signal to exfil. Not long after that, I got his emergency beacon. That means he probably can't get out on his own. I'm looking for your help with that."

Clark heard doors opening and a gust of wind on her end of the line. "I'm just getting to my plane," Mary Pat replied. "What do you propose?"

"For Ding to send a message like that is serious trouble."

"How serious?"

"Serious enough that I'm getting a team together to go get him. Spinning it up now."

"Jesus, John," she answered. "If Campus people charge in with guns blazing, it might play out exactly as the ambassador warned."

"Negative. It will be fully deniable. Master Chief Kendrick Moore has been working on some stealthy new amphibious machines to get us in and out undetected. They'll never know it was us. I'd still like your permission to go, however. I know the situation is dynamic down there."

It took her three seconds to answer. "Yes. You have my permission."

"Good," Clark said. "That's better than me asking for your forgiveness."

16

ARLINGTON, VIRGINIA
2030

LIKE HER FIANCÉ—JACK RYAN, JR.—LISANNE ROBERTSON RARELY FOUND HER HEND-ley white-side work stimulating.

She spent much of her time in the office following through on the details of Jack's various white-side business adventures, which occasionally required meticulous accounting work—especially when it came to Athena Global Shipping Lines.

Earlier in the day, Howard Brennan, Jack's white-side boss, asked Lisanne to gather accrued operating expenses for his Puerto Rican shipping company. Howard was anxious to get conversations started with potential buyers for Athena, which meant providing an accurate set of accounting statements.

Lisanne didn't know much about Athena. Nor, it turned out, did Howard. With Jack incommunicado while traveling, she was forced to track down the Athena managers in San Juan. She spent hours interviewing them in her rusty Spanish to assemble a year's worth of expense receipts that ran into the hundreds of thousands. Before leaving the office that day, she doggedly plugged the numbers into Howard's spreadsheet.

LINE OF DEMARCATION

As a former Marine and Texas state trooper who'd lost her left arm below the elbow in a gunfight, she wasn't wired for office work. On previous similar occasions, she complained to Jack about her boredom and her feeling that her cubicle walls were a form of slow suffocation. Jack's usual response was to remind her that it was the white-side work that funded the black.

She considered it an answer that was all too convenient for her betrothed. While the financial logic was sound, Jack too often treated her with kid gloves, as though her disability would get in the way of black-side fieldwork.

Lisanne didn't see it that way. She was a sharp operator who'd learned to get by with a prosthetic arm, pulling her weight across both sides of the Hendley/Campus operational divide. If there was one source of friction in her relationship with Jack, it was his tendency to act as her protector.

Still, she wished her fiancé was home tonight. After playing accountant for several hours, she would have welcomed the chance to review her work with him. Instead, she returned to their Arlington home to find that Emily—her sixteen-year-old niece—had fired up the oven with a frozen pizza.

Lisanne and Emily ate it in front of the TV as they settled into a streaming video binge. It wasn't as comforting as having Jack at home—but it was close.

When Clark called, Lisanne paused the video.

"When does Jack land?" he asked gruffly.

She thought through the last text message she'd received from Jack in Guyana.

"He's on a red-eye through Panama City," she answered. "I think it connects through Denver to D.C. That would put him back at our place around four a.m. Why?"

Emily took her empty plate to the kitchen, leaving Lisanne alone.

"If he checks in from the airport or something, tell him to call me immediately," Clark replied, his voice clipped.

When it came to black-side work, Clark was Lisanne's boss. Sensitive to family life, the old SEAL was usually more cordial when calling her at home. Though a man of few words, his abruptness had her concerned.

"Mr. C., is everything all right?" she ventured.

"This isn't a secure line," he said. "I can't say."

"Oh." She grew twice as worried.

He changed the subject. "You speak Spanish, don't you, Lisanne?"

"Yes. As it happens, I've been brushing up on it all day. Why?"

A few seconds passed before Clark responded. "I need you in the office, ASAP. And I'd like you to set up a few flights while you drive. I'll explain the rest when you get here."

LISANNE PUSHED HER VOLVO SUV HARD OVER THE CITY STREETS. AT THIS TIME OF night, traffic in D.C. wasn't that bad and she was able to employ her state trooper driving skills. She was on the phone for half the drive, setting up the flights Clark wanted her to charter—though he hadn't yet told her why.

When she arrived at the Hendley office at nine p.m., she found it empty. That meant Clark was down in the basement in the briefing room near the underground shooting range. She used her key card to beep through the sensor lock to make her way downstairs.

"All right," Clark said when she walked through the conference room door. "We've got everyone except Jack now."

By that, Lisanne could see Clark meant her Campus colleagues Steven "Chilly" Edwards, Mandy Cobb, and Gavin Biery.

Like Lisanne, Chilly was an ex-cop. He'd come to Clark's attention when he'd helped free First Lady Cathy Ryan from a gang of terrorists. Mandy Cobb had been an FBI agent before coming on board The Campus full-time. Gavin Biery was up front near Clark with his ever-present laptop beside him, wired to a whirring projector on the ceiling.

"Lisanne, grab a chair and hit the lights," Clark said.

She nodded her hellos and sat down in the relative dark.

The projector bulb popped on, bathing Clark in white light. "Okay," he began, blinking at his big wristwatch. "As of now, twenty-one-seventeen, you're all activated on a black-side op. Copy?"

He was met with a series of nods around the table. Chilly, who was still new to The Campus, leaned forward eagerly. Mandy Cobb sat back with her arms across her chest. They were all dressed casually in jeans and T-shirts, since the call had gone out after hours.

"First slide, Gav," said Clark. A black-and-white satellite image appeared behind him. "Our mission is a deniable, zero-footprint asset recovery on the Venezuelan coast, near the Orinoco River delta."

Mandy Cobb had a reputation as a digger, always looking for more information. "Asset?" she asked. "Do you mean a confidential informant or a nonofficial-cover CIA officer?"

"A nonofficial-cover *Campus* officer, Ms. Cobb," Clark clarified. "His name is Domingo Chavez."

While the rest of the room stared in shock, Clark stepped aside to reveal the screen image fully.

"Okay," he continued. "The compound you see here is my last reported location from Ding. He sent out an emergency distress beacon near this barge that's now about three hours old." Clark looked back at them from beneath his thick brows. "You guys all know Ding. He wouldn't make a 911 call unless he were in real trouble."

Lisanne felt an icy stab in her stomach. She'd become friends with Ding's wife, Patricia Clark—John Clark's daughter—over the ensuing months. She agreed with her boss. There was no way the Domingo Chavez she knew would call for help unless the situation were desperate.

"Mr. C.," she said. "I set up Ding's black-side travel to Colombia. I thought he was in Bogotá working with the Colombians, attached to CCOPE."

"Correct. He was attached to CCOPE," Clark answered. "But you didn't know that that was all part of his cover, worked up by Langley's Legend Wizards."

"Can you give us a little more background?" Mandy asked.

Clark took a patient breath. "Sure. Per my request, the Wizards built Ding's cover as Colombian army colonel Luis Diaz—a Special Forces commander working against the Tiburónistas on the Venezuelan border. The real Diaz is dead."

"Ding assumed his full identity, then," Mandy noted. "We fed disinformation to the Venezuelans so they'd think Diaz is still alive."

"That's right. Ding set up shop on the Venezuelan border, taking payoffs from the druggies, hoping to attract Tiburón's interest. Ten days ago, Tiburón took the bait. Ding was taken blindfolded to the compound on the screen you see here. The big boat is Tiburón's yacht. The helicopter on the bow belongs to a Russian SVR officer. Ding was summoned to a meeting with both on the boat earlier today."

"Has Ding had free access from the compound?" Mandy asked.

"No. He's become a sort of advisor to Tiburón on joint American-Colombian ops in the area. All the men at this compound have been on lockdown, awaiting a large trafficking operation."

"What's Ding's mission?" asked Chilly. "To take out Tiburón?"

"I'll get to it," Clark said. "Next slide, Gav."

The image on the screen shifted to a blowup of an airfield ringed by palm trees that looked like pinwheels from above. "This is Holguin Air Base in Cuba," said Clark. "That cargo plane you see in the center is a chartered Russian An-124. We know it came from the Central African Republic, a hotbed of Wagner Group activity. There's also a Russian army helicopter over here on a hardstand. It's a Russian army Mi-8 attack variant loaded up with missiles. Next slide, Gav."

The image shifted to a man in a suit. Lisanne judged him to be in his mid-thirties, with dark, slicked-back hair and a narrow face. The surveillance photo showed him walking along a dusty boulevard, wearing sunglasses.

"This is Igor Morozov," Clark said. "He's the one who owns the helicopter on Tiburón's yacht. This photo was taken in Niamey, Niger, when Morozov was still with the Wagner Group. He's since moved up the food chain to the Russian SVR, where he runs their Latin Desk. To your question, Chilly, Ding's job was to figure out why a former Wagner leader now in the SVR was dealing with a drug lord who hates the U.S."

"Did he come up with anything?" Lisanne asked.

Clark shook his head. "Ding's reporting told us that Morozov has been bringing Wagner veterans into the country to help Tiburón build up a mercenary force called the Tiburónistas. But we don't know why. Gav, go back to the imagery of the river camp."

When the base was on the screen, Clark said, "We only know they were loading crates onto these boats at the docks, here, and taking them out in the river."

"No theories as to what they're doing? Or where those boats are going?" Mandy inquired.

"Theories, sure. But no conclusions—yet. The boats disappear behind these islands. Ding couldn't figure out where they were going or what they were carrying. That said, Gavin uncovered a few other telling developments earlier today that suggest the Tiburónistas have a larger motive with the Russians. Gav, brief 'em up."

Gavin Biery's work was usually confined to a keyboard, a backstage man. He began with a shy explanation of his AI bot, Princess, which warranted a snicker from the group.

The ribbing stopped when he flipped forward to an image of a Russian warship. "This is a frigate called the *Admiral Gorshkov*," he announced. "According to DIA, NSA, and Princess, she's on a straight-line course at flank speed to the vicinity of Guyana."

"To the vicinity of where?" asked Chilly.

"Guyana."

"Where's that?"

"Right next to Venezuela," interrupted Clark.

"But who cares about Guyana?" Chilly persisted.

"Us," Clark answered. He then explained the gas and oil discovery and subsequent infrastructure development in the Orinoco Basin.

"Neither the Venezuelans nor the Russians want to see any of this Guyanese natural gas sold on world markets," Clark finished. "By exporting it to Europe, the Russians would lose serious geopolitical leverage. It would also screw the Venezuelans out of billions of dollars by keeping prices down. You can imagine how the dictator down there would react to that."

"So we think the Russians might seize the oil field? That's what this Tiburónista force is about?" Mandy asked.

"We don't know. It's why we wanted someone embedded with Tiburón. If the Russians were going to grab it, it would make sense that they'd employ the same tactic they used in Crimea in 2014 with a Wagner-like force. And since Tiburón already has his hooks into Guyana, they'd be able to use the drug lord to help grease the wheels."

"So we're supposed to stop an invasion?" Mandy followed up incredulously. "Just us? Like, tonight?"

"Negative," Clark said. "That's for the higher-ups to decide. But this thing is obviously getting hot. The Campus, this team, is on an asset recovery mission before it boils over. We need to know what Ding knows. We're going to extract him ASAP. That's it."

"Out of a drug lord's compound in a hostile country?" the FBI agent remarked doubtfully. "We'd better have a hell of a plan."

Clark made a circular motion with his head, making it pop. "I've asked Master Chief Moore to put together an insertion plan. Lisanne started the logistics work on her way here."

"That's right, Mr. C.," she chimed in. "We're booked on a charter from Reagan National's private ramp as soon as we're ready. DoD cleared us into Naval Air Station Oceana, Virginia Beach, where we will meet Master Chief Moore. It's only a half hour from here by air. I have a van in the parking lot upstairs to get us to Reagan."

"And after Oceana?" asked Clark.

"I'm still working on it," she responded. "But I think I can get us on a jet to Trinidad-Tobago. Trinidad is just across the water from the Orinoco river delta."

Clark put his hands on his hips. "Good. We'll fine-tune the rest of it on the flight to the Caribbean."

"What about Jack?" asked Lisanne. "He's still in the air. He doesn't know about any of this."

"Right," Clark said. "As soon as he touches down, tell him to redirect to meet us—probably down in Trinidad."

"Okay," she agreed.

Backlit by the glowing screen, Clark surveyed the room. "Any other questions?"

"Yeah," offered Chilly. "Mr. C., you're saying we're going right now? I didn't bring my gear or tactical clothes."

"Maybe you didn't hear me at the beginning of all this," Clark replied, his eyes piercing. "We have a Campus asset in distress. His name is Domingo Chavez."

DAY TWO

17

**ABU DHABI, UNITED ARAB EMIRATES
MARCH 2
0840**

THE LIGHT WOKE PRESIDENT ALI KHASIF.

Though he'd slept in what his host Emiratis had modestly called a *khayma*—a canvas tent—the president had all the comforts of home.

The featherbed was a queen. The floor was a bouquet of silk carpets. The chair and table set up for his use were ornately carved mahogany. In Khasif's opinion, to call it *glamping* would be woefully insufficient. Yet for all of that, the canvas couldn't fight back the strong desert sun, and as soon as he woke up, he was forced to squint.

He pivoted to the edge of the bed and heard the fabric walls bow inward. The wind was rising with the sun—just as well. After his second night in the desert, he looked forward to getting back to civilization. In fairness, he corrected himself as he donned his socks, this kind of living was plenty civilized. But he was growing weary of the royal treatment. As the first president elected from

Guyana's Muslim minority, he was a humble man with humble needs and wanted to get back to Georgetown soon.

He finished dressing and wedged his rolled prayer rug under his arm. Outside, he felt the first flicks of sand stinging his cheeks.

Among the curving dunes, he looked across nine other tents that were of a similar design to his own. Most sheltered the Emerati princes and dignitaries who'd insisted on dragging him out here to the middle of nowhere to witness their big, grand car race. Beyond the royal tents, the president could see a dozen smaller ones for the myriad servants and workers who catered to the caravan's every need. Beyond the tents, he could see the shining metal of the exotic sand vehicles they'd been riding since leaving Abu Dhabi city.

By invitation of the royal entourage, the Guyanese president, chief of staff, and foreign minister were honorary racers in the Abu Dhabi Desert Challenge, an off-road rally of dune buggy–style vehicles that covered two hundred curving miles.

As the crown prince explained to the president, it was one of the many global spectacles that had put the United Arab Emirates on the map. With its lush rainforests and sparsely populated hills, the crown prince had been trying to convince Khasif to make tiny Guyana one of the sport's newer venues. Along the way, he also made his arguments for Khasif to join OPEC, which was the real reason for the royal treatment.

Khasif finished his prayers and returned to his tent. The whipping wind had woken others, and he saw several white-coated servants scurrying through the camp. He had to shoo a half dozen away before making it inside and dressing for breakfast.

"*Salaam alaikum*, Mr. President," Prince Mohammed Ben Sulayem said when the president presented himself. The Emirati leader wore a flowing white bisht cloak. His matching kaffiyeh blew forward, partially covering his face. He stood next to the roaring breakfast fire, sipping strong Turkish coffee and smiling brightly. "You rise early, I see."

"*Alaikum salaam*, Prince. Yes, I got up to pray."

"So did I." The prince poked at the fire with a stick. "Cold this morning. I trust you slept soundly?"

"Surprisingly so, yes," answered Khasif. "I wouldn't have thought it got so chilly here in the Gulf."

"The *shamal* is up," he said. "That might make race conditions interesting."

"Will the wind affect the drivers much?" In truth, President Khasif had had his fill of the dune buggy ride that seemed to enthrall his hosts. He was relieved this was the last day of the exposition.

"It might. But we're headed back, of course."

"Just as well," the president acknowledged. "As you might imagine, I have much to attend to."

By that, Khasif meant the assassination of his good friend Alberto Quintero and his new attorney general, Hugo Suárez. Just before bedding down the previous evening into a luxurious pile of silks, Khasif had taken a satellite call from his prime minister, Guto Castillo, who briefed him on the terrible news. The president had, in turn, informed his Emirati host, telling the prince that the infamous drug lord Tiburón had struck again. He followed it with a request to get back to the city the next day so he could return home.

The prince threw his stick into the fire, causing a burst of sparks to rise and scatter in the wind. "Mr. President, if I may be so bold, the way to deal with a scoundrel like Tiburón is to build up your security forces. You should be able to hunt him down like a rabid dog."

Khasif moved sideways to avoid a shift in the smoke. "Building up security forces is expensive, Prince."

"But something you will soon be able to afford."

"Perhaps. Even so, Tiburón rarely leaves Venezuela. I am left to pursue his shadow rather than the man himself."

The crown prince clapped his hands. A young Filipino servant rushed forward with a fresh coffee for him. "Once you begin exporting your oil and gas, Mr. President," the prince extolled, sipping, "you'll be able to afford whatever security you wish. As OPEC members, we even share in a fund to guard oil assets. Another benefit. You will also be surprised at the reach of your alliances. Who knows? Perhaps the Venezuelans will become an ally. They, too, are in OPEC."

Khasif dismissed the comment with a wary nod. They'd been giving him the hard sell on joining OPEC throughout this journey across the dunes. All he wanted to do was go home.

"Thank you, Your Majesty," he said.

"Ah!" the prince exclaimed jovially when someone new approached the fire. He was an overweight, bald European in a loose, untucked shirt. Khasif hadn't seen him before. "Good to see you, Viktor!"

"And you, Your Majesty," the fat man answered. He waggled his finger at one of the servants, then sat on a stool near the fire, squinting at it. He shifted to retrieve an aspirin bottle from his pocket and threw down three with a dry swallow.

"Have you two met?" the prince asked. "This is Viktor Zhdanov, CEO of the Russian gas exporter, Gazneft."

"I have not had the pleasure," Khasif responded. He introduced himself and offered his hand.

Zhdanov took the hand without standing. He eyed Khasif carefully. "Mr. President," he mumbled. "A pleasure."

"Viktor came in on the supply helicopter last night," the prince explained. "We are honored he could join us for this last day."

Khasif nodded, while the Russian stared into the crackling fire.

LINE OF DEMARCATION

The prince snapped his fingers at an attendant, who brought two additional stools. Khasif wanted to get back to his tent, but now felt obligated to stay. "You came because you have a particular fascination with off-road rallies?" he asked.

"No," replied the Russian. "I came to meet you."

"Yes," the prince added. "You will be riding with Viktor today, Mr. President. I thought it would be good if the two of you got to know each other."

18

GEORGETOWN, GUYANA
0030

WHEN THE DIRT BIKE'S ENGINE DIED, JACK REALIZED THE DREADED MOMENT WAS AT hand: he was out of gas. The bike coasted until it nearly fell over.

Jack dismounted and shoved it into the weeds. As a cowboy might say farewell to a dying horse, he patted the empty gas tank. The machine had saved his life, delivering him here to the rainforest interior.

Jack listened to the jungle as the bike ticked and cooled. He heard screaming piha birds and the occasional monkey howl. The insects made the trees buzz and clack like electric transmission lines. Though it was a clear night, the thick canopy overhead obscured most of the stars. Even so, he could make out the bright waning moon between the leaves.

He scratched his cheek. Based on the moon's position, he was reasonably sure that he was well southwest of Georgetown. Of course, a moonrise was a poor substitute for a smartphone's GPS chip. Jack had left his phone in the restaurant courtyard along with everything else.

LINE OF DEMARCATION

The one thing he'd kept, per Alberto Quintero's dying wish, was the cigar case. It rested uncomfortably in the front pocket of Jack's pants. He took another glance at the moon, then started walking down the road.

Returning to Rancho del Cielo, the eco-farm where Quintero's family lived, was no simple matter. Jack had a rough idea of where it was from his previous visit, and as far as he could tell, there weren't that many roads in this area south of Georgetown. That should have made things easier, but Jack had taken steps to avoid the beaten paths and stay out of the way of the police.

As Jack saw it, the man in the black shirt who'd tried to kill him at the restaurant was probably a cop. He held his weapon the way a cop would. He used concealment well, dashing between the porch pillars with skill. Recalling the minister's warnings about Tiburón's reach into the national police force, Jack thought his attacker was a cop on the drug lord's payroll.

Under the filtered silvery light, Jack stepped into the road and put his hands on his hips, listening and watching. He guessed the eco-farm was near the top of a hill. The road he stood on seemed to be getting steeper, though it was hard to tell under the dense canopy. Without a better plan, he continued in a slow trot.

A half mile later, he was rewarded with a hand-painted plywood sign and an arrow. RANCHO DEL CIELO, THIS WAY.

Thank God, he thought, quickening his pace.

That first sign turned out to be something of a false idol as it was followed by two others, each a quarter mile apart. By the time Jack recognized the modest driveway gate that marked the property, he was out of breath and choking with thirst.

Alberto and Amancia Quintero had taken ten years to build the house. To the left was a three-sided pole barn, where they fed their herd of llamas. Amancia bred the gawky creatures and rented them to her guests for rides up the hill. As Jack stood listening on the drive, he could hear a few of the animals tinkling in the fields, wearing the bells Amancia put on them to ward off the jaguars.

To the right of the pole barn was their two-story house, made of shingled hardwood and glass. Jack walked toward it. He noted that the lights were off, suggesting that Amancia and her daughter, Tallulah, were probably asleep.

He slowed as he neared the front door. It occurred to him that he'd be turning their world upside down as soon as he knocked. He was trying to compose his thoughts when the door cracked open.

Jack leaned forward.

The door swung violently, knocking him backward. A shotgun's twin barrels poked him in the chest. A young man with a dark face had his finger resting on the trigger guard.

Jack held his hands open before him, saying, "Whoa, I'm a friend."

Not sure whether the man bought that argument, Jack estimated the distance to the jungle bush in his periphery. If the gun was loaded with bird shot, he might be able to make it to cover with relatively minor injuries.

Just as he was about to sprint away, the man hollered over his shoulder at the house. "Aunt Amancia! I've got one! Come quick!"

Jack surprised the man by yelling, "Amancia! It's Jack Ryan! Come quick!"

He then looked at the startled shotgun wielder. With his hands still before him, Jack said, "I'm a friend of the family. I thought you were a Tiburónista. I've come to help."

An outdoor light blinked on. He heard a creak on the porch. And then, "Gustavo! Put the gun down. I know him. Jack! What are you doing here?"

Jack shot an angry glance at the man she'd called Gustavo, who had yet to lower the weapon. "Hey. We all good here, amigo?"

"He's my nephew," Amancia explained, rushing to Gustavo's side. She forced the gun barrel down. He relaxed his grip.

Jack got a good look at Amancia in the porch light. The attractive fiftyish woman he'd met the night before had a swollen right eye. Her hair was loose and frayed. She wore a big loose shirt over torn blue jeans and dirty tennis shoes. She was breathing rapidly. Her hands seemed to be twitching, flexing in and out. To Jack, she seemed a completely different person than the one he'd met at dinner.

"What's going on?" he asked. "Are you all right?"

"No," she said, shutting her eyes. "We were attacked. They left an hour ago."

"*Attacked?*" Jack looked around the dark property. As before, he saw the llama barn and heard the tinkle of their bells. The property seemed peaceful. "What do you mean attacked?"

"Tiburónistas," murmured Gustavo. He'd lowered the shotgun to his side. Jack got a better look at him. One of his forearms was covered with tattoo ink. Jack thought he looked to be in his early twenties.

"Tiburónistas," Jack repeated.

"What are you doing here?" Amancia asked for the second time.

"I'll get to it." A cold pang hit Jack when he remembered the terrible news he bore. "What exactly happened here?"

Just as Amancia was about to answer, Tallulah Quintero, the couple's daughter, came out of the house and stood under the porch light. The twenty-three-year-old was wearing a short-sleeved Cal Bears T-shirt and black leggings. Jack was shocked at the damage to her face. Dried blood marred her cheek. She could barely open her left eye. "Tallulah," he said, walking slowly toward her. "Are you okay?"

She nodded and looked down, clutching her arms to her body.

"We were home alone," Amancia said.

Jack looked at Gustavo. "And you?"

"With my girlfriend. In Mahaica. By the time I got back they were gone."

"Tiburónistas," Jack repeated.

"Yes," said Amancia.

"How many?"

"Two," she answered. "They tried to have their way with us. We fought hard."

Jack took another look at Tallulah. The arms folded across her chest were scuffed and bleeding. Her eyes were glassy. His mind spiraled with nightmarish thoughts of what the Tiburónistas might have done to her. And even with all that, she still didn't know about her father.

Amancia seemed to understand what Jack was thinking. "I went after them with a kitchen knife," she said. "They laughed at me, but I cut one while Tallulah fought him off. They ran away before they could do anything serious to us."

"We should get her to a hospital," Jack said. "Do we have access to a vehicle?"

Amancia stared at the porch's floorboards. "Alberto has the Rover. He's staying in town tonight."

Jack knew that on a normal week, Quintero stayed at their city apartment in Georgetown for his government work. But this week was anything but normal.

"I see," he said. "Could we call someone?"

"The men took our phones. Not that it matters. There's no coverage here anyway."

Jack looked at Gustavo. "Do you have one?"

He silently shook his head.

"Jack," she prodded. "What are you doing here?"

"Can we go inside?" he replied. "We need to talk."

LINE OF DEMARCATION

THE HOUSE HAD BEEN ROUGHLY SEARCHED—BOOKS TOPPLED FROM SHELVES, DRAW-ers turned over, dishes smashed. Jack took them to the kitchen and held their hands. He broke the news about the professor to them as gently as he could. Before he could finish, Tallulah rushed off in a swirl of tears.

Amancia took it stoically. While hugging her arms to her body, she asked Jack who else had witnessed it. When he told her that Hugo Suárez had also been murdered, she trudged down the hall to comfort her daughter.

Jack felt like an intruder. But he wasn't about to leave them alone.

He drank some water, then realizing he was ravenous, picked through the pantry and found some dried fruit. While he ate, he could see Gustavo pacing outside in the moonlight near the llama stalls. He was carrying his shotgun.

Jack walked through the living and dining rooms. He didn't know what the Tiburónistas had been looking for—but based on how tumbled the house was, he guessed they didn't find it. All the while he poked through the debris, he listened to the heart-wrenching cries of the two women down the hall. Gustavo found Jack looking out the rear sliding door over a porch.

"Are you sure you don't know the men who did this?"

"I don't know them personally—but I know they are Tiburónistas," he said.

"Why are you so sure?" Jack asked him.

"I was one of them, once." He pulled his sleeve higher up his bicep and showed a series of tattoos. To Jack, they looked only slightly better than bruises. "I tried to remove them," Gustavo added.

Jack gestured toward the mess on the floor. "Do you know what they were after?"

"Uncle was always going on about the Tibs," Gustavo said. "He hated them."

When Amancia emerged from the hallway, her face red and swollen, Jack posed the same question to her. She knelt on the bamboo floor and picked up a shattered picture frame. It was of her, the professor, and Tallulah, about five years old. "They were after my husband," she ventured.

He cleared a spot on the sofa and sat Amancia down. She kept her eyes on the floor. "Did he suffer?"

"No," Jack said. "And his last words were of you and Tallulah."

"I want you to tell me exactly what happened."

Jack kept his voice low so Tallulah couldn't hear. "We were outside, having dinner at the King George Café. Do you know it?"

She nodded.

"Two assassins came at us. The first one was a man disguised as our waiter. The second one carried himself more professionally, like a cop."

She sighed with resignation.

"Amancia, I tried . . ." Jack began. His voice abandoned him. He shut his mouth.

"The murderers got away?" she asked.

"I killed one. The other was still shooting at me when I escaped."

She clutched his hand. "I am sorry you have become a part of this."

Jack lowered his eyes to his shoes and clenched his jaw. He said nothing.

She squeezed his hand tightly and tugged, jerking him back to the present. "It takes brave people to make a country," she said.

"Your husband was very brave," Jack agreed.

"Very," she went on. "One day, Tallulah will come to understand his sacrifice. So will the rest of them."

Like the two women closest to Jack—his mother, Cathy, and fiancée, Lisanne—Amancia Quintero radiated quiet strength. She was sitting up straight, holding Jack's hand tightly. Her eyes were glazed but hard, as though resolve had replaced grief.

"Why did you come here?" she asked. "I thought you were flying back to the U.S. this morning."

"The professor's last words were of you and Tallulah. He said they'd be coming for you. And he wanted to make sure you got this." Jack dug the metal cigar case out of his pocket and handed it to her.

She put it up to her nose and inhaled deeply. Then she unsnapped its clasp and folded back the lid. There were three cigars inside, wrapped in tissue paper and held in place by an elastic band. "I always said these would kill him," she said, smiling sadly and sniffing them. "Why did he ask you to bring me this?"

"I . . . thought you would know. I assumed it was special to you. He was very insistent."

"He knew I hated his cigars."

She put the cigars on her knees, still wrapped in tissue paper. Jack noticed something as she held the gleaming case up to the light. He grabbed the bundle and unwrapped it. A long number was written in blue ink on the tissue: *22302512998296*.

"Could this number mean something to you?" Jack asked, unfolding the paper and showing it to her.

She looked at it, puzzled. "No."

"Maybe the combination to a safe?" he asked. "The professor and Suárez said they were working on a surveillance corruption case. Suárez had evidence of collusion with Tiburón and wanted me to take it back to the U.S. Could it have something to do with that?"

"We don't have a safe."

It was Tallulah who contradicted her from the dark threshold behind Jack. "Yes, we do," she countered. "Papa told me never to tell you about it."

The girl rounded the corner and entered the study. Jack and Amancia followed.

Without another word, Tallulah squatted, shoved some books aside, and pulled back the carpet. She used a letter opener to pry a floorboard loose, then pulled three more clear. With the section of floor removed, she exposed the front of a small safe with an old-fashioned dial pointed up at the ceiling.

"I surprised him last week," she explained. "He told me not to tell anyone about it."

Jack studied the long string of numbers on the tissue paper. "How are you going to know where the numbers break? They're all together without any dashes."

"Easy," Amancia answered, snatching the paper back from him. She went to her knees and perched next to her daughter. "Now that I know what to look for . . ." She spun the dial. "I see birthdays, our anniversary, and the date we bought this land—among others."

When the door clicked open, both she and Tallulah looked inside. Amancia pulled an unsealed yellow envelope free and handed it to Jack. While they continued inspecting the safe, Jack emptied the envelope to find a collection of ten Sony cassettes marked as "DV Premium." Jack remembered tapes like this as a child—they were digital video camcorder tapes. Each case was dated in pencil, going back two years. The last one was dated March 1.

Yesterday.

He guessed Quintero had deposited the fresh tape while Jack had sat on the porch, having drinks with Amancia. "Do you know what these are?" he asked her.

"Wait," Tallulah said, reaching down. "There's something else next to the safe."

She lay on her stomach and extended her hand farther below the floor. She retrieved a Glock 17 9-millimeter and handed it to Jack. He ejected the mag, saw it had all ten rounds, and then slammed it home. He shoved it in his belt.

"That's it," the girl said, getting back to her knees and standing up.

Amancia closed the safe door, replaced the floorboards, and stood next to her daughter.

"What do you know about the tapes?" Jack asked.

Amancia answered, "He was working closely with Hugo Suárez and Martin Croom on the corruption sting, trying to expose Tiburón's network. He must have assumed you could get those tapes to the right authorities."

Jack remembered Suárez's plea to rush his evidence to D.C. Jack had lost the bag Suárez had tried to give him along with everything else in his scramble to safety. "I'll take care of it," he said now. "I'll get us all to the embassy and on a safe flight back to the U.S. You two can deliver the evidence personally."

He tugged at the Glock in his belt to make sure it was secure. He was about to go outside to check on Gustavo when the interior lights clicked off. He saw the young man silhouetted at the kitchen threshold, gripping his twelve-gauge with both hands.

"*Shhh!*" Gustavo whispered. "Truck coming down the driveway."

"Who?" asked Jack.

"Tiburónistas," Gustavo replied. "Coming to finish the job."

19

ORINOCO RIVER DELTA, VENEZUELA
0045

PURELY OUT OF HABIT, DING LOOKED AT HIS WRIST. THE GARMIN WAS GONE, BUT THE code it had relayed may have as well been tattooed to his skin: *5* for "report," *6-1* for "collect all available intel," and *2* for "get the hell out of there."

Exfil time.

Shirtless in the heat, he'd lain awake for hours, listening to the barge's movements. He felt it shudder a few times in the river flow and heard it bump against its moorings. He also heard the footsteps of the rooftop sentry stumping along in his normal way. Twice during the night, Caraza barked orders at the sentry from his berth on the first deck near the door. Otherwise, the barge was quiet—eerily so.

As far as Ding could tell, the hardcase ex-cons and Wagner men who normally departed with full boats and returned with empty ones hadn't come back. Without a window, Ding couldn't be a hundred percent sure—but they tended to be a boisterous crowd. In the ten days Ding had been sequestered on the barge, they'd woken him every night.

LINE OF DEMARCATION

Before falling asleep, he had mentally rehearsed his exfil strategy, trying to picture his actions down to the minutest detail. He'd gone over it in his head so many times in the night that when he finally swung his feet to the floor, it almost seemed like he was reliving a memory.

He tossed his dirty sheet over the small, cheap lamp with the bare bulb. He thumbed the switch on the cord and nudged aside enough fabric so he could see to operate.

Staying low and quiet, he gently pulled his single canvas duffel from beneath the bed and riffled through it. It had been stuffed with the few shirts and pants the Tibs had thrown in when they'd spirited him here from San Felipe.

Ding selected a pair of cotton black pants and a faded olive-green Colombian army T-shirt. The laundry stamp said DIAZ on the back collar—courtesy of the Legend Wizards.

Sitting cross-legged, he opened his toilet kit, removed a tube of sunscreen, and squeezed it onto the floor. Beside it, he snapped off a pencil lead and ground it into a powder. With a touch of water from his jug, he mixed the sunscreen and powder together, forming a dark paste. Once it was sufficiently mixed, he smeared it over his face and hands.

After lacing up his crepe-soled boots—also Colombian army issue—he slid on his back beneath the bed. Reaching up, he removed the twisted pair of metal springs he'd sharpened with a stone and taped to form a shiv. Days earlier, he'd entered camp with a small push-button switchblade concealed in his boot laces, not much larger than his pinkie. The Tibs hadn't noticed it when they brought him here. But they did notice it when Ding used it to ward off the Venezuelan scumbag who tried to steal his food. After that, he made the shiv.

He used its sharp point to open a tear near the duffel's zipper. Then, after a pause to make sure the barge was still quiet, he pulled one side of the zipper off. In the end, the detached zipper looked like a twenty-four-inch brassy chain.

He held it before his face and pulled it tight, testing it.

Satisfied, he slipped through the door and crept down the makeshift hall. When he reached the rear of the barge at the top of the ladder, he caught his first glimpse outside. The moon's watery reflection was behind the stern sentry's head. Just beyond loomed the bow of Tiburón's hulking yacht, the *Gran Blanco*. As far as Ding could tell, the tidal flow wasn't moving very fast. That would make for an easy swim—if he could make it past Caraza.

Carlos Caraza bunked just off the landing at the bottom of the ladder, which gave him control over the Tiburónistas' comings and goings. Based on their earlier conflict that day, Ding expected Caraza's door to be open.

Ding climbed as carefully down the ladder as a leopard coming out of a tree. When his gummy soles touched the deck, he pushed his back against the wall and waited. He heard the barge bump against the dock and a stray laugh floating over the air from the *Gran Blanco*'s bow.

Without a sound, Ding removed the brass zipper strip from his pocket. He wrapped a length around his right wrist and kept the rest of the improvised chain in his other hand. Then, slinking sideways, laying each foot carefully, he approached Caraza's bunk.

The bed was empty.

Ding straightened. He hadn't imagined that Caraza would be elsewhere. He wondered if the thug had been summoned to a meeting on the *Gran Blanco*.

So be it. Though he would have liked to have put Caraza in his place before leaving, it didn't matter. He only had to get past the stern sentry now. Ding crept to the door that led to the fantail and the porta-potties. He watched the sentry and listened.

He could hear the faint creak of footsteps from the rooftop

guard. The Tiburónista up top walked back and forth in intervals as regular as a metronome. The advantage to that, in Ding's view, was that it would make his exit easy to time.

The stern sentry had his AK-12 over his knees and sat with his legs crossed, facing the riverbank. Only ten feet separated the sentry from the exit, and Ding didn't like the odds of slipping over the side undetected. All it would take would be a gentle splash for the sentry to notice. Then he would fire off his AK and alert the people who were making noise behind the barge on the *Gran Blanco*.

Improvising a new plan, Ding turned back and crept into Caraza's room. Snatching a folding travel alarm clock beside the bed, he closed it and weighed it in his hand. Then he returned to the stern door, fingering the clock like a pitcher about to throw a fastball.

When the roof sentry's footsteps had faded to the front of the barge, Ding lobbed the alarm clock over the stern guard's head, making a splash just in front of the *Gran Blanco*. The stern sentry got up and faced the noise. He held his rifle lazily by the sling.

Ding sprinted forward, knocked the rifle into the water with a quick right kick, and whipped his zippered garrote around the man's neck, squeezing tight. The sentry's hands went to the zipper, but its sharp teeth and Ding's overwhelming pressure had already severed his windpipe. Blood ran down the sentry's chest and over Ding's forearms, mixing with his camouflage paste. The sentry kicked and stumbled as Ding dragged him backward.

After the struggle, Ding dragged the corpse into Caraza's room.

He waited for the roof sentry to be at the far end of the barge. When the footsteps had grown faint, Ding lowered himself over the barge's side, quiet as an otter.

The current was slow, only about a knot, weakened by the incoming tide a few miles downriver. Thinking of the roof sentry, Ding lay still. A long time ago, someone had taught him that humans had evolved to detect movement. Dressed in black, his arms, hands, and face darkened, he took in a lungful of air and floated down the length of the barge like a tree limb.

Fifty yards downriver, he risked a few underwater kicks to get closer to the docks where the men kept the metal boats. Since the barge had been quiet, Ding assumed the boats hadn't come back, but now he saw one.

With his days in Venezuela soon to be behind him, he thought through his mission. In his opinion, he hadn't accomplished all that much. Yes, he'd proven the primary objective of establishing a link between Tiburón and the Russian SVR. Then again, he chided himself, he wasn't coming back with a trove of useful human intelligence. Though sequestered among the Tiburónistas for several days, he had yet to understand what, exactly, they were up to.

He looked up at the southern stars while floating in the warm water, and segued into a full-throated condemnation of himself. It didn't seem right to him that all he had to do was ride the warm Orinoco flow to a beach, then make his way south to friendly Guyana. Any candy-ass could do that, he told himself. He needed real, hard intel.

With this thought churning, he angled toward the docks. He submerged and swam hard when he was within twenty feet of them, going for the boat. He climbed aboard it near its outboard engine, cringing when it bumped against the dock.

Aside from a gas can, boat hooks, and a cooler, the twenty-five-foot open metal boat was empty. Ding slid into the driver's seat. There was a chart plotter on the dash behind the wheel. He powered it up and thumbed through the controls. He found an option that showed the trace of prior trips in dotted black lines.

Ding could see that the boat had been going out to an area just offshore. When he zoomed in, he saw a chart labeling the area as

LINE OF DEMARCATION

the Orinoco Reef. It was hashed with several lines, warning of underwater hazards.

He wasn't surprised. His theory had always been that the Tibs were taking the boats with the crates to an offshore freighter. But he still couldn't confirm what the crates held. Hoping to get lucky, he crept onto the dock and looked around. He saw nothing of interest.

Mindful of his exfil order, he turned to leave. But since he suspected this was the last time anyone in the U.S. intelligence community was going to get a ground-truth look at the base, he scanned the shore. A glint of metal in the moonlight caught his eye. He studied it further.

Inside the fences, he saw the silhouette of an eighteen-wheeler tractor trailer at the edge of the road. He crept to the side of the floating dock to get a better view. The truck had a long hood and perforated exhaust pipes coming up from the cab. Along the trailer, Ding could see a corporate logo: PLAYA DEL SOL CERVEZA. He'd seen the beer brand around the camp and knew it was part of the Wagner front company.

He thought of Morozov and the legitimate business interests Wagner controlled in Venezuela and elsewhere. Whatever cargo was in the truck seemed destined for the boats. In Ding's opinion, this was probably the last chance to figure out what that was.

He crept silently up the dock and reached the grassy shore. The final thirty feet to the truck were gravel. Staying low, he spent thirty seconds in the long grass, studying the vehicle by moonlight. With a better view of the trailer's back, he could see that a door was propped open. Below it on the gravel lay three long crates, stacked.

Ding did a silent burpee to hop to his feet. Stooping over, he ran to the crates at the truck's rear and ducked down. They were the size of coffins, with stickers that had the PLAYA DEL SOL label. Ding shoved at the top crate lid and found that it moved. Getting closer to it, he saw a crowbar on the ground. The crate had been popped open.

On one knee, Ding pushed the lid. Inside there was nothing but wood shavings used as packing straw. More straw poked from the two crates below. Ding suspected that they, too, were empty.

From his position by the crates on the gravel, he could now see into the trailer. He thought it worth a look and stepped carefully to check it out. Shoved up against the cab, he discovered another coffin crate on the floor with the same beer label. He reasoned that it was probably unopened since it hadn't been unloaded.

He climbed into the enclosed trailer and walked to the forward bulkhead with the crowbar in hand. It wasn't refrigerated, he noted—further evidence that whatever was in those crates probably wasn't beer.

Once he got all the way forward, he struggled to see, since he was deep in the truck. With a grunt, he slid the heavy crate closer to the open door. Then he pried the lid loose with the crowbar.

There was a second, narrower box made of hard plastic with silver buckles inside. Ding unclipped the buckles and opened it, seeing a long, dull gray tube. Even without the black Cyrillic markings stenciled on the side, he recognized the tube for what it was—a partially disassembled Russian missile. He believed he was looking at the main fuel cylinder of an anti-ship missile that NATO had code-named KAYAK. It could be launched from patrol boats, land, or helicopters.

Satisfied that he'd finally gathered useful intelligence, he replaced the lid and slid the box back to the forward bulkhead.

Once up at the front, Ding heard a creak. Spinning on his heel, he realized what was happening—a moment too late.

A beefy Wagner Russian slammed the rear cargo door shut, locking him in.

20

GEORGETOWN, GUYANA
0050

GUTO CASTILLO, GUYANA'S SOCIALIST PRIME MINISTER, HAD GONE TO BED WITH TWO phones on his nightstand—his official iPhone and his latest burner. The burner was vibrating so hard that it fell to the floor and woke him.

"Yes," he said, answering it, while rubbing his eyes.

"Well, hello, Guto. Why do you sound like you were asleep?" Tiburón's Spanish-accented voice was tinny, and Castillo thought he might be on speaker.

"Because I was asleep," he replied.

"Well, get up," the drug lord commanded. "We have made a decision here."

"Who is *we*?" Castillo asked, jolting upright. Beyond the length of his bed, he could see a long streak of moonlight on the Atlantic.

"Mr. Prime Minister, this is Igor Morozov speaking," he heard through the speaker. "I'm here with Tiburón on the *Gran Blanco*."

As reality seeped in, Castillo felt a chill. He had never spoken directly with the Russian before. He'd barely ever even spoken to

Tiburón directly. Yet here he was in his master bedroom on speaker with them both.

He cleared his throat, shaking off sleep. "Good to meet you, Mr. Morozov," he said timidly.

"Good morning, Prime Minister," the Russian answered.

The formality of the greeting gave Castillo a measure of confidence. He summoned his command voice. "You said you'd made a decision. What are we talking about?"

"We're moving up the timetable," Tiburón answered. "The operation is beginning. That means you need to get out of your big empty bed and shake your ass."

Castillo inhaled sharply. The plan had been to move forward in late April when parliament was back in session and Romero had more time to put his favored, loyal lieutenants in positions of authority. Everything had been orchestrated to minimize risk.

"We can't begin this now," he protested. "We need to maintain the original timetable, beginning on April 26."

"We have no choice," Morozov retorted. "It must happen tonight."

Castillo lay still. In late April, President Khasif was also making a trip to the United States to meet President Jack Ryan. With the Guyanese leader kowtowing to the Americans, it would fit his carefully crafted narrative that the Guyanese had become capitalist puppets, ruining the worker's paradise he'd been advocating.

"I don't understand," Castillo said.

"Let me explain, Mr. Prime Minister," Morozov answered politely. He spoke English with a Slavic accent. "The risk to moving now is substantially less than the risk of waiting. Recent events have forced our hand."

"Events. Such as . . . ?"

Tiburón's voice boomed. "Have you already forgotten why you

called me this morning? You were all hot and bothered. Now you don't care?"

"Do you mean the American Coast Guard boat?"

"Of course I mean the Coast Guard!"

"I thought it was taken care of," said Castillo. "I calmed the American ambassador down. Romero delivered the news to the U.S. director of national intelligence. As far as we can tell, they have accepted our explanation that it was an accidental encounter. We all blamed *you*, Tiburón. As planned."

"Prime Minister, when is the last time you spoke with Director Romero?" asked Morozov.

Castillo glanced at his watch. "I don't know. A few hours ago, I suppose."

"Listen, Guto," Tiburón said. "If you want to be the first leader of the Socialist Republic of Guyana, you'd better talk to Romero now. We'll patch him in. We just spoke to him."

It took fifteen seconds to get Romero on the phone. The NISA chief was still at the Ritz-Carlton in Costa Rica, speaking from his villa.

"Romero, tell Guto what you told us," Tiburón ordered.

Romero cleared his throat. "I am worried the Americans are going to do something about the Coast Guard boat. I think they may be coming."

"*What?*" Castillo seethed. "Why would you say that?"

"I am your head of intelligence, Prime Minister. I'm telling you what I think."

"Based on what evidence?" Castillo shot back. "A few hours ago you said you spoke to the U.S. director of national intelligence . . . and that she accepted your explanation."

"That's right. And it's possible she did," Romero agreed. "But she was supposed to be the speaker at a breakfast tomorrow.

Instead, she left. I checked the airport manifest. She flew back to the U.S. That doesn't bode well for us."

Castillo stared out at the placid water, envious of the calm. "Why? The woman probably deals with three crises brewing on any given day."

"Get to it, Romero," prompted Tiburón. "We're wasting time."

The NISA chief spoke quickly. "Hugo Suárez was trying to establish a corruption case between the government and Tiburón. We suspect he was working with Alberto Quintero to deliver his surveillance findings to the yanquis because of their capital investments in Guyana. Suárez may have been successful in getting evidence to the Americans on the very night Mary Pat Foley flew home unexpectedly."

Castillo clapped his free hand to his forehead. "You led me to believe you handled Suárez and Quintero. You said the Americans would blame it on Tiburón . . . that it would help pave over any further problems from the Coast Guard sinking."

"It would have," answered Romero. "Except that Suárez and Quintero were meeting with an American at the time of the action. They may have given him some intelligence."

Castillo squeezed his temples. "What are you talking about? What American?"

Romero went on. "Minister Quintero had been meeting with the CEO of Athena Global Shipping Lines over the past month—"

"Hold on," countered Castillo. "Athena Global is a legitimate shipping company. Quintero and the CEO, Jack Ryan, were trying to get an export license to off-load the first gas shipments from the offshore platforms. I met the man this morning. I held up the license. My own people took him to the airport. Ryan is no longer in Guyana."

"Yes, well, Ryan never left the country," Romero explained.

"*What?*"

LINE OF DEMARCATION

"One of my officers picked him up on surveillance this afternoon during a covert meeting with Quintero along the port seawall near the half-finished park. He then tailed Ryan to a dinner with Quintero and Suárez at the King George Café. That was when the action went down."

"Dear God," Castillo muttered. He got out of bed, shoved his feet into his slippers, and paced. "Please don't tell me the action involved Ryan. He may be the legitimate president of Athena Global, but he also happens to be the son of the President of the United States."

"Who may likely understand our plans," said Morozov dryly. "And since he's still at large, Prime Minister Castillo, you can understand why Moscow is urging us to move quickly."

Castillo wasn't sure how hard to push back on the Russian, since he'd invoked the Moscow reference. It suddenly seemed like he was making irreversible moves—something that made him deeply uncomfortable.

"With all due respect, Mr. Morozov, Ryan's business is legitimate. He had been meeting with Quintero for weeks."

Romero spoke next. "I agree he is a legitimate businessman. But he was also meeting with Suárez. He had no reason to do that for an export license. Guto, we can't discount that they told Ryan something."

"I agree with Director Romero," added Morozov. "Suárez may have tried to pass information to Ryan."

"Fortunately Ryan never got hard evidence," Romero noted. "He left Suárez's bag at the scene along with his own phone. We have it at the station now for analysis. Suárez's bag contained a hard drive with likely surveillance evidence."

Leaning against the wall, Castillo looked out at the dark sea.

When he first listened to Romero pitch the Tiburón-Russian conspiracy back in February, its implementation had seemed distant, even unlikely. He'd thought of it as harmless musings, something he'd never really have to face. A sickening sense of irreversibility crawled up his gut.

He stood straight. "Well, you have to find Ryan, of course, to make sure he hasn't drawn the wrong conclusions. And you must ensure that whatever's on this hard drive hasn't been duplicated somewhere."

"We'll handle that, Guto," said Tiburón. "But you can't go soft on us. You need to hold up your end."

Castillo closed his eyes. Hearing Tiburón give him the command to hold up his end made him realize that he had hit a point of no return. He suddenly felt the urge to vomit.

Romero added, "I've got my national police force searching the city for Ryan. The Tiburónistas are making sure Quintero and Suárez didn't stash any additional evidence in their homes."

"My Tiburónistas have been turned loose," Tiburón finished ominously. "This will be a night to remember for the people of Guyana."

Morozov broke in. "Prime Minister, given the events of the evening, you can understand why Moscow is pressing us to move tonight."

Castillo swallowed, tamping down the nausea. "What exactly are you suggesting I do?" he asked.

"I want you to declare martial law," Morozov answered. "As a pretext, cite the Tiburónista violence happening as we speak. To quell the violence, order curfews, close the roads and airport, and disable all communications systems. All of these procedures are in your operational contingency plan known as ECLIPSE."

Castillo was stunned that Morozov knew of the top secret security plan. He quickly realized that Romero must have given it to him.

"Mr. Morozov, you are correct about ECLIPSE," he said. "But

in our system of government, it can only be ordered by the Guyanese president. Khasif is scheduled to return in twelve hours or so. Even if I issued the ECLIPSE order, I couldn't close the airport to the president. And when he lands, he could simply reverse whatever I officially enact. This will all be over before it even gets started. I beg you, sir, to get back to the original timetable. Brief Moscow on the difficulties."

"That is where you're wrong, Prime Minister," Morozov replied crisply. "Your soon-to-be ex-president Khasif hasn't left the UAE. My people will handle him. The time to act is right now, sir."

"You hear that, Guto?" Tiburón growled. "Right now. Don't go soft on me."

After agreeing to give the order, Castillo closed the connection. Moments after dropping the phone on his bed, he looked up the beach and saw that a home was glowing yellow, on fire.

The Tiburónistas had struck the first blow to his affluent community.

21

0053

HEADLIGHTS FROM THE APPROACHING TRUCK PROJECTED ODD SHADOWS ON THE wall. After blowing out the candles, Jack urged Amancia, Tallulah, and Gustavo to stay down in the breakfast room behind the kitchen, avoiding windows.

Jack watched the way the shadows moved. It seemed to him that there was only one set of headlights, a single truck. "Gustavo," he whispered. "Can you get to a firing position outside with a good line of sight?"

The boy slid his shotgun in front of him. "I know a spot."

"Is it in range of your shotgun?"

"Yes."

Jack hoped that was true. With good ammo, a twelve-gauge rifle's effective hunting range was about a hundred yards. By the looks of Gustavo's rusted gun, he guessed the distance was substantially less. Then again, the kid had been a Tiburónista himself once. He would know how his weapon worked.

"Good," Jack whispered. "Get out there to your spot. I'll cover the inside." He motioned with the Glock in his hand. "Don't shoot until I do. Okay?"

Gustavo nodded curtly.

"Go on," Jack urged. "Hurry."

Amancia reached out and touched Gustavo's hand as he began to pull away. "Goose," she implored. "Be careful."

Staying low, the boy backed away swiftly. He exited through the rear sliding door and disappeared.

The headlights from the truck suddenly went out. Jack listened to doors slamming shut, two of them. He heard male voices. Next to him, Tallulah began to shake uncontrollably. Amancia threw her arm around her daughter, pulling her close.

Amancia glanced at Jack. "They're the same men as before."

The Tiburónistas out front weren't bothering to keep their voices low. Jack heard catcalling mixed in with the laughter, as though they'd gone and gotten drunk before circling back to finish off the two terrified women.

"Did they come through the front door last time?" Jack asked.

Amancia nodded while clutching Tallulah to her. "It wasn't locked. I didn't know."

The front door was ahead and to the right, on the other side of the kitchen. Jack rose to a knee. "Stay as still and low as you can," he said. "Don't move."

He combat crawled to the front foyer with the Glock in his right hand, listening to the men outside yammering in Spanish. Jack couldn't tell whether it was two or three voices.

He made it to a wall at the side of the door, careful to avoid casting a shadow in a small side window. Propping himself against it, he pulled the slide on the pistol, ensuring a fresh round was chambered. He looked down the barrel and thumbed the sight. It wasn't his pistol, but it looked clean and well-oiled. He aimed it at the door and waited.

He flinched when the kitchen window smashed, showering the floor with glass. A rock tumbled across the hardwood, landing near the women. Tallulah and Amancia stayed quiet, but moved to the side, out of its way. Jack gave them a reassuring look, holding his hand low, gesturing for them to remain calm.

A light flew through the broken kitchen window, startling him. It crashed with a pop. The Molotov cocktail erupted instantly in a burst of blue flames topped by yellow. Jack heard more shattering glass to his right, down the hall in Tallulah's bedroom. Yellow lights flickered on the wall.

So much for shooting them as they came through the door. Staying low, he ran to Amancia's side and squatted next to the two women. With flames rising, there was only one choice—to follow Gustavo's lead and exit through the rear slider. As they backed up on their hands and knees, he heard more wild laughter over the spreading flames.

Once outside, Jack stayed on the porch, pressed to the house's rear wall. He swept the backyard with the Glock. Seeing no one, he pulled Amancia close to him. "Run for it," he whispered. "Let me and Gustavo take them."

"Run for it?" she echoed. Amancia couldn't peel her eyes away from the flames inside her house. "To where? They're blocking the road."

Jack jerked a thumb at the dark thicket of low trees that rimmed the short backyard. "Get through the brush. Get to a neighbor. Let us handle them."

"We can't," Amancia said in a low voice. "There's nowhere to go beyond the acai trees. The ground falls away into a cliff with a swamp at the bottom."

"I'd take a swamp to staying here," Jack argued. "Please. Go. We'll handle them."

Bruised and bloodied, she stared hotly into his eyes. Just beyond her, Tallulah's face was similarly cast, flickering in the firelight.

Jack gave up the argument. "Fine. Get to the edge of the brush and hide. Go. Now."

Amancia led Tallulah to the base of the acai trees. Jack kept his left shoulder pressed to the rear wall of the house while he made his way to the corner. Over his head, he noticed the first lick of flame jutting through a second-story window. He patted the pants pockets where he'd shoved the six small digital video camcorder tapes, grateful he'd gotten them out before the house became an inferno.

He spotted Gustavo. The boy was crouched with his shotgun aimed toward the house, waiting for Jack, as instructed. He was in a position against the llama stall, using a stack of hay bales for cover. The tall square-wire fence behind him was meant to keep the indigenous jaguars away from the herd. Gustavo raised his hand and held up three fingers. Then he shook his shotgun up and down, pantomiming.

Jack took the motion to mean there were three Tiburónistas carrying machine guns. Gustavo swirled his hand, pointing at the back of the house—as if to indicate at least one man was headed Jack's way.

The Campus operative evaluated his options. If reading Gustavo's signal correctly, a Tiburónista would walk right in front of the boy, exposing him and leaving him no line of retreat. Moreover, if Jack took the single Tib with his Glock, he would tip off the other two.

Gustavo would stand no chance against the heavily armed Tiburónistas. In Jack's opinion, massing in a fortified ambush made more tactical sense than trying an uncoordinated assault. He waved his hand quickly, urging Gustavo to run to the acai trees before it was too late.

Gustavo got the message. As the boy rounded the corner, Jack ran to the acai trees, too. They slid in the low brush, landing next to Amancia and Tallulah.

Lying on their stomachs, they watched the house burn. Tallulah was still shaking. Amancia's face was stern, her eyes reflecting the flames.

Jack put his hand on her shoulder. "I'm sorry," he whispered.

She said nothing and watched as the awning of the rear porch went up.

"What did you see?" Jack asked Gustavo.

"Three Tiburónistas," Gustavo managed between gulps of air. "They—" The boy stopped talking when he saw a man at the house's edge. The Tiburónista was walking with his face toward the flames, scanning the walls as if ensuring the Molotov cocktails had done their job. He lingered on the windows, keeping his AK at his hip.

"What's he doing?" Jack whispered to Gustavo.

"Making sure no one got out," the boy answered.

Jack sighted the man's shoulder blades with the Glock. Though he could have nailed the Tib, he wanted the other two to come around the corner so he could ambush all three at once. As he remained still, a jet of flame blew out of the rear sliding door, propelling burning debris across the yard as though fired from a cannon. Glass nicked Tallulah's shoulder. She yelped in shock.

The Tib near the house turned toward them. He saw Tallulah and raised his weapon, firing a burst.

Jack shot him in the face.

A second Tib ran around the left side of the house, staying wide to avoid the flaming debris. Gustavo saw him and rose to a knee, aiming his shotgun. Jack was about to tell Gustavo to wait for a cleaner shot, when he heard automatic-rifle fire to the right. The two Tibs were simultaneously rounding the house on opposite sides, flanking it.

LINE OF DEMARCATION

The leaves over their heads shook with incoming rounds. Wood chips flew from a tree limb. Gustavo fired twice at the Tib on the left side, shooting across Jack.

Jack went low and shot the Tib on the right from a prone position, hitting him twice in the chest.

All three Tibs were down—but it was too late to save the house. The fire was fully evolved, blinding and searing. Jack had seen a propane tank on the other edge of the property, not far from the llama stalls. It wouldn't be long before that would blow, too, going off like a bomb.

"We have to get out of here!" he shouted over the roaring flames. "Goose, check the man on the left for keys!"

As Gustavo ran off, Jack wrestled the AK-47 free from the dead Tiburónista closest to them and searched the man's pockets. He heard a round to his right. The man he thought he'd taken out with the chest shot was crawling and shooting. Jack swung the captured AK and unleashed an automatic burst, shredding the Tib.

A second later, he saw Amancia dashing past him, going through the pockets of the man Jack had just shot. She raised a set of keys and shook them.

Over her head, a fireball blew out a second-floor window, showering the ground with glass that shined like hot lava. Jack could see the roof tilting. The heat twisted the lush green leaves at the edge of the rainforest. The burning wreck would topple over on them if they didn't move.

"Run for the truck!" he roared, urging them forward.

They rounded the flaming house, staying close to the tree line. The front of the property was in worse shape than the back. The silver paint on the four-door F-150 parked in the grassy drive was blistering. After telling the women to retreat farther up the road, Jack threw the AK-47 inside and jumped behind the wheel. He cranked the key. As soon as the engine turned over, one of the eaves that held up a second-floor dormer broke free and bounced off the burning front-porch awning. It struck the truck's hood like a flaming dagger. Jack ignored it and stomped on the gas, racing backward. He skidded into a one-eighty in front of the pole barn.

Gustavo leaped in the truck bed, still carrying his trusty shotgun.

"Where are the women?" Jack hollered out the open window.

"They're freeing the llamas," the boy yelled back.

Not content with burning the house, the Tiburónistas had also set fire to the llama stalls. Jack could see the stack of hay bales burning, sending flames up the main supports of the pole barn like candlewicks.

Squinting through the flames, he searched for Amancia and Tallulah. He didn't see them. "Where the hell are they?" he shouted at Gustavo.

"Probably at the gate."

Thinking of the propane tank, Jack threw the F-150 into park and swung the door open. "We need to get them the hell out of here. Come on!"

He and Gustavo ran past the stalls. As Jack feared, the propane tank was propped on an outside wall. He saw Tallulah at a wire gate, working on a latch. A burning fence post had collapsed, which stretched the fence tight and made the gate impossible to open.

To his dismay, a dozen yards past Tallulah, Jack saw Amancia climb the fence and drop into the llama pasture. The animals had run from the fire and were trapped in a sequestered feeding area rimmed by wooden rails.

Dried straw, meant to ease pasture mud, was scattered freely between the pole barn and the feeding corral. Some of it was already on fire. It was just a matter of time before it all went up and caught the wooden fence of the corral.

"Gustavo!" Jack yelled. "Help Tallulah with the gate!"

He climbed the wire fence and landed with a thud. He sprinted to Amancia's side with the AK-47 in his hand. "We have to go!" he called to her.

"They're stuck in the corral!" she shouted back. "We need to herd them out, or they'll all burn."

Together, they ran to the feeding corral. The twenty llamas were packed tightly together, flaring nostrils, braying, and jumping up on each other. Amancia tugged on their thick hides, trying to turn them around. It looked hopeless to Jack.

He pulled the AK from his shoulder. "Stand back!" he yelled. Jostled at his back by the restless animals, he unleashed a burst at the wood where the planks met a post.

By the light of the fire, he saw the boards shake and loosen. He front-kicked one of them, banging it free. Amancia saw what he was doing and followed his lead, knocking several other planks down. One llama ventured through the fresh opening. The others soon followed and galloped for the gate.

"Follow them!" Jack hollered at her.

She nodded and ran. Tallulah and Gustavo stood to either side of the open gate, crouched low, waving the llamas through. When Gustavo saw Jack, he pointed down the driveway. Jack didn't understand at first. Then he saw headlights blinking between the foliage. Another vehicle was racing down the driveway.

Jack sprinted for the truck. Amancia and Tallulah scampered into the back seat. Gustavo took the passenger side. While Jack fired the engine, Gustavo put two fresh shells in his shotgun. They saw the second vehicle in silhouette. It was a compact pickup truck with a heavy machine gun mounted in the bed.

"Technical," said Jack. "Looks like it has a fifty cal in the bed. Where the hell did they get that?"

"The important ones have them," Gustavo answered.

"Heavy vehicles come over from Tiburón in Venezuela," Amancia added. "Alberto told me about it. The police look the other way, of course."

The headlights made the final turn before the house. The technical was speeding down the driveway straight at them.

"Get down," he urged Amancia. "Please."

With his headlights off, Jack sped forward, hoping there was enough room in the narrow drive to pass by the technical and race away. It soon became obvious to him that it would be too close. Thick rainforest trees hemmed the road in from either side. Jack stopped the Ford, thinking through his options.

He picked one.

"Seatbelts on!" he cried.

Next to him, the boy hurriedly nodded and clicked the strap in place. Jack did the same, threw the truck in reverse, and headed back to the burning buildings.

Navigating by his mirrors, he swung to the left and rammed the truck's tailgate through the wire llama fence fifty feet from the flaming pole barn. He waited with the lights off, idling, hoping the flames to his left would distract the incoming truck.

"Brace!" he shouted.

The technical, an old Nissan, flew down the driveway at high speed. Jack caught a glimpse of three men crammed into the truck's front seat. When it was a few yards from crossing in front of him, he shoved the Ford's accelerator to the floor.

The truck jolted forward and rammed the lighter technical, knocking it sideways and pinning it against thick tree trunks. After the jerk from the crash, Jack threw the beat-up Ford in reverse. Gustavo leaned out the truck window and fired his shotgun at a man climbing out the Nissan's driver's-side window.

Jack slammed the brakes and threw open his door with the rifle in his hand. One man had scrambled free from the opposite side of the technical and was climbing into the bed, swinging the heavy machine gun toward Jack.

Jack raised the AK and shot him in the chest. He veered left to get an angle on the third man. That Tib was rising to his knees, struggling to pull his weapon free of the battered truck. Jack shot him in the neck.

He turned and ran back to the Ford, waving Gustavo in. They scrambled into the seats. Jack threw it in gear and raced down the driveway.

The propane tank blew fifty yards behind him.

22

NAVAL AIR STATION OCEANA, VIRGINIA BEACH, VIRGINIA
0020

THE FLIGHT FROM THE PRIVATE RAMP AT REAGAN NATIONAL TO THE MILITARY ONE AT Naval Air Station Oceana was quick, arriving at the stroke of midnight, Eastern Standard Time.

The unmarked, twin-turboprop Beechcraft King Air had been waiting for them, its door open, engines idling, and props feathered. Lisanne told the charter company she'd pay for the extra fuel if the pilots skipped the safety briefing and jammed the throttles to the stops once airborne. The only tricky business had been to get the Navy to allow an incoming C-12—as the military called it—to land on the sprawling jet base that housed the bulk of the Atlantic Fleet's naval air forces.

A call from Mary Pat Foley to an admiral on the Joint Chiefs of Staff took care of that. The only condition was that the plane would have to disgorge its passengers and take off again without shutting down. That arrangement had proved acceptable to Mary Pat and Clark.

It had sounded acceptable to Lisanne, too—though she hadn't accounted for the miserable weather that had descended on Virginia Beach. She slanted into the brisk March nor'easter, second in line behind Clark, who knew the shortest path to the hangar where they would meet Master Chief Kendrick Moore. The master chief—or just plain "chief," as his Campus peers called him—was the newest member of Clark's squad, having retired as a decorated leader from DEVGRU, better known as SEAL Team Six.

Clark's vision for staffing The Campus was to keep an operative close to each of the special warfare units. He already had an Operational Detachment–Delta—Delta Force—leader in Bartosz Jankowski, whom they called Midas. Clark also had two active-duty Operational Detachment Alpha—Green Beret—operators named Cary Marks and Jad Mustafa, who could be detailed for special duty to augment The Campus on a moment's notice.

But when it came to littoral ops like the one Clark envisioned for Ding's extract, Master Chief Kendrick Moore was the man closest to the Navy.

With a little hocus-pocus from Mary Pat Foley's staff at Liberty Crossing, The Campus concocted a cover job for Moore as an Office of the Director of National Intelligence contractor whose official duty was to evaluate experimental naval warfare equipment. Unofficially, that meant he was to keep The Campus supplied with the latest and greatest SEAL toys.

Her neck stung by sleet, Lisanne saw a bright light coming through a cracked hangar door ahead and to the left. Clark took a beeline for it, nearly jogging.

"Welcome, welcome," said Kendrick Moore from inside the hangar, waving them in. It wasn't exactly warm, Lisanne thought, but at least it was out of the wind. Moore led them to metal folding chairs in front of a table with a flat-screen TV. Looking down the length of the hangar, Lisanne saw that the rest of it was dark.

Moore was a big man with wide shoulders and a shaved head. He wore a faded SEAL assault shirt with camo sleeves that had

Velcro swatches on the shoulders. "It's cold out there," he said. "You guys need coffee?"

"Desperately," Lisanne answered.

The master chief hurried to a side office with glass windows. Lisanne could see him carefully filling Styrofoam cups from a silver percolator. The Campus members settled into the chairs. Still cold, they kept their coats on and sipped coffee when Moore brought over the tray.

"Okay," Moore said. He bent over a laptop hooked to the TV and punched some keys. "Gavin, are you there?"

"I'm here," said Gavin Biery through a speaker. His red-bearded face appeared on the TV screen. Master Chief Moore aimed the webcam at the group in the chairs.

"Can you see us?"

"Yup," Gavin responded. "Hi, guys."

"Let's get this going," Clark said after crushing his Styrofoam cup. He was still standing, looking at Gavin on the TV screen. "Gavin, do we have any new intel on the target area?"

"Sharing my screen," the tech specialist replied.

The big rectangular Samsung lit up with a satellite photo of a river where the black and white colors were reversed, like a photo negative. The picture revealed a series of docks. Among them was parked a long white yacht and a barge.

"This is an AI-enhanced infrared sensor pass from two hours ago," Gavin said. "It's the latest out of NGA. Pulled it down minutes ago."

"Doesn't look like much has changed," Clark said.

"At least the target is relatively static," noted Lisanne. Clark grunted in response.

Moore got closer to the TV and pointed at two dark dots. "These look like sentries," he said. "One man on the stern and another up on the roof. Then I see these guys over here near the fence line."

"Concur," said Clark, eyeing the screen carefully.

Moore asked, "Can we get any tighter on the sentries? Maybe we can see the weapons."

Gavin zoomed in on the roof sentry. The AI-enhanced imagery was good enough to see the machine gun strapped over his shoulder and the ball cap on his head.

"The rifle looks like an AK-203," Moore remarked. "It's Russian military, gas piston, about like our Heckler & Koch 416s."

Clark nodded. "You see anything else in this photo of note, Chief?"

Moore asked Gavin to move the view in and out. He settled the cursor on the empty docks downstream of the barge.

"Do we know what's going on here?" Moore asked, pointing to a tractor-trailer parked near the boats.

"Not really," said Clark. "From older imagery and Ding's prior reports, we think the trucks bring drugs in from the interior highlands. According to the DEA, Tiburón's boats rendezvous at sea with freighters that then off-load in Mexico. The drugs are ferried overland into the U.S. I'm not so sure that's the case now."

"Why do you say that?" asked Moore.

"We started to get some Wagner activity with Tiburón. That's why Ding's there—so we have a heads-up on what the Russians are doing in Venezuela. Now we're seeing some Russian military movements in concert."

"So there might be some sophisticated weapons coming through this base," Moore concluded. "The guy on the stern looks like he's carrying an AK-12. If these guys are already armed with the latest Russian rifles, they're not your garden-variety druggies."

"Correct," Clark agreed. "That helicopter you see there belongs to a head Wagner guy, Morozov. Given his presence, we don't know what exactly we'll be facing when we go in to get Ding."

Moore stood with his arms crossed, thinking. "That eliminates air support. If those are Russian weapons coming in the truck to build up a Wagner-style force, then they're likely to include MANPADs."

"What are MANPADs?" Mandy asked.

"Man-portable air-defense systems," Clark explained. "Shoulder-fired heat-seeking missiles." He turned back to Moore. "We couldn't go in via air anyway. Anything caught on radar would ruin our deniability."

The chief pondered the image on the screen for a quarter minute. He turned to Clark. "You sure you don't want to leave this to DEVGRU? The tasking for all of this is above my pay grade—but this is the kind of shit we used to do all the time."

"Negative. We have to stay fully deniable. We don't want active U.S. forces involved—not yet, anyway." Clark pushed out a short sigh. "And we need to go now."

Lisanne had been hearing that urgency since the first call earlier that evening with Clark. While she was gung ho about moving quickly, she was worried the fuse for this Campus operation was a little too short. In her view, military operations go to pieces when they aren't carefully scripted.

She raised her prosthetic arm. "Mr. C., would it make more sense to wait until Jack gets back? We could use the time to enhance our coordination for this op."

Clark looked up at the overhead lights, frowning. "Well," he said. "That's not an option."

"Why not?" Lisanne followed.

"Because," Clark said. "There's something else that I haven't shared with this group yet . . . and it has me worried."

LINE OF DEMARCATION

Lisanne leaned far forward in her chair. She'd never heard Clark say something that circumspect.

Clark clarified. "Look. A long time ago, Ding and I were involved in an op down in Colombia, disrupting the drug operations of Ernesto Escobedo—if you remember him."

"Scumbag," said Chilly. "Died by the same sword he lived by. Killed by one of his lieutenants, I heard."

"Well, that's not the whole story," said Clark. "Back in the day, I was running the counter-Escobedo op from Panama City. We had a green light for direct action, which was rare at the time. Ding was in an A-team out in the hills, throwing satchel charges into drug factories. It was an undeclared war—and it was working."

The veteran SEAL breathed deeply again. "Well, anyway, amid all that, we took things a little too far. A CIA deputy director authorized an air strike on a gathering of drug heavies with a covert, untraceable bomb. I was there, aiming the laser-targeting beam at the house. It was overkill, not my call." He paused to swallow. "Collateral damage included a crowd of civilians—families and kids. Two of the victims were the parents of Juan Machado—the man we all know today as Tiburón."

"So if Ding gets blown . . ." Moore said.

"Yeah. Ding's cover is very good. The Legend Wizards made sure of that. But with the SVR involved, if they figure out who Ding really is, then, well . . ."

"Now I know why you didn't let me go home to change," Chilly said.

Clark scratched his neck. "Yeah. We have to go ASAP. I'm counting on you, Chief, to come up with something to get us in and out of there fast—and invisible."

Moore nodded. "Well, Mr. C., you've come to the right place. I've got a few special surprises for you."

LISANNE SQUINTED AS ONE ROW AFTER ANOTHER OF THE BLINDING HANGAR LIGHTS came on full blast. Moore led them past five parked F-18s to a cordoned area with several tarped lumps on pallets.

"I had these delivered from Dam Neck as soon as you called," Moore explained as he walked, his voice echoing.

He went to the first tarp, unhooked some cinch straps, and threw it off. Lisanne found herself looking at a hulking, two-seat Jet Ski. It was fifteen feet long, painted flat black, and bristling with antennae. To her, it looked like something out of a Transformers movie.

"We call this a SUDS machine," said Moore. "It stands for surface undetectable delivery system. Highly classified. It came out of the Defense Innovation Unit's Silicon Valley group. DEVGRU has been testing them for about six months."

"It looks like a Jet Ski," Mandy remarked, stating the obvious.

"A badass one, though," added Chilly.

"Well," the chief said, "these are a bit more sophisticated than a Jet Ski."

"Explain," Clark grumbled with a glance at his watch.

"These are completely silent. They're hydrogen fuel cell–based, which gives them a range of five hundred nautical miles and a speed nearing a hundred knots. They're also equipped with UMBRA, specialized radar-reflecting electronics that give them full stealth, even with a rider. You wanted fast, long-range, and invisible. These will give that to you, Mr. C."

"Payload?" asked Clark.

"Thousand pounds. So we can put two operators on each one, fully jocked up."

"I've heard a little about hydrogen fuel cells," Lisanne said. "How does this thing work?"

Moore hefted a long seat on one of the vehicles. After unscrewing some nuts, he used both beefy arms to pull out a heavy box, about the size and shape of a midsize suitcase. He put it on the concrete floor. "The hot-swappable battery is stuffed with metal disks made of magnesium," he said. "Technically they're metal hydrides. That's the battery."

"Metal whats?" asked Chilly.

"Hydrides. The metal acts as an ultradense storage mechanism for hydrogen atoms."

"I thought fuel cells used compressed gas or liquid to store hydrogen," Lisanne said.

"Right," answered the chief. "That's the breakthrough. The metal hydrides allow for more efficient hydrogen storage." He gestured to the case.

The team stood blinking at him. Sensing Clark's impatience, Moore continued. "When a hydrogen molecule touches the metal, it breaks into two atoms. Each atom bonds with the metal down to the crystal level, allowing for very dense storage. A catalyst—heat from a starter battery—releases the hydrogen atoms. The protons and electrons in the atoms take different paths from an anode to a cathode, which drives an electric circuit. That's the battery."

"So they're hydrogen-powered but electric," clarified Lisanne.

"Yes," Moore replied. "We're basically substituting lithium-ion batteries for hydrogen ones. Submarines have been using this tech for a while. This is the first time solid hydrogen has been used to power a small surface vessel."

"Survivable?" asked Chilly. "Seems like you could get electrocuted on that thing in the water."

"The electric motors are sheathed in lightweight, waterproof Kevlar shells. And the metal hydride disks don't explode like a gas tank. These are also loaded up with software to let them operate autonomously. Like surface drones."

"We have to go tonight, Chief," Clark said. "These things are huge. How do we get them to the Orinoco river in the next couple hours?"

"Simple. These pallets can roll right up the ramp of a C-17 Globemaster. We can drop them out the back at sea and parachute in behind them."

"No," Clark responded immediately. "No good. I said deniable. There's a Russian frigate steaming into the area that will have its search radars up. They'll be all over a C-17 coming south. And besides, we don't have the training for an airborne drop at sea like that. Not all of us, anyway."

Lisanne, who'd been quietly thinking that Jack would absolutely *love* to do an airborne sea assault with killer, hydrogen-powered Jet Skis, looked down at her phone to see if he'd texted her. He was supposed to have landed in Denver. But there was no message, worrying her.

She put the concern aside and switched back to her role as the Campus logistics coordinator. On Google Maps, she zoomed into the Orinoco river delta.

"Mr. C.," she said, still looking down at her phone. "If we could hop a civilian cargo charter immediately, we could land on the island of Tobago, next to a port called Scarborough. If these SUDS boats are really capable of five hundred nautical miles at a hundred knots, then we'd be in range for the assault immediately."

Clark looked at his own phone, studying a map. "Still too far," he announced. "It'd be better to launch from a ship, maybe twenty miles offshore. These things may be able to do a hundred knots on a lake, but I'm not so sure about the open ocean."

"Well," Lisanne offered, "Hendley still owns the liquid natural gas sealift company Jack bought, Athena Global. I've been on the phone with them all day tracking expenses. One of their ships, the

Helena, is on her way to the offshore oil platforms on the Guyanese coast. Jack's the CEO. He can order it to Tobago. Or I could do it on his behalf."

This led Moore to ask a few questions about the *Helena*'s capacities. Lisanne pulled up its stats from a maritime registry database. Moore ticked off what it would take to move the pallets from a cargo aircraft to the ship.

"I like it," Clark pronounced, cutting them off. "Lisanne, find a cargo charter that can go tonight. We'll land at Tobago, then launch from international waters. Have Jack make the call." Clark put his hands on his hips. "Where the hell is he, anyway? Have you spoken to him yet?"

"I was just checking on that," she replied. "His connection through Panama City was scheduled to land in Denver an hour ago. I set him up on a flight to Trinidad to meet us there. But he hasn't checked in with me."

"You're engaged, right?" asked Mandy.

"Last I checked."

"Then you probably share your location on your iPhones with each other, don't you?"

"Yeah, we do."

"If he changed planes in Denver, even if he was in a hurry, his iPhone would have registered his location on the network."

As a former cop, Lisanne was mildly embarrassed that she hadn't thought of that first. Then again, she didn't make a habit of using the app because she thought it was nosy. She opened her iPhone's "Find My" app.

"That's weird," she said.

"What?" Clark asked.

"Jack's last reported location was about twenty minutes ago. It shows him as still in Georgetown, Guyana's capital."

"Where *exactly* in Georgetown?" Clark's voice had taken an edge. It wasn't the first time Jack had gone rogue. Probably not the last, either. "Get him on the horn. Right now."

Lisanne dialed and frowned when the call went straight to voicemail. Lowering the device to her lap, she zoomed in tightly on the location app. "Huh," she said. "His phone's offline right now. But its last reported location was in a building that Apple Maps says is the headquarters of the Guyanese National Intelligence and Security Agency."

Clark shook his head, wondering what, exactly, Jack had gotten himself mixed up in.

"At least he's still there," said Lisanne. "That will make it easy for him to meet us."

Flexing his hand and cracking his knuckles, Clark conceded the point. "Right. Get that civilian cargo plane chartered, Lisanne. And pull Cary and Jad in. We're all going on a little vacation to Trinidad."

23

ABU DHABI
1000

GUYANESE PRESIDENT ALI KHASIF SAT ON THE RIGHT SIDE OF THE TWO-SEATER Polaris RZR dune buggy. He gripped the welded handholds on the roll cage like a saddle horn on a rodeo bull, gritting his teeth and occasionally closing his eyes behind his goggles.

Viktor Zhdanov, CEO of the Russian oil giant Gazneft, was behind the RZR's wheel, whipsawing the high-performance machine across dune crests, wadis, and narrow sandstone canyons as though trying to outrun the rising shamal wind that had blown in from the Persian Gulf.

The winds twisted together in one narrow channel after another, raising sand in a blinding tornado. Zhdanov didn't seem bothered by the lack of visibility. He sped straight through them.

"I really think we should be getting back to the main group," Khasif rasped into the lip mic mounted to his helmet. His voice was choppy as the machine thudded over a rutted track.

"In time, in time," the billionaire responded. Khasif could barely hear him over the screaming engine. The RZR was fishtailing up a particularly steep dune.

Khasif locked his elbows and braced his arms against the roll cage when he saw the crest of the dune fast approaching. The RZR soared into the air. A second later, the vehicle dove back to the desert in a sandy splash. The Russian grunted in satisfaction and charged down the slope, burrowing into the cold shadow of a wadi.

"My helicopter will get us if we need it. Don't worry," Zhdanov said while fearlessly running over a copse of prickly bushes in the shade. After slaloming the wadi they broke into blinding light. The Russian added, "I'm taking you to a spot where we'll get a better view of the race."

Khasif leaned forward to glance at the rearview mirror. He had hoped rather than expected to see the rest of the Abu Dhabi Desert Challenge royal followers behind them. Twenty minutes earlier, Zhdanov had veered away from the main trail, insisting he knew a shortcut across the desert that would give them a better view of the racers.

Atop a sandstone peak worn smooth by eons of shamals, Zhdanov skidded to a stop in a brown cloud.

"*Kruto!*" he exclaimed, clapping his gloved hands together. He tugged the gloves from his fingers with his teeth and killed the engine. The brown cloud quickly dissipated. Zhdanov unstrapped his helmet and hoisted himself out of the vehicle.

Khasif followed the Russian's lead. Without his goggles, he squinted against the harsh wind, his eyes nearly closed. The dunes stretched like waves on a yellow sea. The sky was a brilliant blue except for a tan smudge on the horizon.

Zhdanov put his helmet on the sand and sat on it, bending his knees. He leaned against the side of the RZR, which acted as a windbreak. After Khasif settled next to him, the Russian withdrew a small silver flask from his breast pocket and offered it.

"No thank you. I'm Muslim," the president said.

Zhdanov tipped the flask and winked. "*Nostrovia.*"

LINE OF DEMARCATION

After swallowing, he screwed the top back on and returned the flask to his pocket.

"What a place," he remarked with an outstretched arm and a crooked grin.

Khasif looked out at the long stretch of yellow dunes. "Impressive, yes."

"Not a scrap of life in sight," Zhdanov went on. "No trees or animals or people. Like some other planet. Worthless—except for the gurgling black goo under here."

The Russian threw a handful of sand into the air. The wind swiftly carried it away.

Khasif stole a glance at his cell phone. There was no reception.

Catching the movement, the Russian said, "One of the beauties of being out here, Mr. President, is that we can disconnect. Just talk—man-to-man."

Ali Khasif had no interest in disconnecting or speaking man-to-man with Viktor Zhdanov. He'd come to the Middle East in the hopes of learning how best to administer a sovereign wealth fund for his people. As far as he could tell, the Russian administered a wealth fund purely for himself.

Alberto Quintero had spurned a Gazneft export offer because, like many others, the Russian company couldn't comply with the ecological requirements. The foreign minister had backed the decision as well since Gazneft was majority-owned by Kremlin kleptocrats and the last thing Khasif wanted was to put his country down a path that would ally him with the rapacious Russians or their proxy, the Venezuelans.

But he was a decent man who knew he would be on his way home in a matter of hours. While he didn't want to be in business with Gazneft, he also didn't want to provoke its CEO. After a lifetime in politics, he was comfortable operating in the gray space between what one said and what one thought.

"I must thank you for the exhilarating ride," the courtly president began. "And the solace. It is indeed invigorating."

"Of course it is," the Russian said. "Especially for men like us."

"Like us?"

"Oh, yes. You're a president. I'm the CEO of the biggest gas company in the world. Men like us never get to be alone. This is why we should cherish the day, my friend."

Khasif looked across the blazing sands. The prince had said he would be leaving at midmorning. It was now getting on past ten. "Forgive me, Viktor, but I thought we were here for the view of the race. I don't see the rally out there anywhere."

The Russian dug through his tunic for another nip from his flask. "It's coming," he soothed. After a sip, he added, "We're like hunters sitting in ambush. And, while we wait, it will give us a chance to discuss business."

"Certainly," said Khasif, his spirits sinking.

Zhdanov continued. "Namely—I want to know why you turned down Gazneft's proposal to export LNG from your Orinoco Basin."

"Ah," Khasif replied. "For that, I would have to consult with my minister of the interior, Alberto Quintero. Sadly, he was killed yesterday. I must return home immediately to pick up the pieces. I will have his staff prepare a report for you as I'm ill-equipped to discuss the matter myself."

The Russian's long stare made the president uncomfortable. Zhdanov finally broke it by raising his flask. "To Quintero," he said. "May he rest in peace."

The Russian drank alone.

24

ORINOCO RIVER DELTA, VENEZUELA
0220

BELIEVING THAT ALL HE COULD DO WAS DONE FOR THE MOMENT, IGOR MOROZOV HAD allowed himself a few hours of sleep in the *Gran Blanco*'s luxurious guest cabin. His overlords at Yasenevo, the Moscow suburb where the SVR was headquartered, had ordered the operation to proceed on an accelerated timetable.

Here in the drug lord's innermost sanctum, Morozov had tried to convince himself that he'd seen to every conceivable detail of the delicate movement of forces. In his heart, however, he doubted that he had. Much to his discomfort, this operation's execution rested on the shoulders of the Tiburónistas—the same band of ex-cons who shifted the timetable by foolishly attacking a defenseless American Coast Guard vessel.

Led by a small contingent of Wagner veterans, Tiburón's men were out at sea, gearing up on the three staging barges they'd moored to Orinoco Reef, just ten miles from the oil platforms. With a mere twenty-four hours before things were to go kinetic, Morozov hoped they would behave.

Having spent three years as a Wagner manager in the Central

African Republic, the SVR major understood the double-edged mercenary sword better than most. In his experience, the same heartlessness that could terrify a population could just as easily run amok, ignoring orders. To Morozov, the odds were even worse that that would happen in a hybrid operation like this one, where he commanded Wagner and Wagner commanded hastily trained Tiburónistas.

To help even those odds, the Russian had brought over the best Wagner leader he knew from Africa. Yevgeny Zuka was different from the other mercenaries. He'd come up through the Spetsnaz ranks before making real money on the private side. While Zuka was as happy to spread mayhem as any of the desperadoes, he still understood that he toiled under the firm hand of the Kremlin, a hand that could form a fist and smash all of them at will.

With that fist on his mind, Morozov laced his shoes and stepped outside. The Orinoco river was flowing swiftly and silently past the yacht. Since the men were largely out of the camp onshore, even the land was quiet. He watched the moon's reflection ripple on the surface.

He heard a scrape and turned. A sentry walked along a narrow passage on the deck above him. Morozov crossed to the other side of the yacht for privacy. Facing the dark shore, noting the absence of lights, he unfolded the antenna to his satellite phone and dialed.

"*Da*," his Wagner man, Zuka, answered immediately. In the background, Morozov could hear the rhythm of ocean waves.

"What do you think?" Morozov asked in Russian. "Are the Tiburónistas ready?"

"Hold on." Zuka cupped his hand over the microphone and growled a Spanish command that Morozov couldn't quite make out. "They're almost ready," the mercenary said when he came back on the line. "We're all accounted for on the barges."

"The weapons made it out?"

"*Da.* Most of them. We're unpacking and assembling. There are still a few more missile crates that came in on a late truck. I've sent a boat back to collect them."

"*Horosho,*" Morozov said.

His SVR front company, a beer distributor with operations from Valparaiso to Port-au-Prince, had been ferrying the weapons down from Puerto Cabello, Venezuela's main ocean port. They had been coming in via Russian sealift for months, buried in grain, then stored in one of Morozov's warehouses in Caracas. "What about the Tiburónistas? They're . . . behaving?"

"Now they are. I had a troublemaker. One of the Venezuelan ex-cons asked to be paid early. I shot him in front of the men and kicked him over the side."

"*Horosho,*" Morozov repeated.

"I need more Russians," Zuka pleaded. "I have only a few out here. Are we on track to link up with the rest of the troops as scheduled?"

Two hundred Wagner mercenaries were in Havana, ready to land at the Georgetown airport in thirty-six hours via Russian airlift. "They're ready and waiting in Havana," Morozov reassured his best mercenary. "They'll land after the Guyanese political decree."

Waves crashed and hissed on the satellite link. Morozov could hear men shouting in guttural Spanish on the barge. "What about the Navy?" Zuka asked.

Staring at the dark shore, Morozov allowed himself an appreciative grin. In his view, contacting the navy was one of the things Yasenevo had gotten right this time. The frigate *Admiral Gorshkov* was steaming into theater, soon to be patrolling just off the Guyanese coast with a heavy troop helicopter. To Morozov, that ship was an insurance policy—the thing that would keep this operation from turning into the Russian version of the Bay of Pigs.

"The Zircon missiles are already in range," answered the SVR major. "That will keep the U.S. out of the area. The *Gorshkov* will be offshore in the next twenty-four hours."

"*Horosho*," Zuka replied. "And they know about the ship's helicopter?"

"*Da*," Morozov answered. "It will rendezvous as planned tomorrow night. I have seen the order."

Zuka seemed satisfied with that. The Wagner combat leader changed the subject. "What's going on in Georgetown? Are the Tiburónistas doing their job?"

Morozov looked at the black jungle in front of him. He inhaled the swampy air and felt a tingle in his lower abdomen. The mercenary's question struck at his foremost concern—that the Guyanese ground operation was out of his direct control, introducing several dependencies.

The first was the Tiburónistas. For the opening salvo of the operation, the drug gang was to emerge from the rainforests to loot, rape, and pillage. Their actions were intended to create such a sense of lawlessness that Morozov's second dependency—Guyana's weak-kneed prime minister—would declare martial law.

And, as if those points of vulnerability weren't enough, Morozov also had a third dependency on the SVR. It was Yasenevo's job to keep the legitimate Guyanese president from countermanding the order or, worse, inviting American forces in to help stabilize the country. His colonel had assured him that the SVR had an operation in place to neutralize the Guyanese president—but having lived through many African operations, Morozov took the assurance with a grain of salt.

He saw no reason to burden Zuka with such concerns, however. He needed his Wagner chief to focus on doing what he did best: terrifying people.

"The situation on the ground in Guyana is taken care of," he said. "Just be ready when the helicopter arrives."

LINE OF DEMARCATION

"*Da*," Zuka said.

Morozov considered adding an order to keep the Tiburónistas away from the weapons once they were assembled. The last thing they needed was another unsanctioned action at sea. But just as he formed the thought, a voice from above startled him.

"There you are!" Tiburón boomed from the narrow ledge near the sky bridge. "I've been looking all over for you."

Morozov cut the connection to Zuka and looked up at Tiburón. Next to the drug lord, he saw Carlos Caraza, agitated and breathless.

"What?" Morozov called. "Is something wrong?"

"Not anymore," Tiburón said. "But I thought you should know. We caught a man going through your truck, inspecting the missiles. We think he's a spy."

The Russian froze. In all the time he'd been worried about the multiple dependencies he had on Tiburón and Yasenevo, was it possible a rat had been buried in his own end of the operation?

"Who is he?"

"Diaz. He killed a guard on the barge, swam downriver, and snuck into a truck. We caught him red-handed."

Learning that it was Tiburón's intelligence advisor relieved Morozov for a moment. Then again, he had gone through Diaz's background with Yasenevo. If Diaz was in fact a spy, he was a good one—most likely a CIA officer. It didn't seem to Morozov that any of the various Latin countries could pull off a legend so seamlessly.

The SVR major thought of his earlier conversation with Romero and the loose end of Jack Ryan, Jr., who'd been meeting with Quintero and Suárez. Romero had assured him that Ryan would never make it out of Guyana.

With the country headed for martial law within hours, that seemed assured. But with a possible CIA spy in Tiburón's innermost sanctum, it was more likely than not that the Americans knew something about the operation. Were they headed into a trap? Morozov had to find out. Caraza's angry look scared him into thinking he might be too late.

"Where is he?" the Russian asked. "You've taken him alive?"

"He's right under your feet, compañero, in the lazaret. We're about to pay him a little visit." Tiburón picked up a Louisville Slugger and made a mock swing with it.

"Don't!" Morozov exclaimed. "Let me interrogate him first. We need to know what he knows. He's all yours after that."

Tiburón spit over the side of the boat and tapped the bat against a chrome rail. "I'll give you a few hours," he said. "After that, I need to think about my reputation."

25

LOUISVILLE, KENTUCKY
0300

MUCH TO HER DISPLEASURE, WHEN HOLLY PEMBERTON HAD FIRST STARTED FLYING KC-135 air-to-air refueling tankers in the Alaska Air National Guard's 168th Wing, the squadron wags up at Eielson Air Force Base near Fairbanks had tagged her with the call sign "Hollywood."

With her blond-streaked hair, surfer-girl tan, and tendency to wear oversized Ray-Ban aviators, Pemberton, an Air Force ROTC graduate from UCLA, knew she'd have to work extra hard to prove she wasn't just a pretty face—especially with a call sign like Hollywood and a face that was actually, well, pretty.

But that's exactly what she'd done over fifteen years and more than fifteen thousand flying hours, earning the right to wear the star and laurels over her Air Force wings that designated her a command pilot. Having attained that goal, she left active duty as a lieutenant colonel for a job with UPS, where she flew the Asia route a few times a month. Happy to pad her retirement and work on her outdoor tennis game, she was satisfied with her transition to civilian life—though she kept one foot in the door as an Air National Guard colonel to keep from getting too bored.

Despite that background, on this cold Kentucky night, Holly wasn't quite sure what to think of the urgent text from UPS operations when her phone buzzed on her hip. The message came while she was out preflighting her empty 767, prepping for her usual polar route to Tokyo. When she called into base ops she was told that a sister ship would be taking her route, since her plane had been requisitioned for a special mission operation on behalf of the United States government.

She knew UPS had a contract with the Defense Department's Civil Reserve Air Fleet—CRAF. She didn't think it all that strange that the company was forced to participate in a sudden airlift. Several times a year the government called with a request to move equipment from one base to another. The part of the order that puzzled her was when the base ops officer said she had to perform the flight personally—especially when other pilots were sitting at home who weren't about to zip off to Tokyo.

Curious, she rushed to the ops shack and studied the government orders for herself. Buried among the lines of headers, she saw that they originated from the Defense Logistics Agency, as usual. But she quickly came to grips with why she had been identified personally as the lead pilot. One of the header lines identified the Office of the Director of National Intelligence, coded as Liberty Crossing, as a co-originator of the order. To Holly, that meant this was a classified mission, spook business. There was only one other UPS pilot in Lexington who held a top secret clearance and he was off in Kuala Lumpur.

The orders said Holly was to wait for two Army noncoms to arrive in Louisville as passengers, "pax" in CRAF lingo. Once the Army personnel were on board, she was to fly them to Naval Air Station Oceana. In Oceana, according to the orders, she was to take on thirty thousand pounds of palleted cargo and five more passengers. The lift would take them from Virginia to Tobago's Scarborough International Airport.

That was all fine with Holly. She could use a little Caribbean sun.

A few minutes later, after filing a new flight plan, she returned to her massive 767. By then it was fueled, and the big yellow auxiliary power units were screaming nearby. She was about to head up the ramp and inspect the plane's enormous interior when she saw a Ram pickup soaring through the security gate. It careened down the taxiway at eighty miles an hour, headed straight for her.

The truck screeched to a halt and two men leaped out. They approached her with their Army ID cards and identified themselves as Master Sergeant Cary Marks and Sergeant First Class Jad Mustafa. They explained that they had driven over from Fort Campbell, three hours away. Holly flipped open her own ID wallet and introduced herself as Lieutenant Colonel Holly Pemberton. "Call me Hollywood," she said. "Everyone does."

Despite the chasm in rank, the moment Green Beret Jad Mustafa laid eyes on the tall woman in the bright blue flight suit with the blond-streaked hair peeking out of her UPS cap, he was in love. That her name was Hollywood was even more seductive. He listened to her instructions with one ear about loading their equipment, while entranced by the way her lips moved.

Jad smoothed his hair and straightened his posture, trying to look his best. He tried to come up with a charming line, but drew a blank.

For her part, Lieutenant Colonel Pemberton had seen the same look on many a lonely airman's face up in Alaska. To snap the Army noncom out of it, she commanded, "Sergeant! Loadmaster's waiting on you. Get your gear on the scissor lift so we can strap in. We were supposed to be in the air ten minutes ago."

After a "Yes, ma'am," Jad ran to the back of the pickup and started loosening the cinch straps.

Colonel Holly Pemberton spoke authoritatively to Master Sergeant Marks. "What unit are you with?"

"ODA, ma'am," he replied.

By that, Holly knew, he meant Operational Detachment Alpha, a Green Beret. She had already suspected it, since they'd come screaming in from Fort Campbell.

She pulled an empty cargo manifest form from her flight suit leg pocket and clicked a pen. "I'm required to fill out a cargo manifest for air operations. The orders didn't say you would be bringing gear. What is all that you've got in the back of the truck there?"

Cary Marks looked back at Jad, then into the eyes of the woman who'd asked him the question. He was in a quandary as to what to say.

He and Jad had been in the middle of a combat town training shoot over at Campbell when John Clark's call came in. The old SEAL had told Cary and Jad to drop whatever they were doing, gather up a shit ton of combat weapons, and hightail it over to Louisville for an extended Campus op of unknown duration. Marks knew better than to ask Clark too many questions. He and Cary had gone on temporary duty, TDY, on more than one Campus op.

But there was one thing Clark always told them: Campus ops need to remain deniable. They operated zero-footprint and were used only when the full force of the U.S. military wasn't an option. So when a beautiful Air Force lieutenant colonel standing in front of a UPS 767 asked him what he was carrying, Cary wasn't exactly sure what he could reveal.

Wearing Levi's, desert combat boots, and a canvas oil-skin Filson jacket, Marks dug his cold hands into his pockets. "I don't think I'm allowed to say, ma'am."

Holly unfolded her orders. She pointed to the part that identified her as the command pilot with a note about her clearance.

Marks was relieved. As far as he knew, Clark couldn't fault him for telling a cleared, honest-to-God Air Force pilot what he was bringing on her aircraft.

He said, "Well, right now Sergeant First Class Mustafa is loading up six HK416 assault rifles, two M110 sniper kits, six SIG Sauer 9-millimeter pistols, five hundred NATO standard rounds of five-five-six and pistol ammo, thirty thermobaric home-wrecker grenades, and about ten kilos of C-4 with blasting caps and timing fuses. That specific enough, ma'am?"

Holly hesitated with her pen over her paper while the wind whipped the cuffs of her pants. She couldn't imagine that her civilian bosses would let her take off with that kind of dangerous load without filling out at least fifty more forms.

To keep the paperwork to a minimum, she scrawled "construction equipment" on the manifest and stuffed the paper in the breast pocket of her flight suit.

"Let's roll, Sergeant," she said.

"Roger that, ma'am," Marks replied with a snappy salute.

26

**TWENTY-FIVE MILES SOUTHEAST OF GEORGETOWN, GUYANA
0810**

"WHAT ARE THOSE?" JACK ASKED FROM HIS SEATED POSITION AT THE FOOT OF THE front right tire of the F-150 they'd taken from the Tiburónistas. Across his lap was the AK-47 he'd lifted from a dead Tib. Quintero's Glock was in his belt.

"Cacao fruit," Amancia said. As soon as the sun had crested the hills down near Suriname, Amancia pledged to return with breakfast. With Tallulah behind her, she trudged off into the leafy brush of the swampy flatland, away from the clearing in the sugarcane grass where they had parked.

In Jack's view, the cane grass offered good concealment. The green stalks were anywhere from eight to fifteen feet high. The blades grew so densely that they could only walk through them by following the harvesters' paths. Jack found the clearing by standing on the truck cab. From that elevated vantage, he spotted tufts of coconut palms sprouting among the canes, like crabgrass sticking out of a manicured lawn.

"I thought you said breakfast," Jack said, conscious of the pain in his stomach.

"Just you wait," she replied.

She bent to a knee and released the bounty she was carrying in the tail of her upturned blouse. A dozen oblong fruits that looked to Jack like little footballs toppled to the dirt.

"There's a muddy creek down there," she said. "The cacao trees like it."

"Drinkable water?" Jack asked. The smoke from the previous evening had saturated his clothes and left his throat feeling like he'd enjoyed a dozen of the late professor's Cubans.

"Only if we boil it," she said. "It's muddy and slow. But here, eat these. Then we'll figure out water."

"Eat them with the canes," Tallulah chimed in from behind her mother. The younger of the Quintero women held a broad leaf to the bruises on her face. Her Cal Bears shirt was streaked with mud.

The two women sat in the clearing between the canes and sliced the cacao beans with a machete they found in the truck. Jack got up with the AK slung from his shoulder and nosed through the canes with the barrel, looking for a way forward. It didn't seem to him that there were any paths wide enough for the Ford. He thought they should continue heading north to the coast road and drive straight to the U.S. embassy.

Finding no luck with a trail, he turned and saw Gustavo leaning against the Ford's grille, lazily resting his shotgun on his shoulder. "Mr. Jack," he said. "You will like the cacao fruit." They sat next to the women in the shade of the stalks.

"You peel back the skin," Amancia explained. "Inside, you see this white stuff?" She picked out a hunk of pale flesh that looked like a garlic clove to Jack. "If you eat this while also chewing on the sugarcane, it tastes like chocolate candy. Try it."

Jack took the white mass from Amancia and a stalk of peeled sugarcane from Tallulah. The moisture on his tongue was pleasurable. He had to admit that the addition of the sugarcane made it all taste like chocolate ice cream. "I'll be damned," he announced after swallowing. "More?"

With his appetite whetted, he was soon eating as fast as they could peel—until he felt guilty about hogging the stash. "I'm still worried about water," he said, forcing himself to stop.

"Oh, that's easy," Amancia replied. "Goose, go get it."

Gustavo stretched and nodded. "*Si, Tia.*" He turned to the truck. "Mr. Jack, can I use the sling from your rifle?" Jack removed the leather strap from the AK and handed it over. Gustavo stretched it in his hands, testing its strength. "This will do."

He disappeared between the razor-sharp cane blades. Jack's next view of him was when he was twenty feet up the trunk of the nearby palm. The boy looped the sling around the trunk and balanced his feet while his hands pulled the leather. He scurried to the leafy treetop with the ease of a lemur, then batted down a dozen green coconuts, which fell among the canes.

Minutes later, Gustavo was back with five green coconuts the size of human heads. He used the machete to hack off a corner of one, then offered it to Jack to drink. Jack poured the slightly salty coconut water down his throat. Mixed with the chocolate remnant on his lips, he found it shockingly good. He drank a second coconut without saying a word.

Sated, he took a deep breath, stood up, and surveyed the white morning sky. "Okay," he said. "It's after eight o'clock. We need to get to the Georgetown coast road. Is there a way?"

Gustavo used a stick to draw a map in the dirt. He showed their position as a few miles southeast of the village of Baiabu, smack in the middle of the broad coastal patchwork of sugarcane fields.

Jack touched it with his toe. "Let's head northwest toward Baiabu. There are bound to be some roads near the town. That beats trying to get through these canes."

Gustavo shook his head doubtfully and looked away.

LINE OF DEMARCATION

Jack shot a questioning glance at him. "What?"

The boy remained quiet.

"The Tiburónistas are nearby," Amancia said. "They carve out distribution points for processed drugs for pickup on the beach. There are many of them in Baiabu."

Gustavo confirmed her point with a nod.

Five hours earlier, when they'd fled the burning eco-farm, they ran into a road junction guarded by two Tiburónistas standing lazily in the road with shotguns and machetes. In the stolen truck, Gustavo sped past them behind the wheel while Jack, Amancia, and Tallulah ducked in the back seat. Gustavo burnished his Tiburónista credentials by holding the AK out the window and firing manically into the air.

"You think the Tiburónistas will be out like they were last night? In the road intersections?" Jack asked.

Amancia sighed sullenly. "I know from Alberto that Tiburón has long threatened to unleash his people to spread mayhem if provoked. That was his threat to force government ministers to look the other way and ignore his drug factories."

Jack thought of the tapes in his pockets. "Well, if we can get to the U.S. embassy, I can deliver the tapes. We can expose the corrupt cops. We just have to figure out how to get through the cane fields."

"Mr. Jack, I have an idea," said Gustavo, rising to his feet. "Something I saw from the top of the coconut tree." He extended his hands. Jack grasped them and let Gustavo pull him to his feet. "Follow me," said the former Tiburónista.

Heaving the machete, Gustavo hacked a path through the swaying cane blades. After a few hundred yards, Jack felt the earth beneath his feet turn swampy and noticed tree growth ahead. Gustavo stopped at the edge of an enormous trunk.

The boy pressed his hand against the gnarled bark. "This is a silk-cotton tree," he said. "They're the tallest trees in Guyana." He looked up. "If we can climb this one, we might see a path through the canes to the coast road."

Jack tilted his head to look up the enormous trunk. Its first limb was twenty feet above him. Its circumference was far too large to use the leather sling as a climbing brace. "How do you propose we get up there?" he asked.

Gustavo flexed the leather strap again, turning to a skinnier tree ten feet away. Its branches were also high above. "We climb this one, then hop over. *Comprende?*"

The last time Jack climbed a tree was when he was eleven, on his father's Maryland cliff house above the Chesapeake. He peered doubtfully at Gustavo.

The boy grinned. "I'll show the way." As with the coconut palm, he looped the leather around the trunk and hoisted himself up. Once he reached the first limb, he used it as a bridge to another one on the massive tree.

"Look out, Mr. Jack." He let the strap fall thirty feet to the ground.

Jack picked it up and looped it around the thin tree. He bent his knees and shoved his rubber sneaker soles against the bark while holding the ends of the strap. It took him five grunting minutes to gain the first limb.

Using smaller branches as handholds, he made it to his feet and crossed over to the bigger tree. At this height, its branches were close together. Jack was able to climb it like a ladder and follow the boy. After forty feet straight up, he felt the sun on his shoulders. They'd risen above the surrounding trees.

"There," Gustavo proclaimed, pushing aside leaves. "You see Georgetown?"

Jack surveyed the sweeping tableau that rolled out below him. In the distance, glowing under the low morning sun, he saw the brown Atlantic. At its edge, he made out the gray sprawl of Georgetown. The distant city was marked with several columns of dark smoke that rose and slanted inland on the sea breeze.

"What's the smoke?" he asked Gustavo.

Gustavo grimaced and shook his head. "Tiburónistas, I think."

"*All* of that?"

"*Sí*. The bosses always promised we would get to take whatever we wanted one day."

THE HIGH VIEW HAD GIVEN JACK AN IDEA OF HOW TO NAVIGATE THE PATCHWORK OF cane fields to end up near the coast road.

Once there, Jack felt confident they could buy a prepaid phone in one of the many small kiosks he'd seen along the roads. His first call would be to Lisanne. She would help him with a call to the embassy, which could dispatch an American team to scoop them up.

Jack sat in the passenger seat, directing Gustavo through the narrow dirt tracks by the memory of his view from the silk-cotton tree. "Take a right here," he said with a glance at the sun, hoping he'd chosen the right road. "Then, remember? We pass two roads, take a turn east, then catch the last road north."

Gustavo nodded while he twisted the wheel through the green maze. Amancia and Tallulah remained quiet in the back seat. After another twenty minutes, the road got so narrow that the cane stalks blasted the truck's side mirrors. Jack worried he'd misdirected them. "Stop," he said. "I need to regroup."

Gustavo hit the brakes and killed the engine.

The stalks were so thick to either side that Jack couldn't open the door. He climbed out the window onto the hood, then hopped up to the roof of the cab. He peeked over the top of the sprawling sugarcanes like a gopher in a wheat field.

With the truck quiet, he listened to the plants rustling. There was a stiffer breeze than before, and the air smelled of salt rather than swamp water.

Getting close, he thought, proud of himself. Behind him, he saw a depression in the field where a second road joined. Somehow, he'd missed it when they went by it before.

"Goose," he said when he got back in the truck. "We turned one road too late. Back it up and hook a right."

With the canes slamming into the mirrors, they backtracked to the intersection Jack had seen. They turned and were soon moving north on a wider road.

He ordered Gustavo to stop and kill the engine. Again, Jack stood on the cab to gauge their progress. The sun was getting higher, heating up the land and sucking the air in from the cooler sea. Jack listened to the breeze rattling the cane blades.

Over that rustle, he heard something rhythmic—like the steady beat of a bass drum. It was getting louder.

The white Bell 412 helicopter—a modern descendant of the famed Vietnam-era Huey—skimmed two hundred feet over the field. A quarter mile south, it roared by with a throaty growl, scattering the sugarcane stalks in its rotor wash. Jack watched as it gained altitude, then arced into a northerly course. He wasn't sure if it had seen them.

With all the mayhem the Tiburónistas were spreading throughout the city, it made sense to Jack that one of the few helicopters in the Guyanese defense force arsenal would be out on active patrol. He hoped that meant the government was reasserting itself over the Tiburónistas.

He hopped down from the roof, over the hood, and swung back into the passenger seat. "Keep going, Goose. Take the first right turn that comes along. The ocean's just to our north. I can smell it now."

LINE OF DEMARCATION

"*Sí*, Mr. Jack."

After a quarter mile of the blind drive through the canes, Gustavo passed a road on his right. He hit the brakes, backed up, and made the turn. Far, far ahead, Jack saw a pinprick of daylight. It was the first light he'd seen at ground level in the three hours since they'd entered the cane maze.

"Yes!" he exclaimed, slapping the dash. "That's it. Up there we'll be out of the field. That will be the coast road." Amancia reached forward from the rear seat and squeezed his shoulder lightly.

It took another twenty minutes of slow bumping over dried mud ruts before the F-150 broke out into the open.

As soon as it did, a white Toyota Hilux pickup truck moved forward, cutting them off. Behind them, a second truck did the same thing, boxing them in.

An officer in a khaki uniform with a black beret emerged from the forward truck.

"The GNP," said Amancia from the back seat. "Guyanese National Police Force."

"Can we trust them?" Jack asked.

"Some of them," she said. "Certainly not all."

"We're in a Tiburónista vehicle. Hide the guns under the seat," Jack said immediately. "We need to let them know who we are and get them to take us to the embassy."

The officer approached his window with one hand on his holster. Jack could see two men from the Hilux behind them standing off at a safe distance, carrying MP5 machine guns with the muzzles pointed down.

Eager to show they weren't a threat, Jack made his hands visible to the approaching officer. As the man got closer to the hood, Jack saw him referencing a paper. The cop's eyes swiveled between the paper and Jack's face in the windshield.

He waved to his partner on Gustavo's side of the truck. The men in the back were ten feet behind the tailgate.

"You are Jack Ryan?" the officer called in a Caribbean accent.

"I am," Jack confirmed.

The officer pulled his pistol and aimed it at Jack through the window. "It's him!" he shouted.

27

GEORGETOWN PARLIAMENT BUILDING, GUYANA
1145

PRIME MINISTER GUTO CASTILLO WAS A MERE FIFTEEN MINUTES AWAY FROM TURNing a fretful morning into a fateful afternoon. Since the midnight call from Tiburón, he'd worked like a demon, consuming nothing but water, coffee, and Zoloft pills, his favored antianxiety med.

Manning the hardwired phones from the president's emergency operations office in the basement of the pink parliament building, he'd churned through the long list of ECLIPSE chores with only his chief of staff for help. Normally, he would have delegated most of it to an underling—but not today.

Before the sun had come up, hunched over his laptop as if the weight of history curved his posture, he drafted a declaration to the heads of the three coalition parties of the legislature and the commanding general of the Guyanese defense forces.

The decree—which he pictured under glass in a museum one day—told them in carefully crafted language that as the acting head of state, he, Prime Minister Augustus Bolivar Castillo IV, was officially declaring martial law across all of Guyana. In highminded prose, it cited the mutinous assassinations of Hugo Suárez and Alberto Quintero, the murderously rioting Tiburónistas, and the need to move with dispatch.

As acting commander in chief of the armed forces, Castillo had then woken the defense chief, ordering him to keep his forces garrisoned, since the internal strife was more a matter for the security services than the military, whose moves might, he suggested, alarm their international neighbors. With Romero still out of the country, he followed that with a call to the chief deputy of the Guyanese National Police, telling him to have the GNP block road junctions, close the airport, and enforce a twenty-four-hour curfew.

Quoting the very ECLIPSE order he'd written himself, he called the minister of home affairs to order all telecommunications systems offline, except for the hardwired phones that connected him to critical government nodes. Moments later, the switches and routers that controlled the backbone for cellular and landline communications in Guyana went dark.

As a final act, the prime minister ordered himself sequestered for safety in the basement of the parliament building. Castillo's only companion in the bunker was Sheila, his chief of staff.

Sheila poked her head through the door, startling him. "The guards have called on the intercom to say that the American ambassador, Sydney O'Keefe, is at the gate, Mr. Prime Minister."

For two seconds, Castillo held his breath and shut his eyes. He had been ducking O'Keefe's calls all morning, yet here she was, darkening his doorstop despite all his orders to shelter in place.

So American, he thought.

"No," he declared with a brisk shake of his head. "I won't receive her."

"Sir," Sheila countered, placing her finger on her narrow chin. "Is that wise? The ambassador is very insistent. She might well escalate matters. They're already upset about the Coast Guard boat."

LINE OF DEMARCATION

"Give me a second," Castillo said.

He took a sip of water. Sheila had a point. The fear he'd been fighting all morning was that with Khasif silent, the U.S. might intervene on its own, sending in the Marines. If that happened, what then?

"Sir?" Sheila asked while Castillo stared at his water glass.

His mind had wandered to a new thread, triggered by Sheila's suggestion that the American ambassador might escalate.

Was it too late? he asked himself. Could he switch sides and wash his hands of this whole thing? It occurred to him that he still had a way out. He could say that Tiburón was a vile scourge and that they were under pitiless attack from his murderous thugs. It seemed to Castillo that in such a light, his actions were prudent and just.

The alternate course—the one on which he was now embarked—was a minefield. What if he'd missed something? Romero and Morozov had told him that Jack Ryan was still at large, a loose string that might unravel his carefully controlled narrative.

The best course for now, he decided, was to leave his options open.

"Sheila," he said. "Tell the ambassador how sorry I am, but I'm simply too busy working the ECLIPSE orders. We are living through an extraordinary situation here. She must certainly understand that. Give her my most earnest apologies."

"Yes, Prime Minister."

Alejandro Romero, the only other government official with access to the secure operations center, strode in unannounced, passing Sheila as she left. His eyes were a lively blue, his cheeks smoothly shaved, his receding hair slick. In tribute to the historic moment, he wore his Guyanese National Police uniform with a black beret tucked in the crook of his arm. He blithely rolled a chair to the side of Castillo's desk and sat down.

"When did you get in?" Castillo asked irritably.

"An hour ago."

"How'd you get back from Costa Rica?"

"Venezuelan charter. Nongovernment. Don't worry."

It didn't surprise Castillo that Romero had sudden access to a Venezuelan plane. When the smoke eventually cleared, Romero's reward was to be the governorship of the newly established Essequibo province of Venezuela, where he'd be free to line his pockets in various protection schemes in league with his paymaster, Tiburón.

"Well?" Castillo asked. "Is ECLIPSE fully enacted?"

"Per your orders, Prime Minister, the airfield, ports, and roads have been closed. Phones are down, both landline and cellular. We have trusted men on patrol."

"They aren't questioning the orders?"

"No. I have handpicked police commanders manning all the critical spots. They are well motivated, of course. They've been provided the appropriate incentives."

"How can you be sure of all this without phone communications?"

Romero opened his khaki jacket to expose a large radio clipped to his shiny police belt. Its mic was attached to his epaulet. "We have radio antenna repeaters throughout the building. I have one of these radios for you, if you'd like."

The prime minister crossed his arms. "No, thank you. And Tiburón? Have you been in touch with him—personally?"

"Yes. I spoke with him and Morozov before I left Costa Rica. And I must tell you, there has been a development. It's why I'm here, in person. This is not something for the radios."

Castillo was annoyed with Romero's secretive manner. "Get to it. What?"

"We caught a spy. Up at the Orinoco staging base."

A cold pang struck Castillo. "When?"

"Last night."

The prime minister exhaled sharply. "Goddamnit, Alejandro. Who?"

"He was Tiburón's intelligence advisor, a former Colombian army colonel named Diaz. He killed a sentry on the barge and snuck away, swimming downriver, trying to escape. A Wagner man caught him rifling through the anti-ship-missile crates that are to go to the oil platforms."

"Good lord. Where is he now?"

"Morozov is keeping him on the yacht for interrogation. He's going to run Diaz through the SVR facial recognition systems."

"How long will that take?"

Romero shrugged. "You would have to ask Morozov."

The last thing Castillo wanted was to further implicate himself with direct communications to an SVR officer. But the mention of the Russian foreign intelligence service made him think of his own president on his junket in Abu Dhabi. "And what of Khasif?"

"President Khasif is out of the picture—at least according to Major Morozov. You haven't heard from him, have you?"

"No. No one has. But what does that mean?"

"You know as much as I do, Guto. I said exactly what Morozov said. 'The SVR is handling the president.'"

Castillo's Adam's apple bobbed when he swallowed. "If they assassinate him, it's going to hurt our case for legitimacy."

"I'm sure SVR has its ways. Whatever they are, it shouldn't matter to us. The president is a nonissue for the next forty-eight hours. Once we've established the new order, then at best, he's a president in exile. Powerless."

Castillo gulped water, then barked a request for coffee to Sheila.

"You should get some rest, Guto. You've had a long night. Everything is under control."

"Under control!" he exclaimed. "It's entirely possible we've been compromised."

"Perhaps. Perhaps not," Romero replied, shrugging.

"What about the Americans? Have they been in contact with you or your people?"

"With the defense minister away in the Middle East, I fielded a call from the U.S. Southern Command general in Florida. He offered help in battling the Tiburónistas. I assured him that we were more than capable of handling things ourselves."

"Did the American general mention the Coast Guard cutter?"

"He did. I told him that the Coast Guard sinking was the first shot of Tiburón's violence. The same thing I told Mary Pat Foley. I also mentioned that the Quintero and Suárez murders were contributing factors for ECLIPSE, just as you wrote in your decree. The Americans understand that. Oh, good afternoon, Sheila."

Sheila put the coffee on Castillo's desk, smiled, and left.

"What if they're lying?" asked Castillo when she was gone. "The Americans could be lulling you to sleep, baiting you."

"Baiting *us*," corrected Romero.

"Yes. That's what I meant."

Romero ran a hand under his chin before answering. "Well, one of the advantages of the advanced timetable was that we didn't provide any intelligence clues for the Americans to follow. I looked Mrs. Foley in the eye just yesterday. She may have her suspicions . . . but what can she really prove?"

"When the shooting starts, the Americans will want to defend their oil platforms."

"Oil platforms over which you, as acting head of government, Guto, maintain sovereign jurisdiction. If the Americans attempt to bring troops anywhere near us, it would amount to an invasion."

"The Yankees suffer no compunction at invading countries in South America, Alejandro. You know that."

LINE OF DEMARCATION

"Times have changed. With that Russian frigate *Gorshkov* steaming into the area, the Americans won't come. It would risk a war."

"Kennedy took the same risk during the Cuban Missile Crisis. President Ryan doesn't strike me as the type to shrink from a challenge."

"I don't know how much you know about navy ships, Prime Minister."

"Not much."

"The *Gorshkov* carries an arsenal of Zircon hypersonic missiles, for which American ships have no defense. That one frigate could literally sink an entire American strike group if the yanquis come. President Ryan knows that. He wouldn't risk his fleet. Not for a few oil platforms. Or a small country like Guyana."

"What if he doesn't send a fleet? What if he sends commandos or CIA people? If they get to the oil platforms, they'd have a beachhead they know we wouldn't strike directly. Even the Russians wouldn't strike those crown jewels."

"Exactly why we have men staged on Orinoco Reef. They'll take the oil platforms first."

The radio on Romero's belt growled with static. "Forgive me," he said, leaning back to squelch the noise. He fiddled with an earpiece, inclining his head while he listened.

"Give me two minutes," the head of NISA said into the mic. He turned back to Castillo.

"News?" asked the prime minister.

"Yes," said Romero, smiling widely. "Good news."

"What?"

"My men just arrested Jack Ryan, Jr."

Castillo shot him a hopeful glance. "Really? Where?"

"The sugarcane fields to the east. Ryan was taken in along with Quintero's wife and daughter. They were trying to make a run for the coast road in a stolen truck."

"Quintero's wife and daughter? But I thought the Tiburónistas . . ."

"I thought so, too. Somehow, his family wound up with Ryan. Should we bring them all back to Georgetown? You can question Ryan yourself if you wish to see if he knows anything."

While it would be nice to know how deeply Ryan's subterfuge went, it suddenly seemed safer to Castillo to make the man go away. He stared at his cuticles, clenching his jaw.

"Your orders, Prime Minister?"

Castillo looked up, pale in the artificial light of the underground room. "Alejandro. You can't bring Ryan to Georgetown. That would be foolish."

"Why?"

"Think about it. We've gone to great trouble to convince the Americans that Tiburón has been responsible for all the violence of the last twenty-four hours. That violence should include Ryan. Tragically, I'm afraid."

"You don't want to see what he knows?"

"Have your police unit deliver them to a remote Tiburónista camp. Then get out there to question him. You *personally*, Alejandro. Not one of your people. This is too sensitive. I want you to do it. That's an order."

Romero rubbed his forefinger and thumb together, making the hand gesture for *dinero*.

"I'm not going to pay you, Alejandro. I'm not Tiburón."

"No. I mean I have visits to make to my units, to make certain payments. Otherwise, we might start losing a few critical people. They need more motivation. You understand."

"Sadly, I do. How long will that take you?"

"I could get down to one of the Tib camps in perhaps three hours? Maybe four?"

"Fine. As long as Ryan stays in custody."

"I understand. But what about after I interrogate him? What do I do with him then?"

"That's the work you leave to the Tiburónistas, Alejandro. Let them finish him."

Romero raised an eyebrow. "Just to be crystal clear, sir, are you saying you want the Tiburónistas to kill Ryan? And Quintero's family?"

"It is sad," Castillo deflected, "that we have to endure such violence at the hands of a drug lord."

"So that's a yes, then? Kill them?"

"Yes, Alejandro. I want you to kill Ryan. Ensure his body is never found."

28

ORINOCO RIVER DELTA
1200

ZIP-TIED AT HIS ANKLES, WRISTS SECURED TO A STRAIGHT METAL CHAIR, DING COULD feel the heat rising in the cloistered air of the fifteen-by-twenty-foot enclosure beneath the yacht's stern.

Known as the lazaret, the space was just aft of the engine room. It was designed to store rich owners' water accessories—small dinghies, stand-up paddleboards, and other floating toys. From inside the yacht, it was accessed via a hatch in the forward bulkhead. At the rear, a garage-style transom door slid open to reveal a spacious swim platform just above the waterline.

It was off that swim platform, Ding assumed, where they would dump his body when they were done with him.

Caraza had started the interrogation with a baseball bat in his hand. One question after another delved into Ding's legend as Colonel Diaz of the Colombian Special Forces. Each was delivered with a sharp blow. Caraza hit Ding's kneecaps, hammered his shins, and took swings at his ribs.

He did not, however, touch Ding's head.

Vicious though he was, Caraza was deliberate in his choice of target, staying just below the neck. As much as Caraza hated Ding, it could only mean that Tiburón's loyal lieutenant had been ordered to keep Ding alive long enough to figure out who he really was.

Ding grimly held on to his legend as though it were the last rung of a ladder over a roaring fire. The moment he allowed himself to loosen his grip, he would die. From his weeks among the Tiburónistas, he knew their leader delighted in dismembering informants, feeding one limb at a time to the sharks that would inevitably gather off the *Gran Blanco*'s swim platform.

The lazaret's heat was awakening the rest of Ding's body. His head was pounding, his bones throbbing. They had him facing the closed garage door. He could see blood spatters on it.

His mind wandered, thinking about Tiburón. The drug lord had bragged how he liked to bring his family in from their mountain house outside Bogotá for long vacations on the yacht. Tiburón spoke often of his twelve-year-old son, Juan Junior, and his nine-year-old daughter, Imelda. Ding wondered when those kids would next drag their water toys through the blood-spattered garage door.

To stay sane, he tried to guess the time of day. With no outside light, he used the heat as a guide. It had been cool when they first strapped him to the chair around two a.m. Now it was hot.

He replayed the events of the evening. Morozov had arrived in a pressed shirt and gabardine suit pants. He inspected Ding with the mildly aggrieved air of an executive on a kinked factory line.

Using his smartphone, the Russian snapped pictures of Ding's face, maneuvering from multiple angles. Ding could only assume the SVR liked to keep a record of the spies they captured and killed.

Sometime after that visit—Ding couldn't be sure when—Caraza and Morozov returned together. Caraza rocked Ding's chair back to the floor and stretched a pillowcase over his nose and mouth. While the Tiburónista held the fabric in place with both arms, Morozov spouted questions in Slavic English while directing a high-pressure stream of water over the fabric. While Ding choked and sputtered, the Russian didn't bother with questions about his legend. He'd gone straight to the heart of the matter.

What's your name? Who is your handler? How do you report to him? Why were you at the docks? You are American, yes?

Ding had been trained in a waterboarding survival technique at the DoD's survival, evasion, resistance, and escape (SERE) school. The trick, the SERE instructors said, was to hold your breath and let the water flow unfettered through your nose while closing your throat.

Or, in the clinical language of their training manuals, to "block the posterior nasopharynx while keeping the lungs inflated."

Khalid Sheikh Mohammed, the captured al-Qaeda 9/11 mastermind, had invented the technique to frustrate CIA interrogators for weeks at a black site in Poland. In the twisted irony of counterintelligence, KSM's technique had now become doctrinal.

Though miserable, Ding sputtered his answers out as soon as the water stopped. *Diaz. Work for Tiburón. Caught the sentry making an illegal call, killed him, went to the docks to make sure the site was secure. Hate* yanquis*!*

Whether dream or reality, Ding had another hazy image after the waterboarding. Dripping wet, bleeding, bruised, and delirious, he recalled Caraza and Morozov looking at him under the harsh glare of a flashlight like surgeons at an operating table. He remembered the Russian touching his neck with two fingers, checking Ding's pulse. Soon after, he heard the helicopter engines spinning and fading behind the yacht.

"*Oye, americano,*" said the guard entering behind him, jerking Ding back to the present. Ding recognized the Colombian accent of one of Tiburón's long-serving bodyguards.

He raised his head unsteadily, peering through swollen eyelids. The guard stood between him and the garage door. He was holding something up to Ding's mouth.

"*Come,*" he said. Eat.

The guard pried Ding's bleeding gums apart and put a quarter of a protein bar in his mouth.

Swallowing a little food gave him a moment of clarity. He hadn't broken yet.

But that only meant things were about to get worse.

29

**SCARBOROUGH INTERNATIONAL AIRPORT, TRINIDAD AND TOBAGO
1430**

UNDER TOWERING CUMULUS CLOUDS, LISANNE RAN ACROSS THE YELLOW TARMAC, swinging the phone in her hand like a baton in a relay race.

"Mr. C.!" she shouted.

Her voice was swallowed by the UPS 767 hurtling down the parallel runway on its way back to Louisville. She upped her pace, hustling toward the open hangar, where the UPS loadmaster—a C-130 crew chief in the Kentucky Air National Guard—had deposited the Campus team's cargo pallets.

She saw John Clark by the fender of a flatbed trailer. Clark bought it shortly after they landed for two thousand dollars cash from a local freight company. He was guiding Chilly Edwards with hand gestures as Chilly backed their rented van toward the trailer's hitch.

Beyond them, Master Chief Moore, Mandy Cobb, and Army sergeants Marks and Mustafa were prepping to transfer the gear to the trailer.

The four "killer Jet Skis," as the team had dubbed the watercraft, were mated to metal plates with heavy wheeled casters, which theoretically made them rollable. Master Chief Moore and the sergeants had their shoulders behind one of the heavy monsters, shoving it up the trailer ramp like offensive linemen behind a practice sled.

"Mr. C.!" Lisanne shouted again as the 767 lifted off.

Clark was bent over the hitch, attaching a chain and slapping down the tongue latch. Raising his sunglasses to the crown of his head, he stood up and faced her. "Good. You're back. We have a ship?"

"Yeah," she said, bent over to catch her breath. She forced herself to stand straight. "*Helena* is already here. That ship off the rocky crest there. See it?" She pointed over the runway and out at the green Caribbean.

Clark lowered his sunglasses and squinted. Hazy on the horizon, he made out the awkward silhouette of a ship that appeared to have two swollen balls on its deck.

"Those lumps would be the LNG tanks, I guess." Before he could comment further, Moore and the sergeants lost control of the Jet Ski at the top of the ramp. Clark jumped on the trailer to stop it from rolling forward, where it could smash into the van, ruining everyone's day.

Once the killer Jet Ski was back in hand, Clark climbed down, rubbed the knee he'd banged, and looked out at the ship again. "Tell me, Marine. How the hell are we supposed to get all this heavy kit aboard? Did Jack's Puerto Rican captain have any genius ideas?"

"He did, actually," Lisanne said.

"I can't wait to hear this."

"The ship is shallow-draft. It can—"

Cutting her off, Clark turned and barked a half dozen commands at the team at the trailer ramp, telling them where to steer the second heavy watercraft. He shot Lisanne a look of aggrieved patience. "Shallow-draft is great," said the salty SEAL. "But that doesn't mean you can just drive a van and trailer onto it. We still need a crane with a port to load these things. And fast."

"No we don't," she countered with a grin.

Clark cocked his head. "Oh yeah?"

"Yeah. The *Helena*'s a converted landing craft. The captain told me that they land gas tanker trucks ashore. It's how they move propane from the tanks to shore-based island distribution facilities."

"You serious?"

"As a heart attack, Mr. C. The captain said we could just drive right up the ramp. He called it a 'ro-ro' ship, for roll-on/roll-off."

"I know what a ro-ro ship is," he grumbled. "But where does this captain propose to do the ro-ro'ing? In the loose sand on that beach over there? Driving through these shallow waves? Not like we have Seabees standing by to build a ramp."

"Don't need one. The captain said their usual roll-on/roll-off spot for Tobago is about two miles from here. He's steering *Helena* for it as we speak."

Ages ago, Clark had developed a philosophy he called Newton's Law of Military Operations. Its core tenet was that every bit of good news would be inevitably offset by an equal measure of bad. In his view, some other shoe was certain to drop. And given the good luck that they could get their massive weapons load afloat without delay, he worried it would be a size fifteen.

But that was for later. He turned to Lisanne. "Marine, you've earned yourself a reprieve from trailer duty. Hop in the van and call Gavin. Let's see if we have any worthwhile intel updates."

"Aye, aye, Mr. C.," she said. Before stepping into the van, she added, "Maybe our luck's changing." She then slid the door closed behind her.

"Precisely what worries me," Clark muttered into his sleeve.

30

SOUTHEAST OF GEORGETOWN, GUYANA
1600

THE CLOUDS DRIFTED IN FRONT OF THE LOW SUN, SPREADING A PATTERN OF GRIDDED shadows across the masonry wall behind Jack. He heard Tallulah and Amancia screaming.

Hours earlier, the cops had cuffed them, thrown them into pickup trucks, and driven them through the sugarcane fields to the deeper shadows of the rainforest. At the time, Jack had assumed they were heading for a remote police station—instead, they were dropped here, an old cattle farm that had been converted into a cocaine factory.

He'd reached that conclusion when he saw a half dozen native women sitting cross-legged in a circle, ripping coca leaves from their branches, shredding them, and dumping them in big blue vats. He could smell gasoline in the vats, which, when combined with sulfuric acid, boiled the shredded leaves down to the white paste that made their world go round.

Jack shifted his feet, rattling the chain cuffed around his ankle.

On the concrete floor, beneath layers of chicken droppings, he could see the rust marks of old agricultural equipment. Based on the skinny Holsteins he'd seen in the fields where the cane grass stopped and the trees took over, he believed he was locked in a cattle-holding pen with rust left over from milking machines. It was a decades-old building with a pocked concrete floor and a thatch roof layered over a wood frame.

A howl of pain pierced the air. It was Gustavo, roaring out in obscene Spanish. Jack didn't know what they were doing to the poor boy, but since Gustavo was a former Tiburónista, he was sure it was bad.

The sun fell below the towering trees in the distance and the shadow from the welded rebar at the front of Jack's cell disappeared. The chickens walked in front of the bars, sometimes threading the bottom section. They were clucking and pecking at seeds someone had spread on the mud.

Jack flinched when he heard Gustavo wail.

Wanting to pace, he got up. The chain padlocked around his ankle was secured to a ringbolt at the bottom of the masonry wall. The tether gave him a radius of five feet, short of the rebar where the chickens were. Now and then, the hens would scatter when a black rooster drove them off, taking the seeds for himself.

Suddenly and noisily, even the rooster flapped out of Jack's view.

Replacing him was the Tiburónista who'd locked Jack in the old milking stall while the cops kept guard. The Tib was dressed in ragged black jeans over Chuck Taylor sneakers and a stained T-shirt with a hole at the shoulder. He wore an oily red bandana over his scalp and a bowie knife on his belt that went the length of his thigh.

Whoever he was, the cops seemed to know him. After locking Jack away, they'd spoken to him for a long time in Spanish.

The Tib glanced at Jack. Another of Gustavo's wretched cries echoed off the concrete. Jack's guard turned his head to the cocaine processing area. The serious look on his face suggested to Jack that he was in charge of the prisoners.

As further evidence, the Tiburónista with the red bandana tossed a piece of white bread on the floor in front of Jack. He followed that with a plastic water bottle that bounced and rolled. Then he left. The rooster clucked back into view.

Jack squatted and picked the bread up from the chicken droppings. He ate two bites and gulped down the water.

He tested the strength of the chain by tugging on the ringbolt. Frustrated, he stared at the thatch ceiling over his head. It was slanted—higher where it abutted the masonry wall, lower over the rebar gate. He jumped straight up. The roof was too high, out of reach.

Jack sat and sighed. In his opinion, the cops had probably sold him to the Tiburónistas. He was a white man, an executive, someone with value. To them, he was live meat that would bring in a few bucks—not too dissimilar from the cattle that'd once been penned up in this hellhole.

When another of Gustavo's screams echoed off the wall behind him, he got up. The chickens were in and out of the rebar again. Seeing them do that and thinking about his status as a hostage gave Jack an idea. He looked up at the low part of the ceiling, gauging the distance. The more he listened to Gustavo, the more he wanted to try his idea.

Standing with his back against the wall, he slackened up the chain and took a deep breath. When he was mentally ready, he lunged forward in a leap, aiming a fist at a roof support. Just as his knuckles struck the wood, the chain at his ankle yanked him down. He fell to the dung-covered concrete floor with a slap to his ribs.

He stood, dusted himself off, and examined the two-by-four. He'd hit it pretty hard. He could see some exposed nails between it and the stringer above it.

After a few steadying breaths, he leaped again. This time, he felt the board give an inch. He pushed himself up off the floor and studied it. The two-by-four was at an angle.

He leaped a third time.

When his knuckles connected with the two-by-four, it sprung loose, bounced off the rebar, and clattered to the concrete floor. Jack had to lay on his stomach and stretch to reach it. He inspected the old wood. Two rusted nails stuck out from one end. Phase one of his plan was complete.

Phases two, three, and four would be much harder.

He squatted against the wall, tore the remaining Wonder Bread into little pieces, and tossed them near the rebar.

The dark rooster strutted into view sporting his big red cockscomb. He kicked around in the dirt and ate a few seeds. Then the rooster's onyx eyes spotted the bread. Jack shifted carefully to get a good grip on one end of the two-by-four. Going for the bread, the rooster strutted between the rebar into the cell.

Jack lifted the two-by-four over his head with the rusted nails pointing down. When the rooster came closer for more bread, Jack swung the board like an axe. The two nails skewered the rooster's ribs.

The bird squawked, kicked, and jerked, but the nails were sunk deep. Jack pulled the plank back and grasped the rooster's neck. It kicked furiously, scratching Jack's arms with long yellow talons. Partially out of self-defense, Jack wrung its neck, killing it.

He used one of the plank nails to poke a hole in the bird's chest. Dark blood gushed out, leaking to the floor. Jack dangled it by its feet, letting the blood pool. He threw the dead bird to the cell's darkest corner and gathered the stray feathers.

Phase two was done.

For the third phase, Jack lay on his side above the top of the blood puddle, bending his knees into a fetal position. He faced the wall, concealing the two-by-four. He hollered at the top of his lungs when he was in position, imitating the same painful wail he'd heard from Gustavo.

It was about twenty seconds before Jack heard the rebar gate squeak. Inert over the blood puddle, his back to the bars, Jack played dead, like he'd managed to kill himself. He was encouraged when he heard Red Bandana mutter under his breath, then rush across the concrete floor.

He knelt and reached for Jack's shoulder, trying to turn him over. Jack used the momentum of the roll to slam the butt end of the two-by-four into Bandana's face, breaking his nose. He palmed the back of the bandito's head and smashed his face into the wall. Stunned and disoriented, Bandana reached for his bowie knife.

Jack drove the two-by-four nails into the man's temple.

Bandana fell to his knees, clutching at the board, his eyes twitching in confusion. Jack stole the knife and sliced it across the Tib's throat. Human and chicken blood mixed on the concrete floor.

A quick search of Bandana's pockets revealed a set of keys.

One of them had a familiar commercial logo on it. It fit the padlock on Jack's leg.

On to phase four.

THE COP'S TOYOTA HILUX FOUR-BY-FOUR PICKUP WAS PARKED ON THE RUTTED ROAD at the edge of the camp. Sneaking around the backside of the cattle barn, Jack spotted the white vehicle through the thick, shadowed foliage. He crept up behind it.

Radio chatter echoed through the cab's open window. The cop was unmoving behind the wheel. Staying among the leaves, Jack crept farther forward and caught a brief glimpse of the cop in a side mirror. The officer was asleep.

A new scream from inside the old farm made Jack freeze. It was Tallulah. Strong as she was, she sounded terrified. He could hear Amancia screaming furiously at the Tibs. They catcalled and mocked her. Not good.

Jack pushed the horror out of his mind. He crawled along the tires, inching forward. When he was finally below the door, he rose to a crouch with the bowie knife in his right hand.

Springing up, he jammed the point of it into the soft flesh under the sleeping cop's chin. He pressed the point hard enough to draw blood but not do any real damage. In the same instant, Jack stuffed the red bandana into the cop's mouth with his left hand.

"Out," he said.

The cop was shaken. Jack jerked him out of the truck and forced him to the ground, then rolled him to his stomach. He took the cuffs from the cop's belt and wrenched his elbows back, locking the wrists. He reached into the cab and snapped up the MP5 from its holder on the transmission hump. He shoved the barrel against the back of the cop's head.

"Up," he said.

Shaking with fear, the Guyanese National Police officer went to one knee and then got up.

Jack poked the barrel against his back. "Go," he said.

Against the backdrop of Gustavo cursing, Tallulah screaming, and the Tiburónistas laughing, Jack shoved the cop along the back side of the old cattle building. He hurled him into the pen with the lifeless Tiburónista and the bloody rooster carcass.

The cop looked up at Jack, horrified, thinking he was about to join the chicken and the bandito in the netherworld. Jack smashed the butt of the MP5 into his temple, knocking him out before securing the chain around the cop's ankle.

In Jack's tactical view, a cocaine factory in the middle of a rainforest offered some advantages. It provided encircling concealment, plenty of explosive chemicals to set on fire, and drugs to keep the factory bosses high as a kite.

Using the MP5 to part the leaves at the perimeter, Jack got a look at Gustavo. He was between the blue barrels and a shipping container used as a trailer. Gustavo was tied to a chair, his side to Jack. The Tibs were bent over his shoulders, laughing and stabbing at him. Whenever Gustavo cried out, the Tibs smacked him.

Jack slowed his breathing and studied the scene. He'd trained with an MP5 out at Clark's Virginia farm. The weapon's biggest problem was its short range. Jack would have to leave his concealment to shoot the Tibs and avoid hurting Gustavo.

Tallulah screamed from the vicinity of the container. An unseen Tib yelled back at her. The scream had a plaintive, begging quality to it. Jack didn't think she would last long. Time to move.

He sprang from the brush and ran as close to the blue barrels as he could before firing. The moment one of the Tibs saw him, Jack shot him with a five-round salvo. The other three looked up in shock. Jack mowed them down with a sustained burst.

He sprinted full speed to get to the open end of the container. A big Tiburónista with a hanging belly was running out of it, his pants unbuckled and sliding to his hips, a shotgun in his hands. Jack loosed six rounds into him from a few feet away, shredding his chest.

When his ears stopped ringing, Jack could hear Tallulah sobbing.

She was zip-tied to a mattress. Her Cal Bears shirt was ripped. Her pants had been pulled down to her knees, exposing her underwear. Jack dropped the MP5 on the floor, stole a kitchen knife from a greasy table, and crouched by her side.

Without saying a word, he cut her loose. As soon as she was free, she pulled up her pants. Jack could see that her chin and neck were stained with fresh blood.

"Are you okay?" he asked, helping her sit up.

"I bit one of his ears off." She adjusted the bra under her ripped shirt.

Jack helped her to her feet. "Come on. Let's go get your mom and Goose."

She was a little wobbly, but recovered quickly. On her way out of the shipping container, she spit on the shredded Tib, who'd died with his pants around his ankles.

31

ORINOCO RIVER DELTA
1815

THE SHINY BLACK AGUSTA TREKKER HELICOPTER WITH THE TWO DIAGONAL GOLD stripes running over its fuselage flared over the *Gran Blanco*'s bow, then settled gently on the circular helipad.

Igor Morozov, who used the helicopter to look after his beer enterprise across South America and the Caribbean islands, stepped out of the back door carrying a metal briefcase. A *Gran Blanco* deck crewman escorted the Russian to the interior of the two-hundred-thirty-foot motor yacht.

"So," said Tiburón when the Russian joined him at the yacht's highest point—the glass-enclosed sky bridge above the main pilothouse. "You're finally back. Caraza here has been all over me. Are we going tonight or not?"

The Russian glanced at Caraza. Tiburón's security boss was slouched in jeans and a black checked shirt, picking at his fingernails with a knife.

Wearing his pin-striped suit pants and a white shirt with rolled sleeves, Morozov sat opposite, facing Tiburón. "I'm still waiting for final approval as to whether we go tonight or not," he announced.

Tiburón sneered. "Approval from who? I thought you had all the authority you needed when you took me down this path. Now you must have permission?"

"May I remind you, Juan Machado, that it was your mistake to shoot that American Coast Guard boat?"

Tiburón raised an eyebrow. Lounging on the sofa, he wore one of his tropical, short-sleeved linen shirts, four buttons open at the top, revealing a thick gold chain. "With the weapons you gave me," he said.

"Be that as it may. The timetable changed. There are other factors in play now."

"Your warship is close," Tiburón countered. "Our people are out on the barges. Romero has his men spread all over Guyana. Khasif is stuck in . . . in . . ."

"Abu Dhabi," Morozov finished.

"Raghead land. Whatever. We are ready. Tell him, Caraza."

Without shifting from his slouch, Caraza said, "Forty-five men on the barges including five of yours, ready with the boats. All the weapons are assembled."

"We will move when we hear from Moscow," Morozov persisted. He clicked open the clasps of the briefcase on his knees and lifted the lid. "While we wait, I have some information on the man we captured."

He removed a Chinese-made tablet computer and scrolled through it. "Before I begin," he added, "let me separate two issues. First, there is the tactical matter of whether we move tonight. That is a matter of logistics—and of that, I have some confidence."

"What have you got there?" interrupted Tiburón with a glance at the tablet.

LINE OF DEMARCATION

Morozov pressed on. "The other issue is whether we have been compromised. If we have, the spy may have nullified our strategy."

"Spy? What are you talking about? We caught a Colombian drug commando who doesn't give a shit about Essequibo or Guyana. Just drugs."

"Domingo Chavez," said the Russian flatly. He turned the tablet so Tiburón could see the screen. "This is the man you have locked in your lazaret."

Caraza leaned forward out of his slouch, looking. "Who is he?"

"An American operative." Morozov flicked the screen with his finger, shifting through digital dossier pages. "According to our SVR files, by way of Cuban intelligence, Chavez was an Army Ranger sniper. He volunteered for special operations in the CIA. Black operations."

Tiburón flexed his hand on his knee, squeezing it into a fist.

"On a personal note," Morozov continued, "Chavez is married to the former Patricia Clark. She is the daughter of this man, John Clark." The SVR major zoomed in on an old surveillance photo of Ding and Clark.

"John Clark," the Russian continued, "is a very close confidant of both Mary Pat Foley . . . and President Jack Ryan."

Morozov paused and stared at Tiburón. "As an intelligence officer, I will tell you the same thing I told Yasenevo. We find it concerning that Chavez and Foley have both been close to this theater in the past twenty-four hours. In addition, Romero informed me that the President's son, Jack Ryan, Jr., has been in Guyana on the pretense of a business venture. Romero had him arrested. Ryan escaped, killing several of your Tiburónistas."

It was too much for Tiburón. He stood and paced about the sky bridge. He raised his hands before his chest, his face twisted in rage. "They *know*?"

"I didn't say that," Morozov answered coldly. "We certainly need to work harder on Chavez. Our holistic intelligence analysis indicates that the Americans may suspect something. That doesn't mean we won't go tonight. The Americans haven't changed their force structure. We haven't detected any extraordinary communications out of the Pentagon. In other words, Tiburón, we might go tonight precisely *because* it is an accelerated timetable."

Tiburón stopped pacing. "So . . . what? We just wait now?"

"I'm expecting a signal from Moscow at any moment. But I have something else for you, Juan Machado—something you're going to like. Please, sit down."

The drug lord perched on the edge of the sofa, his hands twitching.

"There was an operation in Colombia, years ago," Morozov began. "The CIA called it RECIPROCITY. It involved the direct targeting of drug factories in Colombia, moving specifically against the Ernesto Escobedo cartel."

Tiburón's chest rose and fell more quickly.

"In one phase of that operation, we know from Cuban intelligence that the Americans launched an air strike against a family gathering in northern Colombia." The Russian raised his eyes to Tiburón. "That was the raid that killed your parents."

The drug lord drummed his fists on his knees.

"One of the men involved in that operation was Domingo Chavez," Morozov finished.

"*Aaach!*" Tiburón screamed, rising to his feet, rushing for the steps at the rear of the sky bridge.

"Wait!" barked Morozov. "If you go, I will call off the operation. Listen to me."

Tiburón froze at the door. He looked down at Morozov, breathing audibly.

"Let me question Chavez my way," the Russian argued. "Regardless of when we go, Moscow wants to know exactly what the Americans are up to. They're sending a specialist in chemical interrogation. He's on his way to Caracas, and I will bring him out to the *Gran Blanco*. His methods are foolproof. After I'm done with Chavez, he's all yours."

32

SOUTHEAST OF GEORGETOWN, GUYANA
1830

"STOP!" CRIED JACK.

Gustavo jammed his feet on the brake pedal of the police Toyota Hilux. It skidded to a halt on the dirt road. The sun had set, but there was still enough light to drive without the headlights. They were five miles away in the cane fields, rehashing an attempt to get to the coast road.

"What?" asked Amancia from the back seat. She'd been leaning forward, holding a soaked bloody rag to the back of Gustavo's bleeding shoulders. The Tiburónistas had been tattooing him with a red-hot nail and a ballpoint pen, scrawling LA *RAA*rat—across his shoulder blades in scraggly nine-inch letters. Fortunately, they'd only made it through the L, A, and R.

"I saw something on the roof of that little house we just passed," Jack explained. "Gustavo, back up."

Amancia's nephew threw the Hilux in reverse.

"That's enough," Jack said. "Tallulah, you see that thing by the chimney?"

"I see it," she said. "Is that a Starlink dish?"

LINE OF DEMARCATION

"That's exactly what I'm thinking."

By the chatter on the police radio, they knew the country was on full communications crackdown. They also knew every cop in the area was looking for them.

"We need to use that Starlink," said Jack. "Goose, pull into the driveway."

"Driveway" was a charitable description of the parallel wheel tracks between chest-high cane stalks. Gustavo proceeded slowly toward the modest house with the tin roof and clapboard walls. They were approaching its side. Jack saw another structure, a run-down barn with a midsize Mahindra tractor under the roof.

"Park next to the tractor," he told Gustavo.

"You can't just barge into someone's house," Amancia said, shooting him a look in the rearview mirror. "You're covered in blood. You're going to scare whoever lives here."

Jack tilted the rearview to check out his face. She was right. His cheeks were spattered with blood from the shootout with the Tibs at the cocaine factory. Worse, Bandana's blood left a wide dark stripe over his button-down shirt.

"Amancia, can I talk you into going to the front door? We need that data link, and you look the best of the four of us."

"Okay," she said as she stepped out of the truck. "I'll handle it."

Five minutes later, she waved them in under the bungalow's front porch light. Jack, Gustavo, and Tallulah exited the safety of the pole barn.

At the porch, they met a leathery, dark-skinned man with white hair, a freckled nose, and big calming eyes.

"This is Joshua," Amancia began. "He used to manage the cane fields here. I told him who we were. He understands."

"Please," he said with his hands folded before his belt. "Consider my home yours. The Tiburónistas are the scourge of the country. I will do anything to help you."

"Thank you," Jack replied. "Have other police been by here?"

"Oh yes, they've been by," Joshua said, smiling. "In fact, they said they were looking for an American . . . One that looked a great deal like you, if I may say, sir."

Jack grinned.

"Come in, please." The man ushered them indoors. "Let's get those wounds taken care of."

Once in the house, Jack heard a soccer game on low volume in the main sitting room. When he went to check it out, he could see that Joshua had been streaming a UK Champions League match through ESPN.

Joshua was standing behind him. "I never miss a match," he explained.

"You're streaming this through your Starlink, right?"

"Oh yes. It's coming through that box there. Good thing I have it, too. I don't know if you've heard, but the government has declared martial law and shut down all communications. Fortunately, they don't know about this."

"I need to make a call. Is there a way to do it with this?"

"Here," he said. "Use my phone. It's connected to Wi-Fi and then to the network through Starlink. I have a son in Philadelphia. We speak through this."

Jack looked at the cell phone. "I don't know how to thank you."

"You don't have to," Joshua replied. "Any friend of Alberto Quintero is a friend of mine. Go on. Use my bedroom, if you like, for privacy. It's through there."

Jack thanked him and entered the adjoining room. The bed was tightly made. There was a framed photograph of a beautiful Black woman on the dresser with a cross on a chain hung over it.

He dialed Lisanne's cell phone. It went straight to voicemail. Jack groaned audibly.

"Everything all right?" asked Joshua from the door.

LINE OF DEMARCATION

"I didn't get an answer. Just thinking through who to call next." Jack's eyes drifted back to the picture on the dresser.

"My wife, Beverly," Joshua said. "Died of a tetanus infection, two years ago now."

"I'm sorry," said Jack.

Joshua nodded. "Well. I'll leave you to it." He shut the door behind him.

Jack ran through the other numbers he knew off the top of his head. He tried Clark—same result, straight to voicemail. He called Howard at the office, who picked up.

"Hi, Howard, it's Jack."

"Hey, Jack. How's it going? I hear Gavin's come up with a few targets who might buy Athena. Are you back in the office yet?"

As a white-side manager, Jack couldn't go into the full extent of his current troubles. "Things are in motion," he deferred. "I'm still down in Guyana, working on it. Would you please put me through to Lisanne? She didn't pick up her office line."

"She's not in the office," Howard said.

"What about Clark?"

"He's out, too."

"Howard, would you please check the directory and get me Lisanne's sat phone number?"

Jack dialed the Iridium service number a minute later.

"Lis, it's me," he announced when she picked up.

"Jack! Thank God! Where are you?"

"I'm in Guyana, somewhere outside of Georgetown. Suffice to say, I missed my flight."

"What's going on? Why haven't you checked in? Are you okay?"

"It's a long story. But look, in case we get cut off, let me fill you in. There's some nasty stuff going on down here. Some kind of drug war or something. Place is falling apart. I got accidentally caught in the crossfire. I need your help with an exfil."

"Can you get to a beach?"

"Uh . . . yeah. I'm about fifteen miles from the coast, twenty miles south of Georgetown. I have a vehicle, but I may have to evade. Why?"

He heard her speaking with someone in muffled tones as she pressed her phone against her thigh to shield the microphone. Jack had seen her do it a million times in the office. She came back on the line. "I'll meet you on the coast twenty miles south of Georgetown. Three hours."

"What? How? Where are you?"

"I'm on the *Helena*, your ship, a couple of miles offshore."

TWO AND A HALF HOURS LATER, JACK SAT ON THE DESOLATE BEACH, HIS KNEES BENT in front of him, his hands in the sand behind him to prop him up. The wind had dropped, and the air was still. The surf glowed blue in the moonlight.

Amancia and Tallulah were lying on their backs, dozing. Gustavo sat next to Jack, staring at the stars, listening to the steady boom-crash-hiss of the three-foot waves.

Jack checked the GPS coordinates on the phone Joshua had given them, along with directions on how to get through the cane field. Though the blackout had cut off cell service, GPS still functioned. Confident he was at the exact spot he and Lisanne had worked out, Jack watched the waves carefully. She'd said the watercraft would be completely silent, which Jack didn't much believe.

Until he saw a big black lump ride straight up the water and slide in on the sand like a beached orca.

"Holy crap," he said to Gustavo as a man dismounted from the craft.

"There's another one out there," Gustavo replied, pointing.

Jack saw there were three more watercraft, bobbing and circling in the moonlight among the breakers like phantoms.

By the time he stood up, Master Chief Kendrick Moore had run up the sand.

"I'm told you all need a lift," said Moore, grinning. Against his camo-blackened face, his teeth were glaring.

"Yes, we sure do," Jack answered with a smile. "Is that thing you rode in on safe?"

"Safe?"

"Yeah. Are we really going to head out on the ocean in it, Chief?"

"Oh, just you wait, Mr. Ryan. You're in for the ride of your life."

DAY THREE

33

**GAS AND OIL PLATFORM MARLIN, GEORGETOWN BAY
0015**

JACK OPENED THE HEAVY WEATHER DOOR AND STEPPED ONTO THE GRATED METAL catwalk.

Behind him rose the two-hundred-foot-tall latticework of the oil derrick, glowing in the yellow safety lights. A hundred feet under his beat-up dress sneakers, he could hear the shallow sea sloshing against the boat deck, where Moore's killer Jet Skis tugged at their lines. The slanted orange hulks of the rig's six lifeboats were off his left elbow. In the other direction were the observation deck windows on the billion-dollar structure's living quarters.

Jack inhaled the salt air through his nose and blew it back out with his mouth. He wasn't all that interested in the industrial scenery of GOPLAT Marlin. He'd once been on a bigger one of these monsters in the freezing North Atlantic a few years back, helping take down a terrorist cell.

Rather, his eyes were locked on the green starboard bow and white stern lights of the LNG freighter *Helena* as she steamed back to San Juan. Technically, as the CEO of Athena Global Shipping Lines, Jack commanded that ship. Ever since talking Howard into acquiring the company, Jack had wanted to walk the decks of the *Helena*, Athena's flagship, and, for a moment, feel like a shipping executive. And yet, in the hurry to get busy with planning for Ding's rescue, he hadn't even gotten to board her.

With his elbows propped on the railing, he watched the *Helena*'s lights fade.

As Chief Moore explained over his shoulder during the thrilling, ghostly, high-speed ocean skim from the beach to GOPLAT Marlin, the Guyanese had closed all sea traffic within the twelve-nautical-mile territorial limit as part of the martial law order. The last thing the Campus operators wanted to do was surrender their tactical surprise advantage, so the *Helena* was already steaming back to San Juan.

Before leaving, she'd tied alongside Marlin's floating pier only for as long as it took John Clark to jog up the boarding ladder, flash a memo identifying himself as leader of a team of State Department Diplomatic Security Service (DSS) agents, and order the rig's massive cargo crane to off-load the military kit from the *Helena*'s bow.

The GOPLAT workers—a skeleton crew of American engineers and roughnecks—were happy to welcome the DSS agents aboard. They had tracked the radio traffic about the Tiburónista riots all over Guyana—and were suitably freaked out. To see a U.S. government security team with an army's worth of military equipment coming aboard was an answer to their prayers.

Emerging silently from the dark, Lisanne bumped Jack's elbow with her prosthetic and propped her good arm against the railing, looking out to sea. "Did you enjoy dinner? You ate enough."

Jack had eaten almost nothing besides whatever Amancia Quintero had culled from the land in the past twenty-four hours. At dinner on the rig, he took down half a meatloaf, a pint of gravy, and a quart of water.

He nodded with his eyes fixed on the green and white lights in the distance. "I wish I'd made it back in time to see the ship. Tell me, Lis. What was she like?"

"The *Helena*?"

"Yeah."

"She was . . . okay. The landing in Tobago had its moments. Chilly had to back the trailer onto the ramp and squeeze it between the LNG tanks."

"But the landing ramps worked as advertised?" he asked.

"Oh yeah."

"And her hull?"

"Her hull?"

"Yeah—did her hull look like it was in good shape?"

When the Athena deal first came together, Lisanne repeatedly listened to Jack exclaim about the shipping company's potential. In her view, the idea of walking the decks and playing captain was what really got him pumped up. She smiled knowingly at him. "She is a beautiful ship, Jack."

He remained silent.

She stood on her toes and kissed his cheek.

"By the way," she added, "I came out here to tell you that Mr. C. wants you to jock up. He's starting the briefing at twelve thirty. He's expecting the team to load up and go right afterward."

"Okay," Jack said, looking down at the boats bumping on the dock below his feet. "What do you think of the killer Jet Skis?"

"I had my doubts," she replied. "But they got you and the Quinteros back. Moore was as good as his word. What did you think of your ride out here?"

"I felt like I was on the back of a sea dragon coming in on that thing. I was half worried Tallulah would be tossed off the back. She had a pretty rough time in that Tib camp."

"Yeah. I heard. Poor girl. With the *Helena* almost over the horizon, our best option is to keep the Quinteros here. I put them up in one of the guest cabins. I got them sedatives from the rig's infirmary and dressed Tallulah's wounds."

"And the digital videotapes I gave you?"

"They're in one of the hotel-style safes in their room."

"Were you able to find a player for them?"

"No. Because it's not 1988."

Jack nodded his head once at that. "Do you think Tallulah will be all right? She's not much older than your niece."

"Well, like Emily, Tallulah is a gritty kid. I think she's going to be fine."

"And Amancia?"

Lisanne looked out at the dark sea. She'd been shocked at the condition of the two Quintero women when Jack first led them aboard. The daughter's face was as scratched and bruised as if she'd taken on a tiger. Amancia looked better physically, but her eyes were red, her complexion pale.

"I think Amancia is in shock from the loss of her husband and home," she said. "I know she's grateful to you for safely getting her out of the country. She kept saying she would be dead otherwise. I'm hoping the pills I gave them will let the two of them sleep."

"Yeah. They need it. How about Gustavo?"

"He's giving Mandy, the chief, and Cary Spanish lessons, since they're all relying on their high school coursework. While you were napping, he briefed us on Tiburónista tactics, telling us what to expect up at that river barge and yacht where Ding is." She gently touched the rooster scratches on his forearm. "My turn. How are you doing?"

Jack clasped his hand around hers and held it at his side. He took another long look at the green and white lights on the horizon. "I'm fine. Just thinking about Ding."

She put her head on his shoulder. "Hey, no one would think less of you if you sat this one out. You've had a rough forty-eight hours. Sure you're ready?"

"Lis," he answered. "This thug, Tiburón—did he really lose his parents in that old CIA op when my dad was still the deputy director?"

"That's what Clark told us."

"Then there's no way I'm sitting this one out."

"ALL RIGHT, PEOPLE, LISTEN UP," CLARK BEGAN.

He was standing in front of two rows of computer monitors, leaning against a console of lights and switches in a black Kühl quarter-zip and faded jungle camo pants. They'd assembled in the rig's control room. Since there was no active drilling or off-loading, the rig foreman was fine with letting Clark have the run of the place.

The two-hour-old satellite imagery of Tiburón's Orinoco river delta base showed Tiburón's yacht moored at the docks behind the floating barracks barge. The tractor-trailer was near the small-boat docks. Clark studied the image for a moment, then looked out at his crew.

They were standing, leaning, or straddling chairs, facing him. Moore, Cary, Mandy, Jack, and Jad were dressed in black tactical pants and jungle combat overshirts with pistol belts. Chilly wore his regular polo and jeans with his Glock in a leather hip holster. Each of them held a black lightweight Kevlar helmet with night vision devices, NVDs, snugged to the brackets.

"Before we get into the recovery plan," began Clark, shifting on his feet, "I'll let Master Chief Moore outline the available equipment. The floor is yours, Chief."

Kendrick Moore stood and folded his hands neatly above his belt buckle. "All four amphibious assault craft have fresh hydrogen charges. They're waiting at the boat dock under the platform."

He gestured toward a monitor with a nautical chart. "The Orinoco river delta where Ding last reported is a hundred miles from here. We've got enough battery capacity to ride up at about eighty knots the whole way. You won't even have to steer—the skis are programmed with the ingress route." He took a moment to grin. "Just make sure you stay strapped. The skis will come back for you if you fall off, but you don't want to hit the waves at eighty knots."

He cleared his throat and went on. "Now, including the drop for Jad on overwatch on this eastern barrier island, here, that will make our time-on-target zero-two-thirty. To activate the egress route on the Jet Skis . . ."

Leaning against the console behind Moore, Clark felt his satellite phone rattle on his webbed belt. He nodded at the chief to continue and stepped into the gentle breeze flowing over the oil platform's outer deck. Seeing that it was Mary Pat Foley calling, he strode down the catwalk to the round, spacious helipad for extra privacy.

"So you're in position?" she asked as his boot soles struck the grated metal. "You're on the *Helena*?"

"Hang on." He walked to the curved edge of the helo pad. "We're in position, yeah. But we had a slight change of plans."

"Uh-oh."

"I think we're okay. We caught some static from the Guyanese navy saying they'd closed their territorial waters to all shipping. We hustled to off-load everything to Marlin—the oil platform closest to the Orinoco river delta. The ones to the east of us are both still under construction."

Mary Pat waited a few seconds before answering. "Okay. I suppose staging from Marlin is a reasonable seaborne approach, since you couldn't have gone into Venezuelan waters anyway."

"Correct. And we didn't want to make a fuss and alert any government officials. As Sydney O'Keefe said, Tiburón has access that runs pretty high. So we sent the *Helena* back to avoid tipping him off."

"Good call."

"In the end, I'm glad we're here. Most engineers and roughnecks on this thing are American. They say they've got another fifteen or so staying ashore at their operating office."

"They don't have any clue what you're about to do, do they?"

"Negative. I told them we would be patrolling, making sure no Tiburónistas approached the rig."

"Good."

"But it begs the bigger question, M.P. There are a lot of Americans down here in Guyana. The President may want to get a real security force in here."

"I'm in contact with him. He's asked us to put together contingency plans, but we don't want to escalate unnecessarily. We need to keep Guyana on our side of the ledger, strategically speaking."

Clark's eyes swept the moonlit sea. In the latter part of his SEAL career, boarding and securing offshore oil platforms had been a standard mission profile. Now here he was doing the reverse, launching from one.

"Well," he said. "As to the strategic issue, I'm starting to wonder if this isn't something bigger."

"Meaning?"

"Meaning this surge in drug violence is exactly the kind of thing we've envisioned with a local TALON proxy. The Russians might be using the Tiburónistas."

"The Russians certainly don't want Guyana to start pumping natural gas out of the ground and screw up their hold on Europe. Still, our intel says they'd want to use Venezuela to provide a shield of legitimacy. We haven't seen that. Political and military communications out of Caracas are normal. Russian communications haven't displayed any anomalies."

"I thought the Venezuelan army deployed some units to the Essequibo River. That's an anomaly."

"They've put a few tanks along the Essequibo. But it's not a large force—and DIA says they're not moving. As far as Sydney O'Keefe can tell, this really is Tiburónista drug violence breaking out all over the country."

Clark was pacing the perimeter of the helipad, trying to estimate the size of the waves below. "So you believe the Guyanese intel guy you met?"

"Romero?"

"Yeah, him. You buy his story that the Coast Guard sinking a few miles from where I'm standing was Tiburónistas running wild? I thought you didn't like the guy."

"I don't like him. Part of me thinks he was happy to see us get burned. Maybe he's a secret America hater—I don't know—but I don't have any proof that he's plotting a coup."

"What are we hearing out of our embassy?"

"Long story short, Sydney doesn't trust the guy in charge right now, Prime Minister Castillo. He's declared martial law and cut off all communications. The national police force is running the country."

"What about their defense forces? Who controls that?"

"Castillo does, since they've declared this emergency. So far, the prime minister is well within his right, since President Khasif isn't around. Syd said he's following their emergency contingency plan to the letter."

"Jack briefed me on the crooked cops and the assassinated Guyanese officials. We've got the dead interior minister's wife and daughter with us."

"Wait—what? How on earth did Quintero's family end up with you?"

"Jack was with Quintero and the attorney general when the hit happened. The minister told Jack to get out to his house and protect his family. Jack did. He also collected some tapes that might implicate government officials. Either way, the family helped him get out of Guyana safely."

Mary Pat took a few seconds to process that. "Did Jack give you any usable intel? Or Quintero's wife, for that matter? What are these tapes?"

"We don't have the equipment to process the tapes here. In a nutshell, the wife fears Tiburón's corruption may reach the top of the government. The tapes have something to do with that. But she also said her husband had a lot of faith in President Khasif. Seems to me, if O'Keefe thinks Castillo is shady, then we should be getting Khasif's ass back here right now."

"I agree. Khasif and key members of his cabinet are on some OPEC junket in the Middle East. They're a guest of the Emiratis, incommunicado."

"Who's ever incommunicado these days? The timing sounds rather . . . convenient."

"Agreed. That's why I've ordered a SOCOM unit to find Khasif."

Clark looked up the shaft of the mighty oil derrick, noting the strings of cables, pipes, and drill shafts hanging among the massive steel girders. A ladder went up the side, all the way to the top. "This big GOPLAT I'm standing on was built by an American company. Why not get a Marine QRF spun up right now to secure our interests?"

"That's exactly why I want to get to Khasif. Castillo has formally refused our help. If we send a quick reaction force there, we're basically invading Guyana."

"One man's invasion is another man's security action . . ."

"Said Vladimir Putin. If we send in troops, Prime Minister Castillo could reach out to Venezuela, who could use it as a pretext for the real invasion they've always wanted. Then what? We escalate, the Russians escalate . . ."

"I'll leave the geopolitics to the eggheads. But since you mentioned the Russians. Did that frigate get to Cuba yet?"

"We don't know. The Office of Naval Intelligence last had her about three hundred miles east of you. She went dark and killed all her radars and communications."

"Uh-huh. And those Russian charter An-124 aircraft in Havana that came over from Central Africa? They still there?"

"Yes, two of them. But we don't know anything about the cargo. They've spread netting over the planes. There's an army helo there, too."

"I know I'm the knuckle-dragger here, Mary Pat, not the analyst . . . but I have to ask: You still believe this is limited to a drug war?"

Mary Pat unleashed a ragged sigh. Over the thousands of miles of the satellite bounce, it transmitted to Clark like static.

"Listen, John, you've got enough on your plate. Just get Ding back. Given his time with Tiburón, he'll have the best intel. He'll know what's happening down there."

"Yeah," said Clark, looking down at the bristling black Jet Skis below. "But if Ding's intel is that this is a Crimea-style Wagner op where the Russians and Venezuelans use Tiburónistas as proxies, then we may be a day late and a dollar short."

"Stay on Ding; we'll reassess when you get him."

Clark tilted his head back and studied the three-quarter moon. "I wouldn't have it any other way," he said.

34

RUSSIAN FRIGATE *ADMIRAL GORSHKOV*, ATLANTIC OCEAN
0025

"ARE WE IN HELICOPTER RANGE YET?" ASKED CAPTAIN FIRST RANK MIKHAIL Krokhmal.

He stood just inside the watertight door, bathed in red light. A tall man with wide shoulders, he was forced to incline his head and angle sideways to keep from hitting the maze of cables, pipes, and valves in the frigate's combat information center, CIC.

The lieutenant at the strike-plotting computer terminal manipulated a trackball. "We're not yet in helicopter range. But that depends, sir, on, on . . ."

"On what?" shot Krokhmal, baring his teeth.

"I don't know how much time on station, sir," stammered the mortified lieutenant. "We're two hundred miles from the operating area you asked us to plot. The helo can make it there and back, barely, but it depends on how long it needs to stay in the area. We haven't worked with an Mi-8M before, and it has the heavy weapons pylons, sir, which might alter its range."

The captain scowled, but said nothing.

What was it with the Northern Fleet admirals in Polyarny? Why in hell hadn't they specified what exactly the helicopter was to do? All they'd told him was that the Russian army helicopter was to hoist up a squad-sized unit of troops. What troops? And why was the heavy bird loaded down with a pack of Shturm anti-tank missiles?

Krokhmal bristled at being kept in the dark. Northern Fleet command could trust him with this fearsome war machine that could destroy half the planet with the push of a button. But they refused to enlighten him on why he should send a heavy helicopter gunship out to an uninhabited reef at 0300 on the dot.

To make matters even more confusing, Polyarny told him to stay at battle stations. They specified that he was to keep his Zircon hypersonic missiles on standby. They even went so far as to order him to put the ship in emissions control level Alpha, cutting him off from normal fleet radio traffic. In addition to keeping his air and surface search radars cold, he couldn't use his encrypted satellite radio to communicate.

Captain First Rank Krokhmal always believed that when he was senior enough, the orders that made little sense to him as a junior officer would become much clearer. Now he confirmed to himself once again that however high one got, the orders from the next rung were steadily more obtuse.

He glared at the lieutenant who sat in front of the strike-plotting terminal. Though he knew they were necessary, Krokhmal had a puritan disdain for automated systems like the strike-plotting terminal. When he was a watch officer in the CIC at this lieutenant's tender age, he possessed nothing but a maneuvering board, parallel rulers, reduction tables, and a slide rule to calculate weapons trajectories.

The lieutenant at the terminal pleaded his case. "Captain, I can be more precise if the helo is going in a straight line out and back again . . . or if it is to stay on station for an extended period. I just need to know how long."

The captain couldn't quite begrudge the question, since he wondered the same thing. "Assume an hour loitering time on station," he growled.

If the geniuses in Polyarny couldn't accomplish whatever they wanted from this visiting gunship in an hour, then they'd just have to give him more information.

"Yes, Captain," said the lieutenant. "Assuming we stay at flank speed—"

"Have I said otherwise?"

"No, sir. At continued flank speed . . . then we should be able to launch the helicopter in about . . . thirty minutes."

The captain knew the CIC watch officer had only repeated the information coming from the computer. But since Polyarny had told him to keep his missiles warmed up and his men at battle stations, he couldn't discount the prospect of trouble ahead. Could the hour really be at hand? Would he finally get to use his vessel in combat in an actual naval engagement?

In that unlikely event, once the shooting started, all the fancy electronics in the world could fail them. He'd read a Kremlin analytical paper that said Americans had been developing an electromagnetic pulse weapon, an airburst bomb dropped from a P-8 Poseidon patrol plane that could fry every circuit within a hundred kilometers. And here he was, just a hundred eight clicks from Florida. What if they lost all their fancy electronics?

He glared at the lieutenant. "How can you be so sure of the helo range?"

"Sir, I'm reporting the solution from the strike-plotting system. At present course and speed, with one hour of loiter time, we should be able to launch the helicopter in twenty-nine minutes. You can see it on the display here, sir."

Krokhmal wouldn't lower himself to check the monitor. He kept his eyes locked on the junior officer's smooth face. "I want to see the hand calculations, Lieutenant. We should double-check everything by hand."

"Yes, sir."

"Bring your work to me as soon as you're finished. Shouldn't take you more than two minutes. And no calculators. I said *by hand*."

"Yes, sir." The lieutenant knocked a young seaman in the upper arm, who hustled off for a paper and slide rule.

Krokhmal turned to leave through the secure hatch.

"Where shall I deliver the calculations, when I'm done, Captain?" asked the officer. "To your cabin, sir?"

"*Nyet*. To the flight deck. I'm going to make sure these army pilots aren't as unprepared as our CIC watch officers. We are at battle stations, gentlemen, emissions control condition Alpha. This is not a drill. Act like it."

35

PARLIAMENT BUILDING, GEORGETOWN, GUYANA
0145

PRIME MINISTER CASTILLO SCRAPED THE LAST OF THE LATHER FROM HIS CHEEKS while studying his eyes in the mirror. They looked good, he thought. The whites were white, the irises hazel. The drops Sheila had brought in when she'd gone to get fresh clothes for him had done the trick.

He splashed cold water on his face and dabbed it with a towel. He was dressed in a starched shirt, black double-breasted suit, and solid black tie. Though a bit funereal, he judged the look solemn enough to mark the gravity of the address he would soon give.

When he returned, Sheila was near his desk. She'd brought in a video technician, who set up a camera on a tripod. Cords stretched away from it. Given the deteriorating security situation, Castillo had told her he wanted to be ready to address the country.

"I want a row of Guyanese flags as a backdrop," he said. "Have someone get upstairs and bring down the ones from my office."

"Yes, Prime Minister," she agreed.

"Will the communications blackout interfere?" he asked the technician.

"No, sir. This is going out over broadcast TV. As soon as you tell us, Prime Minister, we will be live over every VHF and UHF television channel."

"I know about broadcast. What about data transmission? YouTube, satellite, all of that?"

"Sir, we'll simulcast on the satellite band and stream over our internet channels. People in Guyana might not be able to stream it—but the rest of the world will."

"Perfect," he said.

"I've alerted the media as well," said Sheila. "They know it's coming."

Castillo stood before the desk with his eyes on the camera lens. The global powers that be—the Americans, the Russians, the Europeans—would all soon be looking at those eyes.

"Nice suit," said a male voice. "Very . . . presidential." Castillo twisted his head to his right. Romero came in, still wearing his Guyanese National Police uniform, though rumpled from his travels. The intel chief removed his black beret and found a chair.

"Leave us," Castillo said to the technician and Sheila. They both hurried out.

Running his blue eyes over the lights and the boom mic extended over the desk, Romero nodded approvingly. "Looks like you have everything set up. For when the moment arrives."

"Yes."

"I would like to see the speech, Prime Minister."

Castillo hesitated. Romero worked for him formally—he'd even appointed the man to the job. For an instant, Castillo considered telling his crooked security czar that he couldn't preview the declaration he would read to the nation as soon as Morozov gave him the word.

But he reconsidered. As Castillo saw it, Romero had far too much sway with Tiburón, and it wasn't worth upsetting him. He pulled the tri-folded paper from his jacket and handed it over. The intelligence chief spent thirty seconds reading it, his eyebrows arching over some of the flowery phrases.

"Well. I suppose it will do," Romero announced.

"Thank you for your opinion, Alejandro."

"I like the part where you say that the druggies who killed President Khasif are from Tiburón's Pakistani distribution arm. Given Khasif's religion, accusing the Muslims will help play down the conspiracy rumors."

"Morozov gave me that wording. I hope it's true. Has he given you an update on Khasif's . . . status?"

"Morozov said his SVR friends are coordinating it. They're building the disinformation campaign, laying a path for the Pakistani heroin angle. They'll filter out the news through Al Jazeera as soon as it happens. It will hit the wires in a few hours."

Castillo frowned. "I'm worried about General Nirani. He's called ten times."

"You ordered the defense forces to stay in garrison. I haven't seen them on the streets."

As the acting head of government, Castillo employed the armed services. But Nirani, the army's commanding general, didn't like being told to stand down when Tibs were running roughshod over the country. Castillo told the general that activating the armed forces would enflame the Venezuelans.

"Nirani keeps asking to speak to Khasif directly," Castillo noted. "When I tell him we *all* want to speak with Khasif directly, he sounds like . . ."

"Like what?"

"Like he doesn't believe me."

"He doesn't have to believe you. By dint of the constitution, he has to obey your orders and keep the army out of this."

Castillo grimaced and looked away. He didn't like the idea that the army's general staff chairman didn't believe him. He said as much to Romero.

"Well, you're the commander in chief. You could just fire him. Put someone you like in the job. You're going to need to do that anyway."

"The optics of that would be terrible," Castillo said. "The U.S. ambassador, Sydney O'Keefe, is already hounding him about the need to protect American citizens. I get the sense he agrees with her."

Romero shrugged and changed the subject. Political opinions bored him. "Essequibo is well in hand."

"Is it?" Castillo asked. He was anxious for some reassuring news. "What's it like there?"

"Essequibo is on fire, as planned. The Tiburónistas are being Tiburónistas. By the way, I found the part of your speech declaring a new relationship with Venezuela to help secure the Essequibo violence particularly moving." Romero smirked.

"I'm still worried about what the Americans might do," Castillo responded. "Let's not forget—you lost Ryan."

"*We* lost Ryan," Romero snapped. "For the moment, anyway. He killed one of my officers, which gave me a reason to arrest him. I might even be able to build a felony charge, since he evaded arrest. You don't need to worry about Ryan. He could turn out to be an insurance package against the Americans."

"I might accept that explanation, Alejandro, if you had him in custody."

"He'll show up at the embassy. Given the security lockdown, it's the only place he can go. When he approaches it, my people will arrest him. Don't worry."

How unbelievably naive, Castillo thought. He knew how tenuous an operation like this could be. History was riddled with failed coup attempts. *If you're going to shoot at a king, you'd better kill him,* went the saying. And here he was, taking a shot at two kings—Khasif and the President of the United States, who had personally built a strategic alliance with Guyana.

"What about that man Tiburón caught?" Castillo asked, his fears of an American backlash in full swing. "Shouldn't we worry about him?"

Romero crossed his legs. "Oh, him. I have some good news there. The SVR has identified him. He's an American spy. His name is Domingo Chavez. A CIA officer, they think."

Castillo's eyes widened. He nearly came out of his chair. "Alejandro, you fool, how could that possibly be good news?"

"*Tranquilo*, as our Latin friends say."

"You just confirmed he's an American spy. How can I be *tranquilo*?"

"According to Morozov, Chavez has a history of operating in the region. He was one of the CIA people who went after Escobedo years ago. That shows that he works in counternarcotics—people like that don't spy on Russians. They only care about drugs getting into the U.S."

"You can't know that. This Chavez person was at the Tiburón base for weeks. He's surely seen the Wagner people, perhaps even Morozov himself. Hell, Alejandro, he may have seen you on one of your visits up there. He may have reported it."

"Well, he's getting the shit kicked out of him right now in the bottom of Tiburón's yacht. He hasn't confessed to working on anything other than drugs. No one could put up with the beatings he's been getting."

"Obviously, Alejandro, he could be lying."

Romero shook his head and frowned. "Now you are in my professional realm, Prime Minister. If he has given the Americans any valuable information, the Russians will find out. They can break anyone. After that, Tiburón will feed him to the sharks, limb by limb."

Castillo clenched his jaw and lowered his eyes, picturing the hell of an interrogation at Tiburón's hands. He shuddered. "From here, timing is everything. Are we sure the Tiburónistas and Russians are ready?"

"Tiburón's yacht left the Orinoco delta about an hour ago. Morozov wanted it to be off the Essequibo coast to help sell the idea that all the violence is driven by Tiburón. I assume you like that idea."

Castillo sniffed. "Yes. I suppose. And the barges?"

"The Wagner team leader, Zuka, reported that the men on the reef are ready to take over the oil platforms."

"I don't suppose we have any intelligence on what the Americans are doing?" he asked Romero.

"I put a call into Mary Pat Foley's office and spoke to a watch officer. I told him to relay to her that we are cracking down on the Tiburónistas and that we'll bring the people that sunk their Coast Guard vessel to justice."

"I hope that's enough," Castillo said.

Romero reached inside his khaki uniform jacket and offered Castillo a long cigar.

"I don't smoke."

"A pity," Romero answered. "These are Venezuelan."

36

ORINOCO RIVER DELTA
0200

JACK REACHED UP TO HIS NVD LENSES AND WIPED AWAY THE SALT SPRAY. STRAPPED to the hulking Jet Ski's seat, his hands were free enough for him to take his time polishing the lenses.

It had been the oddest sensation. He'd raced over the dark Atlantic swells at eighty knots in complete silence. Weighed down by his own body and Jad clinging behind him, the solid-hydrogen-powered machine was heavy enough to plow smoothly through light chop. Occasionally it went airborne, leaping between swells for a fraction of a second, then steadying up on the GPS course without so much as a vibration. When it was aloft, it was in what pilots call *ground effect*. The low, wide flare on either side of the ski acted as wings, letting the machine ride a compressed cushion of air.

He planed over the water so quickly that he could barely hear the tiny wake that stretched away behind him like a dashed line. His helmet and headphones muffled the wind.

The dim green instruments behind the windscreen kept him apprised of their progress. On one screen he could see the four killer skis spread out in a diamond, like a formation of attacking jets.

"Tempest Three," crackled Moore's voice in Jack's helmet. *"You're at overwatch delivery point."*

"Roger overwatch. Departing course," Jack replied into his lip mic. Jad Mustafa, strapped in behind him, tapped Jack on the arm, letting him know he heard the call. "Switching to manual. Departing the pattern," Jack said into the radio. Every time he opened his mouth, wind ruffled his cheeks.

Moore answered with a double click.

Jack looked down at the GPS display. The encrypted satellite link that kept the stealthy skis connected to each other showed Moore in the lead as Tempest One. Following a hundred yards behind the chief was Clark, Tempest Two. Off to Jack's left was Chilly Edwards riding with Mandy Cobb as Tempest Four.

Jack toggled the switch that took him off the preprogrammed course. Then, as the chief had instructed during their brief training session at Marlin, he grasped the handlebars.

The ski slowed to seventy, sixty, fifty knots. Jack followed the automated navigation cursor to a southerly course. He watched a separate display showing underwater terrain features as the depth ticked from ninety feet to forty. A threat console near the base of the handlebars blinked red and displayed an arrow. It was the ski's UMBRA stealth system kicking into gear. It told him that a surface search radar coming from the Venezuelan shore had painted Jack's ski with radio energy. The UMBRA pod buried in the ski's electronics bay picked it up and emitted a reciprocal wave, canceling out the ski's radar signature.

Silent on the water, Jack approached the delta island they'd selected for overwatch. He killed the throttle when he saw the first few shore rocks appear in his NVDs. The ski drifted to a stop. Jack and Jad stayed still, surveying the coast and the ocean waves. Jack smelled the seafoam that hissed around the ski's wide hull.

"I see the beach," said Jad, pointing.

Jack followed the finger and soon saw a curved stretch of light green in his NVDs. From here, he could see the white line of breaking waves.

"The breakers are a little higher than I thought," Jack said, worried about safely beaching the craft. The plan was for Jad to get to shore dry, lest he risk fouling his sensitive sniper optics.

"Are you kidding me?" Jad answered, sounding like the Southern California surfer he was. "This is going to be epic."

"You have any advice on how to get in there?"

"You want me to drive?"

"No. I want you to hop off this thing high and dry. What's the best way to approach?"

Jad studied the waves through his NVDs. "See that flat line about ten degrees east?"

"Yeah, I see it."

"That's a clean break. Ride up the back at a diagonal as soon as one is about to crash. Then wait in the trough. When one of these big suckers rises up behind us, hit the gas—or hydrogen or whatever. Keep running at a diagonal and we'll squirt right into a barrel."

"Jad, we're not going for style points here. I'm just trying to get you on the beach."

"Who's the surfer here, Jack?"

Jack didn't answer.

Jad gripped him from behind by the biceps. "Don't worry, boss. I'll watch the waves back here and move your arms like handlebars. When I squeeze tight, it means speed up. When I pull back, it means slow down. I'll get you sliding right up onto the sand."

Jack watched the steady rhythm of waves rise, then turn into white foam. At the barrier island, he could see two peaks. Jad's mission was to thread them and gain a visual on the Tiburónista base on the other side of the land. "What about getting back out to sea?" he asked.

"You're in for a hell of a ride," Jad replied.

"What's that mean?"

Jad chuckled. "Dude—this thing has reverse, right?"

"Yeah. It has a water-jet thrust reverser."

"Cool. So snap it into reverse as soon as I get off. Do a one-eighty in the white chunder at the beach. Once you're pointed out to sea, wait for a wave to break. As soon as the foam is rushing in, charge straight out. Another wave will be coming by then. Ride uphill before it crests. Should be easy with all the speed this thing has."

Jack looked at the water, trying to visualize how that might go. If the sun were high and he was on vacation, he would appreciate the thrill of it. As it was, he simply wanted them to get back on mission and extract Ding. "Fine," he relented. "Let's get it done."

Jack felt Jad gripping his upper arms. Jad coached him onto the back of a wave, which rose twenty feet. Feeling Jad's tug, Jack slowed, waiting. When the wave surged toward the island, Jad squeezed Jack's arm. They stopped in a low trough of water. The view of the island disappeared; black water rose all around them.

"Okay, man," Jad said. "We got a big bastard coming up behind us. Steer the nose a few more degrees to the right. That's it. Be ready now . . ."

Jack felt the undertow pulling the ski back. Jad squeezed his arms lightly and told him to add just enough power to keep his position steady. Then, suddenly, Jad was crushing Jack's biceps, telling Jack to go.

He twisted the throttle and jerked forward, ripping across the wave at a diagonal. The rising water lifted the ski as Jack cut across it. A moment later, the world tunneled in.

"Woo!" Jad shouted, steadily squeezing Jack's arm. "We're in the barrel, dude! This is so smooth!"

Jack kept the tearing pace steady until Jad squeezed his arm tightly. The ski jetted forward over the smooth water in the barrel as if coasting down an icy hill. Jack felt the ski's stern lift. With a glance to his side, he realized the wave had crashed behind them. The sea shifted to light green as he soared over the foam.

"Steep beach," Jad said, suddenly pulling Jack's shoulders back. "Kill power, quick! Let it drift."

Jack let go of the throttle. A few seconds later, the ski's blunt bow bumped sand. As soon as it touched, the Green Beret leaped off the back into thigh-deep water.

While a spent wave bubbled around them, Jad gathered his sniper gear, gave Jack a hearty slap on the back, and threw his rifle on the beach. He turned and shoved the nose of the Jet Ski rearward. Jack jammed it into reverse. He saw Jad giving him a thumbs-up as the sniper swung from view.

Pointed at the breakers, Jack floated in the shallow foam. He hit the throttle hard when the next wave broke about fifty yards away. The ski whipped forward, rising silently from the choppy foam, going from zero to thirty knots in two seconds. Jack felt the nose rising. A moment later he was in the air. He came down with such speed that the splash of the ski's return to water was left far behind him.

"You nailed that, boss," he heard Jad say over the radio.

"That's a roger," Jack answered, skipping over the swells at seventy knots. "Thanks for the coaching."

"Proceeding to overwatch. See you on the other side."

Jack punched in the keys for the ski's autopilot to take over. On his scope, he saw Tempests One, Two, and Four at the mouth of the Orinoco river, circling and waiting for him. "Tempest Base," he said into his radio. "This is Three. Package has been delivered. Proceeding to ingress point."

"*Roger, Base,*" Lisanne responded from Marlin. "*Report when you get to the rendezvous.*"

"I'M PISSED AT CLARK," SAID THE TEAM'S OTHER GREEN BERET, CARY MARKS, A FEW minutes later.

He was standing behind Lisanne's chair in Marlin's control room. On the monitors in front of him, he could see that Jad was already halfway across the barrier island at the mouth of the Orinoco. Tempest Three, Jack, had made it to the delta along with the rest of the seaborne operators.

"Now you know how I feel on these missions," Lisanne answered.

"But you have a job as the intel officer," Cary said, scratching his ear with his pinkie. "I'm sitting here on my ass while they're having all the fun."

"Someone has to pull security at the command post. Isn't that Green Beret 101 or something?"

He shot her an irritated glance. "Security from what?" he asked. "Sea monsters?"

"You never know," she replied.

37

ORINOCO REEF
0215

YEVGENY ZUKA STEADIED HIMSELF AGAINST THE SWELL BY GRASPING THE EDGE OF an ammo crate. He looked out through the camouflage ghillie netting that shrouded the barge, wondering what had made it tilt. He figured it out when he saw the Tiburónista boat slamming into the floating dock.

"Watch it!" Zuka hollered in Spanish at the Tib behind the boat's wheel. To his further disgust, the Wagner man noticed the boat was only half-loaded. As far as he knew, it was the last one to come from the shore base. And this idiot Tib brought it out half-empty? What a stupid thing to do.

Zuka didn't think much of these Tiburónistas. They were an undisciplined, rowdy lot who would just as soon snort their drugs as execute a sensitive operation on behalf of their boss, Tiburón. While they maintained a healthy fear of the drug lord and depended on him for their livelihoods, they were not cut out for an operation like this.

"Get that gear out of the boat and assembled!" he roared. "We're running out of time!"

Zuka spat into the sea and shook his head. He struggled to understand how these Tiburónistas could be so careless. He'd seen a lot in his fifteen years with Wagner—but never this.

Years ago, as a battalion commander, he led one of the mercenary group's first big successes in Crimea. That operation, he liked to tell the green Wagner recruits, had been nearly flawless. Wearing masks, unmarked uniforms, and heavy combat vests, Zuka and his men walked right up to the Sevastopol naval base and shot anyone who didn't accept their immediate commands. In a matter of hours, his small battalion reestablished Russian control over the port.

At the time, he had mused at the historic shift in fate. It was amazing to him that there had even been such a thing as the Crimean War. Czar Nicholas I lost Crimea to British-backed Ottomans in the nineteenth century. Later, when Ukraine was sucked back into the sprawling Soviet Union, it was in Russian hands again—until the shameful fall of the empire and Ukrainian independence.

After all that history, Zuka's small Wagner force and a battalion of Spetsnaz Alphas had walked right up and annexed Crimea with a handful of rifles. The Ukrainians and their Western puppet masters had been too stunned to do anything about it. To Zuka, the Crimean op was the ultimate example of how to conduct the new way of war. Nursemaiding a band of druggies, by contrast, seemed like a costly bungle.

But like salarymen everywhere, there were times when all one could do was shrug, follow your orders, and check the bank deposits. Zuka considered the Guyana op to be one of these.

"You there," he groused, kicking at a napping Tib. "Get off your ass and unload that boat."

A wave broke over the distant reef. The remnants of the swell rocked the barge. Zuka looked up at the starry sky, wishing he had the rest of the old Wagner troop with him—fellow salty Spetsnaz veterans who knew how to do this.

"Load up!" he shouted, pointing at the boats. A few Tibs stirred. Irritated by their lethargy, Zuka unleashed a furious string of Russian profanity. "We're five minutes out!"

He heard the bang of a crate. A Tib knocked a lid free with a crowbar and pulled a heavy, seventy-five-round banana mag out of packing straw. While a few Tibs made it to the boats, Zuka watched the gunner struggle to put the mag in the RPK, a squad automatic weapon.

He shook his head. The Tibs were only as good as their strong backs. The one thing they could do was hump weapons loads from the trucks to the boats and then here, to the barge. But they had little military value beyond that. The only saving grace to this op was that they were going after a soft, unarmed target. In his experience, fear could be enough.

He walked down the barge's padded edge, stepping over the old tires nailed to the cleats as boat bumpers. Eight metal craft were tied to the cleats, slamming against the tires with the ocean swell. Two of them carried nothing but heavy weapons, the missiles they would erect on the oil platform. The other six had five men each. The plan was for this force to land on the pier below the oil platform, while Zuka commanded the helicopter landing force from above with twenty men.

"Sling your rifle around your back, like this," he instructed one of the young Tibs. He slid the kid's AK-12 from his breast to his back. "That way you can board without it getting in the way."

The kid nodded and stepped aboard.

Messy. Zuka took some solace in the knowledge that his comrades in Havana would be joining the op on the land side. According to Morozov, the Wagner battalion would land in Georgetown as soon as the Guyanese government requested help. The big

An-124 would disgorge more helicopter gunships for air support. By then, Zuka and his men should have the American oil workers on Marlin subdued and locked away. It shouldn't be difficult—even with this ragged band of Tibs.

The Russian looked at his watch, then whistled with his fingers in his mouth. The men aboard the boats looked up at him. Zuka rotated his hand over his head in a circle. The coxswains cranked the heavy outboard engines. Zuka held his hand straight in front of them, signaling for them to wait.

He walked under the overhanging camouflage netting and leaned against the little plywood hut with the towering HF antenna they'd erected at the center of the barge. He didn't like to go into the huts where the Tibs had been living for three days. They stunk.

Sheltered from the breeze, the idling engines, and the bubbling surf, Zuka dialed Morozov on the satellite phone.

"The men and weapons are in the landing boats. They're ready," he said in Russian.

"*Horosho*," Morozov answered. "How are the sea conditions?"

Zuka could tell Morozov was in the back of his private helicopter. He suspected the SVR boss was headed to Caracas, to the station at the embassy. He knew Morozov was waiting for the final word from Moscow before giving them the green light.

"Mild swells," Zuka answered. "Otherwise, calm. Weather looks good."

The line hissed. Helo rotors beat softly over the sat link.

"*Da*," Morozov replied. "Do you still stand by your estimate for their transit to the manned oil platform Marlin?"

"I do. It should be thirty minutes. Have you heard whether the gunship will be overhead on time?"

"It will be there," Morozov said.

"Moscow has approved the operation?"

"Da," Morozov said. "The government broadcast will begin as soon as you subdue the workers on the platform."

"And the American military?"

"Just be ready. We can't be sure how they'll react. You know your business."

Zuka was pleased to hear that Morozov was leaving the tactical decisions to him. Though an SVR major now, Morozov had come up through Wagner, operating shell businesses for the mercenary firm. When it came to military matters, Morozov rarely interfered.

"Can you confirm that you want us to take the platform workers alive? That will make things more difficult."

"Yes," Morozov answered bluntly. "It's too early to say whether the hostages will be an asset or a liability."

"And if they become a liability?"

"Then you will shoot them and toss their bodies into the sea."

38

ORINOCO RIVER DELTA
0223

JACK WATCHED MOORE AND CLARK FROM THE THIRD POSITION IN LINE. TO HIS EYES, the killer skis slithered up the river like crocodiles. Navigating the maze of barrier islands, sandbars, and shallows, the silent craft coasted in at four knots. Up ahead, in his NVDs, he saw the blocky outline of the barge barracks for the first time.

Moore approached the barge, standing off in a ripple. Just behind him, Clark glided in a zigzag pattern, scanning the shore for targets. His HK416, elongated with a muzzle suppressor, rested across his knees. Jack took a quick glance over his shoulder. Chilly Edwards was back there, bringing up the rear. Behind him, Mandy Cobb, a former FBI hostage rescue team operator, had her rifle to her eye.

Moore's voice whispered softly over the net. *"All call signs, I've got the docks to my right,"* he breathed. *"Zero boats. Repeat, zero boats. No tangos on the beach. Area looks cleared out."*

"This is Two," Clark said softly in reply. "Copy. Any vehicles on land?"

"Single tractor trailer. Shows cold on IR. Logo on the side says . . .

Hang on." A few seconds passed before the chief came back. *"I make it out as Playa Del Sol . . . Cerveza.* Saw that beer at the terminal in Tobago, too."

Guiding his ski past a floating branch, Jack pondered that strange detail. The satellite imagery showed a dock where metal boats tied up within a fenced area. Based on the all-source intelligence analysis Gavin Biery assembled, the team believed the boats were used to ferry drugs out to waiting freighters.

"All stop," Moore said suddenly. *"Hold position."*

Jack slacked the throttle. He allowed the outgoing tidal current of the Orinoco to push against the ski's bow and slow him. He studied the barracks barge looming beyond the chief. From where Jack waited, it looked like a long, two-story houseboat.

Checking out its flat roof, he saw movement, a dark shape. It became clear to him why Moore had ordered the stop. It was the roof sentry, just as they'd seen in their imagery analysis.

"Overwatch, Tempest One. You have that tango on the roof?" asked Moore.

"Roger that, One. I've got the roof sentry in my sights," answered Jad from his sniper hide between the hills on the barrier island. It was twenty-five minutes since Jack dropped Jad on the beach. The Green Beret had made quick work of getting to his overwatch station.

By Jack's estimate, having a single man as their recon eyes was risky. For one thing, Jad was working without a spotter, since Cary had remained on Marlin for post security. For another, the Campus team would typically have a drone with a satellite video feed that Lisanne could monitor to keep them updated. This op was too far into hostile territory to afford the luxury.

"Second sentry on the stern," Jad said quietly.

"How are the sentries armed?" Clark asked.

"Stern tango has an AK-12. Guy on the roof has a 203."

To Jack, that confirmed that these weren't regular druggies. They were armed with the best rifles in the Russian inventory, a rarity.

"*Are they wearing NVDs?*" Clark asked.

"*Negative,*" Jad said. "*Regular eyeballs only.*"

"*What about the yacht?*" Clark followed. "*You see any sentries on the* Gran Blanco?"

Imagery analysis showed the *Gran Blanco* moored just behind the barracks barge. Jack still couldn't see the yacht, since the river took a slight curve. Ding's SOS signal had come from somewhere between the yacht and the barge. Clark wasn't sure which vessel held Ding. In their mission brief, they prepared for either eventuality.

"*There is no yacht,*" Jad said.

"*Say again, Overwatch?*" Clark shot back, surprised.

"*Negative on the yacht. She's not there. Copy?*"

That was unexpected. It meant the Gran Blanco had put to sea within the past hour. It seemed to Jack that they could have come within range of the yacht on the trip up from Marlin. Then again, the killer sleds were optimized for stealth, which meant they weren't sweeping the sea with radar.

Moore broke the tense silence. "*Copy. Tempest Two,*" he said, addressing Clark. "*The yacht's too big to have gone upriver. It must have put to sea right before we got here.*"

Jack felt a cold pang. If Tiburón had been working with the SVR, they likely would have discovered Ding's identity. If Ding was on that yacht, he couldn't last long. He might already be dead.

"*Tempest Three and Four, sweep the barge,*" Clark ordered, snapping Jack out of his spiral. "*Tempest One and I will go for the yacht—it can't have gotten far and we have the boarding gear.*"

39

ORINOCO RIVER DELTA
0225

WATCHING THROUGH HIS NVDS, JACK SAW CLARK AND MOORE SWING AROUND WITH the outgoing current. After a few seconds of drift, the bulky sleds were right beside him. In the lead, Moore suddenly catapulted forward. A moment later, Clark followed, streaking silently away.

Mesmerized by the speed, Jack's eyes lingered on them. In seconds, the two Campus operatives were leaning into a turn, disappearing behind the barrier island.

Chilly checked in from the ski behind him.

"This is Tempest Four. We changing tactics, boss? Or do we hit the barge as briefed?"

To avoid confusion and keep their respective missions in focus, Clark and Moore had switched to a separate channel. The net was limited to Jack, Chilly, Mandy, and Jad.

"Negative," Jack said. With the yacht gone, boats out of the harbor, and lack of activity onshore, Jack doubted there were many Tiburónistas on the barge. The roof sentry seemed to indicate that there was something still there worth guarding—possibly Ding. And with so many Wagner and Tiburónista men unaccounted for,

Jack was worried about a surprise coming from outside the barge. "I'm calling an audible," he said.

He heard three mic clicks in response.

"One and Two were going to be on the yacht, covering our six," Jack clarified. "But since they're out, I think we develop a new ingress plan."

"Roger that," Mandy responded.

Jack continued. "We're going to come in the rear, sweep stern to stem, both decks. I'll take the upper, you two have the lower. We'll rally at the barge's rear entry portal, then breach. Copy?"

He heard mic clicks in response.

"Commence gear check," he said.

Checking his own kit, Jack ran his hands over the three flashbangs, three thermobaric, and two fragmentation grenades, ensuring they were within easy reach, but not poised to fall off. He lowered his hand to his thigh, checking his holstered Glock. Finally, he tugged at the sling over his chest, pulling his silenced HK416 assault rifle in tight.

Chilly and Mandy both reported their tactical gear was ready and functioning.

"Okay. Four, I want you to come down from the bank, as briefed, no change. You'll board the barge from landward. Overwatch, splash those sentries when we're in position, on my mark. I'll come up the stern ladder and go for the second deck."

They signaled their understanding with clicks.

Jack went on. "If we find our jackpot, I'll put him on my ski. Four, circle back to pick up Overwatch. You'll have to triple up. The most important thing is to get the hell out of Venezuelan territorial waters as quickly as possible. Any last questions?"

He was met with silence this time.

"Copy," Jack said. "Let's roll."

He twisted the ski's throttle and shot across the river as though on wings. He slowed to a drift in the shadows of the far bank and studied the barge across the water, floating on the current. When he drifted to a position abeam the barge's stern sentry, he touched his microphone and whispered softly. "Overwatch, are we still black?"

"*Roger that,*" Jad answered. "*No change from either sentry.*"

"*Overwatch, you have eyes on us?*" Mandy asked. "*We're feet dry. At the dock.*"

"*Roger, Four. I have you at the edge of the dock. Stay put. Roof sentry will see you if you come out any farther.*"

After a few seconds of observation, Jack spoke softly into the radio. "Overwatch, do you have a shot on the rear sentry?"

"*Roger, Three. I have the shot for the rear sentry.*"

"What about the roof tango?"

"*I have him.*"

Jack considered his options. The rear sentry seemed to be the greater threat, since he would meet Chilly and Mandy at the stern. "Rear first, then roof," he confirmed to Jad. "Execute."

Watching through his NVDs, Jack saw dark mist erupt from the rear sentry's head. The Tib at the back of the barge crumpled and splashed into the water. It took nearly a second for the sound to reach Jack.

"*Rear sentry down,*" Jad reported. "*But I can't tell if I got the guy on the roof.*"

Oh shit, Jack said to himself, his hand poised on the throttle.

He tipped the NVDs up, swung the HK off his back, and eyed the barge roof through a thermal scope. He saw no movement. "Four, you see the roof sentry?"

"*Negative,*" Chilly answered.

"*I lost him,*" Jad said. "*He may have ducked into a barge hatch and gone inside. He was going down when I shot.*"

"Orders?" Mandy asked.

"Go!" Jack barked, now that the rear sentry was out.

He twisted his throttle and sped crosscurrent to the stern. The instant acceleration would have tossed him backward if he hadn't been strapped tightly to the killer ski's seat. He turned the handlebars to put the ski into a sideways drift. It crashed into the ladder with a slosh. Using a carabiner, he secured the ski to the ladder, then jumped on the rusty barge deck.

Running forward, the entrance to the two-story plywood barracks was where he'd pictured it. He slammed into the wall.

"Tempest Four is on the port side," Chilly reported. *"Moving to breach point."*

"Copy."

With his rifle sweeping before him, Jack ran to the bankside of the door. Chilly and Mandy arrived two seconds later. Jack gave them the hand signals that reiterated his earlier orders. He'd go high, sweeping the second deck, while Chilly and Mandy cleared below.

With a final nod, Jack unclipped a nine-banger flash-bang grenade and lobbed it through the door. He waited for the second blaze of light before rushing at the ladder and climbing to the second deck.

At the top rung, Jack pulled his second flash-bang loose and tossed it down the hallway. He closed his eyes, waiting out the flashes and counting down the booms, then pushed himself over the final rung and rolled. On the deck below, he could hear the echoes of Mandy and Chilly flinging their grenades, clearing room after room as they moved forward toward the barge's bow.

In a mash-up of the explosions below and the nine-banger rattling down the hall in front of him, a sudden spray of wood splinters blotted out the view through his NVDs. He realized the thin wooden wall beside him, just above his head, had shredded.

Someone was shooting at him.

He rolled in the opposite direction to the safety of a room with a small metal bed. The wood above the headboard exploded. The defender on the other side of the wall knew where he was.

He reversed to the hall as wood ricocheted all around him. The shooting stopped. His ears rang. He could hear more noise on the deck below, but couldn't tell whether it was coming from ninebangers or the same kind of resistance he was facing.

Wood pulp flew in front of him, nicking his face and blinding his NVDs. The man in the next room was shooting through the wall again, this time from the hallway. Blasting away on full auto, it was just a matter of time before one of the bullets found Jack.

Jack snatched a thermobaric grenade from his vest, yanked the pin, and tossed it into the hall.

As they'd briefed on GOPLAT Marlin, the thermobaric "homewrecker" was only to be used on the barge as a last resort. Given the structure's fragile construction, the team was worried that one of the shock waves from the handheld bombs could bring the building down on their heads. Jack was about to find out if that was true.

He clenched up, careful to keep his mouth open so the pressure blast didn't blow out his eardrums.

The grenade came skittering back across the floor.

Sweeping forward like a soccer goalie, Jack batted it back into the hall, sending it forward. He was on his stomach, stretched out with his rifle at his side, when the wall in front of him disintegrated, followed by a sensation of falling.

Because he was. The thermobaric had blown out the support beam for the second deck. Jack slid at a forty-five-degree angle down the collapsed floor beneath him. A metal bed came crashing from above and smashed his back. A shower of wood landed around him.

He coughed, trying to get up, but slid backward in the debris.

He felt hands on his ankles, pulling him through the pile. Coming to his senses, he yanked his Glock free of his thigh holster and twisted, ready to shoot whoever had his feet.

Mandy, he saw immediately. She released him. He lowered the pistol.

He jerked free of the shattered lumber. Chilly was next to him, shouting into his ear. "*Clear, clear, clear!*" They helped Jack to a knee. He turned around and looked at the junk pile. He could see the dead Tiburónista who'd thrown the grenade back at him. The druggie's eyes bulged. The thermobaric had blown his brains out.

They retreated to the stern. Jack shook his head and rubbed his face. His ears stopped ringing long enough to hear Chilly on the tactical frequency saying, *"Dry hole. Our man's not here."*

Jack nodded unhappily. When he tried to tell Chilly to get back to his ski, he was interrupted by an urgent voice crackling on the link.

"This is Overwatch. I've got hostiles coming down the bank," Jad said. *"I'm guessing they saw that explosion."*

"How many?" Jack asked, his voice rising in alarm.

"A lot. I'll hold 'em off for as long as I can. But you guys better get the hell out of there."

40

GOPLAT MARLIN
0230

"COME ON, GAV," LISANNE SAID OVER HER SAT PHONE. "YOU HAVE TO BE ABLE TO GET something better than that."

She was sitting at the monitors in the control room. Cary Marks was at her side, working the radio. He was tuned into Clark and Moore's frequency as they raced across the ocean, looking for Tiburón's yacht, the *Gran Blanco*. Clark requested a fix on the yacht's position.

Though she hadn't said as much, it seemed to Lisanne that Mr. C. was confusing the oil rig with a Navy ship. If she were on a warship, she could light up a surface ship radar to find the *Gran Blanco* in a matter of minutes. But she wasn't on a ship. She was on GOPLAT Marlin. Its only sensor was a piddly little weather radar. How in the hell was she supposed to find the *Gran Blanco* with that?

Asking herself that question, she'd used her sat phone to shake Gavin Biery awake. He was sound asleep in his D.C. apartment. Fortunately, he didn't need to be in the office to keep up on the intelligence feeds.

"What do you want me to say, Lis?" the infotech specialist

protested. Lisanne put him on speaker while she searched the internet for creative ideas on tracking a private yacht.

"I've hacked into DIA's ship tracker database," Gavin continued. "But I have to tell you, it's not magic. DIA's maritime watch desk looks for military radar signatures, not yachts. What do you want me to do?"

"I don't know," she said, glancing at Cary with concern. "How does the Coast Guard track smugglers?"

"By racing around on the ocean and using their radars. Or maybe search planes. You have a search plane?"

Lisanne sighed in despair. Finding the *Gran Blanco* when they didn't know where to look would be like finding an egg in a wheat field. She couldn't figure out how best to direct Clark and Moore. The last thing she wanted was to tell Clark it was impossible.

Exhausted, she thought of Jack's hangdog expression when he was so down earlier while they were standing on the catwalk together. He had been watching the *Helena* disappear over the horizon.

A light in her head blinked. The *Helena*. "Hang on," she blurted to Gavin. "What about Jack's ship, the one we took to get here? Could we use it for a surface search?"

"You're asking me about naval strategy, Lisanne. I'm a computer science nerd. I don't know what to tell you."

Cary nudged her. "That's a good idea. Maybe the *Helena* could circle back, get between us and the Orinoco Delta. It might be able to find the *Gran Blanco*."

She looked hopefully at the Green Beret. "You think the *Helena* has a surface search radar?"

"I know she does," he replied. "I saw the radar antenna spinning on the mast."

Gavin, who'd heard the exchange on his end of the line, spoke up. "If it helps, guys, I could tell you where the *Helena* is."

LINE OF DEMARCATION

Lisanne cupped her forehead with her hand. "Gav, tell me how it is that you can find the *Helena* but you can't find the *Gran Blanco*."

"Simple," he explained. "Hendley Associates owns the *Helena*. Because of that, I have access to its position through our insurer, Lloyd's of London. Give me a minute and I'll tell you where she is." When he came back on the line, he said, "Got her. The *Helena* is ninety miles northeast of your oil platform."

Lisanne swore silently to herself.

"At her lame speed," Cary said, "the *Helena* would take half a day to get into position for a surface search in the area we need." He pointed to the chart.

"Exactly," said Lisanne. At another dead end, she was about to get up and pour herself a coffee. Her mind was going numb. As she was rising, a thought occurred to her. She dropped back to her chair.

"Hang on," she said tentatively into the phone, blinking rapidly. "Gavin—you said a second ago that you got *Helena*'s position from a Lloyd's database. Can you tell me how it works?"

"Lloyd's tracks its insured assets," said Gavin.

"Yes—but how?"

"They use a signature from the ship's GPS transceivers. Pretty much every ship uses GPS for navigation. Lloyd's detects the signature of the transceivers and matches them up in the database. That gives them a location of each ship in their registry."

"Gavin," said Lisanne, sitting up straight. "Is it possible that the *Gran Blanco* might be insured by Lloyd's?"

After a prolonged silence, Gavin said, "I wish I had thought of that. Give me a minute. I'll call you back."

THE *GRAN BLANCO* WAS NOT INSURED BY LLOYD'S OF LONDON, GAVIN ANNOUNCED later.

However, the infotech specialist learned a much more useful tidbit from an internet image search of the yacht. As he explained, Tiburón had taken delivery of the boat through a broker in the Canary Islands just two years ago. At that time, she was called motor yacht *Valor*, flagged in Malta, owned by a tech billionaire. And the *Valor* had indeed been insured by Lloyd's.

The *Valor*'s new owner had not changed the GPS equipment, Gavin explained. That meant that the yacht, now named the *Gran Blanco*, was still tracked in Lloyd's database as the *Valor*.

Gavin rattled off the precise coordinates of Tiburón's flagship.

After dispatching the numbers off to Clark and Moore, Lisanne traced the spot on Cary's mission chart. "That's weird," she said.

"What?" he asked.

"The *Gran Blanco* is headed right toward us."

41

**ORINOCO REEF
0233**

YEVGENY ZUKA HAD LONG MARVELED AT HOW QUIET THINGS COULD GET JUST BEFORE an operation was about to start. He consistently witnessed this phenomenon during his years as a Spetsnaz Alpha and later as a Wagner mercenary.

He noticed that men on the edge of danger tended to retreat into their minds. They quit talking to one another. They stopped nervously fiddling with their weapons. If there was something natural to study, like the sea or the stars, they pondered it in silence.

With the bulk of the Tiburónista force away on the boats, there was only his helicopter assault team left on the Orinoco Reef barges. Zuka considered them the best of the Tiburónistas, a pack of Venezuelan ex-cons who prized both authority and violence. He had handpicked them because he wanted brutal men who would listen to him, yet scare the hostages on the oil platform into submission. Though they were hard men, Zuka noticed they were quiet on the barge, looking out at the black sea.

"*Vámanos!*" he called a few minutes later, waking them from their collective torpor. Over the hiss of the surf, he heard the steady chop of a heavy Russian gunship. He knew the sound well. He recognized it as the thump of a massive Mi-8 transport.

"Strap up!" he urged the squad. He herded them to a cleared portion at the barge's center. The helicopter flipped on its searchlight, bathing them in a harsh white glare. Peering between his fingers, Zuka saw the helicopter approaching slowly. He was delighted to see it carrying Shturm missiles on stubby wing pylons. He waved his arms over his head.

The gunship flared into a hover, whipping the camo netting and churning up the water like a mini-hurricane. A padded horse collar came down a cable and slapped against the barge deck. Zuka put his first Tib through it. The helicopter crew hoisted the Tib up like a fish on a line.

Zuka repeated the process over and over, twenty times. When it was his turn, he put the horse collar over his shoulders and tugged on the line. Reaching the open cabin door, a Russian aircrewman pulled him inside. Zuka clambered to his knees on the wide steel floor, deafened by the whine of the rotors over his head. The crewman handed him a pair of earphones with a boom mic.

Zuka put the earphones on and tested them. "Where did you come from?" he asked, genuinely curious. Morozov had only told him that a helicopter would come. Now that Zuka saw it was a Russian army gunship, he couldn't quite understand how it had come from the sea.

The pilot responded tersely. "We are deployed on the navy frigate *Admiral Gorshkov*. Came over from West Africa."

The heavy helicopter tilted and lumbered forward. With the searchlight off, Zuka lost his view of the barges. He settled in beside his Tiburónistas. Immersed in the unfamiliar world of the Russian military, it seemed to Zuka that the men were watching his every move. That was good.

After a minute of flying, the pilot came back on the intercom.

"Can I ask, sir, what we will find at the coordinates? Will we have a clear landing zone?"

Zuka was not of the old Soviet school that defaulted to keeping people in the dark. In his Wagner experience, he found that a little context could go a long way. "You're taking us to an oil platform," he replied. "There's a landing pad on it. Should be an easy assignment for a Russian gunship pilot."

After a few seconds of silence the pilot returned. "The coordinates show this platform to be in Guyanese territorial waters. Won't I need clearance to land there?"

Zuka grinned in the dark. "Young man, what do you think your missiles are for?"

42

OFF THE VENEZUELAN COAST
0233

MASTER CHIEF KENDRICK MOORE TIGHTENED THE STRAPS THAT HELD HIM TO THE soaring Jet Ski. On Clark's orders, he kept the throttles open to the stops, jetting over the waves at more than ninety knots. He and Clark vaulted from wave to wave like rocks skipping across a pond.

Though Moore believed in the potential of these stealthy watercraft for naval special warfare, he was privately worried. He saw two problems with running down the *Gran Blanco* at this speed.

The first was battery consumption. When he planned their trip to the Orinoco river delta and back, he assumed a high-speed ingress and a max-efficiency egress. Instead, he was burning through the hydrogen fuel cells at an alarming rate as they followed the coordinates Lisanne had zapped into the navigation computer.

The second problem was more prosaic. Sticking to the same track the *Gran Blanco* had taken put them closer to the shore in slightly shallower water. The waves had risen to three feet with the ocean and land breezes swirling together over shallower seas. No matter how advanced the craft, shooting through the shallows was a risky proposition. He worried they could collide with an unmarked shoal at any moment.

LINE OF DEMARCATION

He felt slightly better when the ski's elevated optical sensor picked up an object. While careening over the sea, Moore noted that it was close to the coordinates from Lisanne. He flashed his ski's rear-facing signal light three times so Clark wouldn't collide with him. Then he put the ski in manual and gradually slowed.

Clark pulled up next to him. They sloshed forward at two knots, speaking to each other through the short-range radio link.

"We're coming up on the *Gran Blanco*'s stern, John. You see it on your optical scope?"

"Yeah," Clark radioed back. "I got her."

"She's dark ship, apparently. I'm not seeing any navigation lights."

"Not surprising," Clark agreed. "I'd imagine a drug lord doesn't usually follow international maritime lighting regulations."

"Yeah."

"You've trained on these things, Chief. How would you suggest we board the yacht?"

Moore had been picturing the approach since leaving the Orinoco delta. He had equipped the boats with boarding ladders, but he couldn't be sure of the best way to use them until he saw the yacht up close.

"Follow my lead," he said. "We'll regroup when we're in range. I need better eyes on her to come up with a boarding strategy."

Clark double-clicked his mic. Moore increased the throttle, dashing forward at thirty knots. After a few minutes, he could plainly see the *Gran Blanco* with his NVDs, a hulking dark shape in the moonlight. "Tally-ho," he radioed. "The *Gran Branco* bears zero-two-three degrees relative."

"I see her, Chief. Let's go."

Moore increased speed. They closed the distance rapidly with the yacht. When Moore was a hundred yards off the *Gran Blanco*'s port stern quarter, he slowed. Clark splashed alongside.

"I have eyes on a few people topside," Moore said. He took his HK416 rifle off his back and held the thermal scope to his eye. "They're up in a glassy area at the top of the boat."

"You see any lookouts?" Clark asked.

Moore shifted the rifle. "There's a guy smoking on the starboard side, leaning on the rail. Not sure if he's a lookout or just a guy taking a break."

"Yeah, I can see him, too." Clark adjusted his NVDs. "Port side looks clear. You come up with a boarding plan, Master Chief?"

Moore dropped the rifle back to his lap. "I think we swing wide to the left and come in at an oblique angle until we parallel the hull. Given the way the first deck bows out over the water, they won't know we're there—if we get in close enough."

"What then? How do we get aboard?"

Moore strapped his rifle to his chest. He kicked a long tube that ran along the side of the black ski. "I have a cable ladder stowed under my seat. We'll marry it up to this painter pole and hook it to the gunwale at the port rear quarter. Then it's an easy climb up. Standard SEAL maritime interdiction op."

"Standard my ass," Clark grumbled. "We normally have a rubber boat coxswain keeping us steady. How do you propose we do this from the top of the ski? It takes two men to set the first boarding ladder."

"Right. I'm thinking we can double up on a single ski. I'll keep it driving steady while you hook the ladder, and then I'll go up."

"What happens to the skis after we get up the side?"

"I'll put them in autonomous mode, following us at a safe distance, maybe a quarter mile. When we get Ding, we jump over the side. The skis will come to us."

"Yeah," said Clark. "If Ding is there."

43

ORINOCO RIVER DELTA
0235

JACK STAYED IN THE SHADOWS ON THE FAR SIDE OF THE BANK, WATCHING THE COL-lapsed barge. His HK416 rested on his knees. Now and then he picked it up and scanned the opposite bank with his thermal scope.

"*All call signs,*" he heard Chilly whisper. "*How are we looking?*"

"Four tangos on the back of the barge," Jack replied. He surveilled the Tiburónistas milling down the dock to the barge's fantail. The Tibs had begun picking through the torn plywood, digging out their dead teammate. They were on high alert, pointing their rifles all around them, trying to find whoever attacked them.

"*This is Overwatch. I've got five standing inside the fence line,*" Jad added. "*They're walking toward that truck. I've also got a vehicle, old Chevy Blazer. It's coming down the hill inside the perimeter fence.*"

Chilly and Mandy had been blocked from reaching their ski in the frenzied egress. When Tiburónistas ashore heard the explosion, they charged out to the docks. The Campus operators took a secondary route by swimming between the bank and the barge, intent on drifting back to the ski they'd hidden in the reeds. But a giant tangle of shattered wood from the explosion had clotted up like a beaver dam, blocking their way. They would need to hop back up on the bank to get to the ski. The risk was that the Tiburónistas might spot them.

"Listen up," Jack said on the net. "If we've got an SUV coming down the hill, then we might be about to lose the only window we have."

"*You're not wrong*," Jad confirmed. "*I think you guys have to make a break for it now.*"

"*Copy,*" Mandy replied. "*Give us a second to discuss.*"

"Make it quick," Jack radioed. "I have eyes on the Chevy."

Mandy came back on the line a few seconds later. "*Okay, when you guys are ready, we're going to get up on the bank and make a beeline for that palm grove twenty yards to our east. We'll need Overwatch to clear a path of anyone who sights us. Chilly's going to dive on the ski and start it. I'm going to strap on behind him, pulling rear security.*"

"*Tempest Three,*" Jad said with a call to Jack. "*I've got a bead on the four tangos closest to them. Can you take the guys on the stern and the docks?*"

Jack double-clicked as he raised his rifle to his eyes. He saw a Tiburónista at the dock and mentally rehearsed swinging his rifle to hit three additional tangos.

Jad continued. "*Tempest Four. You have the mark. Call it when ready.*"

Under the scope's reticle, Jack watched one of the Tiburónistas kneel on the stern. He was gesturing with his hands, talking to another Tib on the dock.

"*Mark,*" said Mandy Cobb, her voice strained from the effort to get to the bank.

Jack held his breath and squeezed the trigger, sending the 5.56 round out the silenced sixteen-inch barrel.

LINE OF DEMARCATION

The man in the crouch toppled over. Jack swiveled his aim a few degrees. His second target hadn't figured out what was happening. He squeezed the trigger and watched. The Tib went down. Jack swung his barrel for his third tango and scored a headshot.

He saw another Tiburónista running on the dock, going for the bank. At this angle, it would be a tough one. Jack allowed for a lead of a few degrees, then pulled the trigger. Miss. He did it again. Hit. The man tumbled forward and landed face down.

When Jack rotated his rifle farther to his right, he could see that five other tangos were down—Jad's hits.

Shouts and screams from across the water reached Jack. Then he heard the Chevy Blazer skidding to a stop.

Jack caught a glimpse of men in green uniforms. He thought they might be Venezuelan army regulars, or as regular as they got at a drug lord's hideout. They placed a heavy machine gun on the Chevy's hood, aiming down the bank at Mandy and Chilly. To distract them, Jack pulled his Glock from his thigh and shot it in the air. The soldier with the heavy weapon swiveled it toward him.

With his rifle still on his knees, Jack gunned the throttle and shot down the river. He saw a few splashes ahead of him and realized the Venezuelans were getting a bead on him. He felt a jolt to his ski and knew he'd been hit.

He leaned over, zigzagged, and raced as fast as the ski would go. He steered so fiercely that his knee touched water. He saw a few orange tracer rounds ricochet behind him. The barge and docks were soon angling away. Even better, when he took a quick glimpse back, he saw Chilly on his ski, darting to the middle of the river.

"*We're clear, we're clear!*" Mandy called on the net.

"Let's get the hell out of here," Jack responded. "Follow me out."

Soaring at fifty knots past the barrier islands, he switched his radio channel back to the link connecting him with oil platform Marlin.

"Tempest Base, this is Tempests Three and Four. We're egressing the target area. We'll be picking up Overwatch in a few minutes, over."

Though grateful to make the egress call, he was chilled by Lisanne's response.

Over the satellite link, she replied, *"Roger, Tempest Three. Be advised we have armed surface combatants inbound at high speed, likely hostile. Tempest Base will check in when we can. For now, we're securing equipment and taking measures to ensure the safety of the crew. Over and out."*

44

GOPLAT MARLIN
0238

"KILL THE LIGHTS!" SHOUTED CARY. HE FLIPPED HIS NVDS OVER HIS EYES AND PICKED up his rifle.

"I put out the distress call," Lisanne said. "What do you see?"

The Green Beret stood at the observation windows. "A couple of wakes now. I saw five or six boats. They must be beneath us. I'm going out for a better look."

He stepped outside onto the catwalk. Through the metal grate, he looked down and saw the line of boats splashing to a stop. They were metal, about twenty feet long, carrying either men or crates. Even from this height, he could see that they were kitted up in combat vests and carrying AK-12 rifles.

Cary hurried back into the control room and reported it to Lisanne.

"Any chance they're good guys? Guyanese military?" she asked.

"Negative. They look like Tibs. Long hair, motley getup, Russian weapons. Take the lights below offline. Fast."

Lisanne threw a handful of labeled circuit breakers, extinguishing the lights on the rest of the decks. She toggled the radio mic and reported in the blind to the Tempest team, which was away on their skis. She knew Clark and Moore were tracking down the *Gran Blanco*. Jack and the rest were egressing from the Orinoco river delta. It would take any of them at least an hour to get back, even at breakneck speed.

"Oh hell," Cary groaned. He was studying the horizon with his NVDs.

"What?"

"Chopper inbound. Russian Hip gunship. The damn thing's bristling with missiles and coming right for us."

"*What?*" she shrieked. "Are you serious?"

"Yeah. We're in the middle of a GOPLAT takedown, apparently backed by the Russians."

"What should we do?"

Cary Marks considered their options. With more than a decade in the Green Berets, he was accustomed to devising unconventional plans on the fly. Few situations required more creative thinking than this one.

"I guess I'm it for armed security," he said. "I should probably get to a good shooter's position while I still can. I faced gunships like this in Afghanistan. They're a bitch to kill."

"I can shoot, too."

"I know. But I'm jocked up. I'll climb the derrick and act as your overwatch. You hustle down to be with the Quinteros and oil riggers. There are thirty men coming up from below. Your top priority has to be to warn the crew of this thing." He looked through the window. "Son of a bitch. We have to hop. That gunship's going to touch down in less than a minute—if it doesn't blow the whole platform first."

"Okay," she replied. "But with Russians coming aboard, we can't leave any of our comms gear here."

"Agreed." Cary pulled a heavy plastic sack from a garbage can, emptied it, and started throwing laptops and radios into it while the beat of the gunship rotors rattled the windows.

"Head below, Lis. I'll dump all this over the side. Good luck."

With the sack of communications equipment over his shoulder, the Green Beret charged out the door into the rushing wind.

45

MOTOR YACHT *GRAN BLANCO*
0255

NEITHER CLARK NOR MOORE HEARD LISANNE'S DISTRESS CALL. THEY HAD EACH switched to their short-range channel and squelched out any emergency beacons for fear of being detected.

Clark maneuvered the long black extendable rod that Moore called a painter's pole. He hooked it over the side of the *Gran Blanco* while Moore cruised along on his ski below him, matching the yacht's speed. Clark's own ski had been sent off under autonomous-drone mode and now loitered a quarter mile astern.

"On the ladder," Clark grunted into the radio. At the top of the painter's pole, they'd mated the end of a flexible cable ladder that now hung down. Clark was climbing up it, hand over hand.

From the cable ladder's top rung, Clark grasped the yacht's side railing and looked over it. "Clear," he whispered. "Don't see anyone."

Moore double-clicked his acknowledgment and watched from below as Clark swung his leg over the side.

Now it was Moore's turn. The master chief programmed his ski to continue at its present course and speed, then fall away in thirty seconds. After that—like Clark's craft—it would keep pace with the yacht, following a quarter mile behind.

With his gloved hand wrapped in the cable ladder, Moore raised a leg, trying to hook it into the bottom rung.

But just then, the *Gran Blanco* veered sharply to port, creating a rift between the automated ski and the yacht. Caught in this nautical no-man's-land, Moore clung to the ladder. His boots dangled over the abyss, the ski retreating as his body thumped and spun against the hull. Above him, Clark peered down. Their eyes met, but Clark was powerless.

The chasm yawned wider; Moore's grip faltered. His muscles screamed; his sinews strained. He reached for the next rung. His fingers grazed cold metal. Desperation fueled his ascent.

With one last pull—a symphony of agony and resolve—he wedged his knee into the cable.

"You good?" Clark asked.

"Yeah," Moore answered, breathing hard as he climbed. After gaining a few rungs, he looped a leg over the gunwale, slid to the yacht's deck, and unslung his rifle. Together, he and Clark crept to the stern. Once there, Moore saw a long wake behind the yacht. Somewhere back there, the two skis were following them like loyal dogs.

They squatted to stay out of view of the rear salon windows. This section of the yacht was dark, which wasn't all that surprising, given the late hour. Moore, in front, saw a moving shadow. Someone was on the stern deck.

He turned to Clark and made the appropriate hand signals. He silently lowered his rifle, withdrew his knife, and crept to the corner. Moore saw a Tiburónista standing there. He had an AK-12 slung over his back and wore a dark T-shirt over jeans. He was watching the wake—about to see the riderless skis.

Rushing him from behind, Moore cranked the Tib's chin with

his left hand while thrusting his right shin into the back of the man's knees. The SEAL jammed his knife into the soft flesh just below the Tib's ear. He twisted it, scrambling the brain, and held the Tib until he stopped moving.

He dragged the body back, leaving a streak of blood on the pristine deck.

"Any intel?" Clark asked.

Moore searched the Tib's body. He found a radio with an earpiece and put it in, keeping the volume low. He'd taken three years of high school Spanish. The new guy, Gustavo, had brought some of it back to the surface.

Over the Tib's radio, a series of people were checking in by answering questions from one main speaker. Moore recognized a few common names as they reported . . . *Sanchez, Gomez,* others. He looked at his wrist. A few minutes after zero-three-hundred hours.

The master chief thought this might not be a navy ship, but it was just human nature to have watchstanders start their shifts at the top of the hour. He listened to the smattering of words he recognized as they reported in: *Puerta inferior* . . . bottom door. *Salón del cielo* . . . sky lounge.

And then he heard something that quickened his pulse: "*Quién está con el prisoner americano?*"

"*Caraza,*" came the gruff answer.

Moore tapped Clark on the shoulder. "Ding is here," he said. "He's alive. They just asked about an American prisoner."

"Where?" Clark asked, eyes narrowing.

Moore held up a finger, still listening.

Clark, for his part, dragged the dead Tib to the edge of the deck. While he was squatting and pulling the body to the lee of the yacht's superstructure, he heard a metal *clank*. Moving his rifle to his back, he flattened himself on his stomach and pressed his ear hard against the teak deck.

He heard the clank again—only this time, it was accompanied by a scream.

Ding.

He hurried back to Moore and whispered in his ear. "You're right. Ding's here. He's on the deck just below us."

46

GOPLAT MARLIN
0312

"IT'S GOING TO BE ALL RIGHT," LISANNE WHISPERED, CLUTCHING AMANCIA'S HAND. "They're not going to hurt us. If anything, they'll want us as hostages."

Lisanne, Amancia, and Tallulah were huddled on the bottom bunk of a guest VIP stateroom two decks below the control room and helipad. Gustavo stood near the door in the dark, listening.

When they saw the huge Russian helicopter land and the men in unmarked green uniforms hanging in the doorway, Cary rushed to the far side of the platform and dumped their Campus laptops over the side.

Armed with his HK416, Glock, and NVDs, Cary climbed a ladder straight up, while Lisanne ran below to the crew quarters and banged on doors. "Armed Russians and Venezuelans coming in by air and sea!" she shouted over and over. "Lock your doors!"

When she reached the room where she'd deposited Amancia, Tallulah, and Gustavo, she entered. She sat on the lower bunk with them, listening, trying to keep them calm.

LINE OF DEMARCATION

"What do they want?" Tallulah asked.

While Lisanne wondered how to answer, Amancia filled the void. "Your father worried about this. He thought the Venezuelans might take everything one day."

"But that would be an invasion," the college student persisted in the dark. "Are you saying we're at war? And the Russians are helping? I thought we were running ahead of the Tiburónistas."

"You were," said Lisanne. After getting the download from Jack, they'd discussed the possible motives and outcomes of the Tiburónistas and crooked Guyanese National Police Force officers they'd outrun. "One possibility is that the Tiburónistas are working with the Venezuelans, who are allied with the Russians."

"Tiburón lives in Venezuela," Gustavo reminded them. "Most of the time."

"But you saw Russian army troops," Tallulah whispered. "This is an American-built platform . . . The Russians wouldn't risk a war with the U.S."

Lisanne could hear voices down the hall, shouting in noisy Spanish, banging on doors.

"American-built, but still Guyanese property," clarified Amancia. "That was the compromise that led to privatization. The American energy companies took the risk because they thought Guyana was a stable partner. Your dad engineered the alliance."

"It's still an invasion," her daughter persisted.

Lisanne cocked her head. "*Shh*," she cautioned. "They're getting closer."

Outside the door, Lisanne could hear American voices. At least one protested. Then Lisanne heard more yelling and bangs reverberating down the metal walls. The American voice screamed. A door slammed somewhere. Ominously, a three-round burst from an assault rifle rattled down the hall. The American was quiet.

Amancia raised her hand to her open mouth.

"Just do what they say," Lisanne said softly, wondering if Jack or Clark had heard her distress transmission.

Another burst of gunfire down the hall broke her concentration.

"We have to play for time," she continued. "We have to—"

A crash and a burst of light interrupted her. A man in an unmarked green army uniform with a mask across the lower half of his face took two steps into the room. He held a breaching tool in his left hand. When he saw the women on the bottom bunk, the intruder yelled something over his shoulder, dropped the breaching tool on the deck, and pointed his rifle at them.

Lisanne automatically initiated a threat assessment. She noted the AK-12, a modern military-issue Russian assault rifle. He had a swarthy complexion, a tattoo on his neck, hair poking out beneath the balaclava. A second assaulter appeared behind him.

"Up!" the second man shouted in Russian-accented English. He wore the same unmarked uniform and balaclava. From what Lisanne could see of his face, she judged him to be a white man in his mid- to late forties.

Russian, she thought—probably Wagner, one of the infamous "little green men" who'd infiltrated Crimea, Georgia, Donbas.

Lisanne stood up. The Russian sneered at her contemptuously, his eyes lingering on her prosthetic arm. He motioned them all to the center of the room, while the Hispanic man who crashed in the door jerked open closets and cabinets. When he got to the digital safe where the video cassettes were, he picked up the breaching tool, ready to break it open.

"Who are you? What do you want?" Lisanne shouted, hoping to distract him.

"Quiet!" the Russian barked at her.

LINE OF DEMARCATION

YEVGENY ZUKA LOWERED HIS AK-12 BARREL AND ORDERED THE TIB WITH HIM TO stand near the door.

These hostages weren't what he expected. They were three helpless women and a South American boy. The youngest woman was wounded and the tallest had a prosthetic arm. None of them looked like oil platform workers.

He took in the young woman's navy-blue Cal Bears T-shirt with a yellow silk-screen logo across her chest. Looking more closely, he saw the logo was stained with blood. He noticed that her jeans were dirty and ripped. Her shoes had been wiped, but still showed reddish-brown mud streaks.

He shifted his eyes to the older woman. She was wearing darker-colored shoes. They, too, showed ample evidence of dirt. If there was one thing that didn't exist on an offshore oil and gas platform, it was fresh dirt.

While the Tiburónista stood by the door, covering them with his rifle, Zuka detected no personal effects or luggage in the room. The only signs of use were the rumpled sheets on the two bunks and the dirty towel by the vanity.

The towel had reddish-brown smears.

Behind the Tib in the hall, Zuka could hear the rest of his platoon herding the platform workers to the stairwell. The plan was to bring them all to the cafeteria. After that, the joint Tiburónista-Wagner force would split up. Some would guard the prisoners. Others would finish assembling the anti-ship missile launchers and distributing the man-portable surface-to-air weapons.

"*Espera*," Zuka said over his shoulder to the Tib at the door. *Wait*.

"Identification," the Russian demanded of the four hostages standing defiantly before him. "Show me."

"No," answered the woman with the prosthetic arm, glaring at him.

Zuka freshly appraised her. She was dressed almost like a soldier in a black quarter-zip pullover, pants with cargo pockets, and Velcro-laced jungle boots. With her high cheekbones and rigid mouth, he thought of the great female soldiers of Russian lore—the all-women "Death Battalion" of the Revolution, the bomber pilots dubbed the "Night Witches" by the Nazis. Her clothes, the fiery eyes, and prosthetic arm suggested she'd seen combat.

He ordered the Tib to move in and frisk her first before proceeding with the others.

The Tib took his time running his hands over the women's asses. He pulled a small nylon wallet free from the Cal Bears girl's pocket. He handed the wallet to the Wagner leader.

Zuka let his rifle dangle at his chest on its sling. He opened the wallet and pulled out two identification cards. One was a California driver's license, the other a UC Berkeley student ID. The name on both was Tallulah Quintero. He was doubly sure the one-armed woman was a mercenary combatant, a hired bodyguard for the Guyanese civilians.

The Russian thought his boss, Morozov, would be pleased. Once he returned to the control room to supervise the arsenal, he would let the SVR man know of the find.

47

OFF THE GUYANESE COAST
0315

WITH JAD STRAPPED INTO THE LONG SEAT BEHIND HIM, JACK KEPT THE KILLER SKI pegged at maximum throttle, bouncing over the water at ninety knots. He could see on the screen that Chilly and Mandy's sled was about a half mile behind him, racing along at the same velocity.

"Moore and Clark aren't answering," Jad said to Jack through the noise-canceling intercom system. "I've tried all our assigned frequencies."

"Could be tactically engaged, unable to call back," Jack replied.

"Copy."

Jack glanced below the windscreen at the chart plotter. Based on the last transmission he'd heard from Lisanne, he was on a full-speed dash back to the GOPLAT. In the forty minutes since he'd picked up the call, he'd already covered fifty of the ninety miles to get back to the oil rig.

"Nothing new from GOPLAT Marlin?" Jack asked.

"Negative."

When there was no immediate reply, Jad added, "Lisanne didn't say for sure they were under attack. We don't know if those incoming surface contacts were hostiles."

"But she hasn't come back online."

"True."

"Try Clark and Moore on the secondary freq again."

Jad switched to the peer-to-peer frequency for Tempest One and Tempest Two. There was no answer.

"I wish this thing could go faster," Jack mumbled.

WHEN CLARK AND MOORE HEARD VOICES COMING AFT ALONG THE BRIDGE DECK above them, they killed the radios and flattened their backs against the bulkhead. The main salon was dark, its bulkhead window reflecting the moonlight. The port gunwale was three feet from them. If any crewman walked aft along this side, there would be a fight. Clark had withdrawn his SIG Sauer and attached the suppressor, while Moore kept his rifle at the ready.

They listened as the voices above them faded. Clark, farther aft, pointed at Moore's face, then patted the top of his helmet with his left hand, using the silent tactical signal for *Cover me*. Moore nodded, took a knee, and listened. He heard Ding scream from below the deck for the third time. He was sure Clark heard it, too.

Creeping sideways, Clark stepped behind the main deck salon's sliding glass door with his pistol drawn. When he was on the starboard side, he found a chest-high white locker with a life ring mounted to it, stenciled with the yacht's name, *Gran Blanco*. Clark opened the locker door slowly, praying it wouldn't squeak. Inside, he found what he was hoping for.

There were two shelves stuffed with generic first-aid equipment and a fire extinguisher. A diagram of the yacht pasted to the door's interior was more important to Clark. He studied it through his NVDs and traced his finger around the boat's lines.

LINE OF DEMARCATION

There was a dot on the aft bridge deck as a *You are here* symbol. The diagram was designed to show the locations of firefighting equipment. What mattered to Clark was that it showed him where Ding's screams were coming from.

According to the chart, there was a space below the main deck where he stood called the lazaret. Clark had never owned or chartered a motor yacht—but in a long career practicing maritime interdiction, he was familiar with their layouts.

The helpful diagram showed dotted lines that revealed that the back of the lazaret was a door that would ease down via an electric winch. According to the illustration, the door would sit flat, like an extended pickup truck tailgate. Clark assumed it served as both a ramp for the water toys and a deck for swimmers when it was out. When extended, it would cover the small, fixed platform they'd seen on their approach, which was more likely used for external maintenance. In Clark's opinion, the Tiburónistas had chosen the spot well as a stronghold to sequester a prisoner. It had no portholes, and the only way to get to it from inside the yacht was to access it via stairs that were forward, close to the crew berthing area.

Based on the yacht's radio chatter, the old SEAL guessed there were as many as twenty to thirty Tiburónista crewmen on the boat. The diagram showed no easy way to get into the lazaret, short of going through the crew quarters. He didn't necessarily mind taking on the whole crew with just himself and Moore—they would have a reasonable degree of surprise and cover. But a firefight would be a death sentence for Ding.

Clark hurried across the deck and returned to Moore's side. He cupped his hand to the master chief's ear and whispered the location of the lazaret and the challenge of reaching it. Moore took it all in, then gave Clark the *Cover me* head tap.

The big SEAL ran to the transom at the back of the boat. Clark could see him looking over the side, studying the closed ramp. After thirty seconds of consideration, Moore returned.

"We can get in there," he said softly, confidently.

"Oh yeah? How?" Clark asked.

Moore bent over and fished around inside a cargo pocket along his right thigh. He pulled out a wrapped piece of black cellophane and spread it out. It looked like four Slim Jim beef sticks packed together.

"What about det cord?" Clark asked.

Moore dug through the cargo pocket on his left side and pulled out a spool wrapped in black wire. "The spool makes a friction charge," he said, demonstrating a twist with his hands.

"You're going to blow it," Clark said.

"You're goddamn right I am," Moore replied.

48

0330

CLARK KEPT WATCH ON THE AFT MAIN DECK, HOPING NO TIBURÓNISTAS WERE OUT for a late-night smoke break.

Moore was lying on his stomach on the transom with a docking line wrapped around his shoulders. To find the correct seams for the eight-inch C-4 charges, he had to lie with most of his bulk over the side. He risked drowning in the enormous yacht's boiling silver wake if he fell.

Moore backed toward Clark, unspooling the detonation cord as he walked. When the det cord was all the way out, the master chief held the spool in his hand, ready to twist it and ignite the C-4.

"Okay," Clark whispered. "You think it will blow the door right off?"

"I don't know," Moore said. "Hard to say how tough the construction is. I concentrated on the top of the door. Hopefully, it will blow straight down."

"Right."

"You want to go over the plan again?" Moore asked.

"Yeah," Clark responded. "After the charges blow, I'll toss a few nine-bangers in the laz, jump to the extended platform, and kill whoever isn't Ding down there. Then I jump into the wake with Ding. You shoot any squirters and leap into the water after me. The sleds will pick us up. That about right?"

"That's about right," Moore repeated with a grin. "What could go wrong?"

Clark fingered the grenades on his chest, making sure he had the flash-bangs ready. Staying on the port side, he crouched at the transom and kept his eyes pegged on Moore. Clark held up three fingers. Two fingers. One.

Moore twisted the detonator, unleashing an electric charge that instantly sparked the C-4, setting off a chain reaction of the four charges.

Rushing aft, Clark looked anxiously over the back of the boat. The ramp was popped open at the top port quarter, sticking out like a dented fender. But the rest of the lazaret door was solidly in place.

Though the charge hadn't worked as planned, Clark saw no choice but to keep going. He hurled the flash-bang through the triangle-shaped opening. When it reached its seventh bang, he jumped through the slot with his pistol in his hand and his rifle fixed to a peg on his combat vest.

Since the door angled out but hadn't come completely down, it acted like a slide. Clark hit the steel lazaret deck hard. Along the way, a bolt snagged the wire to his earpiece, yanking it free and cutting his comms with the rest of the team.

He had no time to worry about comms. The lazaret lights were bright, forcing him to tip his NVDs up. He saw Ding bound to a chair at the forward bulkhead. A man was next to him on the ground, dazed and stumbling from the flash-bang's fireworks.

Clark raised his pistol and shot, but the man had already dived behind a small, white rigid inflatable boat. Clark shot the inflatable sponsons, hoping to remove his target's concealment. But no sooner had the rubber shredded than the man was firing back with an AK-12, forcing Clark to dive behind a refrigerator-sized metal cargo box. He was trapped between the partially open ramp and the machine-gun-wielding Tiburónista next to Ding.

If there was one thing Clark hated, it was a gunfight in a well-lit room. He identified the track of lights running down the lazaret ceiling and shot them out in a shower of sparks and glass. He tipped his NVDs down, ready to move forward and dispatch the tango. As he scanned the area near the RIB, he caught a glimpse of Ding's face.

Chavez was stoic, his eyes open. A gag was over his mouth and his lids were nearly swollen shut. Clark saw no point in calling out to Ding. His longtime protégé and son-in-law would understand exactly what was happening.

Clark heard radio static from the front of the laz. The man at the forward bulkhead by the RIB was chattering, likely calling in reinforcements. Even worse, Clark could hear rifle fire on the deck above him. Moore was initiating a delaying action.

The tango by the RIB unleashed a volley in Clark's direction, plinking off the door behind him, showering him with sparks. Clark saw the muzzle flash and fired a few rounds in reply.

The options to get this guy were limited, he realized. Yes, he had the advantage of the NVDs, but the partially open door behind him was streaming moonlight. His target could see well enough. Then there was the matter of targeting the tango. Normally in this situation, Clark would lob a grenade to get the scumbag out of hiding. But if he did that this time, he'd just as easily kill Ding.

Perhaps the most painful disadvantage was time. Based on the battle over his head and the Spanish radio chatter he could hear from up near the RIB, he knew there were dozens of mad-dog Tiburónistas heading this way, maybe even the drug lord himself.

Clark remembered going after scum like Tiburón—Juan Machado, as he was known back then. He relished the progress he and Ding had made in Colombia back in those days, blowing up drug labs, killing kingpins—until the same CIA deputy director who'd ordered the action pulled the plug to cover his slimy ass.

Yeah, thought the veteran SEAL as he ducked a volley from the RIB and heard a grenade go off over his head. *Maybe if we'd been able to keep going, then we wouldn't be here right now.*

A crash jolted him. It was Moore. The big SEAL slid through the triangle opening and nearly knocked Clark over. He had his NVD tubes over his eyes and his pistol in his hand. To Clark, that meant Moore was out of rifle ammo.

Clark raised his HK and shot at the RIB again, covering Moore.

Moore crawled toward the edge of the door. "Cover me!" he shouted. Clark kept shooting, not understanding what Moore was trying to do, but trusting his brother SEAL.

Then it dawned on Clark. The exterior door he used as a slide started coming down. Moore had activated the switch that lowered it. "No!" shouted Clark. "We can't leave without Ding."

"We're not leaving!" Moore shouted back over the noise of the wake and the electric winch. "We've got incoming friendlies!"

49

MOTOR YACHT *GRAN BLANCO*
0333

AS JACK WAS FLYING OVER THE WAVES IN HIS RETURN TO GOPLAT MARLIN, HE SAW Clark's and Moore's skis on the navigation display trailing the *Gran Blanco*.

He tried to raise them on the radio. "Tempest One and Two, this is Three and Four coming up behind you. We're headed back to base. Say status, over."

Jack was surprised by Moore's strained answer: *"This is One. We're on the* Gran Blanco."

The chief sounded winded. Jack could hear gunshots over the transmission. Bypassing the trailing skis, Jack veered directly for the *Gran Blanco* and fired up the ski's optical sensor. He approached from behind, closing fast. Several flashes of light whited out the optical sensor's screen.

"Tempest Four," he radioed Chilly and Mandy a half mile behind him. "Tempest One and Two are engaged in a firefight on the *Gran Blanco*. Head straight for the yacht!"

"You have any good ideas on how to help Moore and Clark?" Jad asked on the intercom as Jack changed course.

"I figure we'll improvise when we get closer," Jack said. "Moore said we have a boarding ladder on the ski. The painter's pole is down at our feet. Do you know how to use it?"

"Yeah," Jad answered. "They made me do it once during a joint exercise off Korea. But it's been a while."

"Well, get ready."

When they were just a few hundred yards behind the two riderless skis, Jack slowed to keep pace. He looked at the *Gran Blanco* through his NVDs and made out the black opening of the damaged lazaret door. He witnessed flashes that seemed to indicate a firefight from inside the hold. On the deck above the damaged door, he spotted Tibs racing aft, preparing to slide through the opening.

"Jad, you have a grenade launcher mounted to your 416, don't you?"

"Yeah."

"Pop those Tibs. Hit the boat on the fantail."

Jad fired. The thump of the grenade launcher sounded like a hard strike on a bass drum.

The round hit two seconds later with a burst aft of the main salon. Flying glass glittered in a secondary explosion. Two dark bodies lofted over the side.

With the Tibs scattered from the stern, Jack tapped Jad on the leg. "The chief and Clark are behind that stern hatch," Jack said. "You see it?"

Jad held his rifle to his eye. "You mean that banged-up garage door on the back of the boat?"

"Yeah, that one. We need to get in there."

"Well, that should be easy," Jad said, studying it.

"Why?"

"Because it's coming down."

Moore's voice broke in. "*Three. We have jackpot. We're in the lazaret, at the stern waterline. Need more rifles back here. Not sure how long we can hold out. Door coming down.*"

Chilly and Mandy's ski were just behind Jack. Jad fired a second grenade amidships. Another Tib flew over the side in a cloud of splinters and shards.

Jack saw the scene playing out inside as the garage door came down. He raced closer and detected a RIB on a platform. Next to it, he spotted Ding slumped in a chair while Clark fired from behind a locker at the RIB. Moore was working a pistol.

As far as Jack could tell, there were only a few Tibs left on the main deck. They were firing at his incoming ski. Jack zigzagged while Jad returned fire, calling out hits. Mandy joined the melee, aiming at resurgent Tibs on the upper decks.

Jack kept his eyes on Moore at the top of the ramp. The chief was waving frantically, his voice cutting in and out with the gunfire at his back. Jack realized what Moore was trying to say.

"Hang on!" he exclaimed to Jad. "We're going in!"

The ski rose from the choppy water like a sprinter coming out of the blocks. With the throttle maxed, Jack passed through twenty, thirty, fifty knots, holding on for dear life. He aimed at the ramp, going for the tango on the other side of the RIB.

"Oh shit," he heard Jad mutter behind him when the ski was just a few feet from the ramp.

The Tiburónista next to the RIB swiveled his rifle to aim at Jack. Everything in the lazaret got bigger before Jack's eyes. He felt the ski strike metal. For the briefest flicker, the Tib was right in front of him.

Jack felt a terrible jolt to his chest. His head snapped forward. His helmet slammed off the handlebars. Stunned, he heard rumbles and cracks as the ski fell sideways. The crushed Tib lay a few feet from him. Two strong hands were working the buckles at his hips. Clark's lined face peered over him.

The old SEAL was smiling.

Reality rushed in. Jack tried to get up, but fell into a crush of scattered equipment. Clark helped him to his feet. Moore pulled Jad loose. Clark turned away from Jack, kneeling next to Ding. He sawed at Ding's restraints with a Ka-Bar.

Jack made it to his feet. His ribs were sore. When he looked out the open garage door, he saw Chilly at the front of the ski, surfing on the wake. Mandy held her rifle to her eye, aiming above them. She wasn't firing.

"Four," Jack rasped over the radio. It hurt to breathe. "Say status."

Mandy answered. *"We're not seeing any movement on the main deck above you. All tangos are down or retreated."*

Jack double-clicked. He went to Ding. Clark and Moore had stretched Chavez out on the deck. As the team medic, Jad hovered over the wounded man, checking his wounds with a small flashlight. Clark was speaking to him. Jack crouched next to them.

"You okay?" Clark asked.

Ding nodded. Blood pooled in deep bruises on his face. When he spoke, his words slurred through broken teeth. "Don't bother with me right now. Just kill them."

"How many are there?" Clark asked.

"Thirty," Ding answered. "I think."

Clark and Moore lifted their suffering brother operator. Jad put down several life vests stored in the lazaret and used them as cushions. They raised Ding to a seated position, his back to a bulkhead. He winced every time he moved.

"Mr. C.," Jack said insistently when Ding was settled. "We've got another problem."

"You mean the rest of the Tibs on the boat? Right. We need to get forward and help Jad and Moore with an assault."

Jack shook his head. "No. I mean Marlin. The rig is under attack."

"*What?*" Clark shot back, paling. "What are you talking about?"

"Lisanne radioed that armed men in boats were approaching. She was forced to shut down comms. I haven't been able to raise them since her distress call."

"How many?"

"She estimated six boats. She didn't give a head count."

Ding tugged on Jack's sleeve. His voice was lost in the swirling wind and echoing wake bounding around the lazaret's metal walls. Jack and Clark leaned close to his face.

"They're Wagner Group and Tiburónistas," the operative murmured. "My cover was blown. They know who I am. They're going to seize the oil platforms and overtake the legitimate government. They set it up to look like a drug thing. It's not. This is led by the Russians, an SVR guy."

Clark exhaled sharply. "We saw the signs."

"You're not here to stop them?" Ding asked.

Clark and Jack exchanged a look.

"I guess we are now," Jack said.

50

0340

MASTER CHIEF KENDRICK MOORE WALKED SIDEWAYS OVER THE CARPET ALONG THE richly paneled walls. He stepped over the dead Tiburónista he had shot with his suppressed SIG Sauer a few seconds before.

"This is the engine room," he whispered to Jad, who was a half step behind him. Moore tapped his helmet with the *Cover me* signal. "I'm going in."

The SEAL silently twisted the doorknob. After a three-count, he hurled it open. A middle-aged, unarmed man in a grease-streaked T-shirt immediately threw up his arms, pleading in Spanish for them not to shoot.

"Fuse box!" Moore growled at him from behind the Glock's barrel. The man pointed to a metal wall locker. While Jad covered the engineer, Moore worked it open and clicked off the main breaker. The engine room went dark.

"Better," said Jad. The Green Beret tipped his NVD tubes over his eyes and followed Moore down the hallway.

They passed a small galley with several doors beyond it—crew quarters. "You come in high behind me," Moore instructed. "We're going to clear this room on the left first."

Jad scanned the passageway and raised his rifle. He gave Moore two taps on his shoulder.

Moore front-kicked the first door open. He saw three empty, unmade bunks. Jad hurried behind him and kicked open the adjoining head. A Tiburónista sprung from a crouch with a knife in his hand. Jad shot him in the forehead.

"Clear," he shouted to Moore.

They followed a similar procedure in the other three rooms, but found them empty. Moore reached the foot of the stairs. He and Jad waited, listening. Once they ascended, they would be in the dining room off the main salon.

"Clark," Moore whispered into the tactical frequency. Clustered together on the yacht, they had dispensed with call signs out of expediency.

"Go," Clark called back.

"We're at the stairs. What's your pos?"

"We made it out of the hole." Clark didn't bother to add that Chilly and Mandy had ridden up the ramp on their ski and provided Ding medical support and security.

"Can you see anyone in the salon?"

"Roger," Clark said. "Two tangos near the center. Jack and I will hit them with a nine-banger. You and Jad go for the shooters."

Moore remained still, visualizing the sequence, worried about hitting Clark and Jack on the far side of the salon. "As soon as you toss the banger," he returned quietly, "hit the deck. We'll go high."

"Roger that," Clark replied.

Moore looked at Jad, who flashed a thumbs-up.

"Ready when you are," Moore said into the radio.

"On three," Clark answered. "One, two—"

Moore charged up the stairs. He tried to see through the salon's light, smoke, and fury. He spotted two terrified Tibs shooting indiscriminately toward the stern, shattering what was left of the already-ruined glass doors. Moore and Jad took them down with headshots.

Clark and Jack ducked inside, careful not to brush against falling shards. Jack looked at the rolling shell casings on the carpet and the three dead Tibs, each nearly headless. "Nice work, Chief," he said.

"One more deck to clear," Clark added.

"Where do you think Tiburón is?" Jack asked.

Clark tilted his face at the stair landing to the right of the dining room. "I'm guessing he's hiding somewhere up top near the sky bridge. Ding said he did his business up there. I'll take point on the outside ladder with Jack. Chief, you and Jad take the stairs from in here."

Clark and Jack maneuvered outside and waited on the weather deck. Jack looked around the dark boat through his NVDs. He saw a dead Tib on the middle deck and five more lifeless men scattered on the fantail below. The boat was pocked with ragged fiberglass tears, broken glass, and scorch marks from the firefight.

Jack tipped up his goggles and looked at the stars. He glimpsed the Southern Cross, low on the horizon. He made out a streak of land off the yacht's starboard side, distant in the haze. He pictured the map he had studied before leaving Marlin. They were headed south, skirting Guyana's lightly populated Essequibo shore. He mulled Lisanne's last distress call, thinking through the strain in her voice.

"We're set," Moore said over the radio, bringing Jack back to the mission at hand.

Clark turned to him. Jack tipped his NVDs down. "So are we," Clark confirmed. "I'll go up and do a recon. Everyone, stay in your three-foot world. This one's gonna be hot."

With one hand over the other, Clark crept silently up the ladder. Jack watched him peek over the rim of the higher deck before lowering his head.

"Four men in the salon aft of the sky bridge," Clark reported quietly. "The salon has glass walls, already blown. I'm going to toss a home-wrecker to clear the space. Moore and Jad, as soon as it blows, take down anyone left standing."

Moore double-clicked.

Clark hooked an elbow around the ladder to stay steady. He detached a grenade from his vest. "Frag out," he said. He flexed up, threw the thermobaric grenade, then crouched.

Two seconds later, Jack's ears popped with pressure. A cascade of debris flew over his head. When he looked up the ladder, Clark was already gone.

Jack rushed to the top and dashed forward. Clark, Moore, and Jad were in the upper salon, sweeping their rifles. Jad took a few shots into the sky bridge. "All down," he announced a few seconds later.

A Tib with bleeding ears rolled sideways with a pistol. Clark shot him.

Jack kicked over the other three Tibs, making sure they were dead. Clark stepped forward and peered through the door to the flybridge. A fiberglass wall protected the bridge from the thermobaric pressure blast. "The yacht has a duplicate set of steerage controls in here," he said. "And another set of stairs that leads forward and down," he added ominously.

Jack, Moore, and Jad entered the bridge and stood next to Clark. The Tib Jad had shot was crumpled to the deck. Jad pulled him backward into the smashed salon, clearing the room.

Moore gestured at the descending stairs with his Glock. "If Tiburón's on this boat, he's going to be down there." The big SEAL pointed at double doors at the bottom stair landing.

"You sure?" Clark asked.

Moore's NVDs bobbed up and down in the affirmative. "We've cleared every other stateroom and checked the safety diagrams. That's the only space we haven't touched."

"Okay," Clark replied, surveying the double doors. "I'd rather him come out than we risk going in. Any ideas?"

Jack focused on the bridge's console. He saw several rows of neatly labeled buttons under a heading that said INTERCOM. One of them was titled CAPTAIN'S SUITE.

Jack motioned toward it with his rifle. "Why not ask him to come out?"

Clark surveyed the switches. "Sure," he said after a few seconds of contemplation. "What the hell."

The old SEAL stepped forward and stabbed the button.

"Hello, Tiburón," he began, dragging out the syllables with steel in his voice. "My name is John Clark. I came here to find Domingo Chavez. The three of us go back a long time, all the way to the Ernesto Escobedo days in northern Colombia."

Clark paused, then taunted, "You hiding in there, Juan?"

The cabin doors burst open.

An orange fusillade streamed up the stairs, shredding the ceiling with bright sparks. The Campus operatives, already crouched, collapsed to their bellies. Tiburón screamed a string of mixed English and Spanish obscenities over the terrifying roar of his weapon as he barreled up the stairs.

Clark rolled sideways with his arms extended and his pistol in a double-fisted grip.

Mid-roll, he put a bullet through the drug lord's forehead.

The shooting stopped. The yacht was quiet.

Clark slowly rose to a knee. He studied Tiburón's lifeless body, then turned to Master Chief Moore. "Chief, get up to the helm and steer for GOPLAT Marlin. Jack, Jad, clear the decks below to make sure there are no Tiburónistas hiding on this boat. I need to call Mary Pat Foley. ASAP."

Clark fished his satellite phone from a thigh pocket as the other men raced away.

51

ABU DHABI, REMOTE DESERT NEAR SABKAH
1205

PRESIDENT ALI KHASIF WAS HAVING THE STRANGEST DREAM. A LARGE HOATZIN, THE national bird of Guyana, was flying just above him, diving down. It swooped and turned in the air just over his head. Occasionally, the long feathers of its wide chestnut wings tickled his cheek.

He nervously swatted the bird away. The clumsy motion of his hand crashed into his chin and woke him. The earthly world filtered in through crusted eye slits. He blinked.

It wasn't a hoatzin breezing next to him. Rather, the sensation came from the angled wall of a low green tent dipping in the wind. He lay still for another few seconds, letting it brush against his head, not quite sure where he was or why.

He heard a male voice outside the tent. Out of reflex, he checked his watch. It was a quarter past twelve, full daylight. He couldn't understand why he was sleeping during the day.

One memory fragment after another drifted back to him. He was in Abu Dhabi, with the prince. No, he corrected himself—with the Russian, Viktor Zhdanov, the CEO of Gazneft. He angled his torso and leaned on an elbow. His head throbbed. His throat was dry.

He could hear the growl of vehicles outside his tent; the events of the prior day came streaming back.

Since forcing the Guyanese leader to ride shotgun with him in his souped-up, long-range Polaris RZR, Zhdanov had hopscotched from one desert peak to another, constantly claiming to know the next spot along the two-thousand-kilometer course, all the while driving them deeper into the desert.

Having peeled off from the core Emirati vehicle caravan, the Guyanese president had no choice but to cling to the RZR's safety bars while the oil baron invented his own route, bragging about his ability to cross wadi and dune at breakneck speed.

When they entered the no-man's-land of the Rub al Khali, the aptly named Empty Quarter, Zhdanov finally admitted to blundering. He stopped the vehicle and looked around. Khasif could remember it all. Zhdanov had laughed.

"Oh well," he said, grinning while removing his compact satellite phone from his breast pocket. "This looks like as good a place as any. I'll get provisions brought in, and we'll camp here. I bet we're close to the racecourse."

Within the hour, Khasif recalled, two white and silver Eurocopters arrived in a swirl of dust, populating the sand around them with eight men whom Zhdanov described as Gazneft executive staff. As if the billionaire had touched Aladdin's lamp, the newcomers unloaded tents and food from the helicopters.

By the time the sun slipped below the dunes, they stoked a roaring fire under the stars and spread a feast of roast mutton. Zhdanov proposed a vodka toast to the future of Gazneft and Guyana.

Ali Khasif politely abstained. "My staff made you a mocktail," Zhdanov said, "in honor of your religion." After that, Khasif drew a blank.

Mocktail, indeed, he thought heatedly.

He kicked and rolled his way out of the low tent. Outside, squinting against an azure sky, he saw that the helicopters were gone. He noticed two tan Land Rovers parked behind the RZR with five men resting against the tires, a mix of Russians and Arabs. He marched toward them.

"Viktor!" he yelled angrily. The exertion made him cough. "Viktor!" he hollered again.

One of the Russians at the vehicles stood and lazily dusted off his trousers.

"Where is he?" Khasif rasped. "I demand to see him."

The Russian wore khaki pants with cargo pockets. Over that, a long tunic cut like a military blouse. Khasif saw no insignia. "I want to talk to Zhdanov right now," he shouted. "Do you hear me? Now. This is over."

"Mr. Zhdanov had business," the Russian responded in accented English.

"I don't care what he had. You get me back to the prince. Immediately."

"The race is still happening," added the man.

"I don't care about the race!" Khasif seethed. "Get me to the prince! I won't stand for this. Do you understand me?"

The Russian replied matter-of-factly, as if Khasif hadn't spoken at all. "You will ride with Youssef today. He will take you to a better spot to view the race. It's not far." He waved to an Arab in a checkered kaffiyeh who stood near one of the Land Rovers.

"No I won't," Khasif snarled. "Not a chance. You will take me to the prince. Do you know who I am? Do you understand what you're doing here?"

The Arab and the Russian exchanged an uncertain glance. "Get in the RZR, President Khasif."

"No," Khasif objected, digging in. "In fact, I won't get in any vehicle. You will call in one of your helicopters and take me straight to Abu Dhabi. Is that clear?"

The Russian reached under his shirttail and pulled a stubby pistol from the small of his back, pointing it at the dirt. "You will ride with Youssef today," he repeated. "It is not a request."

Khasif froze. A second Russian got out of a Land Rover, wielding a dusty AK-47 with tape on the barrel.

"Get in the vehicle," said the Russian, gesturing to the RZR. "You will ride with Youssef. We will follow you to the right place."

"No," Khasif reiterated, keeping still as a stone. "I won't. As I said, you will—"

A wind with the strength of a monsoon swallowed the rest of his words. So much sand swirled around Khasif that he choked and buried his nose in the crook of his bent arm. In the wall of chalky dust, he lost sight of the Land Rovers, the Russians, and Youssef.

A roaring tear shrieked over his head. He had never heard anything like it—it ripped through the air like a buzz saw. A shower of hot brass bullet jackets pelted him from above, stinging his arms. Thoroughly confused, Khasif dropped into a ball to protect himself, choking on dust. He contracted his body and squeezed his palms over his ears. The buzz saw got louder, seemingly coming from three directions at once. He turned his head to look, but saw nothing but brown. Flying dust blotted out the world.

He felt a painful tug at his armpits. His feet were suddenly off the ground. The dust blew away long enough for him to see that two men were dragging him. They were in desert military uniforms with black gloves and helmets. Clear goggles protected their eyes. One of them had a khaki American flag velcroed to the front of his combat vest, just above a row of hand grenades.

The wind swirled away. In the remaining haze, Khasif glimpsed a helicopter overhead. It was small and black, shaped like an egg, circling them in a tight turn. He spotted a machine gunner at the door, sweeping a thick black weapon back and forth.

"President Khasif!" yelled one of the men holding him.

Khasif swallowed hard against the dust and choked out an affirmative.

"We've been looking for you," the man shouted over the turning helicopter.

"Who are you?" Khasif gasped. "What is this?"

"We're U.S. military. There's been a coup in your country, sir. We're here to get you to safety and put you in contact with your government. Are you willing to come with us?"

The president seized the man's shoulder. "You're damn right I am!" he yelled.

52

GEORGETOWN PARLIAMENT BUILDING, GUYANA
0410

A FEW FEET AWAY FROM THE CAMERA, BOOM MIC, AND PEDESTAL LIGHTS, PRIME Minister Augustus Castillo dozed in his chair with his head canted to one side.

Alejandro Romero darted past the anteroom, where Sheila waited, and burst into Castillo's bunker office with a burner phone pressed to his ear. He was in his police uniform, though he'd removed the jacket. His service weapon was holstered at his hip, bouncing as he walked briskly into the leadership operations center. As soon as he saw the prime minister, he kicked the chair leg and nudged the politician awake.

"Morozov on the phone," Romero said. "Wake up."

"Is it time?" Castillo asked instantly, assuming the moment had arrived when he would get in front of the camera and make his announcement.

"Time for what?"

"My broadcast." He tapped the paper in his breast pocket that would declare to the whole world that Guyana's president, Ali Khasif, had been heartlessly gunned down by a heroin drug lord at

Tiburón's command. The announcement would solicit Venezuelan security forces to crack down on Tiburón, pursuing him and his Tiburónistas into the Essequibo region, if required.

"I don't know. Maybe. But we have other developments. Let me put Morozov on speaker." Romero stabbed a button and placed the phone on an end table, screen up.

"Who's there?" Morozov asked.

Fuzzy from his doze, Castillo shook his head briskly. He felt a tingle in his gut. After all the worry, fears, and efforts, he could hardly believe his ascendance was upon him at last.

"This is Prime Minister Castillo. Good morning, Major Morozov. Are we ready to broadcast? Should I summon the technical crew?"

"No," Morozov replied flatly. "We have a problem. It may delay timing and change the message."

Romero stood with his arms crossed between Castillo and the door, yawning.

"What are you talking about?" Castillo asked with alarm. "What problem? Why change the message?"

"Because I believe Tiburón is dead."

"*What?*" the prime minister spat acidly. "How is that possible? Why would you think that?"

"A distress call came in from his yacht. There were invaders. They hit both his camp on the Orinoco and the *Gran Blanco*. I haven't heard from any of them since their distress calls came in."

"So you're not sure," said Castillo. "He could still be alive."

"I would give Tiburón's death a ninety percent confidence level, simply because he's never been quiet like this. And as I just told you, we got a distress call."

"Does anyone else know?"

"I don't believe so."

"Good."

"Agreed," the Russian said. "At least for the next several hours until the Wagner planes depart Cuba, the Tiburónistas under my command must believe Tiburón to be alive—or we may have problems of allegiance."

"Who hit him, for God's sake?"

"I assume they're Americans."

"Americans?" Castillo shrieked. The fears that had been swimming just below consciousness suddenly leaped up and slapped him in the face. "They can't do that! Under international law . . . that would constitute an invasion!"

"We don't have enough evidence to know for sure that they're Americans . . . yet."

Castillo stood and paced, weaving between Romero and the AV equipment. The head of the Guyanese National Police rolled his sleeves and loosened his police belt a few notches, causing his service weapon to droop.

"And Khasif?" asked Castillo. "Has that issue been handled?"

"As far as I know, the SVR has the matter under control."

"As far as you know? What does that mean?"

Morozov sighed. "Khasif and his staff have been cut off from communications for more than twenty-four hours, as you must realize, Prime Minister. Our intent is that he will be neutralized before any intervention is possible. That part of the plan remains in place."

Castillo stopped pacing for a moment, shuddering inwardly. "When do I broadcast?"

"I need to get confirmation from Moscow, which I expect to have soon," the SVR major answered calmly. "As soon as I do, I will call. You must make the declaration then. That will trigger the other matters. We are not deviating from that strategy."

The prime minister massaged his temples, wondering what other surprises awaited. Much to his discomfort, this fateful day had come sooner than anticipated. He didn't like the unpredictability—an attack on Tiburón's river camp and yacht was beyond the pale, something he'd never imagined.

He ran his hand through his hair.

No Tiburón.

Castillo sifted through the possibilities if the drug lord was really gone. On the surface, certainly, the maniac's death would be a relief. He loathed the outlaw who'd threatened his daughters. His murderous thugs were still running amok, sacking the country. Their mayhem might even worsen without Tiburón to keep them in check.

Castillo wondered how that would play out in the media. In his estimate, he could still justify hiring Wagner. Guyana was in the throes of a drug-fueled meltdown. Was it crazy to hire a mercenary firm to maintain some level of order? In the long term, he calculated, he could still make a case to cut Essequibo off and gift it to Venezuela. He would argue that the lawless province was more trouble than it was worth.

"What about the oil platforms?" Castillo asked. "Have you properly secured them?"

"Yes," Morozov replied. "My men have taken the only manned platform, Marlin. There was no resistance."

"Hostages?"

"About twenty-five Americans, a few Guyanese."

Castillo darted a worried glance at Romero, who stood listening with his arms crossed.

"How can you be so confident?" the prime minister asked the Russian. "You just said Yankee commandos are already here, striking at Tiburón from the sea. What if they're mounting a raid on the oil platforms?"

The SVR man answered like a bloodless accountant. "I would only give that a ten percent chance of success."

"Why?"

"Because we've prepared for that. The Wagner-led Tiburónistas have anti-ship and surface-to-air missile defenses. An offshore oil platform properly armed is a highly defensible position. Any commando force that approaches would be wiped out before they could get close."

"That is true," Romero agreed, nodding.

Castillo looked longingly at the camera on its tripod. "The Americans could send an entire invasion force to take those platforms. I might not keep control of the army if that happens. You don't think we should worry about that?"

"No," replied the Russian.

"Why not?"

"Because the frigate *Admiral Gorshkov* is in range. Any American forces that approach will be destroyed."

53

MOTOR YACHT *GRAN BLANCO*
0422

CLARK BROKE THE CONNECTION TO MARY PAT FOLEY AND TURNED TO JACK, WHO SAT alone on the small built-in sofa behind the helm.

"Good news," the SEAL announced. "A Delta team snatched President Khasif in the desert west of Abu Dhabi. They're flying him down to Doha for a briefing with CENTCOM right now."

Jack frowned. "That doesn't help us with taking the oil platform."

"It will if Khasif can order the Guyanese military into action quickly."

"Quickly?" countered Jack. "They might start shooting hostages if they think this thing is going south."

Clark folded his arms and studied the tops of his boots for a moment. He turned to Moore. "Chief, how far are we from Marlin?"

With his big hands on the wheel, Moore had the yacht's massive diesel engines at full power, chopping through the Atlantic swells at thirty-two knots. He surveyed the chart plotter.

"We're about fifteen minutes from Marlin," he said. "Maybe a little less if I can find a favorable current."

"Still no comms from Lisanne or Cary?"

"Negative," Jack replied. "We're headed into this blind. I think we may have to—"

Mandy and Chilly brought Domingo Chavez in, interrupting Jack. Jad trailed behind them, toting his medical bag.

Clark helped Ding to a spot on the settee. The wounded man's arm was wrapped and splinted. His face was blotchy with iodine stains.

"I'm all right," he said softly, easing onto the seat. "No dancing for a while, though."

"Patricia says you hate it anyway," Clark said, referring to his daughter, Ding's wife.

"True. Now I have a good excuse."

"How is he?" Clark asked Jad.

"He has a broken arm. Pretty severe concussion. Second-degree burns on his chest."

"Burns?" The old SEAL asked Ding. "What'd they do?"

Ding shifted and grunted against the pain of movement. "Jumper cables hooked to a twelve-volt. Don't recommend any of you try it."

Jack put a hand on Ding's shoulder. "Sorry."

"Did they drug you?" Clark asked, concerned about his longtime protégé's sickly complexion.

"They didn't have time," answered Ding. "The Russian, Morozov, ordered the Tibs to keep me alive. I think he intended to return with scopolamine or whatever. He already knew something about my history."

"Like?" asked Jack.

"Like how Clark and I were in Colombia going after Escobedo." Ding frowned, then winced at the pain in his swollen cheek. "The Tib who had it in for me, Caraza, kept telling me how Tiburón was going to tear my limbs off and chum the waters behind the boat."

"I think that's exactly what would have happened," Clark said.

Ding looked appreciatively at Jack. "Hey, man, I liked your Colt Seavers stuntman routine back there. Caraza never saw that Jet Ski coming. You pasted him pretty good."

"Thanks," Jack replied. "But unfortunately, we're not done. We think the Tibs took at least one of the oil platforms, Marlin. For all we know they may be on Mako and Mackerel too"

"Jad told me Cary and Lisanne are on defense," Ding said. "I'm up for a counterattack."

"The hell you are," Clark replied. "What do you know of Tib tactics?"

Ding took a measured breath. "The Tibs have been loading up boats with cargo for the past two weeks. Until last night, I thought they were running drugs. But then I saw a missile right before they nabbed me. A GPS track on one of the boats showed they were headed to a weapons cache out here at sea. Maybe a barge. They have some serious firepower."

"Such as?" asked Moore, looking back from his position at the helm.

"Russian Kayak anti-ship missiles, probably some MANPADs. Safe to assume all that stuff is down there at the oil platform by now. Our approach better be damned careful."

"Maybe we wait until the Guyanese president orders forces to help us," Moore said.

Ding grimaced. "I've seen these Tibs firsthand. They'll have no problem shooting hostages—especially if they don't have Tiburón to give them orders not to."

Clark scratched his cheek. "I agree with you. But getting into a defended oil platform is a serious bitch. I'm not sure we have the manpower or resources for it. If we had air support, then maybe . . . but . . ."

Jack stood up and put his hands on his hips, mindful of the distance to Marlin that ticked down on the chart plotter. "Mr. C., I'm not sure that's going to be necessary."

"Oh? Why's that, Jack?"

"Because I have a better idea."

54

GOPLAT MARLIN
0442

PERCHED MORE THAN FIVE HUNDRED FEET ABOVE THE SEA, FIRST SERGEANT CARY Marks tipped up his NVD tubes and watched the first pink traces of dawn.

He squinted against the breeze. Both sea and sky were still dark. The cloud light was little more than a suggestion of the coming day. But one way or another, his long night was coming to an end.

He glanced down the series of metal girders that formed the tall derrick he'd climbed, then put his rifle scope to his eye.

He watched as men worked to secure their defenses on the helipad below. The main effort, it seemed, involved mating boxy missile tubes to a swiveling launcher. He could hear them grunting under the strain. They'd been at it all night.

Marks studied them from his aerie in the girders. Hours ago, he was halfway to this spot when the heavy Russian gunship touched down. He'd found concealment and watched while men with masked faces spread out in a defensive perimeter. The voices that drifted up to him were a mix of Russian and Spanish.

LINE OF DEMARCATION

As a professional soldier, First Sergeant Marks could admire how swiftly they moved in. Without delay, they used the crane to pull cargo from the boats in the surf, just as his Campus brethren had. The gunship made a few protective laps around the derrick for air support before thundering off. The men had been fortifying their position with missiles ever since.

With defenses like that, Cary had grown steadily more pessimistic about a Campus counterattack. Not that his teammates weren't capable—they certainly were. But as Marks saw it, the enemy he watched below had the tools of a sophisticated army. To his eye, they were far more lethal than the unorganized, poorly trained drug smugglers they set out against.

No. Kicking these guys off the platform would take a real military force—and even *that* wouldn't be a cakewalk. Airborne commandos would be picked off as they floated down. Frogmen could be shot as soon as they put their heads above water. More vexing, the traditional American advantage of air support would be limited. Hitting this thing with a laser-guided bomb would destroy billions of dollars of infrastructure, create an environmental disaster, and kill all the hostages. As Cary saw it, the bad guys had planned well.

Except for one thing: those pros down there didn't know that a Green Beret sniper with an HK416 and prime optics was perched over their heads.

With American hostages below, he was willing to bet that President Ryan would be cooking up a counterstrike. He'd met the President, once, and judged him a man who wouldn't lay down to a hostage situation like this one. If the strike came—Cary intended to be ready.

Until the moment arrived, however, all he could do was plan, hide, wait, and ignore the hunger pains in his gut, the stab at his bladder, and the lack of sleep. He expected to endure the whole day up here in the derrick, dodging the strong sun and shifting to stay out of sight.

Or maybe not.

He suddenly glimpsed a big white yacht on the horizon.

His spirits plummeted when he realized it was the *Gran Blanco*, headed straight toward the platform. Two riderless Jet Skis trailed it at a distance.

HUNDREDS OF FEET BELOW THE GREEN BERET, ON THE MIDDLE DECK OF GOPLAT MAR- lin, Lisanne's eyes flitted around the stateroom, looking for a weapon.

One Tiburónista remained in the stateroom with them, sitting on a metal chair next to a folding desk. On it lay his AK-12, its barrel facing them, the Tib's hands a few inches from it.

The Russian in charge had taken their IDs and seemed to be communicating with someone higher up the food chain, a Wagner commander, Lisanne assumed. Though the probable mercenary's face remained masked, she thought his eyes stayed cool and vigilant.

It wasn't that hard to guess what would happen next. She and the Quinteros were the kind of hostages that would make any terrorist salivate, held in a highly defensible location with provisions to last for weeks.

Lisanne had spent years as a Texas state trooper, working on the occasional missing person case. If there was one thing she understood, it was that kidnapping situations don't end well when the hostages cooperate. In her experience, if she didn't figure out a way to upend their plans, then the man with the cool eyes behind the balaclava would end up killing them. She couldn't recall a Wagner or Tiburónista prisoner who lived to speak of the ordeal.

With this notion very much on her mind, she shuffled to the

edge of the bed, away from Amancia and Tallulah. "I need to use the toilet," she announced to her Tiburónista jailer.

She could only judge the Tib's age by the set of his eyes above his mask. In contrast to the more senior Russian who came and went, the Tib's eyes were unlined. But he had the thick shoulders and chest of a man closer to thirty than twenty. He gave her a hard stare.

"*Ella necesita usar el baño*," Tallulah translated.

"Quickly," Lisanne added. "I really need that bathroom."

"*Rápidamente*," Tallulah said.

Lisanne took a risk by standing up. The Tib grabbed his gun and waved her down. She shook her head and shifted her eyes to the small bathroom door, a luxury afforded only to the rig's VIP guests.

With his eyes fixed on them, the Tib backed to the door and took a quick look. Seeing nothing of consequence in the bathroom, he waved Lisanne in. He tracked her with the AK's barrel.

Once inside, Lisanne shut the door and took stock. There was a toilet and a sink under a mirror. She pulled on the mirror, hoping there might be something she could conceal as a weapon—aerosol, trimming scissors, a razor, anything. But the mirror didn't move. It wasn't a cabinet.

She studied the toilet, wondering if there was something she could improvise from the tank. But it was a pressurized flush system. There was no tank, only a pipe that jutted into the wall. She turned back to the sink, mindful of her limited time.

Squatting, she opened the small vanity. Inside was a trash can with a plastic bag. Using her prosthetic to quietly prop the can lid open, she removed the plastic bag and stuffed it in a pocket of her jeans. She squinted at the gooseneck drainpipe that came down from the sink. It was white with a hand-tightened nut securing it. There might be something here she could use.

The nut was hard to unscrew, but she got the PVC material moving with her single hand. With a quiet grunt, she swung it away and off, exposing the bottom of the sink to the cavity of the vanity. If she turned the water on now, it would splash directly to the base of the vanity.

The Tib pounded on the door. "*El tiempo ha terminado. Sal!*"

"Just a second," she answered. With her head all the way into the cabinet, she glanced up at the metal rod connecting the handle that activated the sink plug. Two wing nuts held it in place. She got to work removing them.

"*Sal!*" barked the Tib at the door.

Lisanne slid the stiff steel rod up the sleeve that covered her prosthetic, flushed the toilet, and opened the door. Under the Tib's gun, she walked back to her position on the bed. Along the way, she feigned a trip over Tallulah's foot, leaned, and pretended to readjust her prosthetic arm. As she fiddled with her sleeve, she shook the rod loose and deposited it next to Gustavo, who hurriedly shifted his thigh over it. By the time she was back at her spot on the bed, the rod lay under Gustavo's leg. Lisanne saw that the Tib was looking at her while she continued to adjust her polycarbonate forearm.

Good, she thought, staring back at him.

The Tib got up and swiftly glanced in the bathroom. Seeing nothing amiss, he slammed the door shut.

Meditating in silence, Lisanne rehearsed her plan. She knew they weren't a large force, perhaps thirty men. Based on the mix of languages, she thought their command structure was likely a weak point—a few professional Wagner mercenaries over undisciplined Tibs. That alone gave her an opportunity.

In the half day she'd spent on the rig, she observed that its designers built it with redundant safety features. The biggest hazard was fire. If the rig were to go ablaze, there were multiple well-marked evacuation routes, especially here on the deck with the crew quarters.

As far as Lisanne could tell, she and the Quintero family were segregated, kept apart from the other hostages because of their significance. Based on the footsteps she had heard earlier, she thought the other passengers had been herded from the crew quarters and taken upstairs to the cafeteria. By minimizing the number of guards, more Tibs and Wagner men could remain on the top deck fortifying their position.

Which probably meant, she reasoned, that this Tib sitting in front of her was the only man standing between her and an emergency exit path. With the attention she'd given to her prosthetic, he would see her as a weak woman, not a threat.

The guard's radio chirped. He pulled it free of his belt and listened through his earpiece, placing the mic close to his lips to mumble a reply. She'd seen him do this before and assumed it was a regular check, but this time, he listened longer.

Lisanne glanced at Gustavo. He gave her a barely perceptible nod, keeping his eyes on her. She extended her palm in a five symbol with her hand on her thigh. Watching the Tib hold the microphone to his lips, she retracted one finger at a time, counting down for Gustavo—four, three, two, one.

When her hand formed a fist, she lunged forward, diving below the table with the AK. Gustavo moved simultaneously. While the Tib dropped his mic and went for the weapon, Lisanne sprung up, knocking the folding table into the Tib's chin. Before the bandito could pull his gun free, Gustavo plunged the sink rod into the guard's neck, hammering it with the rapidity of a sewing machine needle.

The Tib cried out in pain and abandoned the gun.

Lisanne snatched it.

His chest heaving, Gustavo stood, leaving the rod sunk in the

Tib's neck like a meat thermometer. Lisanne kicked the guard out of the chair.

"He's not getting up," she said. "Let's get out of here."

"Where are we going?" asked Amancia, her hand to her mouth. "There's nothing but ocean around us."

Lisanne handed the rifle to Gustavo and yanked the dying Tib away from the door. He offered no resistance. "There are covered lifeboats slung along this deck. It should still be dark out. If we run for it now, we'll be shielded from the rifles topside."

"We're a hundred feet above the sea," Amancia protested. "How can we get to a lifeboat?"

"They're in racks over the water, like on the back of a freighter." She squeezed Amancia's shoulder. "We have to go."

"Won't they chase us down with their boats?"

"They might," she said. "But they need us alive. And when they send men out to get us, I have this." She gestured to Gustavo's AK-12. "We could steal their boat."

Amancia flattened her hand across her chest. "I don't know. Seems like a risk."

"The alternative is certain death," said Lisanne.

"She's right," Gustavo agreed, his hands gripping the stock. The Tib on the floor was still. Gustavo cast his eyes down at the corpse. "Tiburónistas always kill the hostages, no matter what. We go or we die."

55

0445

YEVGENY ZUKA LOOKED OVER THE SHOULDER OF THE WAGNER WEAPONS EXPERT BY the missile launcher. The specialist sat cross-legged on the helipad's nonskid deck, manipulating a ruggedized tablet on his knees.

"Stand back," he said in Russian to a Wagner compatriot. "Powering up."

The missile launcher hummed and growled to life, thanks to a tangle of cables and wires running from it to a separate command module and generator.

"Testing," said the man with the tablet. "Commencing lateral movement."

Zuka watched as the launcher rotated in a three-sixty.

"Setting gimbal limits," continued the specialist. Then, noticing that Zuka stood over him, he explained, "The gimbal limits will keep it from shooting back into the platform. We have a targeting range on this helipad that will give us a semicircle from due west to due east."

"Excellent," Zuka replied, clapping the missileer on the shoulder.

Elsewhere, he saw a Wagner man with four Tibs standing

around him. The Wagner man's Spanish was poor, and the Tibs' Russian was nonexistent. But it didn't much matter at this point in their training. Gestures were getting the job done.

The Russian mercenary had taken the green Verba shoulder-fired missile tube from its case. The heat-seeking SAM that NATO called the SA-25 Willow could knock down incoming aircraft up to twenty thousand feet. Anticipating a possible American helicopter assault, they had brought thirty of them aboard. The Russian passed one to a Tib, and then began unboxing another.

Zuka walked farther along the helipad and saw his two infantry squads, twenty Tibs under a salty Wagner compatriot from the Africa days. Between them, the infantry squads had two dozen AK-12s and three RPK squad automatic weapons, each capable of dispensing six hundred white-hot rounds per minute without the barrel overheating.

Zuka watched the clouds lighten the eastern sky, dusting the sea with pink sparkles. To the west he caught his first glimpse of Tiburón's yacht heading toward them, casting aside a bow wave.

He hadn't quite expected that—Tiburón was supposed to be heading into the Essequibo River delta to expand on the drug violence ruse. But Zuka could understand why Tiburón would want to see the platform for himself, at least at a distance.

The Wagner commander grinned at how well the op was progressing. He looked farther north. Somewhere out there over the horizon steamed the *Admiral Gorshkov* with her Zircon hypersonic missiles. Beyond it, in Havana, were hulking An-124 cargo aircraft with a full Wagner battalion. Once the big jets landed in Georgetown, they would disgorge the men and two additional gunship helicopters like the one that had brought him here. Zuka hadn't seen a layered defense this complete since his last assignment in Chechnya, back when he was still a Spetsnaz Alpha commander.

He inhaled the fresh salt air. He'd never been one to stop and smell the roses—partially because he'd only ever been in hellholes like Afghanistan, Chechnya, and the Central African Republic. But standing here in the tropics, ruling this part of the sea like Neptune himself, he thought the moment worthy of reflection.

His triumphant reverie was cut short when he spotted the American woman, Lisanne Robertson, racing to the edge of the platform with the Quinteros. They appeared to be making a dash for one of the suspended orange lifeboats at the rear. The boy ran with an AK-12 in his hands.

In an instant, Zuka ran through his decision tree. While Morozov had said to keep these hostages as a bargaining chip, Zuka no longer saw the point. His defenses were impregnable. They had already won the battle without firing a shot. He could find no fault in the decision to gun down the women and boy who tried to escape.

"Dmitry!" he shouted to the Wagner man who ran the infantry. "Those four running to the lifeboats—take them out. Now!"

Without a word, Dmitry swung the fire-breathing, blunt-nosed RPK machine gun toward the three women and one man racing for the lifeboats.

CARY HEARD ZUKA'S SHOUTED ORDER, THOUGH HE DIDN'T UNDERSTAND RUSSIAN.

Watching from above, the Green Beret saw the small infantry squad swinging their RPK squad automatic weapon. A moment later, he understood their target. Lisanne and Gustavo were guiding the Quintero women to the lifeboats perched on the side of the platform. Under the blaze of an RPK, they would soon be mincemeat.

Well, shit, he thought.

Tiburón's yacht was charging in. With the riderless Jet Skis at its wake, Cary suspected Moore and Clark had succumbed to a sea battle on the *Gran Blanco*. The odds had been stacked against Clark and Moore from the beginning. Two men taking on a boatload of armed Tibs was damned near impossible. The Campus had lost two of its best.

But Cary didn't have time to mourn. Lisanne and the Quinteros were about to get pasted as they ran for the lifeboats. From his high vantage point, he could see they were almost there.

He raised the rifle to his eye, knowing that as soon as he took out the men at the RPK, all hell would break loose. Every Tib on the platform below would know where he was. He might bring down a few more, but his goose was cooked. If he was going to die, he consoled himself, then he would rather do it helping Lisanne get to safety. Such was the life of the Green Beret.

He mumbled a quick prayer, kissed the top of his scope, and lowered his eye behind it. He sighted in the man at the RPK.

With minute adjustments, he settled the long, silenced barrel and squeezed the trigger. The Tib took the round at the base of his neck and toppled over. Cary moved the reticle a few degrees and fired again. He had thirty rounds in his magazine and would make them all count.

The Tibs were confused at first.

The bullets had come silently from above. But they spotted him in the derrick and began firing indiscriminately. With so much metal latticework below him, the derrick acted as reasonable cover. The bullets plinked and sparked all around him. To hold them off a little longer, Cary yanked a fragmentation grenade from his vest, pulled the pin, and dropped it like a bomb. He did it again as soon as it went off, then climbed as high as he could.

As he scrambled higher, he caught a glimpse of a covered orange lifeboat sliding free. The bulky hard-shelled craft hit the sea with a towering white splash and then righted itself.

But Cary understood with dismay that the lifeboat was only a few hundred yards from the *Gran Blanco*. The Tiburónistas would have a field day hunting it down and taking the women captive.

Angered by the prospect, it took the Green Beret a few seconds to realize that the Tibs had stopped firing at him. A Spanish voice drifted over the air from the *Gran Blanco*'s loudspeaker, echoing on the platform. Cary didn't know Spanish and couldn't comprehend the message.

But whatever it was, he didn't care—the Tibs were standing at the edge of the platform, listening.

He wondered if maybe his prayer had worked.

56

MOTOR YACHT *GRAN BLANCO*
0448

MOORE KEPT THE BOW POINTED AT THE OIL PLATFORM. DING HELD THE LOUD-HAILER microphone to his lips with the volume cranked to max, speaking in rapid Spanish, giving his best Tiburón impression:

> *Esto es Tiburón. Todos ustedes deben deponer sus armas. Hemos llegado a un acuerdo con los americanos. Dejen las armas o los mataré yo mismo!*

> This is Tiburón. Lay down your arms! We have reached an agreement with the Americans. Lay down your arms or I will shoot you myself!

On the *Gran Blanco*'s bow-mounted helipad, Jack and Jad lay prostrate with their rifles trained on separate targets. The two killer skis trailed the *Gran Blanco*, still riding the wake in autonomous mode.

"Cary's at a hide up in the derrick!" Jad shouted with one eye closed, the other behind his scope. "Permission to hit anyone pointing their rifles up."

"Negative," Jack replied coolly. "Hold. Let's see if they buy Ding's imitation."

For his part, Jack trained his rifle on the men at the rear of the platform, who assembled to shoot at the orange lifeboat now bobbing away under its own power.

"The Tibs aren't firing," Jack added. "It may have worked. For now, anyway."

With a ball cap pulled low to disguise himself, Clark crawled close to them on the helipad. He raised a pair of high-powered binoculars to his eyes. Jad described Cary's position. Jack pointed out the men aiming at the lifeboat.

"I don't like the look of this," Clark announced. "It's hard to tell from here, but judging by the hand gestures, I'd say the Russians aren't falling for it. A guy on the helipad has a phone to his ear."

"Do I take him out?" Jad asked. Of the three, he was the most accomplished sniper.

"If all goes as planned," Clark responded, "you won't have to. Let's give it another ten seconds."

STANDING ON THE HELIPAD, ZUKA HELD THE PHONE TO HIS EAR, WAITING FOR MOROzov to answer.

He looked out at Tiburón's yacht, the *Gran Blanco*. It drifted closer to the platform, while the orange lifeboat motored in the opposite direction.

Earlier, Morozov had told him the yacht had been attacked. As he listened to the loud-hailer, he doubted whether it was really Tiburón coming over those speakers. It made zero sense to Zuka that the drug lord would make a deal with the Americans, given how much he hated them.

But whether it was Tiburón or an impostor, the Tibs might obey the order out of habit.

Nyet.

Yevgeny Zuka wasn't about to blow this glorious operation because a cowardly drug lord had switched sides. He wouldn't abide a mutiny. He would sooner kill these Tiburónistas and hold the platform as designated. Even with his small skeleton crew of loyal Russians, its formidable defenses could keep the Yankees at bay, no matter what the Tiburónistas did.

"*Da*," answered the SVR major on the fourth ring. "The line is secure. Go ahead."

"Tiburón's boat is here, at the platform."

"What?"

Zuka repeated himself, then added, "It could be an impersonation, but someone saying they're Tiburón is on the loudspeaker ordering the Tibs to stand down. Is there any truth to this? I need to know right now."

Morozov didn't have a ready answer for him. In the silence while Zuka waited, he heard another command echoing from the *Gran Blanco*. Knowing Spanish well enough to translate it in real time to Morozov, Zuka said, "'The Russians are spies. The Russians have sold us out and are against us. Kill the Russians now or your families will die before sunset!'"

Zuka saw a Tib turning to him, raising his weapon. He dropped the satellite phone and pulled up his AK-12. He gunned the Tib down and aimed at another.

But then Zuka fell to the deck, dumbstruck.

A sniper's bullet had pierced his helmet from above.

NOT A SINGLE COMBATANT THOUGHT TO LOOK UP DURING THE MELEE BETWEEN THE Russians and the Tiburónistas. Cary sighted one target after another, killing anyone in green. With satisfaction, he saw some scurry out of the platform's interior, going for the stairs that would take them down to the Tib boats.

It didn't much matter. They were an easy shot.

THE CONNECTION REMAINED OPEN WHEN ZUKA DROPPED HIS SATELLITE PHONE TO the deck.

Still waiting on the interrogation specialist to arrive from Moscow, Igor Morozov stood in his small soundproof office in the Caracas embassy listening, his eyes widening. For the moment, his cool analytical tools abandoned him. He could hear shots and screams and groans.

His last word from Tiburón was that he'd been under attack. Though Morozov didn't trust the drug lord as far as he could throw him, there was no way the greedy fool would betray the Russians so baldly. He could see no endgame for that. Tiburón, a man ruled by his passions, hated the Americans down to his cells.

This, he decided as he listened, was a clever American trick.

All was not lost, however.

There was still the matter of the *Admiral Gorshkov* and the An-124s now en route from Havana, stuffed with more Wagner men. The army gunship on the *Gorshkov* was airborne, bristling with an array of missiles. If the Americans were going to attempt to take the oil platform back with a force launched from Tiburón's yacht, then Morozov would have the Russian military sink it.

As a mere SVR major, he couldn't order a missile strike on the yacht. But he could send an immediate flash message to Moscow coded with the words that would speed it through the SVR's calcified command structure. Then, with the American commandos humiliated, the Wagner men would land at the airport in Essequibo unmolested.

He hurried down the hall to the secure messaging terminal that went through to the SVR ops center in Moscow. Emphasizing that the Guyanese government would request immediate Russian military assistance, he hammered out the rest of his message in thirty seconds and sent it.

As soon as Moscow confirmed receipt, Morozov texted Romero and Castillo: *Make the announcement now.*

Thinking he'd put all the necessary pieces in play, he decided to fly to Georgetown. He stabbed the intercom button to tell the junior watch officer to ready his helicopter.

The officer's response wasn't what he expected.

"Sir," he said. "You should check VPI TV right now. It's an announcement from the Guyanese—"

Morozov hung up on the watch officer. VPI was the digital Venezuelan news channel. The major usually had it streaming in the background on his laptop with the window minimized. Now he expanded the stream. He wanted to make sure Castillo didn't screw it up, that he followed through with his request for Russian military assistance.

But when he looked at who stood before blue drapery at a wooden podium, he didn't see Castillo's pale face looking back at him.

Instead, he saw Guyanese president Ali Khasif.

With a sick feeling welling up from his stomach, he called the watch officer back. "Call Moscow. We need new orders for the *Admiral Gorshkov*."

57

PARLIAMENT BUILDING, GEORGETOWN, GUYANA
0448

SHEILA CAME IN QUIETLY BECAUSE SHE SAW THAT ROMERO HAD FALLEN ASLEEP IN HIS chair. Since receiving Morozov's message a moment before, Castillo had ordered her to find the AV people so they could stream his announcement.

Now she was back, whispering in Castillo's ear that President Khasif was streaming live on the internet, preempting the prime minister.

Deathly pale, Castillo ordered her away, loosened his tie, and plugged his headphones into his laptop. He opened the Guyanese news channel on YouTube and immediately saw the dark, courtly face of Ali Khasif, his president.

"I have survived an assassination attempt in Abu Dhabi," Khasif began.

Castillo noted that the president was standing in front of blue drapery with American flags to either side of him. A bar of script below him proclaimed, KHASIF NARROWLY ESCAPES ASSASSINATION ATTEMPT.

The president went on. "I am grateful to the United States for alerting me to the threat and delivering me to safety. Further, I am aware of Tiburón's violence in my country. As a result of that, I am expanding on the stringent security measures already put in place by Prime Minister Castillo by extending them to include the armed forces. I am also pleased to announce that the American government has offered further security assistance. As the duly elected president of Guyana, I am—"

Castillo shut his laptop.

He looked forlornly at the camera, the teleprompter, the microphone, and the lights. A few feet behind the chair where he'd planned to make his address hung the Guyanese flags Sheila had arranged.

His eyes twitched back to Romero, still asleep in his chair.

Castillo quietly stood and moved from behind his desk, approaching Romero. In a final pause, he closed his eyes and swallowed, thinking about the few spare moments that define destiny. He'd thought his moment would come from the other side of the camera. He could still see the little line of tape where he was supposed to stand.

Now, his fate would be something entirely different.

Standing close to Romero, he listened to the man's breath. He watched the security chief's chest rise and fall. Castillo quietly tossed his tie over his shoulder so it wouldn't brush against Romero when he leaned over him. He gently squeezed the pistol grip on Romero's belt. He tugged it free.

"What?" shot Romero, jerking awake, confused. When he looked at Castillo, his eyes went round. "What are you doing?" he shouted as he got up.

Holding the gun with both hands, Castillo stood three feet from Romero. The prime minister pulled the trigger. The bullet struck Romero in the shoulder. Though it propelled him back for a second, the country's most senior policeman managed to stay on his feet, his face twisted with pain and rage. He moved toward Castillo.

The prime minister shot twice more, hitting Romero in the chest.

Castillo dropped the gun. It lay smoking on the carpet.

"Sheila!" he yelled. She came through the door and put her hand to her mouth, inhaling, too shocked to speak.

"I've just learned there's been a coup attempt!" Castillo shouted. "Get me General Nirani! Romero has been conspiring with Tiburón all along. Just as he worked with Tiburón to kill President Khasif, he also tried to kill me!"

She expressed the appropriate sentiments of shock and horror and ran to comfort him. He sent her away. "Go, please," he said courageously. "Make those calls. And get the American ambassador on the phone at once. I must tell her of this plot *immediately*."

IN THE COMBAT INFORMATION CENTER OF THE *ADMIRAL GORSHKOV*, CAPTAIN FIRST Rank Mikhail Krokhmal leaned over the tactical action officer who'd computed the missile firing solution for his Oniks anti-ship cruise missile.

The Northern Fleet order revealed exact coordinates and photos of the target vessel. Though the *Gorshkov* was still a hundred miles away, the cruise missile would soar over the Caribbean and then go into active seeker mode before finding the yacht. Krokhmal didn't know who was on the luxury boat or why it had been targeted—nor did he care. An order was an order.

"Show me," he said to the officer who had loaded the Oniks computer with all the requisite information. "Show me how it will work."

The captain watched and listened. For once, he didn't require one of his officers to develop the solution by hand. The order had come in too quickly and without enough amplifying information to drill his officers with a manual backup.

So be it.

He listened to the rest of the explanation and then checked the weapon's status. The missile was ready and waiting on the bow in its vertical launch tube. Though Krokhmal had no understanding of the context, he knew this wasn't a drill. The Oniks would be fired for real, its purpose to sink a ship.

If it went well, Krokhmal would be famous across the fleet. "How long to launch?"

"Thirty seconds," said the officer.

Krokhmal looked at the second hand on his watch. It had never seemed slower.

"Sir!" barked the communications lieutenant. "Flash message, highest priority, immediate action."

Krokhmal ran to the officer's station and read the message over his shoulder, too impatient to wait for the printed copy.

*****STAND DOWN. NO MISSILE LAUNCH.
REPEAT NO MISSILE LAUNCH*****

"Cancel Oniks launch!" he shouted immediately to the officer at the console.

When he heard the man at the watch station breathe a sigh of relief, he grew angry.

Then, remembering his own dictum never to let the men see his emotion, he stomped to the hatch and left.

A HUNDRED MILES TO THE SOUTH OF THE *ADMIRAL GORSHKOV*, THE CANCELED TARGET, motor yacht *Gran Blanco*, pulled closer to the ungainly orange lifeboat that continued motoring for the Guyanese coast.

At the back of the *Gran Blanco*, Moore lowered the bent lazaret ramp and helped Jack board one of the two killer Jet Skis. Jack threw his leg around one, while Clark took another. Seconds later, they were dashing toward the lifeboat.

"Someone's coming from the yacht!" Gustavo cried, alarmed. Standing, he watched through the tiny observation porthole in the lifeboat's domed roof. Tallulah was at the craft's wheel, steering for shore. Her mother sat beside her. Amancia turned and gaped at Gustavo.

"Miss Lisanne," he warned. "There are boats coming from the yacht! The boy leaned and lifted the AK-12 to his side.

Fearing this moment would arrive, Lisanne got up from one of the hard plastic seats and crowded next to Gustavo. She looked through the window with dread.

"Put down the gun," she ordered with a grin. "Those are the good guys."

EPILOGUE

GEORGETOWN, GUYANA
TWO MONTHS LATER

JACK STRODE ALONG THE WALKWAY WITH HIS HAND LOCKED IN LISANNE'S, NOTING the reflection of the midmorning light on the sea. A mild breeze had risen, pushing away the milky marine layer to expose a crystalline, tropical blue sky.

Lisanne's heels clicked on the smooth concrete walkway. Filtered through palm leaves, the sun fell in stripes across her navy-blue dress. "Oh, Jack," she said, gesturing with her prosthetic. "Look how beautiful."

Jack peered at the bright waterfront. The new waterfront plaza was pristine, nearly white in the sun. Beyond it, Georgetown Bay mirrored the dazzling sky. For once, a high spring tide countered the muddy flow of the Demerara River, clearing the water.

"Amancia told me they selected the ceremony date based on the tide," Jack said appreciatively.

"I thought those dark areas in the bay were shadows," she answered. "Now I see they're coral reefs."

"I guess Amancia knew what she was talking about."

Lisanne stopped as their feet touched the sidewalk that would take them to the pavilion. She inspected Jack's suit and straightened his tie. "I want us to make an entrance," she said. "This is a big day."

He grinned at her fussiness and leaned in to kiss her.

She backed away. "My lipstick. You'll have to wait a few hours."

"Then let's get this over with," he answered, pulling her across the park.

A nautical flagpole with a wide yardarm towered at the granite-capped seawall. By the time Jack and Lisanne neared it, the flags were flapping and popping in the sea breeze. They both looked up, standing still in the wind.

Atop the main mast fluttered the Guyanese flag's green, red, and yellow interlocking triangles. Just below it snapped the Stars and Stripes. Jack observed the United States Coast Guard's white service flag emblazoned with a blue eagle on one diagonal yardarm. On the other, he watched a flag with the same eagle atop red and white vertical stripes. It was the ensign the *Harry Claiborne* had been flying when she went down.

A team of Coast Guard divers had recovered the ensign from the seafloor along with the ship's log and bell. The twelve crew members entombed in her hull were left in peace, in accordance with family wishes.

"We'd better head over," Lisanne said with a nudge at his elbow. "It's getting ready to start."

With his fiancée at his side, Jack faced the bright white tent. A hundred people had already gathered, standing around neatly arranged chairs. Beyond them, the men and women of the U.S. Coast Guard band were tuning up on a raised platform.

Gustavo's voice cut through the crowd murmur. "Mr. Jack, Ms. Lisanne," he called and waved. "Over here!"

They ambled to the front row, facing the flags and the bay.

"My God," Amancia Quintero said. "You two clean up nice." Alberto Quintero's widow leaned in and gave each a quick hug.

"You're one to talk," Lisanne replied. "And look at you, Tallulah. Your father would be so proud."

Jack hardly recognized Tallulah Quintero. The last time he'd seen her, she had a swollen face and a jagged cut beneath her eye. Now she stood just outside the tent in a strapless crimson dress, radiant in the bright sunshine. Gustavo, with shorter hair and a smoothly shaved face, was also hard to recognize.

"Mom," Tallulah said. "We better get to our chairs. The official entourage is coming."

On cue, the military band belted out a bouncy brass intro that transitioned to "Semper Paratus," the Coast Guard anthem. The crowd hushed, stood by their chairs, and turned to a procession of government officials.

Leading the way was the commandant of the United States Coast Guard, Admiral Ashley "Ash" Morgan. As she marched stoically, Jack noticed the broad gold stripes on her sleeves, designating her a four-star admiral. The Master Chief of the Coast Guard, the service's most senior enlisted member, walked on her right flank.

Behind them, Jack recognized the American ambassador to Guyana, Sydney O'Keefe. She wore her ginger hair in a smooth lock over one shoulder, a pleasant contrast to her black pantsuit. When she saw Jack in the front row, she briefly nodded to him, but kept her face serious.

When the Americans reached the dais, the band struck up "Green Land of Guyana," the host country's national anthem. Prime Minister Guto Castillo entered in time to the beat, wearing a dark suit and a tie with the Guyanese colors. Senior members of the Guyanese military followed in their khaki uniforms with black berets. The final official to come into view was President Ali Khasif. He walked with his bald dark head bowed contemplatively, like a man in church.

The president stopped at a podium just below the flags. The joint delegation of American and Guyanese officials took their seats on the dais nearby. The band stopped playing.

Khasif glanced at the assembly under the tent. The flags snapped over his head. The sea glittered behind him.

"Ladies and Gentlemen," he began. "As the great Edmund Burke famously said, 'The only thing necessary for the triumph of evil is for good men to do nothing.'"

Khasif glanced up at the *Harry Claiborne* ensign on the yardarm and the clear blue sky beyond it.

"It strikes me," he continued, "that on a day as gentle as this one, it is hard to believe that only sixty days ago, the very evil to which Mr. Burke referred came right here, to Guyana.

"It sprung from the rotten hearts of wicked men who would seek to destroy our democracy, denude us of our natural gifts, and rob us of our freedom for their own ambitions. The evil came as it always does—in darkness. It came from sea and sky, from mountain and plain. It came with fearsome weapons and beguiling smiles. It came for you, and it came for me. But most of all—it came to triumph.

"And, oh, it would have—if it hadn't been for a few good men and women who, when faced with it, decided *not* to do nothing."

The president settled his gaze on the front row. He looked directly at Jack, Lisanne, and the Quinteros. His brown eyes then shifted to the American dignitaries on the dais.

"Ambassador O'Keefe, Admiral Morgan," he continued. "As president, it is my humble privilege to pay tribute to the country you represent—and to the first of those who decided *not* to do nothing on that dark day.

"Because of many good people who came to the defense of

Guyana, evil did not triumph here. But it did claim the crew of the United States Coast Guard cutter *Harry Claiborne*, who were the first to confront it.

"It is my solemn pledge to you, Admiral, and you, Ambassador, that Guyana will never forget the sons and daughters of the United States Coast Guard who gave their lives here. And to ensure that, I dedicate this waterfront to their memories, which shall now be so aptly named the Harry Claiborne Memorial Park. The people of Guyana will never forget that ship, nor her crew whose names I am now so honored to recite."

Khasif briefly looked down at the lectern. The Coast Guard conductor clanged the brass bell recovered from the *Claiborne*. It rang so clearly that a few in the crowd flinched.

"Lieutenant Hannah Mackenzie, captain, Juneau, Alaska."

The bandleader struck the bell again. "Chief Bart Novak, boatswain, Punxsutawney, Pennsylvania."

The bell tolled sixteen more times with crew names and hometowns until the president finished with the last crew member to enter a line in the cutter's recovered log: "Petty Officer Second Class William Gesparek, helmsman, Spokane, Washington."

Khasif bowed his head.

The band struck up the hymnal, "Eternal Father, Strong to Save." Sydney O'Keefe and the two Coast Guard representatives walked with the president to a section of the granite seawall. They removed a black fabric veil to reveal a bronze plaque emblazoned with the crew names.

The delegation remained standing while the band drummed in an honor guard of U.S. Marines. In starchy white trousers and stiff blue tunics trimmed in red, the Marines marched forward with M4 rifles on their shoulders.

The drumming stopped.

LINE OF DEMARCATION

The seven Marines raised their rifles over the sea and fired a twenty-one-gun salute.

JACK ARRIVED A HALF HOUR LATER AT THE EMBASSY FOR THE RECEPTION. HE INTRO-duced Lisanne to Sydney O'Keefe and mingled with the rest of the visiting Americans in the rear courtyard.

The crowd hushed when President Khasif entered with a train of Guyanese officials—including Guto Castillo and Amancia Quintero.

Amancia headed straight for Jack, smiling widely. She carried a broad yellow envelope.

"Why do you look so happy?" Lisanne asked her.

"Because I have something for a Mr. Jack Ryan, chief executive officer of the Athena Global Shipping Lines."

Jack looked up suddenly, nearly spilling the crystal punch glass he was holding. "Oh?" he said, trying to sound disinterested. "And what is that?"

During the ensuing two months, Jack and Howard had yet to find a buyer for the shipping company, which continued burning cash. Making matters worse, the *Helena* blew a boiler on the return trip to San Juan and was laid up for repairs. With the ship out of commission, Jack lost his best argument for getting an export license. Athena was now worth less than Hendley had paid for it. Much to Jack's chagrin, he anticipated his first loss.

"As the new minister of the interior," Amancia said, beaming, "I am pleased to present you with the first and only export license, good for operations with the offshore platform Marlin. It remains exclusive to Athena unless you choose to sell it, which you may."

"Are you serious?" Jack asked. "You're the new minister of the interior?"

"President Khasif made it official this morning. And he signed this export license with his compliments." She presented him with the envelope.

But before Jack could open it, Sydney O'Keefe approached them. "Jack, Amancia, Lisanne. Just the trio I was looking for. Would you please join me in the Americas Room?"

With a sigh of relief, Jack tucked the envelope under his arm and followed the three women into the embassy confines.

Two Marines, still in their honor guard uniforms, stood at the door to the conference room. When the ambassador approached, the Marines opened it and waved them through. Jack took a seat next to a middle-aged man with salt-and-pepper hair and horn-rim glasses. He introduced himself as Bill Rabb, an attorney with the U.S. Department of Justice.

"May I get all of you to stand, please?" Sydney O'Keefe asked. "President Khasif is joining us."

A moment later, Khasif came through the door with Guto Castillo. They sat at the center of the table, facing O'Keefe and Rabb. Jack, Amancia, and Lisanne filled out the rest of the room.

"Thank you for joining us, Mr. President," O'Keefe began. "I know you have a full day."

"It is my pleasure, Madame Ambassador."

"And mine," echoed Castillo. "Though I'm not quite sure of the agenda . . ."

"Yes," said O'Keefe. "My apologies for that, Prime Minister. This is a matter of some delicacy. Please, let me introduce you both to Bill Rabb. He's from our Justice Department."

Rabb rose from his chair and reached across the table to shake hands with the two Guyanese men. After reclaiming his seat, he pulled a letter from a folder. "President Khasif," he began. "After a thorough review of evidence that came into our possession and a subsequent indictment, we are able to bring formal charges against co-conspirators in a criminal action that sought to—"

"I don't understand," Guto Castillo interrupted. "Tiburón and Romero are both dead. Even if they weren't, their crimes were against the people of Guyana—not the United States."

"Yes, Prime Minister," Rabb said patiently. "This is a related matter. It has to do with a conspiracy to murder eighteen American coastguardsmen and your late interior minister, Alberto Quintero, among other things."

"I still don't understand," Castillo persisted. He looked indignantly at Khasif. "Mr. President, is this not a violation of our sovereignty? Our jurisprudence?"

When Khasif didn't answer immediately, the prime minister turned back to the man from the Justice Department. "Mr. Rabb, forgive me. But that crew died—tragically, mind you—at the hands of Tiburónistas and Russians. Tiburón is dead. Are you advising us about sanctions against the Russians?"

"No," Rabb replied bluntly, his eyes fixed on the paper. He flipped a page and resumed reading. "In the matter of the United States versus Augustus Bolivar Castillo, we have issued a federal indictment to—"

Castillo stood up. "What?" he shouted. "You are charging *me* with a crime?"

"Calm down, Guto," Khasif said. "Let's hear the man out."

"As I mentioned," Rabb resumed when Castillo sat on the edge of his chair. "A grand jury has reviewed evidence from the Guyanese attorney general that—"

"What evidence?" Castillo demanded.

Rabb shrugged. "I guess I can show it to you. Your defense counsel will ask for it in discovery anyway." He lifted a remote control from the table and stabbed a button. A projector on the ceiling painted the whiteboard with a video image of Castillo, Romero, Tiburón, and Morozov meeting in a hotel room.

The Justice Department attorney cranked the volume. In the muffled tones of a surveillance recording, they listened to the conspirators—Tiburón, Morozov, Romero, and Augustus Castillo IV.

After Morozov outlined the disposition of forces he would bring in to take Essequibo, Romero added that he would have his police kill Suárez, if necessary, and bury any possible evidence of corruption. Calling in from Venezuela, Tiburón cursed the *yanquis*. Castillo watched and heard himself say, "Please, gentlemen. You must keep me out of this. I am with you, of course; but to maintain legitimacy, this must be our last communication."

The lawyer paused the tape. The frame froze plainly on Castillo's face.

"This is fabricated," spat the prime minister.

Since the failed coup, under the guise of searching out conspirators, Castillo had confiscated every computer Suárez had access to. He had seen the directory himself with the videos—just before destroying it.

"If you bring this to court, you will be humiliated, Mr. Rabb," Castillo seethed. "And you, Ms. O'Keefe. This is all a trick. It's a deepfake."

"It's not a deepfake," Rabb remarked matter-of-factly. "The videos came from an investigation run by your murdered attorney general, Hugo Suárez. We have the raw tapes and several witnesses who saw them recovered. They were backups that the late minister Quintero kept at his house for safekeeping."

Castillo looked around the room with wide eyes. As far as he was concerned, he had proven his innocence when he shot Romero. "I *stopped* the conspiracy," he declared. "Obviously, I had to go along with them, for a time. I even shared my concerns with

Suárez. After he was lost, it was up to *me* to stop Romero. And I did."

Rabb hit play again. After some flickers, a different video sequence appeared on the whiteboard. The attorney froze the frame right after the Department of Justice evidence marker. Castillo recognized himself in the emergency operations bunker. His heart thudded.

"You may not have realized it, Prime Minister," Rabb said, "but Suárez hid surveillance equipment in the ceiling of the emergency operations bunker."

The lawyer pressed play. Castillo heard and saw himself telling Romero to kill Jack Ryan, Jr., and to make sure his body was never found.

"Well—obviously that didn't happen!" Castillo nearly shouted. He glanced angrily at Jack. "I had to say these things until I could safely kill Romero! Ryan is right here, for God's sake. Again, I ask what jurisdiction you think you have, sir? We are *not* in the United States."

"Let me explain," Rabb said. "You conspired to kill Alberto Quintero. He was an American citizen by virtue of his marriage to Amancia."

"I didn't kill Alberto Quintero!" Castillo shrieked.

"You didn't pull the trigger, but the conspiracy you ran directed the murder. Same goes for eighteen coastguardsmen. As for Mr. Ryan, here, we're calling that an attempted murder charge. It's all in the indictment."

"I'm not listening to this," Castillo said. He rose to leave. As soon as he opened the door, the two Marines waiting outside blocked his way.

He turned to Khasif in shock. "Are you going to let this happen? You're allowing the Yankees to run roughshod over our sovereignty?"

The president shook his head. "Not at all, Guto. I am merely letting the United States exercise its rights under our extradition treaty."

"Exactly correct," Rabb agreed. "Augustus Bolivar Castillo IV, you are hereby remanded to American custody. I will escort you back to Miami, where you will face trial in the federal court's eleventh circuit. I would read you your rights—but since you're not an American citizen, you don't actually have any."

The attorney turned his head to Jack. "I understand from the ambassador, Mr. Ryan, that you would like the honor?" Rabb pulled a pair of handcuffs from his bag and slid them down the table.

"Indeed I would," Jack said, rising. "Please, Mr. Prime Minister, give me your wrists. Let's not make this harder than it needs to be."

When Rabb and the Marines left with Castillo, Jack reclaimed his seat at the table. Lisanne squeezed Amancia's shoulder. "I told you we would get him," she said.

"Thank you for your help," Khasif added. "My one regret is that we couldn't get the Russian, Morozov."

Jack shifted in his chair. "Oh, I don't know, Mr. President. These things have a way of working themselves out."

IGOR MOROZOV SAT IN THE BACK SEAT OF HIS HELICOPTER, PONDERING THE GREEN Caribbean Sea.

His beer company, Playa Del Sol, had bottling operations in six countries across South America and the Caribbean. In the two months since the Tiburón operation had fizzled, Moscow ordered him to slip back into his old Wagner cover, grow his business, and look for new ways to bring the region into Russia's sway.

So when a rival beer company, Green Stripe, offered itself for sale to him at a compelling price, Morozov saw an opportunity to reestablish his good reputation with Moscow. Using SVR resources for due diligence, he learned that Green Stripe, a Trinidadian beer, had been acquired by a private equity company called Black Barrel Capital, with a headquarters in the Caymans.

Like most private equity firms, Black Barrel's financial managers were looking to sell Green Stripe in pieces, reaping a series of returns by separating valuable, independent divisions.

One of those divisions consisted of the bottling operations in Trinidad, Grenada, and the British Virgin Islands, for which Black Barrel wanted three million.

Morozov intended to push Playa Del Sol through those distribution networks instantly, adding twenty-five percent to Playa Del Sol's sales. He considered three million an outright bargain and promptly tendered an offer.

To consummate the deal, Black Barrel's managing director suggested a lunch near the airport in Tobago, a stone's throw from Caracas.

After his helicopter touched down at Scarborough Field, Morozov hired a car and arrived at the restaurant a little after one p.m. Smoothing his Savile Row suit, he announced his presence to the hostess, employing his alias.

"Ah yes, sir," she replied. "I was told to bring you straight back to the Calypso Room. The gentlemen from Black Barrel are waiting for you."

Morozov walked with her to the rear of the restaurant. She ushered him through a swinging door to a room with one long table. It was empty.

"They were here a moment ago," she said, confused. "I'll find them. While you wait—I'm told you would probably like a Green Stripe beer to celebrate. We have them on ice in the kitchen. Shall I get you one?"

"Certainly," he said, opening the napkin on his lap. "Why not?"

He was not one to imbibe during the day, usually, but the thought of growing Playa Del Sol's business by twenty-five percent had put him in a buoyant mood.

But when the hostess opened the door on her return, she was not carrying a Green Stripe beer. Instead, she was leading John Clark and Domingo Chavez into the room.

Morozov thought about going for the snubbed Makarov concealed in his breast pocket. But Clark beat him to it, raising a silenced SIG Sauer and pointing it at the SVR officer's head. Ding closed the door.

Morozov was shocked when the hostess expertly ran her hands through his suit jacket and relieved him of his Makarov.

"He's clear," she said to Clark.

"Thanks, Mandy," the SEAL replied.

Clark and Ding sat across the linen-topped table, regarding the Russian with blank stares.

"Well," the SVR man said. "Bravo, gentlemen. I thought Black Barrel was a legitimate private equity company. I didn't realize it was a CIA front."

"It's not a CIA front," Clark returned.

Under the veteran SEAL's steely gaze, Morozov was quick to shift topics. "Well, however you managed to fool me—I came to this meeting prepared to negotiate. The terms may be different—but I would still like to propose a deal."

Clark waited a few seconds before responding. "Which is?"

Morozov composed himself with a long breath. "I know from my research that you and Mr. Chavez are both professional spies. So am I."

"So?" Clark asked.

"So. As one professional to another, I propose my . . . services."

"I don't think so," Clark answered.

LINE OF DEMARCATION

The Russian raised his hands halfway in a mock surrender. "All right, fine. I give up. You got me. I understand I'm short of leverage, here." His voice turned serious. "But be rational. If I work for you, I can tell you whatever you want to know about SVR and Wagner operations in this region. You won't even have to pay me, just let me carry on my business. Not only will I kick in a share of Playa Del Sol profits, but think of the money you'll save by not having to recruit lesser assets."

Clark rested the heel of the pistol grip on the table, still pointing the barrel at Morozov. "We don't accept."

"Just like that?"

"Just like that."

"May I ask why?"

"For starters, you're only a major," Clark said. "We have spies in the Kremlin who are several levels up from you. You're not all that interesting of an asset."

"I'm a professional," Morozov retorted. "I know when you're bluffing."

"No. You're not a professional."

"I'm sorry?"

Clark stared coldly at him. "In the earlier phase of this Cold War, we may not have liked the KGB, but we respected it. And vice versa. That's real professionalism."

"The KGB and the Cold War have been gone for thirty years," Morozov said.

"I think of the last thirty years as more of a break in operations. We're just picking up where we left off."

"I beg to differ," Morozov objected. "What we have now is a new way of war. It's neither cold nor hot, neither black nor white. Let's call it a gray war, continuously operating in the shadows. There is no line of demarcation."

"The answer is still no," Clark said.

"You don't think I can be of use to you as an agent?"

Clark sighed. "There is still a line, Major Morozov—and you crossed it. You knew Ding was an American intelligence officer, and you knowingly turned him over to a psychotic. You can't come back to the other side of that. The line may be a little blurry these days, but it still exists."

Morozov looked at his manicured nails. "All right. How about this? If you give me witness protection, I can help you build a case against Guto Castillo, who remains in office. If you think I'm such a small fish, then let me help you catch a bigger one."

Clark and Ding exchanged a quick glance. "A little late for that," Clark declared. "And we're still not interested."

"Why not?"

"You fancy yourself a businessman, Morozov. So let me put it in those terms for you: you're worth more to us dead than alive."

The Russian paled and glared at Clark. "How could you possibly conclude that?"

"We're going to remind the SVR what happens when they don't respect the rules. The good news, I guess, is that your body will be found. I'll make sure of that. Maybe they'll bury you back home in Russia. Maybe not."

"I see," Morozov said.

"Good," Clark replied. He handed his SIG Sauer over to Ding. "Let's get back to the business at hand. Mr. Chavez, care to finish the transaction?"

"With pleasure," Ding replied.

He raised the silenced SIG Sauer, leveled its black barrel, and pulled the trigger.

HAVE YOU READ THE PREVIOUS, UNMISSABLE JACK RYAN, JR. THRILLER?

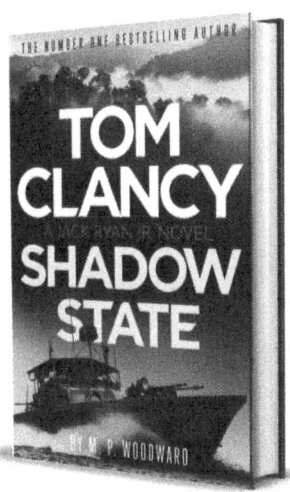

Surviving a helicopter crash in the Vietnamese Highlands is only the start of the challenges facing Jack Ryan, Jr.

The vibrant economy of the new Vietnam is a shiny lure for Western capital. Companies are racing to uncover ideal opportunities. Not wanting to be left behind, Hendley Associates has sent their best analyst, Jack Ryan, Jr., to mine for investment gold. And he may have found some in a rare earth mining company, GeoTech.

But a trip with a Hendley colleague to observe the company's operations takes a treacherous turn when their helicopter is shot down. Some things haven't changed, and Vietnam is still the plaything of powerful neighbours. The Chinese are determined to keep Jack from finding the truth about what exactly is being processed at the isolated factory.

Now Jack is in a race for his life. He's got to stay one step ahead of a pack of killers while supporting his wounded friend. And he'll get no help from the government, because in the jungle, it's the shadow state that rules.

OUT NOW